"A gem of a book. [...] job intertwining a solid nar[...] h a message of real social [...] you haven't had so much fu[...] s" — John Preston, *Gay Chic[...]*

"With the publication of *Street Lavender*, author Chris Hunt has made something of a bid for the throne vacated by Mary Renault as a writer of gay historical fiction" — *Gay Life*

"Chris Hunt tackles many issues, the thin veneer of Victorian morality is scraped away to reveal the ugliness underneath. Clear political comments are made, very relevant to English society today, but above all the book is a good read, with its humour, portrayal of emotions and its captivating story line" — *Bi-Monthly*

"For all its playful mocking, and cherishing, of the gothic adventures and romantic sexual manipulation of pulp Victorian fiction, *Street Lavender* takes its political and sexual cues from Dickens, Edward Carpenter and 19th-century novels based on working-class experience. Sexy, romantic and adventurous reading, a fine merging of history and pride, politics, and cheerful Cockney bravado. Thank you, Chris Hunt!" — *Epicene*

STREET LAVENDER

CHRIS HUNT

◀◀◀GMP▶▶▶

First published in 1986 by GMP Publishers Ltd
PO Box 247, London N17 9QR, England
Second impression 1990

British Library Cataloguing in Publication Data

Hunt, Chris
Street lavender
I. Title
823'.914[F]   PR.6058.H4

ISBN 0 85449 035 3

Distributed in North America by Alyson Publications Inc.
40 Plympton St, Boston, MA 02118, USA

Distributed in Australia by Bulldog Books
PO Box 155, Broadway, NSW 2007, Australia

Printed in the EC on environmentally-friendly paper by
Norhaven A/S, Viborg, Denmark

FOR MICK

PART ONE

CHAPTER ONE

I

A<small>FTER ONE</small> leaf-falling autumn, in the winter that followed, our father died of a fever, and we fell Upon Hard Times. I know we did, because this is what our mum said: "Boys, we have fallen upon hard times."

All I knew was that suddenly we were living somewhere else. It was in Aldgate, near Whitechapel Road, down a little alley. It wasn't in any way the worst sort of place you could live in. It wasn't Bluegate Fields. It was just a street. A lamp post lit the entrance and our house was second along. We had one room downstairs with a fireplace and cooking things, and one room upstairs where me and Charley slept. Out the back was a yard, an outhouse with a copper in it for everybody's washing, and privies that stank, with doors that didn't shut, and nettles growing round the entrances.

My brother Charley was four years older than me, and strong and tough. He had tousled brown hair and aggressive but tender eyes. He was a business-like rebel and earnestly political. He was also distressingly rough on clothes. I say that with real sorrow, because what he wore was due to come down to me. I had to stand by and watch his knee come further through his trouser leg, and his elbows out of his shirt sleeves, and it broke my heart a thousand times over to think what his clothes would be like by the time they were mine. I didn't stand by quietly of course; I kicked him and thumped him and grumbled at him to take more care, only he just kept on growing, and he got muscular real early.

Our dad's Union paid some money for us to start off, but either it wasn't enough or it stopped, because our mum took in sewing straightaway. From then on it was like not having a mother, just someone there sewing. She was up early sewing, she sewed all day, and she was up late at night. She kept us as decent as she could, but we weren't very savoury. We smelt sort of damp and fusty. But we always had boots. We weren't like the kids in the Lane; we never went barefoot.

What she demanded of us was that we be clean.

"We may have fallen upon hard times," she said, "but you will be clean and you will wash your necks, and if I see you dirty I'll lay into you myself."

And so, to achieve this desirable state, either me or Charley – though it usually seemed to be me – had to get up very early and take the buckets to the standpipe each day. This was several streets away and we had to wait for it to be turned on so we could bring the water home. Of this water, we had a bowl in our room so we could wash, though I was more thorough than Charley who didn't seem to mind niffing a bit, whereas I used to get most particular over mucky fingernails. I was like our mum there, keeping up standards.

Our mum told us point blank we weren't like the kids in the Lane.

"They have always been like that," she said. "Dirty and ragged and doing wrong. But you aren't like that, Charley and Willie. You come of decent folk, and your father was a good union man and very clever; don't you forget it. He was a fine carpenter and he could read and write and talk like a scholar, and write poetry too. My family said he was not right for me because of his politics, but they were narrow-minded people and didn't understand. They cast us off but we didn't care; we made our own way without any help from them, and we were very happy. Circumstance has brought us to this place and we must make the best of it. We shall try to live as we always have done, respectably. That means you are not to go down the Lane, ever, because it is a bad place. If you have to do with those people you may pass the time of day politely but no more, and you keep well clear of them."

When we first lived there our difference from the Lane people showed in all kinds of ways. For a start we had net curtains, a tablecloth and a clock on the wall. But the longer we lived there, little by little we lost these outward signs. The net curtains became heavy with grime and half disintegrated; and the last winter they were stuffed into a crack in the wall to keep out the wind. We still had the clock but it didn't tick, and the wall behind it had peeled like skin so that if you touched the place, powdery dust came out.

We lived in that house till I was twelve years old. We started off different from the Lane children, yes, but by the end of that time even an observing person would have been hard put to see any particular differences about us.

I would not recommend selling matches in winter as an enjoyable way to make a living. However, me and Charley both got jobs; I sold matches and he swept roads, and the good thing about this was that we were able to go off together and see a bit of life. We went into the city, which wasn't far to walk, and we went up west, which was farther but more lively. It was during these long strays into foreign territory that it gradually dawned on me that the world was a rich and wonderful place if you had money.

The two of us would leave home after a breakfast of bread and dripping and tea, and sometimes cold bacon, and in all the streets we went through there was food on barrows, all giving off wonderful smells. The street sellers sounded so persuasive that it tugged at your heartstrings not to do them the kindness of buying. Depending on the season there were cockles and whelks, fish and soup, sandwiches, kidney puddings, hot eels, and beautiful baked potatoes. You could follow these with buns and muffins, and plum and apple tarts; and you could wash it all down with ginger beer and lemonade. Clothes and chairs and flowers and tools – you could buy just about anything on the streets.

Bad weather was good for Charley, sweeping roads. We must've covered miles. We had to keep moving because people got funny about anyone taking their pitches. I'd be on the pavement yelling "Any Lights" and "Lucifers" with this hefty tray strapped around me – I must've come up to all of people's waist level – and Charley would be running in and out amongst the traffic, clearing the way for pedestrians. The streets were awful mucky, what with so many horses and straw and wet mulchy leaves and rubbish and mud. It was noisy and busy, things coming in all directions – great carts full of barrels, wagons piled with hay, omnibuses and cabs, and all those wheels grinding and rattling!

We were out in all weathers. There were days when the air was so bright you could see each and every smut floating down from the sky; there were squelchy wet days when the mud splashed up from the road and coated us up to the ears, and there were autumn winds that blew clouds of rubbish round us.

Charley kept running back to me to check I was all right, not lost or trodden on.

"Show your face, Willie," he said, tilting my chin up. "Let the gemmun see your face."

"Why?" I grumbled, permanently cold and tired.

"Don't yer know, yer little sprat?" he laughed. "'Cos you're pretty, that's why, and they'll buy your lights for that."

At that stage in my life I could see no connection between what my face looked like and whether anyone needed a box of matches, but Charley was right. The gentlemen patted my head, and the discerning said I had Unusual Hair. This was true. It was a real auburn, rich and dark, with strands of copper and bronze. It has always caused me to be noticed.

Another tip from Charley was for me was to treat the gentlemen's bounty with an almost saint-like politeness.

"When he gives yer the money," he told me, "yer say: 'God bless yer, mister'. See?"

"Why?"

"Because they likes it, and it's a polite thing to do."

"But me throat's sore with yellin' already."

"You say what I told yer; it's polite."

I looked after him disappearing amongst the great iron-rimmed wheels into the road, and I wondered if he said it when they gave him money for sweeping. I supposed no one would have heard him even if he did. I didn't fancy being out there in all that muddle of horses and wheels and flying mud so I said what he told me to say. No one was more surprised than me when gentlemen came back especially, having heard me, and put extra pennies into my hand, saying: "Keep that for yourself, my boy."

So I said "God bless yer, mister" and my pile of pennies grew. You could get two glasses of sherbet for a penny, and there was all them stalls on the way back home. Trouble was, when I showed my pennies to Charley, thinking he'd be impressed, he just collared the lot, and said:

"See, what did I tell yer?"

My face screwed up with disbelief.

"They're mine!" I screamed. "Give 'em back!"

"They ain't yours, they're ours," he said reasonably. "Ah, don't cry, Willie – people are looking, and you won't sell anything crying."

Charley knelt right down on the pavement, holding my shoulders and looking me in the eyes, and said ever so kindly:

"Look, Willie, don't you know we have to buy candles and coal? We takes it all back to Ma and if there's any over she'll let you have something. We can't *have* pennies for ourselves."

I cried all the way home. Well, we had to pass all the barrows, didn't we? But Charley stopped by one and bought me a baked potato, even though we needed coal and candles, and this shut me up and filled me up, and made me once more aware of how admirable Charley was. He said that keeping pennies that gentlemen had given me was like stealing from him and Ma, so I felt ashamed because he was so good and I was so sneaky. But even though he was so upstanding he was even fonder of me, and he'd bought me the potato because I was upset. He didn't even buy one for himself. He was my very first hero.

II

I NEVER realised that the school we went to was called a Ragged School until some visiting inspector came and told us.

"Oh, ragged children!" he cried, in a big booming voice. "Lucky children indeed, attending this Ragged School. Grateful must you be, and you must show your gratitude by your obedience to those who teach you. Work, work and work. So shall ye prosper."

The school was one large room, and into it were pressed more children than I ever realised existed, all in every shade of poverty.

The first thing I learnt was that because of the colour of my hair I was instantly noticeable. Brown-haired kids merged into the crowd, but I was picked on straightaway with shouts of:

"Oy, Carrots!" "Who set your hair on fire?"

So many filthy little fingers grabbed at the long bits at the back that I was involved in a fight before I'd been there half an hour. I suppose I was about seven or eight years old and slim and small, and I suddenly found myself at the bottom of a pile of squirming bodies who were doing me over for having red hair. Charley slung them off me one by one.

"Anybody touches our Willie again," he said in what they call Thrilling Tones, "and they'll have me to deal with."

It was wonderful having a brother like that.

School was also the first place where I came up against God. I think our teachers must have been quite enlightened, because they didn't put us off religion for ever by making us learn

"The rich man in his castle,
The poor man at the gate"

but managed to introduce us to God without making us dislike him for creating us poor. We sang some happy songs about Jesus loving little children and we heard some exciting stories about boys slaying giants, hearing God's voice when they were asleep, being sold into slavery, imprisoned in a fiery furnace, fleeing into the wilderness, tricking their brothers. We had the Life of Jesus, which was a wonderful story, and out of all this we learned we had to be good, and that meant really good down to the depth of our hearts, because Jesus could see in there; and we weren't to tell lies and steal – all the things that Charley had been telling me all along. So I respected Jesus more because he agreed with Charley, and Charley more because what he'd always said was the same as what God said. I liked God. I didn't think I'd have too much trouble staying good.

As I said, the children were ragged; we were used to bare feet and torn sleeves but one day a boy arrived at school in Only A Shawl. He'd had it pinned around him when he came but someone had unravelled it, and underneath he had no clothes on at all, and everything showed! I stared along with everyone else. A funny feeling came over me looking at that boy, like I half wanted to hurt him for being so thin and vulnerable, and I half wanted to love him for the same reasons. He was trying to cover himself up, and people were pulling his hands away and pushing him around. The teachers were already on their way across to see what the disturbance was, but the boy was starting to shiver and cry, and I wanted it to be me that saved him. I jumped in front of him and punched the boy who was bothering him most, a hefty bloke I'd never have normally dared hit. He was taken by surprise but his two mates laid into me, and as I fell back I flung my arms round the boy without his shawl and we all went down in a struggling pile. When the teachers untangled us I was lying on my front all over this bare boy, holding very tight. Instead of feeling self-conscious and foolish, I felt strong and protective and held on like a dog with a bone.

The boy's name was Matthew Brown, and for a few days he followed me around as if he was my spaniel. The strange thing was, that with his clothes on he couldn't cause a flicker of interest for me. He just seemed like an ordinary boy, weedy, ragged and dull. But the *feeling* stayed. If I shut my eyes and thought about his quivering nakedness I could call it all back, and sometimes in my mind I put myself in his place, imagining myself having a shawl torn off like that. And I knew I'd look nicer than him.

There was a man teacher in charge and a lady teacher who organised the soup and bread, with girls to help her; she also did some teaching in the quiet bits. I fell in love with this lady, deserting Charley who was one of those playing marbles at the back. The lady was so delighted to find someone as gawpingly receptive as me that she gave me all her attention and, with another quiet boy and a bunch of girls, we set about learning to read.

It was awful hard going, but we persevered and after months of grind and mystery it suddenly all came right, and the shapes became words.

Walking through the streets was an entirely different experience, like a new world.

"Leg-of-beef-soup—2d!" I yelled incredulously, running around to read whatever I could lay my eyes on. "Stout-and-light-ale! Brush-up-and-polish—1½d!" And one that mystified me immensely: "Angel and Son."

Now that I had learnt to read, I was hungry for books. And it was this hunger more than the physical one which was the cause of my getting into Bad Ways.

They did have books at the Ragged School. I read out loud from a great Bible with pages that curled at the edges and were tinted brown; and I got to know the names of all the boys in the stories – Samuel, David, Jonathan, even Shadrach, Meshac and the one that nobody could pronounce. Gideon and Joshua were my favourites, because they were so manly. I'd have gladly brought a cup of wine to either of those after the battle, and mopped their sweating brows.

As well as the religious stories we had moral ones. They were generally in the form of poems. There was one about a mouse who ate all of the cake. He didn't share any with his brothers or sisters and he became ill, and the doctor told him that he would die because he was greedy. Thus we learnt that stolen pleasures lead to retribution. The heroes and heroines of these stories were usually chickens and pigs, and over-eating figured largely in the cause of their ruin. None of us who read these tales had the wherewithal to over-eat, nor had ever over-eaten in our lives; given the chance, we would gladly have wrung the chickens' necks and ate them, and fried up the good little pig for bacon. Once when I was reading from the Alphabet of Flowers, about zinnias and water lilies, I heard the lady teacher say despairingly to the man:

"Oh, John! when will they print some books within the experience of poor children?"

Charley had never taken to school like I had. He didn't like book work but active things and standing on his own feet, so he used to skive and go down the docks. At first he just used to hang around down there and listen to sailors' talk and make himself useful; but as he got bigger and stronger he had a wage for his services, lifting bales and humping sacks, loading and unloading; and our mum agreed that was more useful to us than his schooling. So while I went to school, Charley went to work.

He took me down the docks once, but I didn't like it. It was a November afternoon, and already dark. I don't know why I found it so sinister and scary but I did; I couldn't share any of the excitement and lure the docks had for Charley. They were so big and noisy and mysterious – I mean, you thought you were walking on solid ground and there beneath your feet you could see slits in the plankwork, and black lurching water slurping below. In the streets that led down to the dockside the great warehouses soared up black and grimy, and out of the fog, great bales swung unexpectedly on chains, like plummeting boulders, and landed with a crash on the cobblestones. Iron wheels arched past your shoulders, pressing you to the wall where you tripped over tangles of wet rope; above your head the dray horses wheezed and whinneyed, their hooves like great lead weights.

At the quayside the heaving water oozed with threat. The stink of it mingled with the waft of raw fish and that of the beer and sweat from the taverns, whose doors flooded hot air and sudden light and laughter that seemed to me entirely menacing. Sirens wailed and smoke stung your eyes. Finally we reached the water's edge, where Charley's pride and delight was so apparent you'd have thought he'd created the entire spectacle himself.

"See it, Willie, that's the Thames that is, and it goes all the way to the sea!"

"I see it, Charley, and smell it and all."

"Come and see what they're unloading over here; it looks like pineapples. You ain't never seen a pine, Willie, come and look."

"Yeah, all right, I see 'em but I still don't like it. Where I'm standing is wobbling, and I'm scared it'll float away."

"You ain't half a goose, Willie," said Charley. "Come and meet me mates. Ah, no, don't hold me hand; that's sissy down here."

I ended up lifted on to a barrel and sat there kicking my heels against its salty sides, while Charley joked around with people whom I'm sure our mum would have been surprised he knew.

I'd never seen men like these, and I was half alarmed and half fascinated. They must be all right because Charley knew them, but they were coarse and tough and noisy and strange. There was a man with bare arms dripping with oily sweat, and he had pictures on his arms, and when I stared he came and showed me. They were like blue drawings on his skin – mermaids and anchors – and he asked me if I wanted to touch them, so I did, and another man said, "How about me – have you ever felt muscles like this then?"

Blushing hotly, I suddenly found myself feeling sailors' muscles! I vigorously maintain I only did it to be polite, because they wanted me to. They could make their muscles bulge enormous and I do believe my mouth dropped open as I laid my fingers on them.

"That's nothing," declared a sailor with golden ear rings. "Have a look at this!" And he lifted up his vest and unbuckled his trouser belt and revealed his stomach down as far as the start of his crotch hairs, and he rotated the muscles there in an incredible display of hollows and ridges. I was spellbound. Not only by the rippling navel but by the hair. It looked like an animal, furry and hidden.

"Nice, ennit?" they told me, wallowing in appreciation of their own blatant maleness. Then they showed me how I could get muscles like that, all very good humoured, lifting my arm and getting me to clench my fist and telling me that was coming along nicely and I'd be a little devil when I was grown, and did you ever see such hair!

"Like the sun going down!" it was poetically decided.

Some of them then wandered off into a quayside public house and I heard Charley say "No, don't give him a drink," but I rather think Charley had one. I was given a long stick of something sweet and sickly to suck which trickled in brown streaks down my chin, and a couple of the sailors stayed chatting to me as I sat on my barrel. The warm sweaty smell of them filled my nostrils, and I was right up close to the jet black curls of the one with ear rings. He had black hairs in his ears and on the back of his neck, and when he lifted his arm I saw he'd got a whole nest of black hairs there too. Life was full of surprises that night.

"*Like* sailors then, do yer, laddy?" he grinned, noticing my wide eyes and undisguised interest.

"Yes," I blushed, not daring to say anything other.

They hooted with delight.

"Oy, Charley, your little brother says he likes sailors!"

"He's a sharp little bugger, this kid."

"Sailors like *him* and all, don't we!"

Saying these things, they ruffled my hair and pinched my knees, and laughed. I did feel uncomfortable, because I knew they were laughing at things I had no inkling of. I knew you were supposed to be polite at all times, but politeness here seemed to have some kind of double meaning.

"How'd you like to be my cabin boy then?" said the one with ear rings, giving me a nudge.

"I don't know," I gulped, "I don't think – "

"We gunna sail the seas together? See foreign parts?"

This had them in gales of laughter.

"Ooh Charley, we dun half like your little brother – he's comin' to sea with us to learn a thing or two, ain't yer?"

"Yes," I grinned modestly, fluttering my lashes a bit.

Suddenly my friend with the ear rings picked me right up in his arms and started walking about with me. I was overcome with confusion at the closeness of the oily rippling muscles and the dirty vest and the mat of black curls that spilled up from it, and the waft of beery breath that caught me in the face as he bellowed:

"What am I bid for this nice little boy? Wants to be a cabin boy and see foreign parts! Any *Turk* in the audience? Any foreign gemmun want this dainty little boy? This *ripe* little boy? Game for anything and very partial to sailors!"

"Ah, leave off," said Charley, but I know now that he too was laughing when I was being offered. My sailor friend put me down and I ran to Charley. He cuddled me against him, and swigged back his drink.

"He was only joking," Charley reassured me on the way home, still laughing to himself. "Come on, Willie, don't sulk."

"Charley, what's a Turk?"

"A Turk's a foreign gemmun, Willie."

"Why would he want me, Charley?"

"Oh, they says Turks like little boys."

"Why do they?"

"Well, little boys is nice, ain't they?"

This seemed a perfectly reasonable explanation. However, I never went back to the docks with Charley. It wasn't just the indignity of being carried about and auctioned. After all, in its way it was rather flattering, and it had been very jovial and not in any way malevolent. No, what I didn't like was that this noisy disturbing place was somewhere I felt ill at ease in, and Charley felt at home. I was jealous of the docks because they attracted Charley. He'd sided with the sailors and not with me. Secretly I felt hurt and resentful. He'd left me to my own devices while he'd gone and had a drink, and he'd let sailors muck around with me and he'd thought it was funny. Now I come to think of it, I'll bet he knew why Turks wanted boys. And in order not to be confronted with the unacceptable fact that Charley liked the docks as much as he liked me, I never went there again, though he asked me lots of times.

III

MEANWHILE I persevered with my education, and around the age of ten I began to realise that there were books about things other than greedy mice and virtuous chickens. The lady teacher gave me *Grimms' Fairy Tales* for my very own to take away and keep. Of all the books I've owned since, that has always been very special to me because of it being my first ever; and they say you always remember your first!

My enthusiasm for learning didn't mean that I never skived; I did – everyone did. And on one of these days off, something happened to me up west.

I found that it was not so much the food barrows these days as the bookshops which attracted me. I looked in all the windows and read all the titles, and as far as I could tell they were all thrilling stories, and none of them was about chickens. I tried to read them in the shop, but the bookseller rapped my knuckles with a ruler and watched out for me, so I couldn't. The books cost tuppence and had titles such as *Murder in Park Lane*, *The Vault of Death*, *The Forged Will*, *The Squire of Lynwood*, and *Done to Death*.

Well, in this interesting row of shops there was a window with prints hanging – pictures of ladies in flowing dresses, advertising patterned cloth. I had been gazing in there for a while, lost to the world, when a gentleman beside me struck up a conversation. I answered politely, and the man asked me whether I'd like to earn two shillings and sixpence. Needless to say I nearly collapsed with eagerness, and so I went off with him walking along the street. We didn't have to go far, just into this house; and up a whole lot of stairs till we were right at the top. It was a long low room under the glass skylights, and you could see the chimney pots real close. All round the room were prints and drawings, pinned up, mostly of similar ladies in long skirts, showing quite a lot of their bodies.

The man took off his coat and put a sort of smock on, and started fiddling around with sheaves of paper.

"You an artist, mister?"

"That's right, my boy."

"You drew all them pictures?"

"Indeed I did. Do you like them?"

"Yes, mister."

"And how would you like to be on one of those pictures yourself?"

"Yes I would, not half!"

"Let me explain," said the man.

He was thin and tall, with pale-coloured hair hanging wispily over his collar, and he moved around in a way that made me think of a hen on long legs. He said he drew pictures to make people buy materials, and that his pictures were not realistic but created to capture the tone of the material.

"Ottoman," he said, "satin, finely decorated with flowers. I've represented it by this damsel," and he brandished a sketch of a voluptuous lady in a curtained tent. She had a transparent veil across her face, and a sultry gaze. You could see all the top part of her body. When he saw me gawping at that he whisked it away and showed me the next one.

"Algerine," he said, "shot silk in gorgeous colours." This one was a plump little girl in a short white dress, with flowers in her hair and a bunch of grass in her hand.

"Sultane," he said, "silky soft and striped." This was two ladies dancing, in long loose dresses, and in the background some camels and a palm tree.

"And so we come to Pekin point," he declared. "A lovely white and gold silk. And for this I need a boy."

He'd got a large unfinished drawing of a lady reclining. She was extremely pretty and languid, and she trailed a garland from her drooping hand. To one side there was a space, with a vaguely boyish shape loosely sketched.

"Do you think you can pose for me? You are exactly what I want."

I thought about this.

"My clothes ain't right," I came up with.

"How astute it is!" he beamed.

He hunted around and produced a shaggy goatskin. Amazingly enough, I was thoroughly comfortable and enjoying myself immensely. My artist chatted away lightly while he moved around, either thinking he was putting me at my ease or pattering on to cover up his own guilt. He must have been not a little uneasy at the social acceptability of dragging a boy in off the streets, and planning to ask him to take off his clothes. Because that's what he did next.

I hesitated. Through my mind went what I knew our mum's reaction would be. But she wasn't here, was she? And stronger in my mind was excitement and the unashamed desire to see myself drawn on a picture to sell Pekin point.

"All right, mister," I said. "And I get me half crown after."

"Let's have a look at you," said the artist, fixing the goatskin around my front.

I put my hands on my hips and stuck my chest out and looked as important as I knew how. At the back I was Completely Bare!

"Yes, dear," he said, half amused and half assessively. "Whirl around for me."

He liked what he saw; you can always tell. He darted around me, kneeling, looking up, sketching, squinting, muttering.

"Nice . . . good . . . keep your head still; I want your neck . . . ah, that curve . . . that is a most exquisite posterior . . . "

Then we heard footsteps coming up the stairs, and into the room came a lady. It was obvious to me immediately that she was the one on the drawings, but at the moment she was simply a lady who had been shopping. I held my pose and let him do the explaining. She was horrified and alarmed.

"Ernest! What are you thinking of? In the street? What if his parents – ?"

" – but he's exactly right – "

" – damn lucky if you don't get into trouble – "

" – perfectly all right, Charlotte – "

" – I see he's what you wanted, but . . . "

" – and he has *no natural modesty!*"

My mouth dropped open. Charlotte burst out laughing. Suddenly it all came nice. Charlotte swanned over to me, streaming false fur and smelling like a bunch of flowers, and cuddled me and said I was a sweetheart. When I got back into my clothes Mister Ernest gave me two shillings and sixpence. He said the print would be on sale in the bookshop and it would cost one shilling. It cost so much because it was Art.

Owning half a crown was dizzying. I knew what I wanted: books. So, keeping one shilling back to buy the print, I bought six books, half fainting with excitement as I chose, and caused a caustic remark from the bookseller who'd rapped my knuckles:

"Come into a fortune, have you?"

They were called Gem Pocket Novels. They all had manly heroes, bright of eye and muscular of limb; and terrible villains who would Stop At Nothing. They were not wicked books at all, and they were refreshingly free of exhortations to piety. However, because I'd bought them in secret and from "immoral earnings" they did seem wicked. I think I came to associate the possession of money – particularly money that was easy to earn – with secret pleasure and deceit and, quaint though the word may sound, shame.

IV

WHEN THE artistic print came out on sale I bought it and brought it home. It was late at night when I showed it to our mum. I came down in my nightshirt, barefoot, and without any preface I said it was me. She just didn't believe me at first, and then when I pattered on about Mr Ernest and Charlotte, the horrible truth dawned on her and she had to believe.

She got up from her chair and called for Charley. He came down in his nightshirt, rubbing his eyes and grumbling. One candle burned on the edge of the table, lighting up all the shirts, cottons, pins and scissors. For the first time ever, I realised our mum wasn't well, and she looked old and gaunt, the candle making the grey hollows under her eyes look cavernous, and I thought oh lawks, now I bin and gone and done it.

"Have you seen this, Charley?" she demanded, flicking her finger at my print. "You seen this *indecent* thing?"

I watched Charley anxiously. I knew him well enough to work out what he was thinking. He liked it! He went all absorbed and interested, and had even started an appreciative grin until he realised our mum didn't approve and was waiting for him to confirm her disapproval.

"That lad's your brother," she said in clipped tones, "that lad showing his behind. And he's just had the nerve to come and tell me he went into a house with a man and took off his clothes in front of him and let him draw what he could see. What do you think of that?"

"I dunno, Ma," said Charley, playing for time. He looked at

me, curious. "*Is* it you?" He peered at it. "The hair ain't right. Yeah, but the bum is."

"Charley!" shrieked our mum.

Charley couldn't help grinning, and I grinned back, a bit sheepishly.

"I brought you up decent. I thought I did. You go to school. I thought you were learning things. I thought they taught you how to behave right. And then I find you've been out of school. You've gone with a man who's no better than he should be. A wicked, wicked man who should never have asked you to go with him. All that was bad enough. But taking your clothes off, Willie – don't you know that's *wrong?* Don't you know that? Haven't you any shame?"

I twitched around squeezing my fingers together.

"It didn't *feel* shameful . . . " I began, wriggling. "Well, only a bit."

"Charley, you'll have to belt him," said our mum flatly.

"Owww!" I wailed protesting.

"He doesn't know the difference between right and wrong," she said, "and that's the only way I know of bringing it home. I'm too tired to do it myself; I haven't got the strength. Do it, will you Charley? Do it as if you were his dad."

"Ow, Ma!" Charley groaned. "Do I have ter? You know how he howls if anyone lays a finger on him. Half the street'll hear."

"*Do* it, Charley," said our Ma.

The sound of the belt swishing through the air was horrible, and the slap of it landing on my squirming flesh was more horrible still because it stung sharp, and I yelled and yelled. You'd have thought I was being murdered the noise I made, and I hoped Charley was embarrassed. Afterwards I ran upstairs. What upset me was that it was unfair. I was awash with confusion, accepting their right to punish me, but not sure that I had done wrong.

I was still sulking when Charley came to bed, and I snatched the blanket off him.

"Ah, come on, Willie, give us it," he grumbled.

"Fuckin' lousy bugger," I muttered savagely.

"I had to," he said reasonably. "I'm sorry."

"You hurt!" I accused.

"I know I did. I did it hard 'cos she said to do it like our dad.

I thought he'd do it hard. Being as we ain't got no dad, there's only me to keep you right."

"And who does it to you?" I exploded.

Charley sniggered.

"Well, I don't go around taking my clothes off, do I?"

I turned my back huffily.

"Ah come on, Willie," he cajoled, pulling me back to him. "I'm sorry about belting yer. I thought you looked real nice in that picture."

"Did yer?" I said pleased in spite of myself.

"Do you forgive me about what just happened? You know I didn't want to do it."

"I do forgive yer. But I wish you'd gerroff me."

"Not yet, Willie," he said, in a muffled sort of voice, and he was moving his hips around on me, his shape distorted by the bundle of blanket. I whimpered a bit from being pressed into the bed. He put his mouth down and sort of kissed me, still grinding his hips about. He gave a shuddering groan and dropped his face in my neck. I put my arms round him. I could feel his strong shoulder blades through his thin nightshirt.

"Did yer mind me doing that, Willie?" he asked.

"No."

"Did yer like it?"

"Yes."

He got off me and lay on his back, breathing hard.

"Your mouth's just like a girl's," he said.

"It is not."

"It is, it's soft and very nice."

He pulled me up against him, and the blanket around us both. His strong arms held me.

"I'll make it up to yer," he told me. "I never wanted to make yer cry."

I would have been quite content with that, but Charley was as bountiful as the sea and he went in for grand gestures. He gave me a day out!

We got up when it was still dark and went down to a place he knew by the river's edge, and we stole a boat. I was so sleepy I fell asleep in the boat; otherwise I would have spoilt things by worrying about falling in. But as it was, when I awoke it was like magic. The sun had come up and the sky was blue. Charley was quietly rowing, moving us along quickly, past banks of trees. It was like a different world. I couldn't remember ever having seen a proper tree, not for years. And now here they were hanging over the river, trailing into the boat.

We got out and we were in fields. We ran about, and lay in the grass and rolled. I wanted all my clothes to smell of grass. I couldn't breathe in enough. Charley had brought cheese and hard biscuits wrapped in a handkerchief. We could see these tulips growing the other side of a garden wall, and we nipped over and picked a couple. We had to go back after we'd had our cheese because Charley had to get back to work. We couldn't put the boat back where we found it in case we were seen returning it, so we left it with some others and had to walk miles back home. I carried those tulips the way boys carry candles in a procession, like they were lighting the way. And all that beautiful time was a present to me from Charley.

When I say what he did next, there might be some as think he was a bad lot and very much to blame. but I don't and it was me it concerned.

It happened soon after the day out.

CHAPTER TWO

I

THE BED where we slept, me and Charley, was a wooden one, and the mattress was stuffed with straw. We suffered terrible with bed bugs in hot weather, itching and scratching and waking up sudden, but I used to think our bed was a special place, bedbugs and all. We slept tight against each other in cold weather, huffing on each other and down our nightshirts to get warm. Through the walls we could hear next door coming to bed and getting up and having rows; we could also hear creaking from the bed, and manly groans along with the creaks.

"You know what he's doing, don't you?" said Charley one time.

I nodded and said: "No."

"Do you want me to show you?" he offered.

"Yes please," I said, a pleasurable surge of excitement tickling me at the realisation that one of life's mysteries was about to be revealed to me, and anticipatory gratitude that someone as reliable as Charley was the one to initiate me.

"You're the girl," Charley began briskly.

"Oh no," I whined, "not *that* again."

"For this someone *has* ter be," said Charley. "Now d'you want me to show you or not? Because," he added, with a glittery look about the eyes, "I'm going to show you anyway."

"Well, maybe I don't want you to," I resisted provocatively.

"Well, maybe you can't stop me," he responded at once.

I lay underneath him on my back, pleasantly squashed, and let him kiss me as much as he wanted. He was working himself up, hanging over me, rubbing his crotch on mine and I was getting lovely sensations there.

"Give us yer hand," Charley panted in my ear. "Put it *here* and keep holding."

His hand closed over mine, and he thrust quick and sharp.

"Charley I'm all wet!" I squeaked.

"Shurrup, it's all right, it's supposed to be like that."

We lay in the darkness, hot and sweaty under the blanket.

"And that's what they're doing next door, is it?" I asked.

"Yeah, that's what. Did you like it?"

"Yes, it was nice. Charley . . . you know you said I was the girl?"

"Yeah, you went underneath."

"I know, but I was a boy, and you still did it."

"What d'yer mean?"

"Well, you liked it, didn't yer?"

"Course I did!"

"But you were doing it to a boy. So it still works if you use boys?"

"Yeah, but only 'cos there isn't a girl. It's only pretend if you do it with a boy; you're pretending he's a girl. I can do that with you because you feel all soft and your mouth is so nice. I couldn't do it with a tough sort of boy, all bony and hard. I was pretending with you."

"Yeah, but Charley . . . "

"What?"

"If you was pretending, I shouldn't have got wet."

We had another think.

"I couldn't help the wet," said Charley reasonably. "After a bit there's nothing you can do ter stop it, it just comes out itself. It's all right to do it with boys if there ain't no girls, but you'd be stupid to do it with a boy if there was a girl. It's better with girls. Girls is made for it." Then he added mournfully: "The trouble with girls is that they have babies after, and you has to provide for 'em."

I thought about the girls at the ragged school. They had yappy voices, and they weren't half bossy; they elbowed you out the way when the soup came round and they were quick and clever and secretive. I couldn't imagine them taking seriously what Charley and I had just done or keeping still long enough for him to be able to do it.

"I don't know," I said earnestly, "I think I'd rather do it with you."

"You won't!" Charley laughed. "Not when you're growed. You'll want girls then. You see if you don't."

Some time later that summer – I would've been ten, and him fourteen – I was educated a little further. The nights were very hot, and the bugs were biting, and even the air in the room smelt of the street – a grimy smoky smell overlaying a smell of rotting fruit. The lads selling strawberries on the barrows said they'd rather sell them than eat them, and there were flies everywhere, and if you had to go past a butcher's you hurried.

"You too hot?" Charley asked.

"Baking."

"Take yer nightshirt off; I'm going to."

Well, after that we never bothered wearing them and I got used to the feel of him naked, and that's when I learnt to do little things he liked. One of those nights when we were lying close, Charley said to me:

"Willie, I want to do something different with yer. It's something that lots of people do, and someone might do it to you, someone you didn't like, because sometimes this gets done to pretty boys whether they want it or not. So I'm going to be the one who does it, and it'll be all right from me because I loves yer."

So I lay how he wanted, on my stomach, and he started stroking me. I could sense he was very excited. His palms were sweaty and, if it hadn't been Charley, I'd have said trembling. Then he did things with his fingers and I wriggled.

"Stay still, darlin'," he said.

I gasped being called that. It seemed to make what he was doing into something else, elevate it to a different level, make us into lovers – people who met secretly, people whom the world would try to separate, like in the Pocket Gems.

"I'll be gentle," he said. "You see if it ain't real nice."

I believed him and I lay still and quiet, and he moved very slow and smooth. I never felt so close to him as then. I felt his heart beating on my back and his excitement growing. He moved quicker, panting in my ear. I was excited too and scared, but pleasurably. I sighed. I knew exactly when he'd finished. We were both gasping, and my teeth started chattering.

"What's up?" Charley panted.

"I dunno – I'm all of a tremble."

"Are yer? So'm I."

We lay close, waiting for our breathing to steady. Charley asked me cautiously if I was all right and did I like it.

"Yes I did," I replied.

"You ain't half good," said Charley, possibly with relief. "You really liked it, did yer? You did seem to."

"Yes thank you."

"Can I do it again sometime then?"

"Yes, if yer want."

"You are nice to me, Willie, you are a little darlin'."

The funny thing was that it was me as much as Charley who wanted to do it again. Some nights I'd pester him in bed and wake him up specially.

"Do it, Charley, do that thing to me, that thing I like."

It was very much later before I wondered whether it was an all right thing to be doing. I suppose I was following the logic of it being wrong to take off your clothes for an artist and this was something you did without clothes.

"No, it ain't wrong," said Charley. "Because I love yer and I wouldn't hurt yer, and anyway you like it."

"I know I like it, but I liked posing, and I got belted for that."

"This is different. It's something we do private."

"I know it's all right between you and me," I agreed, "but what if our mum found out? Would *she* think it was right, or would she think it was like posing?"

"You ain't *never* to tell ma!" said Charley, going dead white. "D'you hear, our Willie? You ain't never to tell her!"

"I won't tell her," I hurriedly assured him.

"See, Willie," said Charley relaxing a bit. "She wouldn't understand. Women don't know about these things. She ain't very well and we don't want to make her worried. So we don't say anything to her, right?"

"Yeah, right."

"Not ever," he insisted, very serious.

"No, all right. I wasn't going to anyway. I just wondered what she'd think, that's all."

"Willie, I don't think she even knows about it. It's something private, between men."

"Do they do it down at the docks then?"

"Some do, yeah. But they got girls as well. You know, girls

specially for it, who live down there in houses and wait for the ships. *And* there's boys."

"Boys specially for it . . . same as the girls?"

"Yeah . . . You know them poor lads they call mudlarks, them as pokes around in the mud for driftwood and scraps that come off ships? Well, they can earn more push going with a sailor and they won't get half as muddy."

"They get *money* for it, Charley? For doin' what we just did?" My eyes were certainly being opened tonight.

"Course they do, and the girls do."

"Get money for doing something so nice?" I marvelled.

"Oh Willie, you ain't half stupid," Charley groaned. "D'you think it's nice with a drunk old sailor? You think it's nice because it's me and we love each other. But what do you think it's like takin' yer britches down for someone you don't know, and without feelings, and not even a word said between yer and no lovin' care? You think that's nice?"

"No I don't," I said. "But I think it's an easy way to make some money."

"Go on with yer," Charley laughed, thumping me. "Else I'll have ter give yer another belting for not knowing right from wrong."

II

IT MUST have been the year after; and it was a boiling summer day, everything stinking and everybody sweating. I was kicking a stone down a gutter when I saw Fadge sitting on a wall, eating peaches. I stopped dead in my tracks, gawping with lust at the sight. You could hear the slurps of his spit as he sucked; you could see the juice trickling down his chin, and the flies buzzing to get a lick.

Fadge is an old street name for a farthing, and Fadge the boy was about thirteen, a Lane kid, the sort we weren't supposed to know. I knew him from school. He was skinny and tough and always skiving, and he had no boots. His filthy feet swung against the wall and his trousers were all ragged. The soles of his feet were completely black. They were on a level with my chest. I stared up at him, captivated by the peaches. He'd got one that he was eating, and two more on the top of the wall, just as big, bigger even.

"Know me again, will yer?" he remarked sarcastically, a comment on my stare.

I was affronted to have him think I was wasting a stare on him, so I hurriedly put the matter right.

"Where'd you get them peaches?"

"Fell from the sky, wotcher fink?" he sneered.

"You pinched 'em, I'll bet," I said enviously, practically dribbling.

"No I never and it's bugger all to do with you."

I turned to go past. I didn't like him and I was already annoyed I'd betrayed such interest.

"Oy, Carrots," he said, "Want one?"

I spun round, open mouthed.

"What, all of one?" I couldn't believe it.

"Wotcher give me for it?"

"Wotcher want?"

"Come here."

I put myself close to him, and he leaned down and I could smell peach juice from his sticky face.

"What?" I said.

"I'll give yer a peach if you'll come behind the wall with me," he said mysteriously.

"What for?" I asked a bit stupid.

He hooted with laughter, and whispered wetly in my ear.

I blushed bright red. I was astonished that he knew about that sort of thing; I even wondered if he knew about me and Charley. For a startling moment it even crossed my mind that it somehow *showed* – that if you did it fairly often, other people could tell.

"You done it before?" I asked cautiously.

"Course I have. Will yer?"

"Will you tell anyone after?"

"Nah!" he said, licking his lips.

"*Two* peaches," I said.

"All right," he replied. He backed over the wall like something out of a Punch and Judy, and I had a quick look in both directions and strolled round to join him. He was on to me like a shot, with all the finesse of a rutting tom cat. I whistled through my teeth, half upside down, my head within inches of a particularly evil-looking nettle.

"Oy, easy on," I winced.

A moment later it was over and, red-faced with bending and exertion, we separated, making no communication other than a swift business transaction. He even reached the peaches down for me, which was decent of him, as he was tough enough to have welched out of the deal and sent me packing. I walked away, and he went back to sitting on the wall.

I ate both peaches walking home. They were beautiful – over-ripe, dripping with juices, practically disintegrating with sweet mulchy softness. The streets were dusty and the peaches were a wet satin waterfall on a dry throat. Wasps pursued me so enthusiastically I looked like I was dancing.

But oh my goodness! How Life imitated Art that night! All those schoolbooks about the specific punishment of sins must have had me in mind. All those mice with gut ache, all those cut fingers from delving into sweet jars that broke, all the wasting illnesses that struck fat lads who didn't share their pies, they all came to my mind that night which I spent half dying on the privy, wracked with gripes like I'd never known. No use then to bewail my stupidity at taking half-rotten fruit from a Lane boy who lived where the water was bad, in high summer and the air thick with flies. I didn't half pay for them peaches; but even out there suffering I could see the humour of my predicament, considering what I did to get them.

I was lucky I got nothing worse than a night in the open air, and in the morning I felt properly chastened, and resolved to be more discriminating.

Just my bad luck. Instead of keeping it to himself, it seemed like Fadge had told just about everybody in the world, and it was a hot topic of gossip running round the school, that Willie Smith would go behind a wall with you if you'd got something nice to swap. I knew, because boys came up and asked me about it.

"Is it true about you and Fadge?"

"D'yer do it with anyone?"

"Will yer do it with me?"

"I could get yer some peaches too."

"I'll swap two marbles for it."

I was awful embarrassed at having found fame in this way, and petrified the lady teacher would get to hear and I'd lose for ever my reputation of being a sensitive, serious boy who liked reading. So, somewhat late in the day, I took refuge in modest refusals and a possibly tantalising and insufferable coyness.

"Why won't yer?"

"I don't want to."

"You wanted to with Fadge."

"Today I don't."

Several of them gave up, deciding I was a disappointment, and went back to pestering the girls on very similar lines. In fact, my indiscretion seemed to have reached their ears too because one of them said, in a voice I was intended to hear:

"And I told him no I wouldn't. I said why dontcher ask Willie Smiff, he'll do it for a coupla peaches!" which roused shrieks of horrible high-pitched laughter from her friends.

"Here, Willie," they teased. "Come and sit by us and we'll give you some tips."

"Want ter borrow a ribbon?"

"Or a petticoat?"

"His face is going as red as his hair!"

"Willie Smiff's a Mary Anne!"

I never heard that stupid name before. I hated all the teasing. It sounded jokey, but underneath it was barbed. Considering that what I'd done was really nobody's business but mine and maybe Fadge's, it surprised me the effect the ripples had. I don't know if it was what I actually did, or because I'd done it for peaches, but people seemed to be personally affronted and to need to let me know it.

I suppose I found out early on that if anyone gets to know that you're a boy who goes with boys, and if you get a present for your favours, you can be certain of reaction and hostility from people with whom it has no connection at all.

As to what a Mary Anne was, although I'd never heard the name before, it didn't take much imagination for me to work out what it meant.

I SHOULD'VE realised that the boys who had become interested in me weren't going to take no for an answer.

I was safe enough inside school, but going home I had to resort to evasive tactics, walking miles out of my way so they wouldn't realise where I lived. Then one evening Fadge and two others abducted me and carried me off to a place of Horror and Despair – the Lane itself, where they lived.

I was hustled along, my boots splashing in a gutter where soggy lumps squelched under my feet. If this place had ever been a lane there was no sign of it whatever. We turned off down a narrow court, houses crowding in on both sides and lines of grimy washing slung between. We passed a public house, people sitting on the steps and sticking their feet out, yelling at Fadge, who yelled back. I know I was in a state of shock, but I could hardly understand the language of the people here – they sort of snarled slang abuse; and then some tiny kids joined us and trooped along, all barefoot and squawking like chickens, and a couple of girls I knew from school came sloping up in curiosity. I got a hard thump between the shoulder blades to direct me through a doorway, and gasping I found myself in a room with no way out.

The three boys drove off the noisy kids and slammed the door, but the girls came in and they let them.

The room smelt, but everywhere smelt here, and it was dingily dark and fusty. Without any more ado, just a few exchanges as to who'd be first, they pushed me over a bare table. I tried to get up and someone took hold of the back of my neck and slammed my face down on the table. They grabbed hold of me and hoiked me about till they'd got my trousers down, and they started working themselves up on me, leaning and grunting.

I hadn't realised that someone had come into the house after us, until Fadge yelled from being hit. I was alarmed to see a man there, the more so when he laid about him with the flat of his hand; he slapped them round the heads and slung two of them out of the house, leaving Fadge very uneasy backed against the wall.

"Don't hit me, Harry," Fadge whined, disintegrating into pathetic subservience.

Impressed, I tugged my trousers back up and fixed my braces. I stared admiringly at Harry.

I would say he was about nineteen and he was flashy and gorgeous. He had coal black hair and gipsy ringlets curling down long, and I'd never seen anybody dressed so brilliant. He had dark blue trousers and a crimson waistcoat and a black corduroy jacket. Around his neck and hanging down was a huge yellow neckerchief that must have been silk.

He stared back at me, his eyebrows all curved up quizzically, his eyes shining and merry, and a most provocative grin.

"Well, my little chavy," he said, as if the admiration was mutual. "And what's caught *your* eye then?"

"I don't half like yer jacket, mister," I said frankly.

"*Do* yer now?" he said pleased. "Well, I liked it meself and I see you're a gemmun of Very Refined Taste – *not* like the nasty little bleeders hereabouts," and he glowered darkly at Fadge and made as if to hit him. Fadge ducked. "Sara," he continued authoritatively to one of the girls, "go and get us a nice drop of You Know What, sharpish."

Sara went out, and Harry asked me most politely what my name was, as if we'd met in the most proper circles.

"Willie Smith, mister."

"Well, Willie Smith, if we are to become closely acquainted you may call me Mister Harry, and I think we shall be acquainted, don't you? If you ain't the loveliest bit of young male flesh I ever seen in my life, I'll eat me neckerchief and that would be a waste of a nice bit o' cloth."

Sara came back with the Nice Drop in a jug which she carried carefully in both hands. Harry poured some out for me into a cracked cup. While Fadge clamoured for some and he and Harry argued, I sat and sipped it. It was gin.

To my delight and awe, Harry drank his from a real wine glass, one with a stem and a wide fluted top. Everything about Harry impressed me immensely. I couldn't believe he lived here. He was like a jewel in a puddle. He was so flashy and bright he seemed to spangle and shine. Best of all he liked me, and he somehow signalled that he and I were special and better, that he recognised in me a fellow spirit. A heady glow suffused all my limbs as I drank.

One elbow on a shelf, Harry leaned with one leg crossed over another, knocking back his gin and chatting to me very friendly. Fadge squatted nearby, quiet, half sullen, half tolerant, and Sara and her friend sat without speaking, still as a picture.

"I has ter tell yer," said Harry. "I never seen a face like yours on a boy, more like something out of a church, I'd say. You got them great big eyes, what they call a Wondrous Shade Of Blue. Open 'em wide, go on, see how you look. Tell yer what, look *up*, as if you was blinkin' at an angel. Can you make yourself cry?"

"Whaffor?" I asked blankly.

"Never you mind what for. Can yer? Can yer make me a big fat tear as'll trickle slowly dahn them pretty cheeks, and touch the heart of a passing lady?"

"I don't think I can," I said, screwing my eyes about.

"I could make 'im!" Fadge offered generously.

"Ah, yer ugly little villain, go punch yer head," growled Harry quite affectionately. "No finesse you ain't got, not like me and Willie. Well, we'll use an onion for the tears."

All this was beyond me, but I felt peculiarly contented, and continued to sip my gin, sorry to see the bottom of the cup.

"You ever been up west, Willie?" Harry asked.

CHAPTER THREE

I

GOING UP west with Fadge and Sara was a very different experience from going there with Charley, and if I may say so, it was a lot more fun.

Through their eyes, I saw the rich part of London not as a place where I could earn an honest sixpence, touching my cap to the kind gemmun who put a coin in my tray of Lucifers – no, but as a great tumbling whirlpool of pickings, a shifting treasure hoard where if you were quick, anything at all was up for grabs.

Not that we were haphazard. Griddlin', it was called, and we took it very seriously. Mostly what we did was this. We walked across the city with a little barrow and, when we got near the big streets, we dived into an alley and sorted ourselves out. I took off my boots and hid them in the barrow under some sacks, and I stripped off my shirt and put on a horrible tattered one, more rag than shirt. Sara ruckled up my hair, blacked my face with grime from the street, and squeezed onions into my eyes till I was crying vigorously. Then I sat in the barrow and she wheeled me into the streets, and all I had to do was to keep crying and sitting there with one foot twisted up as if I was crippled. I had to be sure to look angelic, and let the people see my face. Mister Harry trained me in looking soulful.

Day after day I sat and sobbed in different parts of town. We had to keep moving because the policemen – "crushers" we called 'em – took a dim view of begging. Sara was in charge. She was a long stringy girl, taller'n me, and older. She had straggly hair and a white sad face, and she was real good at begging.

"Mister, mister, can yer spare a penny? Me brother's a cripple and we lost our mum and dad. There's only me to look after 'im and I ain't that strong. I ain't properly well, and I can't get no work. Ah, but he's so patient, he's a little angel, but we ain't had no decent food for a week, and he cries at night for hunger . . . "

"God bless yer, mister," I wept, fifty times a day.

No wonder Harry could afford posh clothes and gin.

When we got back to the Lane, Harry counted out what we'd got, and gave us each a share. I regularly had a shilling.

One time when we'd done a day's begging, Fadge pinched my boots out of the barrow and wouldn't let me have them back. He put them on his own feet.

"Give us them!" I screeched, thumping his chest with both my fists.

"No I won't! Do yer good to go barefoot. I has to."

"You're used to it. I ain't used to it."

"You will be by the time you've walked home."

"Ow, please, Fadge! Please!" I wailed.

"No chance," he gloated, stomping off with the barrow.

I was nearly hysterical with pain and outrage by the time we stumbled into the house. Harry was waiting for us, amused at first at our blatant discord, and then frowning.

"What's up, Willie? What's up with him, Sara?"

"Fadge has got my boots," I gulped almost incoherently. "He made me walk – "

Harry looked down at my filthy feet, and at Fadge taking off my boots. Then he beat Fadge pretty well senseless. It was terrifying to watch. It wasn't what I wanted. I'd never been close to a real beating before. My legs shook and I cowered back against the wall.

"No – don't!" I choked, appalled at the awful retribution, but Sara told me to be quiet. Harry didn't stop till Fadge was coughing and writhing on the floor, blood all over his face. I could hardly do up my bootlaces for how my hands trembled. When Harry told me Fadge wouldn't ever do it again I didn't find that at all comforting. Harry was still panting and glossy with sweat, examining his fine hands for damage.

"Listen," he said, "you got water at your house, have yer?"

"Yes," I croaked.

"You wash your feet good and proper. Boil up the water nice and warm. Sit dahn and soak your feet in a bowl. You got a bowl?"

"Yes."

"You do that then, and you see, your feet'll be good as new."

Pleased at his concern, I went home. The obvious never struck me, that Harry for his own purposes needed to keep me sweet and docile, because I'd only go round there if I felt secure. He didn't want to risk my swanning off in pique; he was busy making plans for me. In his book, how he reacted was normal. Sara accepted it, and so did Fadge. It was only me that was shocked.

Fadge was all right; he had two black eyes, and bruises, but nobody bothered.

It was chastening to me. It showed me another side of Harry. He'd got the fingers of a lover, but you didn't cross him. At least I learnt that early on, so I curbed my initial admiration. Though I still found him glitteringly attractive, I knew he was heartless and I was wary of him.

II

ALL THAT autumn and winter, I was rich.

All those months when I was involved with the Lane – that place of Horror and Sin – I had money to spend. You see these pictures of poor ragged boys looking in bakers' windows, at heaps of cakes and buns, and a sign says 7d and you know the boy can't afford any, and in his eyes there's resignation and a sort of dull ache. Well, when I was with Fadge and Sara and Harry I wasn't like that poor boy. I could have any cakes I wanted. I could buy baked potatoes on a cold evening, and roast chestnuts in the December twilight, and hot coffee from a stall – I could do all those things.

I used to get twinges of guilt because I couldn't share my modest wealth with our mum and Charley. I got round this problem sometimes by bringing them things and saying a man in the street had given them to me, but I could only do this so often – I couldn't daily pass by bountiful gentlemen who showered me with gifts, could I?

But how could I ever have admitted what I'd got involved with? I'd got belted for posing. What would they say about organised begging? Accepting gin? Mixing with common children – which our mum still thought I wasn't – swearing, missing school?

Although I had a good time spending my money on street food and sweets, what I was really interested in was clothes and books. Milliners' and drapers' fascinated me, and I'd go inside and feel any material I could before I got my fingers slapped.

When lady customers asked for rolls to be unwound, I considered myself especially lucky, and I'd stand and sigh and watch all that silk and satin come spilling out and rippling like coloured water. Ladies, I thought, were much to be envied, able to wear yards of shimmer and colour. Myself, I fancied dressing like Harry. I was obsessed with corduroy and in love with brocaded waistcoats.

As to books, the more I wandered around up west, the more I realised what a wealth of them there was to be bought. My taste was still for melodrama – adventures on the high seas, dastardly doings in secret rooms, horror, blood, villains of darkest degree, and terrible natives who tried to boil their victims in a bubbly cauldron, in the darker regions of our Empire.

However, as I poked around the back streets by Holywell Street, I began to realise that there were other sorts of books: Tales of Twilight. Many of these were sold from under the counter, but by positioning myself in a shadowy cranny I could often glimpse the books in question, and watch the furtive purchasers. One dark little shop, with bottle-green whorled glass in its windows, did not even hide its selection, and I read all kinds of things which I did not properly understand at all.

"*Nymphomania, an essay dealing with this illness in Young Girls*, its degenerative influences on mind and body, including details and diagrams of the female parts. There follows a genuine account by several hapless women of their Trials and Tribulations resulting from febrile excess. Price 2s 6d."

The diagrams were very good.

"*The Sad History of Amelie* – an innocent young heiress who finds her trust betrayed, and through monstrous mistreatment falls eventually to a life of shame and degradation. Contains beautiful illustrated plates."

Yes, for a moment I really did expect to see dinner plates in it, nice patterned ones, with bare ladies on them.

"*How I Saved my Virtue, the Tale of Sweet Primrose*" – 10s 6d and probably not a best seller. And there was one I'd have done well to absorb:

"*Onanism Revealed* – many illustrations of the Serious Results of this Disgusting Habit; 3s 6d"; but unfortunately that one had a paper binder around it, which would have to be broken before you could read the book.

This bookshop was called Pinker's, a name which struck me as particularly funny – I don't know why; I suppose because pink is light and frothy, and that bookshop was deep and dark and full of hideyholes behind piles of books where a small person could be overlooked. In December, when it grew dark soon after midday, that shop was a cave of secrets. Later I began to realise that Mr Pinker had not been unaware of my sneaky presence and that he tolerated it with indulgent amusement. I suppose I was quiet and inoffensive and I did actually spend money. Not on *Onanism Revealed*, because I didn't know what it meant. Because it was described as a Disgusting Habit, I vaguely connected it with eating snot or shitting in one's britches, both of which were common at the Ragged School. The books I bought in Pinker's were *The Cruel Hangman, The Butcher's Knife, Foul Doings at the Grange, The Mad Monk of the Ruined Tower*, and *Secrets of the Prison House*.

But Mr Pinker knew I leafed through the books about Ladies and Young Girls, the ones with pictures, and he shocked me one day by slipping me a book called *The Seduction of Sarah*, price 1d. I went scarlet to think he had been observing me all this time. He chuckled like anything. To make matters worse, there was a gentleman in the shop too, leaning on the counter, looking at *How I Saved My Virtue*, and they both had a jolly good chortle at my expense. What embarrassed me was that I knew they approved. We were all men together; it was quite right and proper that we should be sniggering together at pictures of ladies in corsets, and reading about how they were seduced and shamed. I remember one extract particularly; it was on the lines of:

> "The three men ripped off the shreds of her clothes, twisting her this way and that, until her majestic breasts swung free, as she stood clad only in her drawers, her wild eyes glittering with rage."

This sort of thing happened frequently in these books. Breasts were everywhere! The heroine always had Alabaster Globes, and sooner or later they were Revealed. She was usually called a Nymph, and she was White and Soft. Her skin was Ripe and Velvet Smooth, her lips as Red as Rosebuds. She always – whether golden haired, auburn or chestnut – had fleshy, swelling globes, and these tipped from the confines of her bodice, coyly, or burst forth dramatically as she struggled in a threatening embrace. When the hero was fortunate enough to reach her thighs, he found that they were large and sensuous. Thin ladies had no love-life.

Well, feeling that Mr Pinker and I now had a nodding sort of acquaintance, the next time I went back to the shop, I was very bold. I waited until there were no customers, and I slunk up to the counter and caught his eye beyond a pile of ornate geographical text books (*Our Beautiful World*).

"Yes, my boy?" he enquired.

I took a breath for my big moment.

"Mister," I said hopefully, "have you got any stories about *boys?*"

I do believe that for a moment he did not quite understand what I meant. He looked at me so blankly I nearly thought about asking again. I just waited patiently, expecting yes or no, but not the reaction I received when it dawned on him that I was interested in Unnatural Vice.

His face went as hard as nails; his eyes malevolent and hostile. He swelled up and leaned forward and he spluttered: "Out!" and pointed over my head to the door.

"Out, you filthy little brat," he said, "and don't you ever come back into my shop. Be off with you!"

After that, instead of spending my money at Mr Pinker's, I bought bags of bullseyes and sticks of barley sugar, and very nice they were too.

III

IT WAS beautiful to be on my own up west, with money in my pocket, merging with the late afternoon crowds in the Haymarket and Piccadilly, and down the Strand. Darkness fell early, and soon gaslamps were lit in the gloomy smog; everywhere there was light and shadow. A russet glow showed all along the streets where the ground floor stores were alight. The roads were jam-packed with hansom cabs and growlers and omnibuses jostling each other half off the road. People struggled home from work or began to come out for the night.

What I particularly liked were the Ladies. They weren't like the sensuous languid females in the books, with alabaster globes, and skin as white as ivory. They were very much alive and real, and funny, and good-humoured, and big and pretty. They let you feel their dresses! They were rather like female versions of Harry, almost unnaturally bright. Their hair was brilliant yellow or flaming ginger or glossy overripe chestnut, and decorated with ribbons and sprays of flowers. Their faces were painted so that they had bright spots of colour on their cheeks, and glowing lips. They laughed a lot, answered folks back, nudged each other cheekily and flounced their skirts so you could see their shapely black boots and black stockings. Their dresses were lovely colours – scarlet and purple and green; as they moved along such perfumes filled the air it was beautiful to sniff. They also always had half an eye on the street, where the hansoms prowled hugging the kerb, and suddenly the lady who was flirting with me would ruffle my hair and remark: "Oy, looks like I'm in luck," and leave me standing, feeling very young and glum.

I longed to be transported by a hansom cab. They were so lean and beautiful; they gleamed, swift, sleek and elegant, coming out of the gloom, their headlamps alight, their bridles jingling, a white gloved hand at the window, a gentleman's silhouette. I envied the ladies, the ones who were chosen, who disappeared into the night to unknown destinations. It must be very gratifying, I thought, to be so gaudy and bright, and have a man peer at you and say "That's the one for me", and whirl you off down the glimmering, shadowy street.

I found it very cheering and comfortable being a part of it all. I was teased, praised, and ignored at the drop of a hat if a cab drew up, but I loved it. The ladies in the books were created by men who dreamed up these plump submissive objects of desire as they sat in seclusion and wrote. But these ladies on the streets were noisy and jokey, sentimental and coarse, warmhearted and oh, ever so pretty and bright. If anyone had said Alabaster Globes to them they'd have laughed in his face.

There was something else that happened around this time, which was important to me because of what it meant and warned and threatened, and how it was concluded. It concerned some boys whom I had never thought of from one day to the next and whom I assumed were as indifferent to me. They were "respectable poor" like me; some of them I quite liked.

I was walking home from school when, from out of nowhere, this stone hit me between the shoulders. I whirled round, picked it up and flung it back, the stone slithering against the ankles of the boy who'd thrown it. Almost as if he was glad of my reaction having provided a reason, he pointed at me and yelled "Get him!" and several of his mates gave chase. I belted off down the street, bootsoles clattering on the stones. Then I heard someone else yell "Oy, they're gettin' Willie Smiff!" before somebody fetched me sprawling and I was on the ground. I grazed my chin awful. Hands turned me over.

This boy dropped on my stomach and sat astride me and thumped me hard in the chest.

"You're a Mary Anne, ain't yer!" he accused, with such venom and rage that it sounded like something personal to him.

"Aaah!" I yelled from the thump.

"Ain't yer?" he yelled back. "It's all round the school. You go with boys."

"I don't!" I gasped. "It ain't true."

"Everybody knows it; you're a Mary Anne."

"I ain't," I maintained in indignation. "Gerroff me, I ain't done nothin' to you."

"I'm going to smash your face in," he said. But he didn't, because a whole gang of kids from the Lane had surrounded us; they pulled him off me and started a running fight up and down the street. There were stones flying and boots kicking, and as I scarpered out of the way, I saw my previous aggressor come out much the worse for it. He had to be taught a lesson. I watched half appalled and half delighted, as they banged him about; he was streaming blood.

Fadge sloped up to me, also bleeding.

"He won't trouble yer again," he told me panting. "He knows you got mates. Don't yer forget it, Willie. You don't never need be beaten up. We'll see yer right. You got mates now."

"Ta," I said gratefully, "It's real nice of yer, Fadge."

He shrugged modestly, meaning anyone would have done the same.

It was a chastening thought for me. Boys I had much in common with by background had turned on me for what they'd heard about my private life. That life allied me with the kids from the Lane. Because of it, I was one with thieves and villains and violence. There was the respectable and there was the lawless; and suddenly I was on one side of the fence.

IV

GRIDDLING IN January was no joke, and Mister Harry could tell I hadn't got my heart in it. He had been nurturing other plans for me all along. Little did I know, I was like a goose being fattened for the table.

One dark afternoon, Mister Harry said to me: "Well, young Willum, I got a little proposition for yer. How'd you like never to go griddlin' again but earn more in half an hour than yer did in a day? And earn it indoors!"

"Doin' what, Mister Harry?" (But I daresay I had an inkling.)

Harry sat closer to me, and I noticed the shape of his knee in his tight trousers, the bone of it, and the creases taut along the seam.

"You know, don't yer, that there are some gemmun very partial to boys."

"Yeah, I did know that." I felt worldly wise, saying it. I remembered Charley telling me about the ones down at the docks, who hung around especially, for the sailors.

"Did yer?" he laughed, not believing me. "Well, I could get hold of some, real easy. And they'd pay the earth."

While I sat and thought, Harry went on. "See, boys ain't very easy to come by if yer don't know any. So these gemmun as specially likes boys is very hard put ter know where ter turn. Ah, Willie," he said, laying on all his charm, which was devastating, "a boy like you! With that hair like leaves in autumn, and them great big blue saucers and them dear sweet lips, they'd be all over yer. Your cheeky little ways, your teasin' and your flirtin' – we could lay our hands on a fortune, Willie, and no mistake! What d'yer say?"

I noticed the plural. Oddly enough, that it was a business proposition reassured rather than alarmed me. I realised that Harry's considerable powers would be directed to looking after me and ensuring my welfare.

"You'd be there with me, would yer, Mister Harry?"

"Not 'arf," he assured me warmly. "What I was thinkin', see, I knows this ahse, I knows this lady who runs it; she's an old friend of mine and she'd see us all right. You and me'd go there together, I'd wait for yer, and then we'd come home clankin' our push."

"I couldn't stay out all night; Charley'd ask where I'd been."

"We could fix up something. You ain't said whether yer fancies it. Does yer? If I looks after yer and sees yer right?"

His lovely glittery eyes were all concerned, but twinkling, like someone who doesn't expect to be refused.

"All right, Mister Harry, I'll give it a try."

"There's my little lovey," he said, cuddling me. "Let's have a little drop to clinch the deal then!" And he filled me the little cracked tumbler and his own glass goblet, and we drank to our partnership, in gin.

It was an evening in late January when Harry and I first went to earn money in this new way.

It was cold and dark, and without him I would have felt anxious in the dim-lit streets. There was always a chance of people lurching out at you from alleyways. Naturally if they meant to rob you they'd go for a proper toff, but even so, there could have been some villain who'd have murdered anyone for tuppence, and I never told Harry just how scared I was as I accompanied him on these trips. He let me hold his hand in the specially dark bits. Sometimes a couple of patrolling crushers wished us goodnight. They didn't pace on their own round Spitalfields, they paced in pairs or groups. Drunks'd come staggering by us, hiccoughing and singing; and on corners you might find bundles of rags that turned out to be tramps bedding down for the night. They used to lie on the hot grilles where the air from the underground railway came out.

The house that Harry knew was up in Holborn, in one of the streets off Gray's Inn Road. The lady whom Harry knew well was called Madame Rosa! It was said she had Spanish blood. Certainly she was sallow-skinned and had thick black eyebrows, astute brown eyes and strikingly black hair too glossy and vibrant to have been dyed. She wore scarlet, which made her look even more exotic. I took to her at once.

She hurried us indoors, and as we went down a high narrow corridor my senses were assailed by the unusual smell. It was an odd mixture but very striking, and I know it very well now. It comprises lust and perfume and sweat and soap and cigar smoke and coffee, and it's always different, depending on which girls are there and which perfume they use, and yet it's always the same.

She took us up a back staircase. There was wallpaper on the walls, patterned all over with monstrous roses, and from the doors we passed murmuring voices came, and pencil thin slats of light. Rosa was chatting to Harry about trivia, and I followed with a thudding heart. We ended up in a small warm room, with a fire lit in a grate, and before the fire was a bath! It looked not unlike a nursery, as if it were nearly bedtime.

"I thought you'd want him bath'd," she said briskly. "I think you'd be wise . . . You'd like a bath, wouldn't you, sonny? What's his name – Willie? Oh my gawd, *wouldn't* it be!"

Between us, we got me stripped and into the water, which was pleasantly warm, and I sat down and soaped myself with a nicely scented soap. Madame Rosa poured out drinks.

"How about it, Harry, can he take a glass? It's a cheap Bewjolly; will it go to his head?"

"Give 'im a glass, Rosa."

Sitting in the bath I drank wine from a glass – a real glass with a stem. The wine was dark red and warming.

"How about that hair!" admired Madame Rosa, eyeing me up and down. "That'll be his making, or his ruin!"

"Out yer get," Harry said, handing me a towel. "Shall I give 'im some scent, Rosa?"

"He pongs of soap," she declared, "I think that'll do. This one likes 'em innocent. Gorblimey it makes yer wonder – innocent! And he comes *here* for it!"

"Step over here, Willie," said Madame Rosa, and I went to her, and she put her hands on my shoulders. I swallowed. I was being assessed.

"You're lovely," she told me, smiling encouragingly. "A little peach. How old are you? No, don't tell me, then if I'm asked I can say I thought you was older!" She heaved with a sort of dry laughter. "Nah listen: just be polite and quiet and do what he says. He's very proper, this one. No quirks. You'll be fine." She let me go, and walked away and opened a door. "Just wait in here, and he'll come up to yer."

My throat went dry.

"Harry," I croaked, "Don't leave me!"

"Nah! I'll be right here, waiting for yer."

I went through the door. I heard Madame Rosa say: "Harry! What a lovely little arse!" and then the door closed.

The room I was in was bigger and rather sombre. The heavy dark curtains were drawn, and a lamp was lit on a table beside a bed. It all seemed very rich and strange, though of course it wasn't; it was just very much better than I was used to. If I hadn't been against a wall before we'd come in I'd probably have needed a piss, I was that nervous. It felt peculiar being naked in a rich dark room, and seeing all my flesh, tinted by the fire.

And then the door slowly opened, and in came a stranger. He was wearing a top hat and high-collared coat.

"Shall I take yer coat, mister?" I said; and walked towards my first gentleman.

Maybe this all sounds shocking. All I can say is that there were boys younger than me down the coal mines every day of their lives, and boys with bleeding limbs forced up chimney flues, with brine rubbed in their wounds to harden their flesh. That's true immorality; so save your pity and revulsion for that.

CHAPTER FOUR

I

KNOWING WHAT I know now, it amazes and troubles me
that when there are randy lads of seventeen and upwards
to do for him, a gentleman still wants to go with boys. I
talk from my own experience, thinking how gauche and wooden
I was in the bedroom of Madame Rosa's, within a month of my
twelfth birthday. But maybe this was what they sought – the
illusion of innocence? Strong imagination then, to seek it in the
backstreets.

However, I didn't feel a poor little victim that night, and I
don't in any way blame Harry. I didn't have to accompany him
there. But although I did it for money, from that very first night
I know I regarded it as an art, and I wanted to do it well.

My first gentleman, though, was a bit of a disappointment.
He didn't want me to fuss over him, and he was rather terse and
severe. I think it was the strain and worry of being where he
was. I would have known how to ease him if I'd been older.

Out of that little business I got two shillings – not bad, hey?
So I thought. I was in fact very much exploited. Madame had
ten shillings; Harry had eight. They were very pleased with me.
Madame Rosa gave me a cake and some coffee while I got
dressed, and on the way home Harry called into a public house,
and we both had a small gin.

Money was what tempted me to Madame Rosa's house. But
given that, how can I explain the prickly little thrill I felt when
the door opened into that lamplit room, and my gentleman came
in? Already I was sensing the powerful sympathy I felt for such
men. They were furtive and ashamed, sidestepping the law,
risking imprisonment – for me! Reputation hung in the balance,
social ostracization, ruin. But desire was so strong, it amounted
to a torment. But I'm saying what I learned later; I hadn't
worked all this out at twelve. I just felt a polite and instinctive
wish to please.

My third gentleman was fat and blond, and he joked and

laughed a lot, but I knew perfectly well that it was to cover up his uneasiness at being where he was. He was younger than the previous two, about thirty, and like the others he wanted to begin with me sitting on his lap. Why did they like that so much? Did it make them feel as if they were kindly uncles, and then did it add to the pleasure to take liberties? Were they carrying out fantasies, pretending I was some desired lad within the family whom they lusted after and could never ever have? He patted my head and thanked me. I definitely felt he was an improvement.

"I had a nice one this time," I chatted to Harry on the way home.

"Did yer?" he said, amused.

"Yeah, he talked to me. And he wasn't arf cuddly. He had a big fat tummy, ever so comfy."

"Garn, Willie, you ain't arf a caution!"

Suddenly, then, without warning, Harry shoved me into a doorway.

"Stay still, ssh!" he said, half squashing me. It was a shop doorway, the blinds down for the night.

"What – ?" I mumbled, muffled.

"I'm avoiding a bloke."

"What bloke?"

"One o' them bleedin' do-gooders. I seen 'im before. Bleedin' 'ell, they gets all over the place!"

"Who is it?" I wriggled, peering through the crook of Harry's arm. All I saw was the gaslit street, wispy with darkness, and, slowly walking between the narrow houses, a tall upright figure in a long coat and a tall hat. His steps echoed firmly, like a crusher's, and he carried a walking cane, which he tapped against his leg sometimes. He was walking away from us, down the street.

"Harry, yer squashin' me!"

"I don't want 'im to see yer."

"Why? What'll 'e do?" I gasped.

"Ask bleedin' questions, that's what. He picks up boys off the street and takes 'em to a hahse."

"Cor! Like Madame Rosa's?" I said, impressed.

"Nah yer silly bleeder, a do-goodin' ahse. Boys with no homes. 'E collects 'em and takes 'em home and makes 'em sing bleedin' hymns!"

I sniggered. Then I said: "Anyway, I got a home. He couldn't take me; I wouldn't go."

"Yeah, but he'd have asked yer who yer was. 'E'd have asked wotcher was doin' aht here at night, and I didn't want that, did I? I don't get on too well with do-gooders; we don't seem ter hit it orf! So we can do wivaht him!"

We waited a while, till the echoing footsteps grew distant. Oh! How different would my future have been if Harry had not been so quick, or if the stranger had turned back. But it was not to be. Besides, I wasn't destitute, as many were. He would have ascertained this fact and let me alone. But unknown to me then, our paths would cross again.

II

I ONLY went one more time to that bedroom in Madame Rosa's house.

As usual, I waited by the fire, stark naked, warming my limbs in the reddish glow and savouring the feel of carpet under my toes. I heard Harry and Madame Rosa laughing in the next room. Everything seemed just the same as it ever was. But it wasn't.

The different thing was that my visitor wasn't a gentleman. I don't mean he was in any way a lout: far from it. He was clean and smart and spoke in neat clipped tones. Also different was what he did with me.

"Right, boy," he said. "Let's have a look at you."

But then instead of what I was accustomed to, he ran his hands around my ribs and my spine; he opened my mouth and put his fingers inside, feeling my teeth and the insides of my mouth and along my lips. I did think he was strange. He certainly asked me to lie on the bed, but again, it was more exploratory than lustful, probing me, everywhere, rolling his fingers around, pressing, like he was feeling for something.

"Good," he finally decided. All he said was: "I've finished with you for now – but I expect we shall meet again."

Well, I was partly bewildered and partly relieved. I was only concerned about whether I'd still get paid for something so undemanding. I got two shillings as usual. I suppose they wanted to be sure I didn't suspect anything.

On the way home, Harry was rather preoccupied with his thoughts. Then he suddenly said: "Willie, yer hasn't *got* anybody, has yer?"

"How d'yer mean, Harry?"

"There's just you and yer brother and yer widdered ma."

"Yeah, that's right."

"An' yer brother ain't much older'n you . . . an' yer ma's ailin'."

"Yeah, she ain't bin well for months. She keeps on workin' though. She's always aht, sewin'."

"But yer ain't got nobody else," he said, and added: "as'd come *lookin'* for yer."

"I ain't got no one," I said, "'cept ma and Charley."

"That's what I thought," he said, mostly to himself.

Then a little while later, he said, out of the blue: "Should yer ever like ter travel, Willie?"

"Ooh yeah!" I said cheerfully, having never thought about it.

"I bet you'd like ter see the world, eh?"

"I speckt I would."

"Would yer be sick if yer went on a boat?"

"Yeah, not arf!" I said feelingly. "I only 'as ter see water and I thinks abaht drownin'. I reckon I'd be sick as a dog if I went on a boat."

"Nah!" said Harry, "Not you! Yer'd love it!"

"I ain't ever gonna, though," I remarked practically, "so it don't make no difference."

"Well," said Harry enigmatically, "who can say?"

The drift of his words only sank into my thick skull long after we'd separated, and I was alone at home.

Blimey, that house was cheerless to come into on a winter night! Ma never got in till towards midnight, Charley not much before. I had to light the fire and the candle before I could make a cup of tea, and there I'd sit, by the spluttering little fire, eating my bread slab, drinking tea and reading my murder stories. *The Battered Gamekeeper . . . The Poisoned Maiden . . . The Mangled Corpse . . .* THE STOLEN BOY! . . . . What? That wasn't a title in my series; that was a phrase in my mind! Suddenly I came over really cold, shivering all over, and scared as hell.

"You ain't got no one . . . as'd come lookin' for yer? How'd yer like ter travel? On a boat? . . . Who can say?"

"Oh! Oh!" I screeched, jumping off my stool and spilling my tea, tealeaves and all. "Oh bleedin' 'ell!"

I was in a state. To think there I was, all alone, surrounded by leaping shadows, and outside, the pitch black night pressing in, while I was reading about grisly goings on. *The Vault of Terror* I'd just got to. It was like the words had jumped off the page and hit me between the eyes. Come alive. Drawing me helplessly into A Horrible Net. The blackness outside seemed crawling with sinister villains – sailors with ear rings ready to abduct me to a ship, gangs with knives and axes, and lurking in a doorway counting his money – *Harry*, ignoring my cries! Anyone could break into the house – a good kick would drive the door in, and there I'd be, a Cowering, Terrified Wretch, a Helpless Victim to their Wicked Purposes. But oh! What *were* their wicked purposes? Were they going to sell me to the Turks? It must be that! Those people the sailors knew about, who were partial to boys, yes it must be them! I would be sold overseas, on a boat that would make me seasick – I could drown – I would never be heard of again – I would be Lost At Sea. Or if I survived – Prisoner Of The Turks!

I was so overwrought that I could not bear to stay there any longer, so I went next door, and sat with the Webbs, our neighbours on one side, and I stayed there till I heard Charley come home. You could hear the door bang.

It was awful at the Webbs', though not as awful as being at home on my own, a prey to ghastly imaginings of riotous colour and abandon. Mrs Webb harped constantly on the theme of death; who'd died, who else had died, and then again who else. You wondered there was anyone left alive at all. She went on about cholera and diphtheria and double pneumonia, and questioned me closely about our mum till I was even more depressed than I'd been panicky.

Finally after an interminable age I was able to yell: "Ooh, there's our Charley," and get up and run out back to our house, where I instantly received a tirade for having let the fire out.

"Oh Charley, I gotter talk ter yer," I gasped, jumping up and down like someone badly needing a pee; but Charley wasn't having any till he'd lit the fire.

Grumbling a lot, he got the fire going. Overcome with guilt and remorse I got down on my elbows and knees and started blowing vigorously to help it on. Then I felt all hot and ashamed because it was the same position I'd been in for that man who – of course! He was *examining* me! He must have been some kind of doctor! Was he seeing if I was good enough to sell? Not damaged? I came over all cold again, at this apparent verification of my fears. I crawled up into a crouching position, staring uneasily at the fire. I heard Charley reassuringly pottering about.

"Tea, our Willie?" he asked, cheerful again.

Next thing I knew, I'd got a cup of hot tea in my hand, and Charley was pulling up a stool.

"Nah then, sprat, what's this all about?"

Would I ever have told, if I hadn't had that bad attack of panic? Or had guilt and shame finally caught up with me? I'd hardly even realised it, but I felt my secret life had got out of hand, unwieldy and too much for me to manage. I needed to confess. Although my lurid visions of Abduction and Captivity were based on the flimsiest evidence and fed by my own imagination, there was some genuine fear in my mind. It was all right when it was just me and Harry, and sixpences; but other people were involved now, and a house of ill repute, and gentlemen and shillings. I was up to my knees in deep waters, and I was scared of drowning.

"Charley, I've been awful bad."

"Yeah? Wotcher done?"

I put my tea down and knelt by Charley's knees; the penitent position seemed appropriate. I groaned. Where to begin, on a tale of such sordidity and deceit? But I must go on now; it was weighing on me so much.

I had the impression that with each fresh revelation of my wickedness, Charley thought that was the extent of it, and yet there was always more. He listened quietly and seriously, drinking his tea. That was the sound I particularly noticed, him slurping, and then my droning husky voice going on, stiltedly, and the Webbs next door poking their grate, clearing the ashes for the morning.

I told how Fadge and me and Sara had gone up west and I'd used my angelic looks pretending to be a cripple, and how I'd spent the money on books. I told how Mister Harry had said I

could earn big money in a house where gentlemen came. I heard
Charley sort of groan, but I didn't stop; I hurried on, about how
I'd gone there and been bathed and put in a room, and gentlemen
had come to me and that's how I'd got the shillings as'd bought
Charley's boots. And I said how walking home Harry had asked
me if I'd got anyone who'd come looking for me and if I'd like
to travel, and how it seemed to me the last client had been
examining me for a purpose. "And I'm scared now, Charley," I
wailed. "I'm real frit; I don't know what ter do."

"Is that the lot?" said Charley grimly.

"I reckon."

My brother said slowly and with feeling: "You stupid little
bleeder," and he hit me round the head both sides, with hands
like spades, knocking me over. I lay there wailing, knowing I
deserved anything he felt like laying on to me, half wanting to
be punished and redeemed, half resentful of his righteousness
and strength.

But Charley was always fair; he never mouldered on bearing
grudges and wasting time recriminating. He was a man of action,
Charley.

"Gerrup, yer little bugger," he said, "I won't hit yer again."

I put my head in his lap and my arms round his waist, and
cried and cried. He held me tight and patted my shoulders. He
felt fierce and protective. When my sobs grew less noisy and my
back was heaving less, he said: "You ain't half been a bloody
fool."

"I know," I wept, muffled in his crotch.

"Let's get it straight," he said. "Tell me everything you can
about this Harry."

I dredged my memory and recounted all I could, between
sniffs and hiccoughs. Then I had to tell him everything about
the house, and he even wanted to know what I actually did –
and here I think genuine curiosity and even fascination motivated
his questions.

"And this last one," he said, "and yer thinks he was a doctor.
Well! At least he said 'Good!' You'd 'ave wanted ter worry if he
hadn't. Sounds to me he was feelin' you for clap." At the look
of blankness on my face he said angrily: "Bleedin' 'ell! Didn't
they tell yer abaht that? Lousy bastards, they wants guttin'!"

My eyes went wide and anxious.

"Don't worry," said Charley, "you bin examined and he said 'Good!' Any road, gents who goes with boys is likely to be clean."

I sat down on the floor at his feet, chastened and thoughtful. I felt that Harry hadn't played me fair. As a hero, he was rapidly developing cracks in his pedestal.

"You ain't never ter see that man again," said Charley firmly. "Or at least, maybe you can go and tell him that. Yeah, and I'll wait for yer while yer does it. Best ter get it straight. D'you hear?"

"Yes, Charley."

Ah, the beautiful peace I felt, at having him take charge. He said I'd got a leaning sort of nature: well, I certainly leaned just then. Everything seemed right in the world with Charley in control, looking after me like he always had done. I snuggled against his leg.

"I don't know whether he did have any plans ter take yer away, but it does sound very odd, havin' yer examined and all. You can forget abaht the Turks – see, he wouldn't even need ter send yer so far. There's always a market for boys. There's hahses in London, so I've heard, and there's dealers from Paris who come over special. They wants little girls and all. A stupid trustin' boy like you is just what they're lookin' for, and if he goes willin', so much the better. I feel bad for not havin' warned you more. I thought you was at school!"

"I was, mostly."

"It comes of us havin' no dad. I oughter 'ave been more careful of yer. I see yer don't know the difference between right and wrong. I thought yer did. You're someone as needs lookin' after. You're such a blame fool."

"I'm sorry," I said penitently. "I can't help it. I'm in it before I realise it."

"Well, not any more," said Charley. "You're breakin' with that life. Termorrer yer goes to this Harry, and yer tells him politely that you're done with him. And if he thinks you ain't got nobody, you tell him this: you got an uncle, who's very important in the city"

"Eh?" I grimaced.

"Yeah, it's true . . . Ah, Willie, I wasn't goin' ter say anything about this to yer, but dontcher know our mum ain't well?"

"Yeah, *course* I know," I protested, confused at the direction of the conversation.

"I mean *badly* not well. I mean like ter die."

"She *ain't*," I cried hotly. "She's walkin' abaht."

"Well, if she goes," said Charley, "you oughter know, she's arrangin' for this uncle ter come and see us, and talk abaht providin'."

"*What* uncle?" I disbelieved.

"I dunno, do I? You don't suppose our mum and dad dropped out the sky, do yer? They had family. They all split up when she married our dad, because he was no good or something. But our mum's got a sister, and she's wrote to her; and that's how we got an uncle. Now you tell Mister Harry. I think if you tells him we got an uncle who's important in the city, the type of man he sounds, it'll scare him off. You see if I'm not right!"

"Is he really important in the city?" I marvelled.

"Course he is. You tell Harry he knows the Lord Mayor! You tell him he's coming to ask us all about how we been livin'. You won't get Mister Harry pesterin' you no more."

"Yeah, right," I murmured impressed.

I looked gratefully up at Charley. In that moment, before my adoring eyes, he became my ideal. The strong man, the provider, the one who would look after me and fight my demons. Working down at the docks had made Charley into a man at sixteen. He was beautiful. His neck was thick, his shoulders were full of power. He was someone who could look after himself, who knew what he wanted. He was rough and warm and strong and affectionate. There was another thing too – he was Good. He made Mister Harry seem brittle and tarnished. I realised all this that night, along with a sharp physical stab in the guts that made me want to love him and stay with him. It was an unforgettable moment, seeing it all so clearly. The combination of lust and nobility, of mastery and friendliness, it welded itself into my being as an image of perfection: the image I was searching to recover all my life.

Next day I went and said my piece to Harry. You had to hand it to him; he took it very well. I don't know to this day whether he had evil plans for me, a boy brothel lined up somewhere which ended up disappointed. But Charley was right – at the mention of our uncle in the city, Harry went not exactly pale green but nearly, and just said: "Fancy that, eh?"

"And I can't come and see yer no more," I added apologetically. "Me brother says. Me brother's waiting for me dahn the street."

"Well, I calls it a shame," said Harry. "We was a jolly pair, we was, and I shall be sorry to see you go."

"So shall I be, Mister Harry," I replied, but I wasn't really. I was relieved to have got away – like a little fish through a tear in the net.

Mister Harry and I shook hands. I suppose in his business he had to cultivate a philosophical attitude.

Well, Charley stuck to his word to look after me. Seeing as how I couldn't be trusted and didn't know right from wrong, he fixed up a little job for me. We set out together each morning in the dark cold February dawn, and on into March; I was left to help a shopkeeper. I had to sort nails. Batches of them would arrive and I had to sort them into smaller boxes – ten inch, six inch, one inch; separate the screws, label the boxes and write down what I'd sorted. The shopkeeper was nice to me, though strict, and I had a small dinner with him and his wife. Charley told him to keep an eye on me and I'm afraid he certainly did. I wasn't allowed to leave the shop. I sorted nails and screws in a back room, I swept floors, cleared away straw and sawdust, rolled up string and twine, tidied up; things like that. I got sixpence a week and paid a penny back for my food. In the evening Charley collected me on his way home and we walked back together. I did my honest job with serious application. It was boring, but I looked upon it as a sort of expiation for my sins. Maybe if things had been different I would be an ironmonger today!

III

IT WAS bronchitis that carried off Ma, and it was Mrs Webb who saw to everything for us. The whole street turned out in fact to help us through. It seemed like no one was taken by surprise. Charley and I were there at the end, and we sat seriously by while the bustle went on around us.

The funeral was plain and decent – everything done proper but cheap. Someone gave us violets to throw on the coffin. Our uncle paid for it. Knowing our uncle as I do now, I can understand he would have had it done that way – holy but basic, his duty but no trimmings. Also, he didn't attend, none of 'em did who were supposed to be her family. So it was all neighbours and us, and we came back to Mrs Webb's house for tea and hard little cakes.

We were feeling very bleak of heart, Charley and me, when we left the neighbours and came home to our silent house. The first we knew of the presence of our uncle was when the door opened and a wan light fell across the room. Then this pale oblong was blotted out by a big dark shape.

"Good afternoon!" it said loudly and clearly. "If I am not mistaken, Charles and William Smith. I am your uncle!"

Charley and me, we must've looked like the artists' impressions of the Princes in the Tower, transported to modern times. Charley was sitting on the stool, I was on the mat by his feet, leaning on his knee, and he had his arm around me. Our sad white faces must have turned very poignantly to the intrusion, and the tear streaks on mine would have added a delicate touch to the general impression.

Our uncle came into the room. He wore a black top hat and he had those bushy cheek whiskers that crept across the face and bunched out strangely from the skin. He was all in black, as befitted somebody in mourning. These features all struck me more than his actual face, neither harsh nor kind, but adaptable to either. He was not alone.

Holding his hand and looking like a radiant angel was a boy of about ten years old, in a black velvet suit. (Velvet! I itched to touch it!) He had the most beautiful face I'd ever seen and hair of a soft pale gold.

"And this," said our uncle, "is your cousin, Georgey."

Georgey stepped forward and held out his hand. I jumped up and took it, instantly responding to a gesture I sensed he was finding scary to make.

"I'm so sorry to hear you are bereaved," he said in a sweet soulful voice, looking up at me with huge pale blue eyes that melted me to confusion.

"Thank you," I said gratefully, and I know my attitude endeared me to our uncle – the deserving poor showing proper humility before the benefactor. My swift response to Georgey's gesture, my meekness and subdued respectfulness, though seeming attractive and appropriate to my uncle, were in fact all caused by the instant bloom of love I felt for Georgey – the most beautiful little thing I'd ever set eyes on. We stayed holding hands and smiling tentatively, Georgey in genuine sympathy and warm-hearted generosity of spirit over my predicament, myself in the glowing warmth and ardour of sudden love.

Charley didn't fare so well. He stood up resentfully, hostile and sullen, and my uncle didn't like him; his attitude was wrong.

Our uncle made a speech.

"I have come to be your benefactor," he told us. "Your mother – God rest her soul – wrote to my wife, your Aunt Louisa, and all is now arranged that you should come and live with us. We have a modest but comfortable establishment in Putney, which is very different from what you are used to. It will seem a very great improvement. I will undertake to educate you and place you in a trade. You, Charles, we can place immediately – why, you are almost a man. William, you shall take lessons with Georgey, and live exactly as one of the family. You will have a room of your own, and you shall learn from books, with Georgey's tutor, Mr Irving. I think I can promise you an environment beyond your wildest dreams, of comfortable God-fearing family life. I am not a rich man but I am a Christian, and I believe it is my duty to do well by you and I think you will find you have every cause to be grateful. In return, you will be dutiful too, and show obedience, and the arrangement will be of benefit to all."

He then enquired into the details of our daily life, to which Charley said that he worked at the docks and I worked in a hardware shop and had done well at school; and my uncle said it would not do for him to continue at the docks, but he was pleased to hear I had been a good pupil.

"Our family name is Armitage," he said grandly. "You may call Georgey by his name, and you will call your aunt Aunt Louisa."

"And I'd rather be called Willie," I added, since it seemed to be naming time.

"No," said our uncle. "I shall call you William. I think it will inspire you to improve."

"*I'll* call you Willie," whispered Georgey in my ear, his lips touching the lobe and giving a sweet sensation – both to my ear and to my state of mind.

My uncle then declaimed to Georgey: "Georgey, I have brought you here with me, as well as to meet your cousins, in order that you should see the face of Poverty. Poverty is like a Pit of Snakes that lies beneath the floorboards of Society. Into this Pit anyone may fall. The way to avoid it is by Honest Endeavour. *Toil*, Georgey. Charles and William are blessed. This day a Helping Hand reaches down to them, and they have the chance of a better life. They will come with us on Sunday to give thanks to their Maker and you and I, Georgey, may feel we have done a little good."

Everyone looked impressed and pious, except Charley, who scowled throughout, and picked his teeth.

"I will come for you tomorrow," our uncle told us, "at eleven o'clock. Then you shall see your new home."

After that, he and Georgey left. Charley and I stayed quiet most of the evening, thinking our own thoughts. Myself, I was thinking about Georgey. My feelings about him were pure sensation, like smelling a rose, or touching silk. I was permeated with a sunny warmth from him, as if our place was indeed a pit of darkness and Georgey was a sunbeam penetrating. The images my uncle had conjured up were wonderful to me. Book learning – studying with Georgey – it was so miraculous, sprung on me like that. Georgey liked me, I knew it. I had bathed in his warm gaze. His hand had been hot and smooth. My emotions, raw and numb from the funeral, flared into a strange and beautiful throbbing, almost like a pain, in the contemplation of my cousin Georgey.

Charley's thoughts were totally different.

I am glad he didn't tell me till the early morning, because I would never have gone to sleep, and I'd have cried and pleaded, and my last night in Charley's arms would have been spoiled. As it was, I had a good memory to look back on, of lying close to him, excited and even hopeful, thinking about the future.

"Willie," he said, as we lay there, the early pallor of dawn lightening the dark, "I ain't comin' wiv yer."

My heart missed a beat. "What?" I said blankly.

"He don't want me, it's plain. He don't like me and I don't

60

like him. He thinks I'm a lout and I don't think much of him neither, and he'll have me sent off to some trade he chooses sooner'n you can blink. Well, that ain't for me. I ain't gonna be pushed around; I'm grown now and I chooses for meself. I won't be looked at that way, that sneerin' sort of I'm-better'n-you look; and I'm gettin' aht."

I leaned up on my elbow. After the initial stab of terror – and it was no less – I knew that I wasn't at all surprised.

"What will you do?" I said.

"Run away to sea. There's any number of ships as'd take me. I fancy Australia. I always have. It ain't like here. Once you gets off the boat you're, like, free. You ain't battin' yer head night and day against how things *are:* you make 'em for yourself. It's like goin' into clear air. It's what you *are* as matters, not what people make yer. I think that'll suit me dahn ter the grahnd. I'd have gone long ago if it hadn't been for you and ma."

"Didn't you never think to take me with yer?" I said quiveringly. It was my only reproach. Otherwise I took it very well.

"You wouldn't like it," he said. "You don't like the sea, nor the docks. It takes months, Willie, to get to Australia – on the sea all that time, in heat and storms and rain, and it's rough and dirty. I'd be that worried about yer I wouldn't be able to work me passage. It'd suit me, but it wouldn't suit you."

I was silent; of course it was all quite so. I don't think I took in the full implication of it all; it was too much. I blocked out of my mind the frightening thought that I might very well never ever see Charley again in the whole of my life. As always, I trusted him completely. He always knew what was best for me. What he said seemed entirely reasonable and I accepted it, fighting down the panic and alarm that buzzed at me like a little swarm of flies coming and going.

"I know how it'll be at our uncle's," said Charley. "One o' them nice hahses where it's all clean, and full of things you knock over if yer swings yer arms. I wouldn't fit. But *you* would, Willie. I'd go off easy knowin' you was there . . . You like that little Georgey, dontcher?"

"Yes," I said, with a renewed feeling of warmth and pleasure at the memory of his hot little hand.

"Well, you'll be learnin' wiv 'im, and playin' too, I daresay. It's the best thing as could've happened. I honestly do think so.

They'll learn yer how to be posh, give yer a good start in life. You think big. You'll be able to get a *proper* job, the sort where yer moves up. I'm ever so glad for yer."

He went on, convincing himself, and I daresay fully believing it. "Even all that God stuff needn't get yer dahn. You like singin', and it won't be too bad prayin' and that. They won't do it all the time I don't suppose, just Sundays. And you'll get to wear decent clothes. You'll be happy as a pig in shit. See, Willie," he said earnestly, "you got a *leanin'* sort of nature. You needs lookin' after. When you go and live with our uncle you'll be looked after. Neatened off, like, made nice. They'll teach you things you need to know to get on in this world. You know – manners, and ways. Then when you're like groomed and polished, you can do anything! You can turn yer back on them or not, as yer pleases, 'cos you'll be yer own man. Same as me! Each in our own different way, we'll be all right.

"But we 'ad ter leave this 'ole, Willie, there ain't no future *here* and that's for sure. This is dead end, no good. We're well aht of it . . . Willie, this ain't a *fair* society. Things ain't *right* here. Me I'm gettin' aht, startin' a new life in a new land. I couldn't get on if I stayed. But you, you can. You can learn how to get on, inside, how things are. You can play their game; you'll be good at it. All right, Willie?"

"Yes, Charley," I said, biting both lips hard. I refused to let him down by a display of weakness now. I smiled pluckily if rather wobbly.

"Just one thing, our Willie," he said grinning. "See yer don't swear, eh? They won't like it where you're going . . . And, I don't have ter tell yer, do I, there ain't no need to let 'em know anything more than they needs. I mean, let 'em keep thinkin' you're a nice little boy!"

"Yeah," I grinned back. As if I'd ever tell!

"Then come on, we'll 'ave a cuppa tea, and then I'll be off."

Charley worked hard to make our leavetaking appear perfectly normal. I do believe I hadn't fully absorbed the finality of our separation, and fortunately I was prevented from this by a shell of numbness which lasted for several weeks, although I didn't realise it. Charley and I parted with a manly handshake and a brief hug, and he strode off down the street.

"I'll come back," he called, over his shoulder.

He did and all, though years were to pass before I saw him again. By then he was a grown man, a partner in a shipping company, a big burly Australian with a wife and *five* children! But that was far ahead.

After Charley had gone, I spent the time slowly and carefully burning all my Pocket Gem books, one by one, and the print of me on the advertisement, and the Twilight Tales from Mr Pinker's. I was not desolate. Like Charley, I had to make my own life in my own way, and I saw the sense in what he said. I thought more about Georgey than about Charley. It was only commonsense to think to the future and I was very much looking forward to my new life. I felt extremely lucky that I was to leave Aldgate, and I was determined to make best use of my chance.

Although it is more customary to burn boats than books, I thought that by doing so I was destroying those parts of my past best forgotten. Little did I realise that you take the past with you wherever you go. This truth was spared me as, hopefully and optimistically, I sat, scrubbed clean and waiting for the hour of eleven when my uncle would collect me.

PART TWO

CHAPTER FIVE

I

I LIVED at the Armitage home for four years.
When I first arrived it was the month of April and everything was blooming. And so appeared my life to be, sunshine and light taking the place of darkness and gloom.

My nefarious wanderings had never taken me to Putney. It was another world. The streets were wide and pleasant, well lit, with views – as the road sloped – of rooftops and trees. The houses were all quite new, bright red brick with painted window frames and ornamental doors. Each house had a small front garden with shrubs and flowers, and a gate and a little path. And within a short walk from anywhere there was Putney Heath, which was like the real countryside. It had a furzey common and copses and spinneys where all kinds of wild flowers grew in their seasons – it was big enough to get lost in.

My uncle came alone to fetch me. When I explained about Charley, he questioned me carefully and, though he said that it showed a sullen ungrateful nature in Charley, I sensed only relief on his part at the way things had fallen out. He put a firm hand on my shoulder, looking down at me with munificent approval.

"Come, William," he said, "let us be on our way."

Round the corner of our street – and surrounded by gawping kids and passers-by – a growler waited to take us to Putney. I learnt later that my uncle, normally fastidious, made use of these heavy cumbersome cabs when he had an unpleasant job to do, and collecting a grimy boy from a disreputable back street was one such. I've never liked them – four great iron-rimmed wheels and a vast bulk swaying and creaking, and everything noisy – the slam of the door, the gruff shouts of the driver – the drivers always coarse and aggressive. Ah – all so different from the hansoms! I found it a bit alarming to climb up inside it to sit opposite my uncle.

I was of course thoroughly uncomfortable in his presence. He didn't chat, but sat severe and impassive, leaning forward slightly on his black walking cane. Part of me wanted to bounce and exclaim and gasp, and to admit that I'd never ridden in one of these before, and part of me supposed that I should model myself on him and sit in dignified silence.

The strange novelty of the journey took me over. I stared absorbed through the window, watching the streets and people. Sometimes my uncle pointed out a landmark. I had no idea Putney was so far. Or that London was so big. We seemed to be in that cab for a very long time.

Then I began noticing the sky; and the buildings receding. I craned my neck to look.

"Ain't it clean!" I marvelled, impressed.

My uncle was pleased. "It is a pleasant place to live," he said. "I think you will like it here." He meant: how could you not, coming from where you do!

Eventually the cab drew up, and I was to see my new home for the first time.

Cor, though! It was like a bleedin' palace! So I thought then; in fact it was simply a nice well-appointed family home. It was in a row, but not the same way as ours had been, squashed up tight. These houses had bay windows, and lush flowering trees where one house joined another. They were three storeys high. Georgey's house had a mahogany front door with a shiny knob and a little stained glass window. When the door opened, all down the hall you could smell apple and cloves.

The door was opened by the maid, but before I had time to stop and marvel, my Aunt Louisa herself came to the door. Taking one look at me standing there on the step, my uncle's hand on my shoulder, she rushed forward and scooped me into her arms. I can see now I probably did look a solitary little waif and I must have touched her kind heart.

"Louisa!" said my uncle, half fondly, half reprovingly. He meant: the boy is filthy!

Ah, she was ever so pretty, my Aunt Louisa. She looked sweetly young, like a mother in a children's book, benign and gentle. She smelt wholesome, of eau de cologne and soap. She had blue eyes like Georgey, and a rosebud mouth like his, and her cheeks were moist with poignant little tears. She would have been thinking "Oh, my dead sister's child!" and her tender heart was affected by the sentiment.

"My poor little lamb," she said, extremely moved. "I am your Aunt Louisa. Shall you like living here with us?"

"Yes, thank you," I said politely. My face was against her black silk dress. She had a little round brooch with a pressed violet embedded in it. She straightened up, and I saw with pleasure that Georgey was behind her. He smiled and held out both hands, which I took gladly.

"Ah, the pets!" said Aunt Louisa fondly. "Friends already. Let us go inside. There's much to do to make Willie feel at home."

With a little surge of delight I realised that in fact my uncle would be the exception in calling me William. We went into the large tiled hall.

My aunt took me by the shoulders and looked at me earnestly.

"Willie, you'll think it very odd, I know, to begin our acquaintance thus, but the first thing that I am going to do is to see that you have a bath and wash your hair . . . And listen! I have a lovely suit of clothes for you! Come with me!"

I followed her upstairs. Georgey came too, and, shock after shock, the bathroom! A bath fixed to the floor, on four little feet, with big round taps and an intricate series of water pipes. A lady was filling the bath with water, her sleeves rolled up, and billowing clouds of steam half hiding her. This was Mrs Braddon. She came in each day and helped Aunt Louisa run the house. She had big brawny arms and she was Indispensable. There was also a live-in maid called Lucy, who got up early each day to light the fires and scrub the front steps, and who answered the door and did the dusting.

I learnt quickly about Aunt Louisa that she did nothing dirty. She might embrace me on the doorstep and she might oversee my transformation, but when she contemplated the actual me as I stood there on the black and white tiled floor, she pressed the back of her hand against her forehead in a theatrical gesture of stress and despair.

"Mrs Braddon!" she cried. "See to him."

Georgey giggled. I grimaced.

"Mamma, may I stay?" Georgey pleaded.

"How does Willie feel about such an impudent request?" asked my aunt who adored him.

"Yeah, stay," I appealed to my sweet little friend. I needed some support at the idea of being seen to by Mrs Braddon. She had the inevitability of a machine. In no time and without preamble she'd got me stripped and bundled into the bath where my screech at the heat of the water went unnoticed and I rapidly became boiled lobster coloured. Aunt Louisa drifted in and out with towels while Georgey sat on a little stool and beamed wickedly every time he caught my eye. Mrs Braddon, with all the finesse of a washerwoman heaving sheets, turned me round this way and that, lathering me all over as if she had never heard of personal modesty, and soap was literally coming out of my ears.

I never saw my clothes again; they were burnt. In their place I had some new ones. To my alarm we started off with underclothes. Cor, they weren't half itchy! They were followed by a very neat smart black suit and a white shirt, very starched and stiff. It was a mourning suit, which explained why it hadn't been much worn. We all wore mourning outfits, and I had a black arm band to wear after that. And then there were shoes and socks.

"Ah, Willie!" cried my aunt. "You look splendid!"

They were not the kind of clothes I would have picked for myself – being formal and sombre – but then, I'm a flashy lad like Harry at heart, and left to myself I'd always add a scarf or a buttonhole or a splash of purple! Still, I appreciated the good intentions, and I smiled at her compliment, though I was prickling from them drawers!

Next, I was to be shown my room. That day one wonder fell on another, thick and fast. My room was up another flight of stairs, under the eaves. It was only a small attic room but for just one person it was big. The roof sloped, which made a very pleasant effect. It had a window, with green curtains, looking on to the back garden. I could see trees, blossom, smudges of bright flowers.

There was a slim bed with a white cover, a wardrobe for my clothes, a washstand with a cold smooth top, and a beautiful bowl and jug with roses painted on the sides. A handtowel hung on a rail at the side, and I had toothpowder and a toothbrush, and my own soap! I wandered around, touching things.

"It's beautiful here," I concluded; and my aunt gave me a big hug, because I was turning out just as she'd hoped. And then we went down to eat.

II

I DON'T know what I'd have done without Georgey that meal, and those first few weeks. I must have done countless wrong things without knowing it, but they didn't come down on me hard; they let Georgey point things out. How to hold a knife, fork and spoon properly, when to leave the table, what to do with a serviette, and all the other things, like how to work the lavatory (an entirely white one, with a pull chain!), and hang my clothes, and which rooms to use at which times of day. The thing that struck me particularly was how tightly controlled that household was. It ran to order, exactly the same each week, and once you'd learned the sequence of events, it gave you an oddly pleasant feeling of security.

It is a strange business, being the cause of somebody else's salvation. My uncle took me in from strong religious fervour, to perk up his chances of getting to Heaven. I don't mean to criticise his actions – I was grateful and appreciative – but I simply state his motive. Because Aunt Louisa was a nicer person, and had the old remembered feelings for my mother, her attitude was much warmer, but her motive was the same. Fortunately for us all, I was an attractive accepting child – I knew I was lucky and I was properly humble and shy, and so we all got on unusually well. I accepted all their directions as correct and tried very hard to please. This meant that they basked in a complacent self-congratulatory warmth, and emanated an image much sought after in those days, of the haves giving their bounty to a have not. We looked like the illustration to a moral tale. It could only work with us being as we were. If I had been Charley or Fadge, or anybody with aggressive spirit, refusal to adapt, or downright ugliness, the arrangement would have collapsed about our ears.

That first evening, my uncle sat at the desk in his study, and I stood the other side. He told me he was happy to see me so much improved already and he asked me how I liked my new surroundings. I was properly grateful and mumbled my appreciation. He told me that we must now make a start on the way I spoke. "I suppose you can hear for yourself," he said, "that we in this household form our words differently from you. Your speech is a blight from your old way of life, amounting almost to a physical handicap. I shall start with kindness. I want you to listen to those about you and model your language on what you hear. Every time you make a mistake I shall stop you and I shall instruct Georgey to do the same, and you must correct yourself before you go on. At the end of each week you will read me a passage of prose, and I shall see how you are improving. Your dreadful accent, William, is not native to you. It is caused by your environment. I know that with diligent application you will succeed."

That very next day I was introduced to Mr Irving, Georgey's tutor. We had our lessons in the dining room which was cleared to make it look like a schoolroom. We all sat at the table. Family portraits – real live photographs – looked down at us from their frames, and it was a strange sensation to realise that some of these people were my relations too. In a vase there were some tall white plumes, soft and lovely to feel. There were long windows that opened up like doors out into the back garden, and heavy dark blue velvet curtains.

Mr Irving was quite young, late twenties I would say. He had a pleasant face, a large nose, brown eyes and flat straight hair which he somehow combed across his head so that he had more on one side than on the other, and when he shook his head the hair flicked about like a cloth.

"Let's have a little talk about this language problem, Willie," said Mr Irving. "I expect you know that I've been told to stop you at every 'ain't' and lapsed h. This may well reduce you to stuttering incoherence. Suppose I make a promise to correct you in general rather than particular, and then see how we go?"

"Yes, sir," I said, enunciating beautifully.

"By the age of fifteen," said Mr Irving, "a boy is expected to be able to write well, to have mastered grammar, to have arithmetical skills at his fingertips, history, geography, a foreign language, and possess more than a nodding acquaintance with book-keeping. The lives of great men should also be familiar to him, and a smattering of Latin would be no hindrance. I think, Willie, we should be getting our heads down."

"Yes, sir!"

"If you call me Mr Irving," he said, "you can be using it as speech practice."

"Yes, Mr Irvinggg."

And thus I began my Education.

I soon worked out that what I'd learn at the swishing skirts of my previous lady teacher was a haphazard hotch-potch of unrelated knowledge. My best achievement was being good at reading but my writing was, said Mr Irving, like tangled string in ink. So I spent hours at my copperplate, broad downs, slim ups. To keep my interest he let me copy out of *Tales of Chivalry*, a mixed blessing, as I couldn't write fast enough to learn what happened next, but at least I learned about Roland and Thor and Lancelot and Perceval.

To think what Georgey had been brought up on! He'd had poems coming out of his pretty little ears, and they were all dreadfully moral.

> Have you not heard what dreadful plagues
> Are threatened by the Lord
> To him that breaks his father's law
> Or mocks his mother's word.
>
> What heavy guilt upon him lies,
> How cursed is his name!
> The ravens shall pick out his eyes,
> And eagles eat the same!

In another book there was one to make comfortable children contemplate the plight of the poor. Georgey confided to me that Aunt Louisa had sat down with him and reminded him of it, in order to persuade him to agree that I should be brought into their home.

> While some poor children that I meet
> Have very little food to eat
> Thanks to my heavenly Father's care
> I have enough and some to spare.

And now these homeless little boys
In the cold archway sleep.
Poor children! When the morning comes
They will awake to weep.

Oh children in your happy homes,
Pity the children poor
Who have no friends, no home, and who
Such misery endure.

*Our readers can help the poor of London by subscribing to the Ragged
School Union, at the Strand, or the National Temperance League.
Both these Societies are working most actively in reclaiming and
helping the children of the poor outcasts.*

"I did have a home," I protested. "I never slept in a cold
archway. It ain't about *me*."

"You went to a Ragged School, so it's *partly* about you," said
Georgey. "And you should say *isn't*."

"Isn't," I grumbled.

"Oh, don't be cross, Willie! It doesn't matter whether you
ever slept under an archway. Don't spoil it. I wanted so much
to help you. Your life's been so hard, and mine's been so easy."

"My life weren't that bad," I began. "*Wasn't*."

"Oh, Willie, it was! I saw where you lived. But it's all over
now — don't let's talk about it. You're safe now — you're with
us."

I flicked thoughtfully through the book. We were in his
bedroom, which of course was furnished a lot more luxuriously
than mine. We were sitting on the floor by his toy cupboard.

"Do lots of children read books like these?" I wondered, a sort
of realization occurring to me.

"Of course they do. It teaches them to know about the world."

"I always thought rich people didn't *know* about poor people.
I thought that's why we went begging, to bring ourselves to
people's notice."

"Oh, Willie! You surely never had to go *begging!*" Georgey
was appalled, and the full force of his blue-eyed gaze turned on
me.

"No," I said hurriedly. "I mean *beggars*. I thought rich children
didn't know about them and that's why everything is like it is.

Only it's just that if there are poems like this, which troubled *you*, Georgey, then everyone knows abaht – *about* the poor. But they don't do nothin ter – *to* change it."

"They do, Willie. Everyone gives to the church and the Poor Box. You see them, on Sundays."

"It can't be enough though, can it? Else why is there still poor?"

"But there are so many things to help as well. Look further on. The missionaries in China – have you read that poem? *They* need our help. And the black people. Do you know about the Horrid Rituals in India? And the fierce New Zealanders who eat each other? You would be giving all the time if you gave to everything that needed money. Every cause is good. Where do you start and where do you stop?"

"You starts on yer doorstep."

"You *start*. But Willie, that's what we did do. With *you*. Willie," said Georgey anxiously, "I hope you don't think that our family is rich?"

"Well, I don't know – how can I?"

"We aren't! You mustn't think we're wealthy and we're holding back our wealth for ourselves, and not helping the poor. We're only ordinary. We haven't got a private carriage. We have to make Many Small Sacrifices. Don't think we're mean and selfish. We do try and help people, we do!"

"Yeah, all right," I said embarrassed. "I don't mean to pick on you personally. I just mean, well, I hadn't thought about it before, but if there are a lot of rich people who like givin-g, well, if they gave a little bit more, in the end there'd be less poor. Like if everyone got together and didn't give in dribs and drabs, they could, like, change things quick, and then go on to something else."

"Willie, it can't be that easy," said Georgey seriously, "else somebody would have done it already."

III

MY SUITS of clothes were replaced as I grew. They had waistcoats – but not crimson ones! Grey ones to match the jackets, with tiny little buttons all the way up, and a black necktie. The best part of my outfit was the shoes. They were black and slim, in a soft leather, laced like boots, with neat criss-cross laces which were most attractive. Georgey had the same kind of clothes, though as he was younger he sometimes wore his black velvet suit. It was astonishing to see the clothes Georgey had been wearing throughout his childhood. There were photographs of him. At the age of about five he wore a little suit with a round collar and knee breeches and leggings and sweet little boots and a huge round hat. At three you would have sworn he was a girl. His hair was long and curly and he wore – well, there is no other word for it – a dress. It was trimmed with braid and was worn with a sash. Below the hem hung little scalloped-edged drawers. It was all I could do not to burst out laughing.

My Aunt Louisa was a warm-hearted and sentimental person. She was like someone living within a picture frame. Within the limits of social convention and accepted expressions of feeling, she acted out a happy pleasant role. Go outside the picture frame, and you were beyond her reach. She could help no one who had a real problem; it was outside her experience. But I'm hesitant to criticise her, because I value so much what she was able to give me, things which have seeped into my nature. She did have a very tangible sweetness.

Sitting with Aunt Louisa was a regular part of the organised routine of life at that house. The parlour was a lush and beautiful heavily furnished haven. Above the fireplace, the mantelpiece had a dark red fringe dangling curly tassels, and each side of the hearth the shelves were crammed with ornaments and small brown photographs in round red velvet frames. It was a dark room because of the heavy dusky-red curtains and what seemed like several thicknesses of yellow-creamy net. Small fringed cloths hung over all the armchairs, and there were vases and lamps, little tapestried footstools for Georgey and me to pull up, and a mulberry coloured chaise-longue on which my aunt reclined. The room was lit at night by gas flame in exquisite ornamental brackets, and Aunt Louisa would sit and sew. I'm afraid she unwittingly stirred some bad memories for me. The things she sewed were the frivolous stuff that ladies do for pleasure – bits of cloth for chair backs, embroidered initials on serviettes, little bouquets of anemones to look like a picture. I daresay she never sewed a shirt buttonhole in her life.

Religion figured heavily in our lives. It governed everything we did. It stemmed from my uncle, who was head of the house, the fount and source of all wisdom.

On Sunday we all went to church, twice a day, and sometimes three times. When we weren't at church or walking to and from it, we sat about silently studying our souls for flaws, even during meals, and there was a half hour in uncle's study when we all sat with folded hands and downcast eyes, while uncle directed our thoughts to matters of sin and gloom. Here we learnt that God hated pleasure and fun, and that the virtue he most prized was obedience, particularly in children, who had to obey just about everybody, as opposed to adults who had to obey God. We heard about the necessity for meekness and self-control, and of the looming importance of Work. If we filled all our waking hours with Toil we would have no time for Sin and we would not fall into Destitution. We were reminded that we might well die during the night and we were asked to consider how prepared we were.

Uncle also spoke about a mysterious work with which he seemed comfortably familiar, called the Lord's Book of Life, and he frequently enquired if we thought our names would be in it.

In between church services we also learnt hymns, and thus we could be shown off as being particularly holy, because we could sing without using our hymn books. Disturbingly enough, Georgey and I did *look* holy. With our pink faces, blue eyes and long wavy hair, you would have thought us candidates for the cherubim. Ladies patted our heads.

My uncle's dire warnings about doom and retribution did not trouble me over-much. I did think about Hellfire and Eternal Damnation, but I didn't relate it to *me*. Of course, I had sinned at Madame Rosa's, but I'd repented by working at the iron-mongers' and I wasn't sinning now. In fact I was continually doing God's will at the Armitage's – attending church, working hard, obeying my elders, being polite – and so I let the threats pass over me. Meditating about Sin and Retribution was just one more thing that happened in the course of a day at the Armitages, like eating with a knife and fork and learning about the Horrid Rituals in India. We'd managed all right without it in Aldgate and so I didn't worry about dying in the night; at bedtime I curled up to sleep in the clean scented sheets, with the companionable sound of the hot water tank gurgling under the roof nearby sending me quickly off to sleep.

IV

ONE SUNNY afternoon Aunt Louisa and I walked out into the garden and sat on the wooden seat upon the two cushions which I had carried out, and we looked at photographs.

The photograph album was a beautiful book bound in dark leather. The pages were of stiff card, painted gold at the edges, and the book closed with a metal clasp almost two inches square. Inside, the portraits were very formal and posed, and on the pages that surrounded them there were curling trailing plants drawn, and delicately coloured flowers.

I stared into the eyes of a frowning gentleman surrounded by lilies, trying to penetrate beyond the frozen rigidity of the pose.

"He is the one who – drove my mother away . . . " I began.

"You mustn't think of it like that," my aunt reproved. "Yes, this is your grandfather Hillyard, and he only did what he thought was right. He wanted the best for his daughters, you see; he wanted them to marry well. If a young girl marries well, the rest of her life takes care of itself, if she works diligently in the sight of the Lord. He does look stern, I know, Of course, he didn't always frown so; he could be quite merry. He was awfully fond of us. Maybe even this caused the intensity of feelings on his part when Emma left home. It was like a slap in the face for all his care."

"And grandmother . . . she agreed with him?"

"She always accepted his judgement, as a good wife should. Of course, she was dreadfully upset, but she knew my father was right. They could never accept that man – your father – into the family. They made that clear to Emma from the first."

"But she has a nice face. I would imagine her putting her hand on his arm and saying 'Oh, for my sake do not be so harsh,' " I said earnestly, unconsciously remembering a line from *The Squire of Lynwood*. "And maybe he would have been diverted from his Cruel Purpose."

"Ah no, Willie, it wasn't like that," she half laughed. "He didn't throw Emma out into the snow on a December night, you know. First of all, no, it wouldn't have been proper for Mamma to try and divert Papa from his decision. It would have undermined his authority. The husband, you see, is head of the household. On him the burdens of care and worry fall, and on his shoulders lie the responsibilities pertaining to the correct management of a household and family. My father remained calm throughout. He was a man of principle, and he always knew what was right and wrong. It was wrong for Emma to disobey him, and it would have been wrong for Mamma to intervene.

"You mustn't think, Willie, that Emma was a poor weak drooping sort of girl. Your mother as a young lady was very headstrong and difficult. To be quite honest, she was rather boisterous, and she thought nothing of slapping me and taking away my toys – I was very much younger than she . . . She announced flatly that she would marry this Charles Smith, and that if nobody agreed then she would leave home with him and make her own life."

"Did you *see* my father then?"

"Yes I did; but remember, we are talking of some twenty years ago, and I was not very old – I only knew what I was told. But yes, I did see your father – only, I think, twice, because he was not welcome at home."

"And – ?" I pursued eagerly.

"What was he like? Well, he was a very handsome young man. And he had hair the same colour as yours. He was quietly spoken and, I think, shy; but I believe his reserve covered a strong and stubborn nature. He came to our house to mend chairs."

"I wish his photograph had been taken!"

"Believe me, if it had, by now if would have been removed! We were supposed never to mention his name again."

"Why did nobody like him? He sounds most attractive."

"*Personally* he was, dear; very attractive. But he had no home, and his occupation was so precarious. He went from house to house mending furniture. He was, you see, not exactly a vagrant, but I believe grandfather classed him with tinkers and those road travellers who hawk their wares from town to town. He was an Unsettled Person; he didn't even come from this part of the country . . . oh, the Midlands, I believe. And then, you see, when we learnt that he belonged to one of those dreadful Unions, well, it could not be tolerated."

"Why not?"

"Surely you've heard of these things? If we *must* discuss it, Willie, all I can say is that it's a nasty business, and decent people don't involve themselves in it."

"I'm sorry – I just don't understand."

"They come from up north. They band together and they smash machines, and attack the men who give them work. They're ruffians who drink heavily, and who try to bring down their employers, and work secretly against the Queen. Bad men, Willie, sullen and ungrateful. I'm sorry; I'm sure your father wasn't wicked, just very misguided, and maybe he was tricked into believing the best . . . If he had kept it to himself, it would have been better, but unfortunately he took Emma to a Meeting."

A Meeting! Her tone suggested a Ritual Desecration of Graves, with an Orgy to follow.

"Yes?" I said. "What kind of meeting?"

"Apparently there are bad men who travel round the country and make speeches to crowds, and try to persuade them to agree with their way of thinking. *That* sort of meeting."

I frowned and thought. To me it sounded eminently reasonable.

"No more, Willie," said my aunt. "It's not a pleasant topic and there is no need for you to pursue it. Suffice to say that your father was a man with ideas of which your grandfather disapproved, and so he was not encouraged to visit at our house."

"Yes, I see," I said politely. "I'm sorry I persisted."

"Let us finish turning the pages," she said, changing the subject with a pleasant smile. "This is your uncle's father. Don't you think Georgey takes after him a little?"

"Who do *I* look like?" I wondered.

She thought.

"I think you must take after the Smiths, don't you? I see no likeness to you in these whiskered gentlemen! Even the ladies have a different shaped face – round, like Georgey's. Yours is more pointed – elfin, even."

"Georgey has all his grandparents in that book," I sighed. "I've just got half. I may have grandparents alive, and cousins and aunts, with dark red hair and elfin faces, and I'll never know. It's like I shall always have a part of me missing."

There was no answer to this obvious fact and I started feeling rather sorry for myself.

"My intention today, dear, was to make you happy," my aunt pointed out, "not discontented. Why, listen Willie, it means that you have something none of us has: a Mystery! Into that space where you don't know your relations, you can put whatever you like. You can put something beautiful. You can fill it with what might have been, and that way it will be always changing, and always special."

I was rather pleased with that idea. I incorporated it into myself. I was different; I was mysterious. Like a changeling prince, I thought modestly, in a fairy tale.

V

NEXT DAY, in lessons, as I was sitting at the table making laborious lists of things we imported from foreign countries, it suddenly struck me that Mr Irving knew about large and important issues. "Are trades unions wicked, Mr Irving?" I enquired.

"What makes you ask that question?" he said.

"My dad was in one, and my grandfather said if our mum married him she'd have to leave. She did marry him, and they went to union meetings. Aunt Louisa says it's not a pleasant topic."

"Indeed, Willie, I tend to agree, when it occurs halfway through a geography lesson. Please continue making your list."

"Yes, Mr Irving," I said in disappointment.

After a short while, Mr Irving said: "Now, Georgey, I'd like you to go to the kitchen, and without being any kind of nuisance or bothering Mrs Braddon, I'd like you to see if you can bring me five examples of food we import, and five examples of home grown produce. Just small samples, Georgey, not sacksful! Can you do that?"

"Ooh yes, Mr Irving," said Georgey, pleased, while I grimaced in jealousy at his getting out of the lesson on such a jolly task.

When the door had closed after him, Mr Irving said to me: "The answer to your question is no, Willie."

I blinked, trying to remember what my question was.

"What was your father's trade?" he asked me.

"He was a carpenter."

"The General Union of Carpenters is perfectly reputable; you need feel no shame about any connection with it. Let me put something to you, Willie." He spoke quickly and in a low voice. "However kind and well meaning a person is, he or she can only form an opinion from the facts at her disposal. If, rather than facts, a person has heard wild rumours or biassed talk, then she will pass on distorted information. There are two sides to every question, and what for some people is wicked is for other people a struggle for justice. I feel very strongly about this."

He was not making complete sense to me, but I understood the urgency in his voice, and I realised with a bit of a shock that he'd sent Georgey out of the room on purpose, so we could talk. I felt a conspiratorial thrill, like being in the little room at the country manor where it was rumoured the Roundheads plotted the death of the king.

"Can you tell me more about them?" I said.

"No, I cannot," he replied, with a crooked sort of smile. "If you think about it, you may understand why. I daresay if anyone heard that the subject had even been *mentioned*, I would be called to account. It is very strictly regulated what I may teach you."

"You wouldn't teach us wrong things?" I cried.

"No! Everything I tell you is honest and genuine. It's limited, that's all. It *excludes* things. I have to teach within a framework dictated to me. I spoke up just now because I feel it is an unnecessary burden for a child to bear, the doubt and dread that his father may have been wicked, when his supposed crime was in fact difference of thinking. So rest assured on that score. When you are older and out in the world, question and explore, find out, and form your own opinions. Do not let society impose its views, but seek the answers in your own head and heart. Do you understand me?"

"Yes, mostly. Thank you very much."

CHAPTER SIX

I

I MUST have been about fourteen when Mr Pearson came to speak at the church. Came and went, without ever suspecting the trouble he caused at the Armitage household.

Spectacular changes had occurred to me by then! I had got hairs! They were lovely. I lay in bed stroking them and ooh, it was nice. I knew it was a good thing to happen because of having seen Charley's, so I wasn't startled or bothered, just very pleased. They weren't exactly the same colour as my head hair but browner and curly, which was a surprise as my head hair was sleek and smooth. They gleamed with coppery bronze tints and some bold little hairs were actually red, like a thread of silk when you curled it round your finger. They shone real glossy after a bath. And along with this beautiful manifestation everything else down there had got bigger and heavier, and there were curly coppery hairs under my arms and dark brown, like Charley's, on my legs. How very interesting it all was!

These changes had obviously been observed by other people, because I had to stop having baths with Georgey. Up till then we'd sat facing each other in the suds and steam, but suddenly without explanation we had separate bath times, and Mrs Braddon stopped coming in to check if I'd washed behind my ears.

Exploring my bodily secrets touched old chords from my past. I relished my unsavoury knowledge. I thought I probably knew more about real life than my aunt and uncle. I knew things ordinary people didn't know – like that there were gentlemen in the City who spent their evenings in places like Madame Rosa's, and how desires could be translated into fact. And I knew that men screwed other men and that it was commonplace, and that it could be nice, and that it left you messy. And another thing I realised was that if I thought about these things in bed while I was stroking myself, sooner or later the juices would spurt into my hand and this was very nice.

In fact I did this so often that I became very slick at leaving no mess. At first, when it took me by surprise, I was left with a clammy puddle, which dried and marked the sheets even though it was white. I learned to use my handtowel. This made a lovely firm place to do it into, and afterwards it dried and looked like soap or washing-wetness.

At first it was mostly just a way of keeping close to Charley, like keeping him alive in my head. If the day hadn't been very nice I could keep happy by looking forward to the night. Then going to bed would be a real pleasure, and I teased out the dregs of sensation by putting off and putting off the moment of actual abandonment to delight. It seems to me that it was after Mr Pearson's address to the church that there came a cross-over point, and Charley receded to being a firm, kind, strong, loving friend. For my fantasies, it started to be Georgey.

Let me explain about this Mr Pearson.

On some Sundays, as well as the sermon (never, unfortunately, *instead* of the sermon) we had a Visiting Speaker, who came to try and induce people to give money to a Good Cause. There were ladies wanting money to train other ladies to be nurses, and a gentleman appealing on behalf of seamen's widows, and any number of missionaries, some from as far away as China. We'd seen pictures of The Heathen in Georgey's books. They usually held spears and cavorted with crazed grimacing faces, while the missionaries stood by holding Bibles and looking digni- fied and pious. The Heathen wore little drawers. This is a pictorial convention so as not to upset small children and offend ladies. In reality their behinds are quite bare.

It was October. We had squelched through the leaves and now sat in the pew in a row. I was on the end, having gone through a series of complicated manoeuvres to avoid sitting next to my uncle. Our Visiting Speaker, Mr Pearson, was going to talk about Goff Street Boys' Home.

Suddenly, as he was talking, I realised who he was. He was the figure I had seen when Mister Harry and I were coming back from Madame Rosa's, that dark cold night when I'd been with a gentleman. At least, I was ninety-nine per cent sure. Harry had bundled me into a doorway so quickly and I'd only seen the figure from the back, but I remembered very well watching the figure walk away, tall and inevitable, with steps like a policeman's. A tall top hat he wore, and a long flowing coat. Was it him? I stared, mesmerised. "I want to tell you what it's *really like*," said Mr Pearson.

Aunt Louisa stiffened. I could feel her stiffen and she was the other side of Georgey!

Mr Pearson stood very straight. He had brown hair – dark, thick, almost shoulder length – and his clothes were shabby. His suit had been so much worn that his trousers were full at the knees where his knees had made a shape in them. The jacket had shiny patches where the material had worn thin. I wondered how old he was – thirty? He had an impressive profile with a firm chin. He spoke very well and gestured at the poignant parts – and believe me, there were many. He had a lovely melodious voice and he was using it as an actor might, working almost theatrically to tug at our heartstrings. Pauses for effect. Clear round vowels – oh yes, he spoke very proper, none of your ain'ts and wasn'ts. I absorbed the tone of him. His message then began to filter through.

". . . Unimaginable squalor . . . rats . . . twenty boys in one wretched derelict room . . . filth . . . rags . . . crust of bread in the gutter."

One o'them bleedin' do-gooders, Harry had said, they gets everywhere. He takes boys in and they sing bleedin' hymns. I'd sniggered. But now that I was an educated boy I was more aware. I listened to what Mr Pearson actually did for the boys – provide some education, fit them for the Army, enable them to emigrate to Canada and South Africa to be farmhands. He spoke about his walks around the night-time streets; about half-starved bundles of rags that were boys too scared to go home; about others who had no home at all but slept down by the river huddled together, dying from cold, boys who were so destitute that they did not even have clothes. *Naked boys*, was what he said. I gasped. Nobody said "naked" at the Armitage home. To my alarm I found myself shamefully excited. Naked boys! My cock actually twitched and I had to put my hymn book over it in my embarrassment.

Whether anyone else was shocked by the sound of that word in church I do not know, but there was a tangible atmosphere of Sentimental Concern, a sort of Shocked Sympathy, associated with the well-meaning and distanced. As if he could sense it too, Mr Pearson instantly set out to wreck it.

"I want you to forget the pious pictures," he said. "Let us look truth in the eye without flinching. I am not talking about saintly children clutching their picturesque tatters about their slender shoulders and looking skyward. I am talking about changing an attitude, thwarting a monstrous inevitability of vast scale crime."

He told us that these were not Tiny Tims with pretty faces, but boys who would turn to crime as a natural outcome of their indescribably grim situation. He told us a true life story of a boy born in a Whitechapel rookery, familiar with gin palaces, beaten by his father, cast aside by his drunken mother, stealing and filching on a small scale, till a vicious network of organised crime got hold of him and used him to rob and steal, and finally he was knifed in an alley and left to die. For these boys, he said, there is Nothing, no hope, no escape, not until the pattern is broken into and the boy is removed from the physical situation. Such boys, he said, grew up with an unattractive and thoroughly understandable attitude that society was against them. They were hostile, angry, suspicious of help. "This is reality," he said, "this is how it is. How much harder for you to try to aid them than if they were humble and grateful. They are bitter and warped; but how desperately are they in need, unlovely, guilty victims."

Goff Street Boys' Home, he said, was only small: a drop in the ocean. It functioned on a charitable grant. It took in boys off the street, and no one was ever refused admittance. Stay was short; the boys were helped to better things and more came in their places. Money was always needed, and there was never enough, because the city threw up destitute lads as the sea churned up driftwood and scum.

"*If we gave all we had,*" he said in thrilling tones, "*it would not be enough.* It will never be enough."

Oh! I thought, spellbound. *I* was won over. *I* would give all I had – not that I had anything. I thought he was like Jesus standing there, out at the front saying things people didn't want to hear, with the altar behind him, and the tawny sunlight catching the gold of the solitary cross.

The audience wanted to hear that the boys were humble and

weak, happy with scraps; he told them the boys were savage and resentful of them. They wanted to hear that a small collection would make all the difference; he told them that whatever they gave it would hardly ripple the surface. But how forcefully he told it – how unafraid and frank! He was like a martyr. I almost expected someone to hurl a spear. His words were vibrant and disturbing; he had thrown down a challenge to the comfortable people about to go back to their Sunday dinners. They could not pretend they hadn't heard or didn't know. He was the best Visiting Speaker of all; he was exciting. He was much better than the missionaries from China.

I looked along the row, beyond Georgey's curls, curious to see how my relations were taking it. They sat with very dignified expressions, my uncle poker-stiff, and Aunt Louisa with a protective arm around Georgey, her chin tilted up, in obvious disapproval.

Mr Pearson was concluding his talk. His voice was now quiet and serene, yet *smouldering*, I thought, with controlled passion. I suddenly thought of Mr Irving saying "I feel very strongly about this"; Mr Pearson felt very strongly. I remembered Charley saying "This ain't a fair society, Willie." It's nice when all the people you like agree with each other.

Mr Pearson was now reading out extracts of letters from his boys who'd been successful. ". . . Thanks to you I am making a fresh start . . . I am a farmer now, I own land . . . If it had not been for Goff Street Boys' Home I would be in prison by now, or worse . . . " He was proving what a good thing his place was. I pictured him, walking the dim-lit streets, bringing hope and a refuge. What a risk he took! He could be attacked by a lawless gang! But he looked as if he could take care of himself, I thought assessively. He was beautifully built, lithe, broad shouldered, lean of thigh . . . Before I knew it my wayward mind had stripped off his unflattering clothes and stood him there naked. Yes! That word! I flushed crimson and my collar constricted my throat. I had to open my hymnbook out over my crotch like a fig leaf. I longed passionately to touch myself up. I was shocked with myself, but the horrors persisted. I put my hand under my hymnbook. Sinner, sinner! I told myself. I was in church! But I could still see him naked.

He thanked us for our kind attention.

Little can he have realised that he had aroused desire in a member – in every sense – of the congregation. As I sat hot and flustered, there came the general rustling and shuffling as people prepared for the final hymn. Then we were all standing up, and in the singing I was able to compose myself. We sang "To Be a Pilgrim." I joined in enthusiastically, relieved to lose my arousal in religious fervour. How appropriate it sounded for Mr Pearson! Who would true valour see, let him come hither! No foes shall stay his might! There's no discouragement! Oh, I did hope so! I did hope that Mr Pearson went home to ease and contentment and did not feel bowed down by the enormity of his task.

After all the prayers and blessings and private kneelings for the perusal of the soul, we all filed out and gave our offerings. Uncle, after a secret amount on his own behalf, gave Georgey and me threepence each to put in. I frowned. It didn't seem very much, considering the horrendous bigness of the problem. As we walked home, we were as usual silent. The idea was that you thought about the sermon and let it sink into your mind, like treacle around a baked apple. However, it was fairly clear that my aunt was annoyed. It was over the Sunday dinner that we had the conversation.

"It is monstrous," said my aunt, "that a talk like that should have been allowed inside a church, with children present. I feel most aggrieved. I will not have Georgey exposed to coarse accounts of the lives of vicious people."

Georgey Exposed! What was the matter with me that day? Even that phrase gave me a cock twitch.

"The fellow was exaggerating," said uncle dismissively. "He was after money, remember. He had to make a case."

"That story he told," said my aunt, pressing the back of her hand against her forehead in a gesture of despair. "I've never heard such horrors – but to mention them in church! Gin palaces indeed! Violence! The insistence on the fact that they are unclothed – it was obscene."

"I tell you, he was exaggerating. Let us put it from our minds. Apple sauce?"

"Willie!" insisted my aunt. "Did *you* ever see anyone stabbed on the street?"

"No, aunt."

"There, you see," shrugged my uncle. "And now, Louisa – "

"Boys who lie in a row under a blanket all day because they have no clothes?" my aunt persisted.

"No, aunt."

"Well!" cried my aunt, "if it was exaggeration then that is almost worse, that he should embroider facts to suit his purpose!"

I went hot. I couldn't sit by and let Mr Pearson be accused of lying. "I didn't see those things," I said, "because I didn't live in that sort of place."

"You lived in a slum house," protested my aunt. "You would have seen them if they were as prevalent as he made out."

"No," I said, "there are all kinds of poverty. We tried to keep decent. But there was a place near us, called the Lane, and it was like how he described. I never saw anyone stabbed – "

"Exactly," said my uncle.

"– but a boy did come to school who had no clothes," I said defiantly. "Just a shawl. When it came off he was – " (I took a big breath) " – naked underneath."

There was a sort of communal gulp and everybody clicked their knives and forks busily.

"What happened next?" gasped Georgey, shining-eyed and absorbed, mouth open and fork frozen in mid-air.

"You see!" cried my aunt. "This is just what I wished to avoid. It's disturbing the child. We shouldn't begin to speak of these things."

"At least," said uncle sanctimoniously, "we have done *our* duty. By taking William into our home, we have made it possible for one boy to have a decent start. *One* boy will not sleep roughly tonight."

"Owww!" I burst out. "*One* boy – but there's more!"

Everyone stared at me and uncle in particular looked very forbidding.

"Explain that remark, William," he said.

He always had the effect of drying up my mouth. I licked my lips.

"Only, sir," I began bravely, "that while I have a good home now, even while we are sitting here, there's boys still starvin', stealin' and cold, wivaht homes."

"*Without*," corrected Georgey importantly.

"Is this *ingratitude?*" uncle demanded coldly, staring me in the eyes.

"No, sir."

"I am relieved to hear it. And now suppose we cease this distressing conversation. It is not conducive to good digestion."

"Sir," I groaned, "can we *give?*"

My aunt looked uneasy, and flashed me a warning look.

"We have given," said my uncle in chilling tones.

"Yes, once," I said, "but there are *always* boys – it keeps going on. If we give once, we forget."

"William, you are beginning to overstep the bounds of politeness," said my uncle.

"I don't have any money," I plunged on, "but I could give up my Sunday dinner. I know meat costs a lot, and what I saved could go to the Boys' Home, and feed a starving boy."

"Be silent, child," my uncle snapped.

"But, sir – "

"William, I order you to be quiet, and after this meal you will come to my study."

Flattened and glum, I lowered my eyes and ate my dinner.

"I'll give up my Sunday dinner too," Georgey piped up generously. "I'd like to feed a starving boy."

That only made matters worse.

"Playing on Georgey's good nature," my aunt seethed. "Sweet susceptible child, prey to anyone who can sway his tender feelings . . . "

After the meal, I faced my uncle in his study. His shelves were lined with well-bound books, giving a tone to the room, the topics mostly botanical and medical. Beyond, through the window, you could see a dull yellow-leaved tree, drooping from recent rain, and a sky like a grey water-colour wash.

"I did not wish to hold this conversation over dinner," said my uncle, sitting, arms folded, at his desk. "I suspected, however, that sooner or later it would occur."

I stood, hands by my side, presenting, no doubt, a slightly shifty appearance. I always found it very difficult to look him in the eye.

"William," he said, "your aunt and I discussed at length the question of whether or not we should take you into our home, all those months ago, when we first received your dead mother's communication. We were well aware of the difficulties involved. Up till now, you have, on the whole, borne yourself worthily.

We have been pleased at the improvement in your speech and at the way you have applied yourself to your lessons. I give much credit to Georgey and Mr Irving. Now I know that there comes a time when a child begins to question and look about him. In your case, the background you have had puts you at a terrible disadvantage. I am not only thinking of the degradation your family endured as a result of poverty, but also of the malign influence that the opinions of your father may have had upon your forming mind. I am going to put the matter to you clearly, William. I will not have it here!"

I frowned, trying to decide which aspects of me he was attacking.

"Disruptive talk," he elaborated. "Provocative ideas. They must be nipped in the bud. While you are in my house, I want it understood you abide by my principles. That means, as far as you are concerned, obedience to your aunt and myself, and lack of meddling in notions which you know nothing about."

"I do know something about poverty," I muttered.

"If you are grateful for your home here, for your food, clothes and education, for the chance it gives you to progress in the world later on, then you must surely agree that the least you can do in return is to respect the views of one much wiser than yourself, who is acting entirely out of principles concerned with your own best interests."

"Yes, sir," I said guardedly.

Appeased, my uncle calmed a little. "You know nothing of the world, William. All that we can do is to fill the space we are in by living according to our Heavenly Father's dictates. Goodness, obedience, prayer – He loves these things. You cannot change the world. The poor will always be with us. Our Lord said so."

"But sir!" I burst out rashly, "*Jesus* changed the world. He went out and did good. Just like Mr Pearson. Mr Pearson is like Jesus. He *touches* the poor – he's with them on the streets – "

I dried up. I had of course gone too far.

My uncle stood up slowly, and his brows loomed dark. He ordered me, in a doom-laden voice, to recite the Ten Commandments.

Dutifully I began, counting them off on my fingers. I heard the sound of my voice saying them. At this stage of my life I sounded as if I had a permanent sore throat; my voice kept going husky. Mr Irving said it was a phenomenon which occurred in boys of my age; it showed particularly when I was reciting out loud. When I arrived at the third my uncle ordered me to stop.

"There is no excuse for blasphemy," he said. "You took the name of the Lord Thy God in vain."

"I didn't mean to. I only meant . . . " I felt misunderstood.

"This has been a very sinful Sunday for you," my uncle observed. "Unseemly arguments, petulance, and the culmination: the breaking of a commandment. I have no choice but to chastise you. An offence toward God – on a Sunday – is a shameful wicked act, and sometimes, William, I feel that mere words make no impact on you. It pains me do to this, but I know it is for the best. Hold out your hand."

I wonder if it is possible to feel a person's dislike for you down the length of their arm and through a slim taut stick. I thought so. Or should I say, I thought so afterwards when I went over it in my mind, nursing my throbbing hand. At the time, I was much taken up with preserving a manly fortitude, and failing. I'd never had six before. I'd had three a few times – all for persistent carelessness in my speech and a couple of Blimeys. ("Do you in fact wish the Good Lord to strike you blind? I will remind you that you are using an oath.") After the fourth, my whole arm started quivering, and I had to put my right hand underneath to hold it steady for the welts to come. My eyes watered, and when he'd finished I felt like I was holding the hot end of a poker.

"You will spend the rest of the day in your room," my uncle said. "You will not come down to tea nor to supper. You have been offensive in the eyes of God and in the eyes of those who care for you. I hope you feel shame."

"Yes, sir," I said – what else could I say?

"Will you ask for guidance to keep you from further sin?"

"Yes, sir," I had to wipe my cheeks. My hand felt like it was made of rubber, several sizes too big. I still didn't see anything wrong in comparing Mr Pearson with Jesus. I only meant it loosely.

"Now, I want to hear no more silly talk from you. Go to your room and examine your conscience. Tomorrow begin a new day, with Our Heavenly Father's aid, and curb your sullen rebellious nature. Show proper obedience to those who know best; and sin no more."

No tea! No supper! I was shocked. And then I remembered guiltily how all my childhood I'd gone without, and now here I was, sulky and affronted because I had to miss my tea. Up there in my room, I reflected that unawares I'd grown very soft and cushioned. Was this life here at the Armitages spoiling me, teaching me facts at the expense of my integrity?

Well, this is hindsight, because the answer of course was yes, and I didn't see it quite so clearly that particular afternoon. I just sensed I'd been punished for having different ideas rather than for being wicked. They didn't want me to be difficult, but to pass through their hands with the minimum bother. I can't tell whether my uncle welted me because he genuinely thought I was a sinner, or because he was intelligent enough to see there was some truth in what I was saying but it didn't suit his philosophy to accept it.

However, I certainly felt that he had been glad of a reason to hit me and I had been caned because of personal dislike. It made me think about the peculiar servitude of my situation. There were benefits to me at the Armitage home and I passionately wanted them, but they had a cost. I was being educated and bettered, but slapped down for thinking. If I wanted to stay I would have to learn to suppress. I would have to seem obedient and never disagree.

And so I divided myself into two people. I had an Overlife and an Underlife. In the Overlife I was proper and compliant and I worked hard at my lessons, and went through all the trappings, duties, pleasures even, of the week. In the Underlife I was rapturously wicked. I let thoughts come and go as they wished, and I dwelt on sordid details from my past and, best of all, invented the stories that brought my release. They centred on Georgey.

II

I LIE in bed and concentrate. Close to, his hair is shiny gold, a little curl touches his cheek. His cheek is hot and soft, his neck is small. Quickly I transfer him to a different setting. A turretted castle and I am its lord. My courtiers bring in Georgey in a long blue cloak, daisy chains in his hair. When I lift back the cloak he is Quite Naked. I've seen him naked. He's like when you make a cake and put butter in a bowl and add sugar and it goes fluffy mixed together, that's the tone of Georgey naked. Fine pale down on the back of his neck, small shoulders. His tummy is plump, his whole texture peachy soft. Oh rosebud mouth, oh eyes of sapphire blue, oh softly swelling velvet smooth bum! I lead him to the bed. An ornate structure with brocaded hangings. Come give yourself to me; you will find me gentle. I lie down upon the bed. I kiss his neck and his little pink nipples. I LIE UPON HIM. All that smoothness. I quiver. I put my lips on his, not gently like saying goodnight, but hard, till it hurts. He whimpers, but I've got him, he's mine and I shall cover him with love juice.

I had several illnesses when I was thirteen and fourteen. Illnesses were treated with pomp and ritual. I don't know that it's a good thing to pamper sickness. I feel my illnesses were partly to do with the fact that I had the facilities for being ill and was encouraged to indulge. They took the form of hot fevers, and my aunt wiped my face with a cool cloth, and a medicine tray came in three times a day, along with much hot milk and blackcurrant cordial. One time my neck swelled up and hurt, and as I recovered Georgey read stories to me, sitting in a chair on the other side of the room. Then his neck swelled up, and I read stories to him. My aunt said we must have caught it from some children in church. Georgey in bed with a swollen neck looked more than ever like a peach. The doctor had to come in to Georgey, as his constitution was not so strong as mine. For weeks after he was better, everyone treated him as if he was a wisp of thistledown which might blow away, when anyone could see he was a plump, indulged little boy.

In balance, though I had these illnesses in the winter, I completely lost the perpetual cough I'd had for most of my childhood, due to the clear air and regular walks and three big meals a day. With all those baked apples and steamed puddings and hot milk sprinkled with cinnamon, I grew nicely rounded. I was very interested in the shape of my body and studied it quite a lot. My hair was shoulder-length and curled under like a Renaissance page-boy, fringed across my forehead. My basic shape was slim and willowy. I never had much weight round my ribs and my stomach was very lean; my hipbones showed. Once, later, I was told I was like a Moreau nude. You see them in the paintings, beautiful androgynous youths, slight of build, with longish backs and well-rounded arses and girlish thighs. *Unlike* a Moreau nude I had a hefty wodge of coppery brown crotch hair and an obvious cock.

And then in my Underlife:

A cold November night, and me and Georgey lie tightly pressed together under a coarse rough blanket. A lean-to wooden slab is all that protects us from the night air. We are somewhere in Whitechapel. Villains stalk the streets. The wood is roughly pulled back. A dozen ragged ruffians surround us; they tear the blanket off. Ah, they cry, Naked Boys! They drag us away, into a Thieves' Kitchen. Warm and steamy, full of ragged people crouched around the grate. Georgey stands quivering, his hands clasped like a lady angel. They laugh. They lay hands on him; they *feel* him. Give the baby something to suck, cries one, open your rosebud mouth; and Georgey, who has been brought up to be obedient, opens his mouth to a big round O. His face is like somebody surprised. A dirty ragged man pulls open his filthy breeches. Georgey is a pink and golden kneeling cherub. His little throat gulps but he never takes his lips away. Suck, suck, the thieves all shout, and the man shoots forth his load.

One winter Mr Irving had a fever too and couldn't teach us for three weeks. In order for us not to slack, my uncle gave us an hour of his time every evening. He began by testing us on our general knowledge, walking up and down importantly. I knew the dates of every king and queen from Alfred to Victoria, and the capital cities of every country in Europe. I knew the name of the prime minister and the ships that fought at Trafalgar, and I could explain how the Battle of Waterloo was won. I knew about polar bears and kangaroos and elephants. Naturally my uncle kept on until I didn't know something, and I stuck on three influential French philosophers. He was easier on Georgey but of course, as we all knew, Georgey was two years younger and wasn't expected to know so much,

Then my uncle turned to the two piles of written work. "William," he said pompously, and picked up the pile he thought was mine. Georgey's top paper was covered in blots and crossings out. He had been supposed to write it out again but he didn't because Mr Irving was ill and couldn't check it. Georgey had a lazy streak and usually shirked if he could. My uncle's expression as he saw that the paper was in fact Georgey's was a joy to behold. He controlled it pretty quickly, but not quickly enough, and he knew I'd seen. He'd been made to look a fool and he was sore about it, and I don't think he ever forgave me for the knowing way I was looking at him, showing I'd realised. He'd assumed I was a messy worker, and was all prepared to lecture me on slovenliness – and it was Georgey's!

In reproachful surprise he turned to Georgey, and "more in sorrow than in anger" he spoke about his distress. But how can you berate a rosebud? Georgey sat there small and pink. "It was the pen's fault," he whispered meekly.

Fortunately for my uncle, as he went through my papers he found enough spelling mistakes to be able to castigate me severely, and so he felt better. He set us dictations, at which Georgey was better, and he made me write out my mistakes fifty times.

"Lawks!" I muttered.

My uncle turned on me.

"Control your language! You are not in Spitalfields now!" He found Spitalfields more satisfying to say than Aldgate. He spat the word so forcibly that a blob of saliva landed on the table near my elbow. He stood over me while I corrected my mistakes. However, I was a neat writer, and he could not fault my copperplate.

At night:

Georgey and I are walking hand in hand down by the docks. Pausing innocently to look at the fish barrows where the ranks of scaly white bodies still twitch and glare glassy-eyed, we are seized from behind by sailors in the pay of Turks. "Just the kind of boys we're looking for!" they cry. They drag us to a wharfside warehouse and bundle us inside, among the strawbales, tea chests and pineapples. "*Examine them!*" orders a sort of slave driver. "The blond one first!" Before my eyes Georgey is stripped by eager leering sailors. His clothes are wrenched from him, his little drawers come down, he stands before us Exposed. Unceremoniously he is upended and placed on a tea chest. "Oh," they cry, "what a pretty sight! We will get a good price for that!" We all look, and sailors *feel* him with their fingers, in turn. Then a Turk steps forward, bristling with ear rings, turbanned, and wearing baggy oriental trousers, and shoes that curl up at the end. I am afraid he's going to use Georgey badly, but no, he turns to me. "The boy shall do it," he orders. The sailors shove me forward. "Do it or it will be the worse for you!" I have no choice. Georgey lies spread before me, offered up like a feast. "I have to do it, Georgey," I tell him. "I do not mind," he answers bravely. The sailors shout encouragement. It's like velvet in there, and I groan with happiness.

III

ON MY fifteenth birthday Aunt Louisa gave me a book, *The Idylls of the King*, and with it a gift far subtler and as beautiful – the awakening of my Erotic Nature. I don't mean by this the awareness of lust and pleasure – obviously I had known that for some time! Bound up with the mystic world between the pages of that book, the other gift was an emotional perception, sensuousness, a way of being.

It happened like this. One winter's evening when Georgey and I were sitting about the fire, and Aunt Louisa was sewing, she said teasingly: "And now what's all this about our William not liking poetry?"

"Oh," I grimaced. "I do try, but it's all about Nature, or how to be holy."

"Ah," she laughed, a little rebukingly, "and you know all about how to be holy, do you, so the poems do not interest you?"

"I prefer stories," I said, "and I hate learning by heart. That seems to be all that can be done with poems – learn by heart."

"Spoken very feelingly," said Aunt Louisa.

"He means *Lycidas*," said Georgey. "He's never recovered from learning it in full. It was one hundred and ninety lines."

My aunt looked smilingly mysterious.

"It's a sad thing, it seems to me, not to enjoy poetry. I may have to take you in hand."

I thought she meant she'd persuade me to learn more poems; but she didn't. She had in mind something much nicer.

My birthday falls in February, and we had a special tea, with presents by my plate. That particular birthday, it happened that Georgey had a bad cold, and so after tea he was put to bed with ceremony and a strong smell of camphorated oil. My uncle retired to his study, and so it was just Aunt Louisa and myself who sat down on my birthday evening by ourselves in the parlour.

Long since out of mourning, my aunt was wearing a dress of powder blue silk, with a cameo brooch at the neck. She reclined on the dark red chaise longue. At her elbow on a small table was a glass vase of purple and crimson anemones. "Come over and sit on the stool," she said. "You may be almost a young man but you are still boy enough for me to mother you."

Only, she not being my mother, it did not feel like that. I pulled up the stool, as we'd always done, and sat there, my head level with her shoulder. She opened my new book and said: "Now you shall grow to love poetry or I shall consider myself to have thoroughly failed."

She told me this work was written by Mr Tennyson, and indeed there was an engraving of him in the front, an impressive bearded gentleman. She said that a little bird had told her I liked King Arthur, and she began to read aloud. From the first I was won over. I knew I would like it. It was a story, but poetry, and spellbinding. And while my aunt read it to me, she had one arm round my shoulder. Her soft hand played with my collar, her pale blue silk sleeve brushed my hair. I must insist that all my feelings (and certainly hers) were entirely pure in intention, but in effect were extremely arousing.

The room was very red. The heavy curtains were drawn against the winter night, and the fire and the gaslamps cast shadows. She was stroking my hair. Her fingers touched my ear and sent sensations all down my shoulders. The nice thing was, she didn't pretend she hadn't touched my ear but stroked some more. She could because she was supposed to be mothering me, and mothers may stroke their boys' ears. But I was fifteen and she wasn't my mother. My senses were startlingly alert. The anemones, the firelight, the pale blue silk, the clock-ticking silence, and the air heavy with magic from the story – all braided themselves together in my consciousness. She stroked my forehead. It made me sigh.

"Not *sad*, Willie?" she asked, sure that I wasn't.

"I always . . . " I confessed emotionally ". . . wanted a mother like this . . . like in a story."

She was pleased and touched; she was very sentimental, and anything to do with mothers and babies affected her. It was the same for me; I felt affected myself and it was true what I said. I longed for this sort of sweetness and I never had it in childhood. I'd have loved to have been like Georgey and have had it from infancy, cuddling into silk against a warm bosom. Only, when this happens to you at fifteen, well, the innocence is lacking. There was a *seeming* innocence, the trappings of mother-son affection, but I was, I must admit, erect as a flagpole, and when she cuddled my head to her breast, my feelings were not childlike; they were erotic. My cheek could sense the actual breast. My instinct was to put my arm around her waist, and I had to fight down this highly improper notion.

I would love to think that she too felt an uneasy stirring of desire. It sounds boastful to say I knew I was beautiful and to assume therefore awareness on her part. A married lady, wife to a severe, straight-laced city gentleman, she would have been heavily defended against a sudden sneak attack of carnal stirring. And yet I think she did feel it, unconsciously. I think she felt possessive of me, and that we shared a sensitivity that uncle didn't have, and nor did Georgey, for all his winning ways.

I read the book whenever I could, by candlelight in bed and in the summer in the garden, pressing rose petals between my favourite pages. I loved the places which the knights encountered – the gloomy glades, the forest pools, the ivy-covered castle walls, the wilderness and the sea. And then there were the clothes they wore – the gold, the shining satin, the sparkling jewels, the play of mingling blues and greens. I loved the mighty language and the characters with their strengths and weaknesses, the sunlight glinting upon chalices and armour.

SHORTLY AFTER the gift of the book, my aunt and I went shopping for dress material. She needed, she said, a dove grey silk for Sundays. Now there was a drapers in Putney, but she said we would have a change and go into town, because it would Do Us Good to Go Out. Georgey was not included in this trip because he was recovering from his cold. He was going to stay behind and help Mrs Braddon make toffee. I was partly envious of that, but mostly elated at the strange jump in status. It was as if Georgey was still a child, but I was Nearly a Man, and was to accompany my pretty aunt into town. And that's how she treated it too. I was as tall as she was now, and when we crossed the roads she took my arm in a nestling sort of way, as if I was her protector. It was very nice, very flattering.

We went into town in the omnibus, inside as the weather was cold. It was the beginning of March, and there were a lot of daffodils about. The shivering flowersellers wrapped in shawls had all kinds of spring flowers standing in buckets and bunched in baskets.

The drapers' shop was a long deep room with counters on both sides, and shelves stacked with rolls of material. There was a lit stove in the centre of the room where people were warming their hands, as we did too before we went to make our purchase.

"Oh aunt!" I whispered agonised. "Let's pretend we want cherry red or peacock blue!"

To my delight Aunt Louisa was in the same mood as me. We were frivolous. We were never like this at home, but somehow we were very merry and free that day. She asked the man to show us cherry red, beautifully serious she was too, sparkling under the serious front. Yards and yards of cherry red cascaded before our eyes, and we felt it between our fingers. Then she said she wondered about peacock blue . . . and the man fetched us what she required. Oh! It had a shimmer – it rippled like a limpid pool. We stroked it as if it were alive.

"Now lilac," said my aunt.

And this is what she did – she gathered up the lilac silk and put it against my cheek and observed me. "Ah!" she said. "I knew it would be your colour." And to the staring shopman she explained: "It's for his sister. Her colouring is just the same."

My aunt was making me blush at the attention I was getting. It suddenly struck me that none of the young men in the shop had hair as long as mine, and I was conscious of it touching my shoulders. What did they think our relationship was? I blushed hotter. Could I pass for her son? I didn't think so. Suppose they thought she was buying silk for *me* and that I was – I could hardly form the words, even in my head – her young lover. Blushing wasn't helping either. My aunt was dressed so respectably but she was acting very whimsical, not like a serious matron at all. Taking pity on my embarrassment she asked to see some dove grey silk and was shown it, and ordered enough to have a dress made up. The draper asked if she would like it delivered, but she said: "No, my young friend can carry it, won't you, dear?"

"Yes," I mumbled, blushing all over again at being called her young friend. I felt eyes were all over me as we walked out of the shop; I was convinced they would all gossip as soon as we were outside and assume I was her kept boy. A flighty duchess in one of the Twilight Tales had had a kept boy. He was called her Petit Ami. The duchess took poison in the end. The gentlemen who seduced young girls rarely if ever took poison, and therefore the reader was induced to believe that ladies who act so will come to a bad end but gentlemen will not.

When we came out of the shop, I found that although I felt flustered, I was flustered in a very agreeable way, and my aunt's instant return to sober dignity did not deceive me a bit. She had enjoyed playing with me, and her lips twitched as she enquired was I all right, and was the material too heavy for me? I assured her everything was fine. "Delightful," I added, "it's a wonderful day."

A shocking thing about that day, I realised afterwards, was that I never thought about the social injustices I saw, only about myself and my sweet confusion. It never bothered me that the flowerseller girls had cold blue fingers and threadbare shawls and would be on the pavements maybe from six in the morning till well after dusk. We saw street sweepers, lads such as Charley had been, and I hadn't pestered my aunt to give them shillings. We ignored some beggars, we hurried past. And in the shop, so taken up was I with my delicate sensibilities and my lust for silk that it didn't concern me all the trouble we put the shopman to for nothing, for a whim; nor did it bother me that young men not much older than I were behind the counter, subservient to our dictates. Maybe they had wives and families at home, and every day they would have to come into the shop and remain polite and never answer back, while ladies made them unroll not just silks, but cottons and coarse cloth and ribbons; afterwards they must re-roll it and if they were anything less than impeccable, they could be dismissed.

I realised soberly that I had been guilty of the casual behaviour of the comfortably off. It was a chastening thought to me who had once sold my arse for peaches.

V

MR IRVING set Georgey and me an essay entitled "Paradise".

I must admit I enjoyed writing it. It began with a grandiose flourish: "Paradise is a conception in the mind of men". I explained about its religious significance and the angels with harps, but I didn't dwell on it. "Paradise is perfection," I wrote, "and perfection must be perceived by the senses and the mind. These are not active after death, therefore perfection must be sensed *before*, which is, on earth. For perfection, that is Paradise, to exist on earth, certain things must change. There can be no doubt that existence on this earth for the teeming hordes of humanity is not perfect, is not Paradise."

I went on here about social ills, poverty, unfair distribution of wealth, including a few examples from my own experience. I then went on to some suggestions as to how that could be remedied – pooling of wealth, destruction of slums, housebuilding schemes, limits by law upon how much wealth one person should be allowed to possess. I finished with an idyllic description of what life would be like, humankind at one, no wars, no crime, no struggling for success at the expense of others, but a sort of generalised bliss, in fact Paradise.

Mr Irving slung it straight back at me.

"Are you trying to get me dismissed?" he demanded. "What kind of answer is this?"

"The one that came into my head, sir."

"I seem to have taught you decent English and somewhat less

of common sense. I can see by your idiotic smirk, Willie, that you expected a reaction like this. Whatever are you playing at, boy?"

"Oh? Did I say anything you don't agree with, sir?"

"Behave yourself, Willie. My political views are not at issue. I will simply point out that I am engaged here at the discretion of Mr Armitage, and that if he believed I had been so careless as to pass on these ideas to you, or to treat your essay as a serious work, he would have no hesitation in terminating my employment."

"I'm sorry, sir. I truly didn't think along those lines. I just thought I would answer as seemed appropriate to me."

"I may agree with your sentiments," said Mr Irving, "though you have not followed them all through to fine detail. I am criticising you for a kind of cheery bravado. You know your uncle sees all your work sooner or later, and I would be held responsible if I let this pass. You know what I'm going to ask you to do, don't you?"

I pulled a face.

"You're going to rip it up," he told me, "and get your head down and write me an essay on 'Paradise' that is simply crammed with angels and archangels and souls, and packed with wise and pious injunctions as to how we may all attain that happy place."

"Yes, sir," I groaned.

"If you are stuck, read Georgey's. His is a little gem."

I sniggered. Yes, I thought, smuttily, that's very true.

And so I wrote about the angels.

That night I lay in bed imagining. I find myself separated from my Roundhead troop. The moon, high in a pitch-black sky, illumines the old manor house, a Cavalier stronghold. I climb the wall, I sprint across the flower beds crushing petals beneath my leather boots. With the speed of light I climb the ivy and I'm in through the mullioned window. I tear aside the curtains, and drop into the room. In a four-poster bed a Cavalier lad lies asleep. Ha! Just the sort I like! Georgey! His golden curls lie tousled on the pillow, his pink cheeks are smooth as alabaster. His eyelids flicker and widen with alarm. He sees me. "Silence, brat! My men are without!" "Have pity on me," he whimpers.

"That depends on you," I tell him grimly, "O scion of misbegotten wealth. Do you not know that peasants starve while you sleep here in silks?" "Oh, sir, what shall I do?" Slowly I pull back the cover, until he is Exposed. I see his white back, the alabaster globes of his behind. With my leather glove I thwack his arse; I leave a scarlet imprint. He stifles a cry. I welt him again. Six times. He wriggles and writhes; I am inflamed. "Get out of bed," I order. He stands quivering before me. "Get down on your belly" – oh! another wicked word, and Georgey's is so sweet! – "and lick the mud off my boots." "Oh sir, must I?" "Yes, you must; you have No Choice!" I watch him kneel and bow his golden head. "Lick!" I command. I stand feet apart and watch his little pink tongue come out and taste the mud on my boots. "Eat it!" I order, implacable. He eats it! He licks my boots clean, dribbling brown spit on to the leather, utterly obedient. I unbutton my trousers. "Lift your head up, slave, and look at me!" Carelessly, as a conqueror would, I make myself spurt. I aim at his big blue eyes and his rosebud mouth. Docile, he lets me. He has to. He is my victim.

That autumn it was constant frustration for me – always in the company of my love object, but never allowed to treat it as I longed to. My life was illuminated with small panting incidents, hardly anything in themselves, but treasured by me as isolated pearls, and set on fire at night in the heat of my heaving imagination.

Mr Irving took Georgey and me to see Westminster Abbey. We saw the tombs and memorials of Milton, Jonson, Dryden, Spenser, Pope, Sheridan, Gray, Addison, Handel and Isaac Newton, also the organ and the Henry VII chapel. We came back on the omnibus, upstairs. It was crowded so we had to sit close, and I was squeezed against Georgey so tight I was welded to him all the way down, shoulder to ankle. I pretended I was jostled, and put my arm round the back of him. My face was close to his hair, and I could see the texture of his suit, the little grey roughnesses in the cloth, the pale gold curls lying on his collar. He wriggled; my thigh experienced his wriggle.

"Willie! You're *pressing* me!" he grumbled.

"Sorry," I lied, pasted to him all our entire lengths. His trousers were pulled tight over his round thighs, but all puckered in the crotch, where his drawers were. His knees were perfect ovals.

"Willie, you're making me hot," he said, his lips so close that I had the sensation of his breath on my cheek. I thought with a sigh of all the bits of him that would be hottest and the rumbling jolting of the omnibus wobbled us together and gave me fresh sensations.

"Move *off*, Willie," he said, pushing me. So I did, amused and contented and aroused all at once.

One day when Aunt Louisa was out making purchases, I came into the dining room where Georgey was sitting at the table, perfecting his handwriting.

"I've something for you," I said nonchalantly.

"What?" he asked looking up.

"Something I was making yesterday, in the kitchen."

"Ooh! I *know* what you were making yesterday!" he cried happily. "Marshmallows! Is it that?"

"You have to close your eyes," I told him.

"Yes, I will."

"And open your mouth. No, it's no good with you sitting at the table. You have to stand in front of me."

"Oh, all right."

Georgey came and stood before me, twinkling and pleased.

"Have you been a good boy?" I enquired.

"Don't tease me! You know I have."

"Well, to get your reward, you have to kneel down, and look very pious, like a choirboy."

Georgey knelt down on the floor and clasped his hands. He assumed a holy expression for a moment, but I giggled and so did he.

"Oh, come on, Willie, please. I love marshmallows, and you make them so beautifully."

"You heard my terms," I said masterfully.

Georgey closed his eyes tight and opened his mouth.

"Wider, Georgey, as big as you can."

Oh! Georgey on his knees, eyes closed, his rosebud mouth opened to a great big O, his pink tongue showing, his throat a little arched . . .

I sighed and took out a marshmallow. Ever so gently I touched his lips with it, and popped it into his mouth.

"Mmm," he said appreciatively, opening his eyes.

"Georgey, you are a trusting fool! It could have been a dirty potato!"

"You wouldn't do anything so nasty," he said confidently.

I just laughed. But I felt a little twinge of guilt about my bedtime fantasies. He really did not know me at all.

CHAPTER SEVEN

I

A s my sixteenth birthday drew near I was encouraged to
think about my Future.

I was old enough now to leave the Armitage household
to earn my living – Make My Own Way in the World. I contemplated the prospect with both pleasure and alarm – I had no
clear idea of what I wanted to do. Half flippantly, because I
knew the answer would be complicated, and half in earnest
curiosity, I asked Mr Irving how one went about becoming a
social reformer.

"One has money," he replied caustically.

"You mean one should come from the upper classes?"

"Not necessarily. Starting poor need be no handicap, as long
as you accrue your wealth rapidly. Let us look at Robert Owen.
This great socialist started out as a poor boy in Wales and
became a wealthy manufacturer quite by his own efforts. His
fortune came from his cotton mills and he used it to further his
ideals. Where your money comes from is irrelevant, but you must
have it. Otherwise the business of personal survival is going to
sap your strength and divert your purpose. Obviously a family
fortune is the most convenient source of wealth – you have it
behind you from birth, and need not waste time earning it."

"So you mean that without personal wealth you stand no
chance at all?"

"No. You could start at the roots and work as it were at
grass level! Shall we consider George Howell? His background, I
believe was humble; he was a bricklayer. His attitude to this
work led to clashes with his employers on a theme dear to
your heart, the rights of the working man, and eventually to his
involvement with universal male suffrage. Logically, one then
develops a political commitment and becomes elected as a parlia-
mentary candidate. Again, you need funds, and total dedication.
A life's work, in fact. I still maintain that a private income is the
most secure base from which to work for social justice. Unfortu-

nately, from that position, you are usually constitutionally unfit to notice such injustices exist! You might even actively work against the notion of change. There are too few like Lord Shaftesbury."

"How about if one went to university? Would that help at all?"

"Education has to be paid for. One doesn't see many gowned farm-labourers, nor many cloistered chimney sweeps!"

"Mr Irving! Are you treating my questions seriously, or being frivolous?"

"Are you contemplating full scale social reform, or have you in mind one particular aspect? I must point out that to reform the entire social structure is rather a mammoth undertaking. Maybe I should point you in the direction of Mr William Howitt's works. He proves rather conclusively that five-sixths of the good things which are given away in this country are bestowed upon the aristocracy: pensions, appointments, clerical, naval and military promotions. Where did you imagine one would break into the spiral in order to instigate change?"

"Oh," I said glumly. "It's impossible, I suppose."

"Are your questions hypothetical, Willie? Or do you have yourself in mind?"

"Only in ideal terms."

"These days, unfortunately, my boy, one cannot simply brandish a flaming sword for the devils to flee. I believe that chisels do more good."

"I don't know what you mean. With reference to me?"

"Are you asking me, in indirect terms, whether you have any chance of doing some good in this life, and helping to change society?"

"You know I am shortly to leave here. I would like to do something useful."

"Then I will be perfectly fair with you, Willie, you deserve at least that. I think you care about the poor in your way, but I don't see in you dedication; nor do I think you enjoy hard work and total commitment. I'm telling you this kindly, you understand. You have a certain indolence, a self-indulgent streak, a preference for clean hands. Be honest, Willie – would you *want* to be a Member of Parliament? Could you stand to mix with gentlemen's sons and landed gentry, and abide by formality and accepted standards of behaviour? You'd hate it. You'd never be at ease there – conventions, correct clothes, dignified behaviour. I don't think you've the sticking power to devote your life to something so austere as principles, and I don't think you've the right personality to mingle in those spheres of society."

I listened to all this very serious and thoughtful.

"Mr Irving," I said, awed. "I ain't fit for *anything*."

"No, I didn't say that. I told you what I thought wouldn't suit you."

"Yeah, but look, I've been taken from one place and been given learning and comfort so that now I've grown used to it and come to expect it. I wouldn't want a slum in Whitechapel now I've lived in Putney. But though I'm educated I can't fit in; I'm not one thing nor another."

"Education is never wasted. What you've learnt with me will be of value to you wherever you are."

"But what can I do?" I said appalled. "What is there for me?"

"When I said just now," he replied, "that chisels were of more use than fiery swords to change society, I meant that one can start with the individual. Do you know what I think would suit you very well? I'd like to see you helping boys like you once were. I see you down at street level, bringing all the benefits you've acquired, to share with disadvantaged boys. Amongst them."

"What, like a teacher?"

"You could lead their minds to improvement while understanding them, through your own experiences."

"Yeah, I see . . . it would be useful, like I want."

"You consider it, Willie. It's within your capabilities."

"Yes – but – " I grimaced. "It takes me straight back to where I was."

"It's merely a suggestion. It's up to your uncle, of course, ultimately."

"Am I as bright as Georgey?" I wondered.

"That's more than my job's worth to reveal! Georgey has a conventional, adequate mind. Yours is more quirky and enquiring. Between ourselves, you are more interesting to teach, and more complicated. Georgey is an open book; *you* have some dark corners."

"Will Georgey go to University?"

"Your uncle would like it."

"What will Georgey *be?*"

"Your uncle would like him to – er – enter the church." Mr Irving did twinkle there just a little.

"I appreciate your talking to me properly," I said. "I don't know whether I fancy being back with poor boys, teaching. I think you're right, I ain't really a social reformer at heart, just someone who wishes things was different. I suppose I'd like to be rich and idle really, and have time to read books and wear all the clothes I was partial to. I hate grey suits! I once knew a feller who wore a black corduroy jacket, with a crimson waistcoat, and a great yeller neckerchief so big it come down to *here!* I always wanted to dress like that."

"Do you still?" laughed Mr Irving.

I had to think. "Well, yes, I suppose I do! Only, for the jacket I fancied green. Not bright green, more subtle. It might be jade, it might be olive – sort of dark."

"It's important to get it exactly right," said Mr Irving, amused, but pretending to be serious.

"Yes!" I cried. "Ain't it always? – I mean, in life."

"Ah," said Mr Irving, "in life that's rarely possible. In life one chooses the most acceptable compromise."

II

FOR MY birthday when I became sixteen, I had some very serious presents, all to do with my Going Out Into The World. The largest and most expensive was a new grey suit. There was also a carriage clock and a framed picture of a heron dipping in some water, for the room I would presumably want to furnish with such things. Aunt Louisa became a little tremulous, all her sentimentality coming to the surface at the idea of my going; and Georgey had to retire early, suffering from earache and a sore throat.

A few days later I was seated (seated! a very formal occasion) opposite my uncle in his study, while he outlined the shape of my future. For once I did not feel particularly antagonistic. I was glad to be leaving, and curious as to what he had lined up for me.

"I have found two very suitable openings," he told me. "I think you will find they are both positions that accord with aspects of your character, and it is simply a question of choosing which you prefer."

In all fairness I do believe he did think he was doing me a favour and had come up with two little gems. I really don't think it crossed his mind that I'd have set my sights on higher things, or that I had considered myself equal to Georgey, who was all set to go to university however suited he was. I don't think he meant to insult and degrade me, and it just shows what a jumped up little prat I was, to take it that way.

The two suitable positions were a clerk and a draper's assistant. Instantly into my mind came the memory of those wretched young men who'd waited on my aunt and me when we bought dove grey silk. Permanently polite, ingratiating, bowing and scraping, smiling, rolling up muslin, climbing little ladders to the silks. I knew that in such a situation a person could grow to hate the lovely cascading cloth. My uncle was saying something about your Aunt Louisa tells me you were a great help to her when she bought the material for her Sunday dress . . .

"What does a *clerk* do, exactly?" I said expressionlessly.

He told me they worked from seven in the morning till six at night. My beautiful handwriting would be an accomplishment that would stand me in good stead, and I could manage book-keeping. The wages were not high, but it was a secure and steady job, indoors, and the people would be civilised and intelligent. It all sounds so reasonable as I write it. How can I explain then the helpless rage I was feeling, the fury and hatred, the anger, jealousy and resentment, horrid feelings boiling in me and stirring me round and round? I was livid; I felt bitterly betrayed and shamed, and burning with aggressive and vicious emotions. I can see that it was my pride and conceit that was hurt, and I do condemn myself for my ingratitude. Why should I think I deserved better? How had I become so vain of my worth? To be a clerk or a shop assistant was very much more acceptable than sorting nails in the backroom of a hardware store, or sweeping crossings or selling matches. I would be *lucky* to be a clerk. It was clean and you worked indoors, and doubtless you grew used to the long hours and being cramped up to a desk all day under the eye of a master . . .

"I was wondering about teaching," I began.

"Teaching? What could you teach?" he said surprised. "You don't know enough to teach anybody."

"I mean teaching poor boys, like I was," I said, almost apologetically, not exactly timidly, but genuinely wanting his opinion.

"It would be ridiculous," he said, "to take you from the hovel you grew up in, to teach you manners and social graces, to let a civilised education enter your mind and work its improving effect, only to send you straight back to Spitalfields. These four years might just as well never have been. I cannot agree to such a notion. The intention was to improve you; I feel it has succeeded. You can go amongst decent people now, William. You responded well to nurture. I would even go so far as to say I am pleased with your progress. It would be a monstrous waste of your accomplishments if you went back."

In fact these were my own opinions, and so I allowed him to persuade me away from Mr Irving's suggestion. Had I become something of a snob at heart?

"Besides," said my uncle contemptuously, "a teacher is a nothing job. It has no status, no respect. Any oaf may set himself up and call himself a schoolmaster. They're a blackguardly crew, who take your money and then please themselves what they do for your child. We've been satisfied on the whole with Irving, but one has to be watchful. It has a very poor reputation, that trade – attracts a bad class of person. Believe me, William, you will be more comfortable as a clerk."

I maintained a detached and blank exterior. I told my uncle I thought I preferred clerk to draper's assistant; but I ask you, would you like to work eleven hours a day for a pittance and be grateful for it? No account was taken of my personality, with all its questioning and covert rebelliousness, its *mixture* . . . I was too *complicated* to be a clerk, too *restless*, emotionally and physically. I couldn't sit at a ledger sheet for hours on end in some office in a neat suit and short hair, missing all the hours of daylight and be too weary for the evening. I suppose deep down I would have liked to have been *considered* as someone who could have gone to a university, even if I turned out not to be clever enough. But I wasn't worth the money. I wasn't really family, just *toler-*

ated, while Georgey, whom I couldn't help feeling was less intelligent than me, would have all these opportunities presented on a plate.

III

AS USUAL at this time of year, Georgey was in bed with a cold. At the slightest snuffle he was sent to bed because he was considered delicate, and though he looked nothing worse than a little red around the nose, he was tucked up in his blankets and horrendously bored.

I went up to read to him that evening. I decided it would be more fun for me if I sat close to him, so I arranged myself on the bed, legs and all, my arm round Georgey and both of us propped against the pillow. I could feel his body all warm through his nice clean nightshirt, and smell his neck – he had been freshly soaped before he was put to bed. After a while I put the book in my left hand, and with my free right hand I started stroking the bedclothes somewhere above his crotch.

"Ooh!" he said, "that's my – " and stopped and giggled.

"D'you like it, if I just stroke through the bedclothes?"

"Yes, keep on doing it."

I kept on, just ever so slightly pressing. I could feel the tops of his thighs and a little twitching bulge.

"Maybe I better stop," I said hesitantly.

"No, don't; no one will come in. Listen, mamma is playing the piano, so as long as it plays we know she's downstairs. No one else will come in till it's time for my medicine, last thing at night."

"If I keep strokin' yer, something might happen."

Georgey gasped. "Do you know about that?" he said, going very pink.

"What, Georgey?" I said innocently.

"Something wicked," he whispered. "God makes your hands wither if you do it."

"That ain't true, Georgey. I'll do it for you, if you like, and then it won't be your hand, it'll be mine."

"Oh! Willie! Should we?"

"We might as well."

"All right. But don't tell."

"Course I won't. Only you'll want something to catch it in. Shall I get your towel?"

When I came back to the bed, Georgey had pulled the covers aside, and to my immense gratification I saw his bare knees and his bare thighs. I sat on the edge of the bed.

"I ain't seen your legs for ages," I remarked, putting his legs flat, "not since we had baths."

I felt his knees and squeezed them gently, and I slowly lifted his nightshirt back, all the way up.

"Oh, Georgey!" I gasped awed. "You got *hair* now!"

A little dewy triangle of blond curls it was. I had to touch, I had to stroke it.

"Ain't you pretty! Ain't you a doll!" I marvelled.

"Have *you* got hair?" he asked, anxiously I thought.

"Yeah, lots, but it's a different colour."

"Show me,"

I showed him. I got no end of a thrill standing there with Georgey studying me and my lush coppery curls. When he reached out and touched my cock it jumped in excitement.

"How did it get so big?" he said. "You weren't stroking it."

"It got big thinking about yours."

"That's funny; I thought you had to think about girls to make it happen on its own."

"I dunno. With me it's boys."

"Willie, do you . . . ever do that wicked thing, in your bed?"

"A coupla times," I said shiftily.

"If I do it I feel so awful," Georgey confessed.

"Do yer? Why?"

"Because of God watching. I'm scared he'll send a thunderbolt down and strike me. Afterwards I'm so frightened; I lie and count to a hundred. After a hundred I feel I'm going to be safe."

"Ah, yer mustn't be scared. Who told yer God minded?"

"Well, it's obvious! It's a sin and sin is wrong."

"I dunno," I grimaced, tucking my cock away. "I know sin is wrong, but dontcher think we wouldn't have had 'em in the first place if we wasn't supposed to test 'em out? It's only like, practising, isn't it?"

"Do it for me then," Georgey invited, wriggling, "and stay by me after, and then we'll be sure none of us gets struck."

I lay down on the bed. I never saw the moment as fulfilment of my fantasies – it wasn't, because they were so exotic and violent, and I was very much aware of being in Georgey's room, with his bookshelves and his old sofa and his small rocking-horse, with his framed pictures of mice and ducks. But I felt I had a free hand with Georgey at last, and before I got down to work I wanted the extras. I kissed him. He tasted so sweet. A smell of warm, clean, confined skin rose up from his nightshirt neck. I did lots of small erotic things to him till I was sighing ecstatically.

"I'm getting cold," he grumbled.

You fat indulged baby, I thought; I wish you were totally in my power, I do.

I stirred him back to full stiffness; I'd only been doing it for a moment when he came. All the time it went on, Aunt Louisa was playing Traditional Airs. It was "Greensleeves" as Georgey finished. "Did yer like it, poppet?"

"Yes thank you," he gasped. "It's rather different when someone else does it. It's like very fast running down a hill."

"I know some other things," I said.

"What things?"

"Nice things people can do to each other."

"What! More than that?" he said, wide-eyed.

"Yes! And all lovely."

Downstairs the music stopped. We tensed guiltily.

"Shall I come down again later tonight, and show you them?" I offered.

"Oh!" Georgey gulped. "Will you be very quiet?"

"As a tomb!"

"All right, then! All right!"

We tidied him up rapidly, and I rinsed out his towel. He pulled the covers up to his chin. It was bedtime. I was ready to go to my own bed too. I badly needed to do for myself what I had done for Georgey.

IV

AS TO what happened later that night, all I can say in my defence is that I was in a very disturbed state. I know it's not much of an excuse, because what I did to Georgey was unforgiveable. I feel ashamed, but at the same time I feel truculent and sullen. That night I sort of erupted, and became myself. I stopped being this false pretending person who spent the day politely fitting into a sphere which wasn't his, and the night giving way to crude abandoned lust affairs – instead I merged. I never went in for deception afterwards; I always acted honest and true to myself. But I'd never have been so vile if I hadn't been, as I say, very disturbed. To this day I'll never know if I did it out of dreadful frustration and need for Georgey, or out of vicious spite and jealousy because he had so much and I had so little, and I felt we deserved the same.

For all that Georgey was pretty and dimpled and winsome he was spoiled and weak. He never got caned. He was always forgiven. If he made blots he said it was the pen. If he didn't want to do something he cajoled and simpered. He was pampered like a lap dog when all he had was a runny nose. And he was going to university, and I was condemned to be a clerk. I was boiling with so much violence I had to hurt someone. I was like a long suppressed volcano, frustrated by constant smouldering, exhausted by simmering, and needing to erupt.

In the middle of the night, with icy cold feet, I crept through the darkness down the top stairs, and let myself silently into Georgey's room. It was a creaky house at night, and a few more sounds went quite unnoticed. As I slid into his bed he gave a sleepy little snort, and murmured: "What? Oh, I think I've changed my mind. I don't want – " but I wasn't going to let him change his mind, he was going to be mine, mine at last. To make sure he was weak and docile I set about tossing him off, kissing his ear till he shivered. I was merciless, using every accessible part of my body to stimulate his. Something I had suspected became clear to me that night – that I was good at it! That I could take someone half asleep and tease them into arousal, and all the time I muttered sweet rough endearments, the kind of things I'd spoken with Charley and never out loud since. I stroked him off. Warm fat Georgey lay in my arms like a dream come true. But it was his arse I wanted, and I rolled him over, and in savage delight I gripped both plump buttocks, and squeezed. "Ow!" he said. "Don't!"

"I'm going to show you something nice," I panted, out of

myself with lust and excitement. "I'm going to have you, my darling, like I've always wanted."

He couldn't do a thing. I was so much stronger than him. He grizzled and wriggled.

"Go limp!" I hissed. "If you're tight it'll hurt; now do as you're told."

I slammed my hand over his mouth as he cried out. I laughed out loud. "I'm fucking yer! I've got yer now, my fat little plum, you're mine to do with like I want; you're my boy, my minion, my slave . . ."

I panted and grunted over him, and he began whimpering and snivelling: "I don't like it, Willie; it hurts, it's horrible, take it out."

"Shut up and lie still!"

"You beast – you hurt!"

"Lie still then, else it'll hurt more. And stop that silly noise."

"I hate you – you're horrible!" Georgey wept, but I took no notice. He squealed. Alarmed, I hit him round the head and, wincing a bit, I pulled out, shaking.

"You filthy beast!" he spat at me. "You foul filthy beast! I hate you, I hate you!"

And then he burst into a full flood of tears, heaving and howling and shaking the bedsprings. I panicked and ran upstairs.

I was breathless and trembling. Still in the dark, I washed myself clean, no clear thought in my head. I knew I'd got to leave, and so I started getting dressed. I could hardly do up my buttons for my shaking fingers. When I was completely dressed I sat down on the bed and wondered what to do next.

It was at this point that sounds and images penetrated my senses. I heard footsteps on the stairs, I saw a beam of light from down below as the door opened and my uncle came in. The horrible nearness of him, vast in his dark green dressing-gown, froze me into numbness, and his great black bulk in my room was like a monstrous nightmare. He reached out and grabbed hold of me by the back of the neck.

"Owww!" I yelled, wriggling, but he forced me across the room and out of the door, holding a fold of skin and the clump of hair above it at the back of my neck. I was in great distress all the way down the stairs, stumbling along with him. A lit lamp illumined the landing, and he hustled me down the next flight of stairs. I could hear Georgey having hysterics as we hurried by. The doors were all open on the landing, the lamps lit. I was shoved along the hall, yowling and wriggling, and I was only released when we arrived at the cellar door, which my uncle unlocked, opened and thrust me forcefully through.

The door slammed shut and the key turned. I was in complete darkness. My legs started shaking, so I sat down on the cold stone steps; then I found I was trembling all over. I just sat there, hunched, my arms tucked across my chest, fists under my chin, for ages and ages. Even when my eyes adjusted to the blackness I could see nothing. I knew what was in the cellar; it was stacked full of coal; solid, from the bottom of the steps all the way across. You could smell it, and the stale damp smell of stone. I wished I could stay in the cellar for ever, just sitting there, and never have to face anybody or talk about what happened. I wished day would never come and I would never by judged.

When the key turned in the lock and the door opened up, I realised by the fact that lamps were still needed that it was either still night or very early day. My uncle was outside the cellar door, like a huge black crow. He gestured with his arm that I should come out. I stood up reluctantly and came out into the hall.

The front door was open and my uncle gestured me towards it. The sky was still dark but it had the feeling of near morning. In a rather trance-like way I moved to the door and I saw that beyond the front gate there was a growler waiting, a big black shape with two men – the driver and someone else, the horses stamping and blowing and rattling their harness. My uncle had his coat on, and top hat. I was mystified, but still accepting. I wanted to ask where we were going, but I didn't. It would have connected us. I dreaded he would speak to me. I preferred the silence; it separated us.

How sinister that growler seemed, how uninviting its open door! The morning air was very chill, and it startled me into more of an awareness. I heard my uncle say something about "to the school". The driver and the man and the growler all seemed black, like bits of darkness broken off. The house I was leaving seemed like no kind of haven but just another black shape. The shrubs in the garden rustled harshly. All the curtains upstairs were drawn, the street silent.

I climbed into the conveyance and sat, and my uncle came in and sat opposite, slamming the door. On the floor there was old straw. The seat felt dirty. With clankings and rumblings the vehicle groaned into life.

"My aunt . . . " I suddenly said, startled.

"Your aunt wishes never to see you again."

In silence but for the noises the growler made, we continued. As we journeyed, daylight began to penetrate the gloom and the streets came awake. The shouts of the milkman rang out, and maids began to swill the steps and fling back the shutters. Gradually the roads filled up with traffic, and the street sellers took positions on the pavements.

School? I thought, school? But no images came to mind.

It seems incredible to me now, that I went with him so *meekly*. At first I can't think why I did, but the stupid reason was in fact, out of habit. My own mind wasn't reliable, and so I trusted convention. I was used to doing as he told me, it was polite, and we were very dignified the way we set out. I was incapable of imaginative thought at that point, and could not possibly guess what was coming; so, habituated to trust, I just did as I was told. I saw no reason to dodge under his arm and go belting down the quiet respectable streets to lose myself in an alley. I'd lost all my street sense now anyway; I was a domestic animal, used to a hearth. I didn't want to rough it. I would have had to push past him, *touch* him even, maybe cause a chase that woke up the neighbourhood, the driver thundering after me, and an embarrassing recapture. But really I don't think these things even occurred to me, or that there was any urgency about it. I simply wanted to get right away from the house and everybody in it, and start again somewhere. If I thought anything, I thought my uncle was going to take me far away and dump me, and that suited me all right. Just as long as he didn't *speak* to me, *talk* about it, make me have to admit it happened, something so private that had become so public, and which I didn't really understand myself.

Well, sitting as I was, with my back to the way we were going, I didn't even realise that we'd gone through gates until they closed behind us. There was a man in some kind of uniform standing by the gates, and there were great high walls with iron points along the edges. We had driven into a courtyard, and the growler door was opened by a man in uniform.

"This is the young offender," said my uncle smoothly. Turning to me, he spoke at last of his own volition: "Perhaps that which decent people have failed to teach you, you will learn more surely in the Reformatory."

PART THREE

CHAPTER EIGHT

I

A BRIEF glance was enough to see what kind of a place this was. It looked like an institution – high walls, rows of tiny windows, and warders prowling about. Not exactly a prison, not exactly a workhouse, but something in between, a place for young offenders – people who had committed crimes. I couldn't believe this was happening to me.

I was handed over to this warder. We went across the court-yard and in through a door, and down corridors which were all painted dark brown. Right at the end of these, there was a room of dark brown tiles with a great network of pipes all over the walls, and in the corner an immense stone bath built into the structure. Into the room from a further door came another warder, not the dull mechanical sort like my escort, but the sort you noticed, brisk, aggressive, full of self-importance. I grew to know him very well. Firth his name was. He had horrible bright eyes and a blunt nose and a face without any redeeming sensitivity. He was quite alert enough to know what he was doing; you couldn't even excuse him on the grounds of stupidity.

"Oh," he said, actually rubbing his hands together. "Is this him? Our little sodomite? Right then, darling, off with them clothes and into that bath."

I stared at him in disbelief.

"Deaf as well as twisted," he leered to the other warder.

"I'm clean," I said. 'I don't need no bath."

"Ooh, he's got a lot to learn," said Firth shaking his head. "Now, look here, laddie, suppose you tell me what this is, hanging at my belt, this here."

"Looks like a truncheon," I muttered.

"Very true. I'm only telling you this once. When I give an

order you obey it. If I hear hesitation I don't tell you again. I trounce yer. Now it so happens that every mucky little cove as comes to be edified within these walls begins his time by washing off his fleas and his filth in that there bath and you ain't no different. I won't repeat the order. If you ain't in that bath before I draw three breaths . . . "

He puffed himself out, playing to his audience, strutting like a lead soldier, comfortable in his power. He didn't half make his point though. I'd never got undressed so hurriedly in all my life, and he accompanied me to the bath. I slung a leg over its rim and screwed up my face in revulsion. Ugh! I couldn't help saying it out loud. The water was not just stone cold, it was slimy brown and scum-covered, and even as I moved my leg a line of fawn rimmed my limb. I could not hide my revulsion, for all that it played into his hands.

"Down!" he ordered, putting his foot on the side of the bath to better watch me go in.

I made myself sit down. The water came up to my armpits. I could see things floating on the surface – dead insects, clumps of brown foam, hairs. I started getting up. He put a hand on my shoulder and held me down. He slung some soap in and told me to wash. The soap disappeared in the murk. I couldn't find it. Shivering I groped around for it, trying to keep my chin above the slimy surface. I grabbed the soap and loosely sloshed it around my neck.

"Hair and all," he said.

I looked at him stupidly.

"Wash your hair," he explained long-sufferingly. Extending his great hand and dropping it flat on the top of my head, he pressed me down into the water. I went right under and he held me down. I struggled and splashed wildly, pushing up, arms splaying, retching and spluttering, nauseated and furious.

"Right," he said. "Out!"

I climbed out, revolted by myself. The first warder was waiting with a towel and some clothes slung over his arm. He handed me some trousers, coarse grey cloth and very tight. Pulling them up my thighs was like peeling an orange in reverse. The shirt by contrast was too big. It was of similar rough cloth and smelly under the arms from a previous inmate. It hung round me as if I was a Chinese paddy-field worker. Three pairs of boots were offered for my inspection, two of which had laces. One pair was a good fit lengthwise but too broad; however, they were the best, so I got into them, and there I was.

To my relief it was the first warder who took charge of me. Up a staircase we went. Everything was painted this shit-colour, wall after wall. As we walked you could hear this echoey chanting which, from its rhythm, sounded like a psalm, lots of sullen resentful voices all in unison, saying prayers.

Finally we arrived at a sturdy wooden door with a brass plate on it saying "Ernest Sheldon". The warder knocked and we were admitted.

The spider at the heart of the web, the director of this vile establishment, Mr Sheldon, was the sort to give anybody the jitters. It was strange; in his way he was really quite good looking. He was about forty-five. Slim of build, he wore a black well-cut suit and a starched white shirt, and his grey hair was combed flat – you could see the comb marks. He looked the sort to have a wife he loved dearly, and three neat attractive daughters to whom he was devoted. He had long piano player's fingers and well manicured nails. Why did I consider him so evil then? He was frozen into a bigoted way of thinking that left no room for doubt and possibility. He wore immaculate clothes and made you appear before him dressed as a scarecrow and smelly from other people's sweat. And he did everything to you in the name of God. I've met a lot of repulsive people in my life but the thought of him still makes me shudder.

"William Smith," he said to me, "aged sixteen, and already deeply degenerate."

I don't think I was expected to deny or justify this statement. I just stood there, stiffly. The warder lurked behind me, by the door.

"You have committed an abominable offence," he told me. "Your action places you lower than a beast. I cannot pretend to treat you as if you were a human being. You are obviously immune to reason and the standards of civilised behaviour. I am appalled to learn of the exact circumstances, that in fact your heinous offence took place in a situation where obedience and gratitude should have been your strongest characteristics. I can say nothing to one so early steeped in depravity." He coughed delicately behind his hand, and forced himself to continue in my foul presence. "You have been brought here for correction and cure," he announced. "Correction seems in every way appropriate, for natures such as yours are beyond normal discourse. Cure I believe to be impossible but I have given my permission for its attempt. Have you anything to say?"

"I know I done wrong, sir," I said, "but I ain't as bad as you say. I don't think I should be condemned so completely all at once."

"How dare you question my judgement!" he said icily. "You shall learn proper humility here."

"How long have I got to stay here?" I demanded.

"I see you are of a disruptive and aggressive nature," he observed. "I fear very much for your chances of salvation. Can you read and write?" he asked me.

"Yes, sir."

"Be seated at that desk. You will take some notes at my dictation."

It was a single desk and seat in one, much marked with ink and initials. I sat down, with some relief, because my legs had started feeling weak at the knees with all that hostility and disgust directed at me, and I tried to compose myself.

"Do you know what this book is?" he asked me.

"Yes sir, it's a Bible."

"You know that, do you?" he marvelled. "And yet you still behaved like a beast. I fear your sin may be more deeply ingrained than I even at first suspected. Take up the pen," and he handed me a sheet of paper, "and write down the words I say. If you find any of them difficult, say so."

This is what I had to write:

"Know ye not that the unrighteous shall not inherit the Kingdom of God? Be not deceived: neither fornicators, nor idolaters, nor adulterers, nor effeminate, nor abusers of themselves with mankind. Nor thieves, nor covetous, nor drunkard, nor revilers, nor extortioners, shall inherit the Kingdom of God. *1 Corinthians 6: 9–10.*

"If a man also lieth with mankind as he lieth with a woman, both of them have committed an abomination. They shall surely be put to death, and their blood shall be upon them. *Leviticus 20: 13.*

"Knowing this, that the law is not made for a righteous man, but for the lawless and disobedient, for the ungodly and for sinners, for the unholy and profane, for murderers of fathers and murderers of mothers, for manslayers. For whoremongers, for them that defile themselves with mankind, for menstealers, for liars, for perjured persons, and if there be any other thing that is contrary to sound doctrine. *1 Timothy 1: 9–10.*

"But the fearful and unbelieving, and the abominable, and murderers and whoremongers and sorcerers and idolaters and all liars, shall have their part in the lake which burneth with fire and brimstone: which is the second death. *Revelation 21: 8.*"

This covered both sides of the paper, I might add. Although my hand was a bit shaky I completed it in very attractive copperplate, and never asked him to stop for a word. He took it from me and read it, and for a moment he treated me perfectly normally as if he'd forgotten I was vile beyond belief but just an ordinary lad.

"Your handwriting is very neat," he remarked. "You have made several spelling mistakes – deceived, effeminate, extortioners, whoremongers – whore has a 'w'. Otherwise all is correct."

Then he recollected that I was abominable and handed the paper back. "Do you understand this?" he asked.

"Yes sir."

"You realise, then, that your offence is abominable in the eyes of God."

"Yes sir," I muttered.

"It is conclusively proved so, by these readings from Holy Scripture."

"Yes sir."

"It fixes you for ever with murderers, perjurors and lawbreakers of every kind."

"Oh, sir – " I groaned despairingly. I thought: this is crazy! If he makes me admit this I can't help but disagree with him, despise him even. It was awful what I did, but it wasn't like murder, nothing like murder.

"Silence!" he hissed. "Do you presume to deny the word of God?"

There was a horrible little silence while his words hung in the air. Outside the window noise suddenly erupted, boots on stone, and barked commands. My eyes flicked towards it. But when I turned my gaze up to that man I realised he was standing there with a fixed penetrating stare, waiting to hear whether I disagreed with God.

"Sir," I began desperately. "I do agree I acted wicked, but I never took anyone's life, and to me they don't seem the same sort of crime."

"You presume to make judgements!" he said. "I believe your degree of sin is very great indeed. I believe it has penetrated your Immortal Soul. It is fortunate for you that you were brought here, for you *shall* see the light, yes, even you."

His tone went rather mystical. He told me to get down on my knees, so I did, and he told me to shut my eyes and put my hands in an attitude of prayer. I did that. Then he took a book from the shelf (I opened one eye) and stood in front of me and read out of it. It wasn't the Bible; it was some other holy work. In fact it wasn't too bad to listen to. I suspect I got more out of it than he realised. It was about the philosophy of sin, and the necessity of awareness of sin before the act of repentance. He walked about while he read, and all the time I was down there kneeling like I was praying, and half listening to him and half to the sounds outside – it was a drill class. Having succoured their souls by psalms, the boys were now benefiting from the exercise of the body. I do believe that for them out there in the courtyard and me on my aching knees, a whole bleeding hour went past.

I was ordered to stand up and then he told me I had to learn by heart everything I'd copied down, and that tomorrow I'd come to him for more spiritual instruction. I folded up my paper and put it in the pocket of my shirt, and the warder took me away.

II

WE THEN went into a schoolroom where I sat down on a bench and looked around.

The windows were too high up to see out of, and there were rafters across the roof. All along one wall was a strip of lettering saying "The Blood of Jesus Christ cleanseth us all from Sin". Along the other walls it said "I am the Way" and "I am the True Vine", and along the opposite wall to the first it said "Are you Ready to Die?" The walls were the same shit-brown. There were benches and desks, and a blackboard up front.

I took out my Biblical extracts and applied myself to learning them. I had been about it just a few minutes when, with a great noise of marching boots, everyone returned from drill and filled up the room.

I would have found this daunting to the point of being over-whelming if I had never been to a Ragged School, but old instincts rose up to help, and I was able to face this influx calmly. About forty boys, from about the ages of seven to eighteen, marched in with about four warders, one of whom was Firth. The boys were all wearing ill-fitting grey shirts and trousers, and boots in varying degrees of repair. They looked underfed and ugly, and their hair was all cropped short, which startled me because it looked so awful and because mine had been left long.

The boys filled up the benches, a teacher appeared and put himself at the blackboard. Firth spoke to him, and the teacher looked at me and called out my name. Anyone who hadn't been staring before stared now, and not for the first time I wished my hair wasn't so distinctive. I went and stood before him.

The teacher was a thin weedy man who seemed to me to be the pawn of the warders. Only due to their presence was he able to conduct a lesson and exert his authority. No one would have obeyed him out of natural respect. "What have you been doing?" he asked me.

"Sitting here learning things," I said.

"What things?"

I showed him that I'd got a piece of paper in my hand.

"Give it to me."

I handed it to him, and as he read it, I found myself colouring up crimson. It was like I was giving him a reference of character and, since it was all about abominations and ungodliness, I felt I was handing over my rights to be treated decently. I think he took it that way too. He handed it back to me between finger and thumb, as if he didn't want to touch my hand by accident.

"By all means learn it," he said, in a choking sort of voice, "but put yourself farther off where you do not contaminate the rest of the class."

I did so, conscious of Firth smirking and the frank interest of the people nearest to me. I slouched to my place and turned my back. Behind me, a travesty of a lesson got under way. Obviously I listened. Chanting repetitive words, chanting arithmetical tables, chanting historical dates and capital cities, and then shuffling silences and the scrape of pens while the same facts were written down. I was just perfecting the section about fire and brimstone when we were all ordered out and, as no one said otherwise, I went too. In a horrible kind of marching line we all went for lunch to the dining hall at the other end of the same corridor.

This was a similar room to the schoolroom, with benches and tables, but the texts in here read "Be Sure Your Sins Will Find You Out" and "The Eyes of The Lord are in Every Place". We had bread, a dollop of meat and gravy, and two potatoes (small) – but not before a half hour reading from the Bible while we stood and watched it get cold and then it was an undignified scrabble to eat. The warders paced between tables fingering their truncheons and clipping the ears of anyone who spoke. Someone was ejected snivelling and his half-eaten meal was belted down by the two next to him before he'd hardly got off his bench. After this meal we had another horrible march, past the privies, stopping for which was accompanied by thwacks on the backs of the legs for anyone dawdling. Then we were back in the schoolroom, not for lessons but for oakum picking.

We sat on benches in rows with piles of this tar-encrusted rope on the floor at our feet, hard as wood to hold and prickly as needles, and bent over it picking it to shreds. I suppose I had been doing it about an hour when I realised just what it was doing to my fingers. Every one of my nails was broken, split across the top, and the ends of my fingers were raw and scraped. It hurt. It was at this point that the full extent of my misery and humiliation struck home. I shouldn't be here . . . I shouldn't be doing this . . . what would I become? What about my hands? My beautiful fingernails all wrecked, my fingers throbbing, a coil of foul rope waiting between my feet. Full of self-pity, my eyes filled with tears and I couldn't see what I was doing. I wiped my eyes but more tears came. I hadn't even noticed I'd stopped picking; but a warder had. He pulled me off the bench by my ear and stood me in front of him. "Think you're hard done by, do you?" he said.

"No, sir," I said, fisting my wet cheeks dry.

He grabbed my wrist and shook my palm extended and welted me across the hand with a cane. Then he did it to my other hand.

"That's how I reward slackers," he said. "I don't want to see you look up from your work once – not once – and if I do I'll have my stick across your shoulders so fast you won't know what hit you. Is that clear?"

"Yes sir."

"Get back to your place."

I hurried back to the bench and bent over the stinking stuff, tears pouring down my face, my hands on fire. I couldn't see a thing, but all afternoon I daren't look up and my shoulders and neck ached from stooping. My fingers made ineffective attempts at the horrible job and my tears fell onto my hands. As the afternoon wore on, someone's knee nudged mine, and the person next to me slid some of his picked rope on to my pile. I felt overcome with gratitude. This boy was called Jerry Parfitt. He was in here for sticking a knife in someone.

Next we were marched off to eat, and on the way two boys managed – without the warder seeing – to kick my shins on the bare bit between my trousers and boots, and so hard and nasty I got a cuff round the head from the warder for the noise I made. Right into my ears when they went for me, the two boys said, "We know what you're here for. We'll be getting you later", so I wasn't in any doubt what I was being kicked for.

We had a tea of bread and butter spread very thin, and two hours of prayers in the schoolroom. Around seven o'clock all forty of us were locked into a great long dormitory and there we stayed till we were let out twelve hours later.

III

I DON'T know what Mr Sheldon thought happened when the door was locked on the dormitory. Could he really have supposed that everyone lay down flat on his bed and went to sleep, or did he think we all deserved each other and everyone being scum it made no difference anyway? What it all came to was that for twelve hours we were ignored out of existence, safely penned in, forgotten about. Whichever of the warders was on duty stood in the room until everyone had undressed and put on a nightshirt; then they left, turned the key, slid back a bolt, and disappeared.

On the bed were two stiff stained blankets; up against the wall were two large pails, and a feature of each night was the sound of people getting up to piss.

At first I was left alone, and I certainly didn't encourage any kind of contact; I didn't speak to anybody, and turned my face away from any approach. After about half an hour the bolt was drawn, the key unlocked and a warder called round the door: "Oy – Smith!" Another boy near the door, whose name that was, started getting out of bed and the warder said: "No, not you – the little pervert."

Out of principle I didn't move.

"If I have to come and get you," he said, "you'll go limping."

He didn't specify how but his logic persuaded me, and I slouched out of bed and went with him, everything being locked up again after us. We went along this corridor, up a small flight of stairs and entered a warder's room. It contained a stove of warm coals, a table and chairs, and Firth sitting eating bread and cheese. They'd got bottles of ale as well, you could smell it.

"Well," he said to me, grinding away at the cheese like some predatory rat. "And how's my little sweetheart settling in then? Making lots of nice friends? Getting the feel of this high quality establishment? Learning new skills?"

I stayed quiet. It doesn't take long to learn you get belted for anything that can be interpreted as insolence.

He surveyed me, assessing me.

"Show your hands," he said, and I complied sulkily. He took one by the wrist and turned it over and back.

"You been living very soft, ain't you?" he remarked. "Finding it not quite what you're accustomed to, no doubt. I daresay your tender little fingers never even knew what hit 'em. You wait – they'll harden up. A couple of months here and you'll have hands like a bloomin' bricklayer's, eh, won't he, Frank?"

"Do you know how long I've got to stay here?" I demanded, hopefully, alarmed into speech by what he'd just said.

He laughed nastily. "Why? Don't you like it here? Listen to that, the ungrateful little pervert, free food and lodging, and he isn't happy. If you don't like it here," he added in a heavy meaningful tone, "you shouldn't be going around screwing little boys then, should you? And speaking of which, that's what we had in mind when we sent for yer. Turn him round, Frank."

I got hustled around by the first warder and, not resisting much, I found myself with my arms behind me and the hard touch of metal on my wrists. To my shock and alarm I was handcuffed. Firth checked them in place, and then sat down again and poured himself some beer. I stared at him trembling with rage and panic; I expected at least an explanation. "Why?" I screeched.

"Don't you *know?*" he leered at me. "We've all heard what sort of thing your type gets up to in bed. D'you think you're going to go back there and give yourself a treat on the sly? *Oh no!*"

As I worked out what he meant I blushed crimson. I felt revolted to the guts at the idea of that man connecting me with that. Not only hinting and referring, but doing this to me – it was like being branded on the forehead. It didn't hurt me much, the confined wrists, but for the reason he gave I felt shame as burning as if it was a physical chastisement.

Firth sniggered at my obvious discomfort and understanding.

"You can see he knows what I mean! Can't have you contaminating my other little charges, can I? No boy would be safe."

He chortled comfortably and leaned back in his chair and stuffed another hunk of cheese down his gullet.

"Please don't send me back in there like this," I said quiveringly. "How can I sleep?"

"You'll have to learn, won't you?" he remarked.

"You lousy stinkin' bleeder!" I yelled. "You don't give a cuss for the other boys – don't think I don't understand how your bleedin' mind works – "

He got out of his chair and thumped me in the belly with a fist like a brick. I doubled up with a grunt, sagging in the middle so much I had to drop to my knees with it. I was in awful pain. I heard him say "Get him out of my sight!" and Frank took hold of me and forced me to my feet, but I couldn't straighten up, and all bent over like that I got shoved out and down the steps and along the cold corridor. I was groaning and wincing so much I hardly knew where I was. Frank unlocked the door and opened it and I stumbled through. The door clanged shut and bolted, and I shuffled across to my bed like an old tramp, and curled myself on to it, knees up, aching. Even through my pain I could feel the interest I'd caused.

"What've they done to 'im?"

"What've they done to yer?"

"'E's 'ad a thump in the guts, ain't 'e?"

"Ay! 'E's got cuffs on! 'E's got ruffles!"

"Tell us wotcher done, Willie."

"Did yer 'it 'im?"

"Oh piss off," I groaned. "Leave me alone."

It was dark now. Jerry Parfitt came and sat on my bed.

"Look 'ere, Willie," he said. "We're all in this together; you can't go around as if you was on yer own. Yer needs ter know fings."

"I know all I want," I snapped.

"What they put ruffles on 'im for?"

"You bleedin' dangerous, Willie?"

"Course he ain't. He's one o' them Mary Annes; they ain't dangerous – they're soft."

"Is yer, Willie? Goes with boys, does yer?"

"Leave 'im, Alfie. We'll find out soon enough."

"Hammer's got plans."

"Hammer'll sort 'im aht."

I buried my face in the stinking blankets and tried to wriggle them around me. I ached all over, but my guts burned so savagely I started crying with it; I felt so humiliated and angry and hurt. I cried a great wet patch on the stiff rough cloth; I couldn't stop. I tried to cry quietly, but how do yer? And I was pretty down at that point.

"Oy, Willie," said Jerry. "Hush yer racket, yer silly bugger."

"Bleedin' fuck off," I told him.

"See if I ain't right," he said illogically.

I took no notice of anything. I was so far gone in general misery I'd hardly even realised how cold I was; now I noticed my feet were perished and I kicked some blanket around them.

A situation I hadn't known for years now nudged up into my consciousness – bleedin' bed bugs in the blankets! That didn't half sober me up. I'd forgotten all that, the itching and the scratching that was so usual in my bed of childhood. Living very soft – yes, that bastard was right; I had been, and it wasn't any kind of practice for this. If I'd been brought here straight from Aldgate I wouldn't have lain blubbering in the blanket. That's what living comfortable did to you, made you weak. It was a chastening thought.

Sometime later during the night someone got on to my bed and lay on me. I mumbled a protest. He said: "Wotcher going ter do about it? 'It me one?"

"Gerroff me, yer lousy crud," I said.

"Lie still, yer little tart," he said, "else I'll black both yer eyes."

I lay still; such language is very persuasive.

"Oy, Smiff," he said. "Do you know who I am?"

"No; who are you?"

"I'm Hammer. D'you know why I'm called that? It's because I got very strong fists. D'you know what I'm in here for? I lost my temper one day and I beat a bloke's head in. Afterwards," he added juicily, "they couldn't tell who he was."

In the daylight when I observed him later on, I found that Hammer was an ugly youth with short straight hair and a squat nose, narrow pugnacious eyes close to his brows, and thick well-shaped lips. His skin was all mottled and discoloured; some of it was freckles, which continued all over his neck.

"I want ter know abaht yer, Willie Smiff."

"Yes? What?"

"You was sent here for fuckin' some boy, right?"

"Yes."

"And was it your first time?"

"Yes."

"How did yer know abaht it then?"

"People had done it to me."

"Ah, so you wasn't virgin. I didn't think yer was. Well! You and me is going to make a deal."

"Oh yes?" I said warily.

"I fancy having you for mine. An' if you're smart you'll take me up on this offer I'm makin'."

"What would it mean exactly?"

"It'd mean you was my moll; you'd belong to me. See, Willie, you badly needs protectin'. If I don't take you on I'll tell yer what's likely to happen to yer. You'd be anybody's, as many as fancied yer. How'd you be then, eh?"

"One boy I know," interrupted Parfitt, "had that happen to him. Shall I tell you what it was like for him after . . ?"

"Shut yer noise," said Hammer. "He can work it aht for himself. An' there's a couplar other fings, Willie. Larkins is aht ter get yer and do you over cos 'e don't like yer long hair and yer pretty face. If you ain't got me to look after you, you're going ter get somefink broken, and some of yer beauty spoiled. Ah'd yer feel abaht that?"

"Worried."

"Course yer does!" he assured me. "The other fing is, yer need *guidance*, yer really does! You'll never last in this place how you're going on, makin' enemies of friggin' Firth, and blubbin' all over the place. There's loads of fings you got ter be told. You stick wiv me and you'll find fings a darn sight easier."

"Hammer's a good boss," said Parfitt. "Very fair. Tough but fair."

"Yeah, that's me," Hammer sniggered. "Nah, my little doll, what's it ter be? You goin' ter be my tart, while I look after yer?"

"Yeah, all right," I said; it was as easy as that.

"You hear?" Hammer called out gleefully. "You hear, Larkins? You wanna fight me for 'im?"

Larkins muttered something ungracious which amounted to a refusal. With a tangible sense of relief I realised he lived in dread of my protector and wasn't going to touch me while I was Hammer's moll.

"Come with me," Hammer told me, and I got up, and he put his hand on the back of my neck in a proprietary sort of manner, and escorted me round the dormitory, up and down, past the dark shapes of the beds. As we went, he was declaiming: "You all hear this. Willie Smiff's my tart now, and anyone who touches 'im 'll have me ter reckon wiv, and if you're keen ter 'ave yer teef knocked dahn yer froat that's what you'll do. You hear Anstey? That means you and all, I know you fancied him. *And* you, Gappy, you asks me first. This pretty redhead tart is mine. Tell him, Willie."

I squinted into the darkness at the shape sitting up in bed. "I'm gointer be Hammer's tart now," I told him, "just like he says."

"Will yer be lendin' 'im aht?" Gappy asked.

"I might," said Hammer loftily. "Dependin'."

Gappy, I later learnt, was in here for theft – the spontaneous and stupid sort. He was caught running past a policeman, arms full of stuff. Early in life someone had punched in several of his teeth. I shuddered for him. Any mention of violence and teef dahn froats was enough to petrify me rigid. My own teeth were so nice. The idea of not having any scared me stupid.

When we came to Larkins, Hammer said: "This is Larkins and he's a bastard, but he ain't as tough as me, lucky for you. He'd rather fight than fuck. If he lays so much as his stinkin' finger on yer, yer tells me and I'll do him over an' he knows it. Dontcher, Larks?"

Larkins spat and missed. "You was lucky, Smiff," he said. "We'd have got you, just like we said."

Hammer took me back to my bed. If I say he tucked me in it would sound like it wasn't, but he certainly fixed the blankets around me. "I'll see after yer," he told me.

I drifted into a weird doze, lying how I was left. The next thing I knew it was the half light of early morning and the door was being unlocked, with a warder supervising everyone's awakening. It was he who took the cuffs off me, and he passed no comment at all.

There was a washroom at the end of the corridor, with a sort of counter with bowls sunk into it. We queued up, stripped off our nightshirts, and washed as much of ourselves as we had time for before we were hustled along. Some people settled for a quick dab round the face and ears, but others were very thorough and even took pleasure in a good soap. We were all shivering with cold, and the water was never more than tepid. I was one of those who took trouble, and certainly I needed to that first morning. As days went by I learnt to wash at breakneck speed, and nicked soap regular to make sure I stayed cleanish.

We dressed and marched down for breakfast. So began my first full day at the Reformatory.

CHAPTER NINE

I

We had some lumps of stiff porridge for breakfast, and after two hours of prayers we marched outside for drill. Horrible as these exercises were, and pointless insofar as we ran miles on the spot and around in circles, they did at least warm up our perished bodies. This day the whole business was enlivened by a dramatic event: a boy tried to make a break for it.

Everyone could see it was a doomed venture, and we just gawped in stupefaction, waiting for the moment of his recapture. The reformatory building rose up on all sides out of a courtyard, so that there was space all round it, and then the wall. The wall had two gates, with warders always positioned there. Of course, we weren't actually a prison, so security wasn't first class, but it was pretty obvious to work out you would be caught just running for the gate. The stupid boy must have been desperate and he was caught real easy, but we'd all seen it and I heard Anstey say there'd be a flogging over it.

We were marched back inside, and while everyone else went to lessons I went to Mr Sheldon, to recite.

"Good," said Mr Sheldon without expression. Then he flicked his eyes over me coldly.

"Your presence here," he said, "has aroused the interest of a professional man who may be able to promote your future well-being. Myself, I hold grave doubts as to that but I shall nonetheless be interested in the outcome. Take him to Dr Jameson." He added, darkly, to me: "You will, of course, submit yourself entirely to him. You will be severely punished if I hear anything otherwise."

Swallowing apprehensively, I went with the warder along the corridors. In the mornings they smelt of disinfectant coming up from the privies. All afternoon they smelt of stew. By evening they smelt of sweat and privies. You could tell the time of day from the smells.

I was taken up a little staircase to a small room, identical in shape and position to the warders' room, and containing table, chairs, and a stove. As usual the walls were painted brown. Cold pale sunlight came in through the bare window. At the table sat two men. I was brought in by the warder, who positioned himself at the door and folded his arms. "William Smith," he announced.

"Sit down, William," I was told, and a chair was offered.

Astonished and nervous, my heart going a bit, I sat down cautiously in the chair.

"I don't want you to be nervous," said this man. "There is nothing for you to be afraid of. I am Dr Jameson and this is Dr Grey. We are here to help you."

I stared at these two men.

Dr Jameson was quite young, maybe thirty-five. He had an eager intense lively face, bright eyes, and thick black hair. His face was quite round, sort of babyish and smooth, and his eyebrows thick and dark.

Dr Grey was somewhat like his name, of rather forgettable features, watery in comparison with his more vital companion. He had straw-coloured hair and pale eyebrows and light-coloured eyes. His lips were large and droopy, his neck very thin. Most of the time I saw him he had a cold and he was constantly dabbing his nose, which consequently was always reddish at the tip.

"Yes, William," agreed Dr Grey. "We are here to help you."

"To get me out?" I gasped, with a thumping heart.

They looked surprised, even amused. "No, my boy, to help you."

"Help me what then, if not to get aht?"

"Help you to understand yourself. And help us to understand you."

I relapsed into disinterest.

"Now," said Dr Jameson in a brisk pleasant voice. "Let us begin by finding out a few basic facts. Your name is William Smith. Do your friends call you William? Or Will? Billy? What would you like us to call you?"

"I'm usually called Willie."

"Right. Right then, Willie, and how old are you? Do you know?"

"Sixteen. Just. My birthday's this month, early."

I was stabbed by a sudden remembrance of my birthday, in a different world, last year when my aunt gave me the *Idylls* and stroked my hair in the firelight. It shook me, remembering that.

Then they asked me where I was born and who my father and mother were, and where I'd lived during my life. I answered very briefly, keeping detached, as if I were talking about somebody else.

"Apparently, Willie," and it was always Dr Jameson who did the probing, "you were brought here because you committed a certain offence upon your young male cousin. I'd like you to tell me, Willie, whether this was – how shall I put it? – an act of aggression or an act of desire."

I stared, silent.

"He isn't ready," began Dr Grey hesitantly.

"Did you want to hurt your cousin, or did you want to love him?"

I must've looked a halfwit, sitting there, saying nothing.

"Come, Willie, you must *know*. Tell me what your feelings were towards your cousin."

After a long horrible silence, I blurted out: "Why do you want to know?"

"Let us try to explain *our* position," said Dr Grey, almost timidly. "We are interested in certain mental phenomena – "

"Diseases of the mind," interrupted Dr Jameson firmly.

". . . and we are particularly interested in discovering all we can about a certain type of male. We have been led to believe that you may be such a one, and because you are here, you are available to us for study. Talking to you could help our research, and our research could help you. But the situation is complex. We need to be sure that you are one of these people. Willie, what you did was an action which is open to more than one interpretation. Some wicked, wicked boys do it out of a perverse wish to hurt, or even out of animal bestiality, because they are halfwits and lunatics. But some men – some particular men – do it because it is their way of expressing physically a strong emotional desire. There are names for such men. Would you like to hear what they are?"

"Yes, all right," I said rather blankly.

"I daresay you already know the term sodomite, and even pederast? These terms, particularly the first, are usually spoken in a derogatory way. Society en masse experiences such a strong disgust that it condemns and very strongly so." This was Dr Grey talking. He spoke very feelingly. "But other names," he continued, "are spoken with different connotations. Platonists, for example, is a classical and literary reference, because long ago it was considered possible for one man to love another. The other names I have for you are Urning . . . The gentleman who coined this term also coined *Mannling* and *Weibling*. They are labels for different aspects of the Urning. Sometimes it is called the Female Soul in the Male Body; or the Third Sex. Dr Jameson and I would like to know whether any of these terms apply to you, or whether you are a plain and simple wicked boy. And that is the reason for our questions. We must establish this fact before we can proceed."

I was half impressed at his polite manner and half cynical at his earnestness and the silly words. "I never thought about it," I shrugged.

"Willie, have you ever felt desire for a girl?" said Dr Jameson bluntly.

I laughed in embarrassment. Fancy asking anybody that, straight out, when they didn't know you or anything! It was peculiar.

"Answer us, please," Dr Jameson insisted.

"No, I ain't," I said. I didn't mind admitting it. It was a hundred times easier than answering what were my feelings for my cousin.

My reply overwhelmed my inquisitors with delight. Dr Jameson glowed with bright excitement, and Dr Grey gave a little quick smile. They even swapped a glance with each other, as if it was too good to be true.

"Ah, but wait," cautioned Dr Jameson. "Maybe he has had limited experience. Willie, have you ever been regularly in female company?"

We spent a few moments clarifying my various encounters with females. Dr Grey made notes.

"Do you ever *think* about girls?"

"No."

"What, *never?*" teased Dr Jameson in an unpleasant intimate sort of voice. "Not in your daydreams? Not even at night?"

"No," I said irritably.

"But do you ever, in those circumstances, think about *boys?*" enquired Dr Grey almost breathlessly.

"What I think is . . . "I began with difficulty, ". . . is private."

They hesitated. I made it easy for them. I said, with a surge of anger: "I'm wearin' filthy clothes, I'm eatin' stinkin' food, I'm made to go where I'm pushed; but nobody gets rights over what goes on in my head – nobody's got that right."

"Quite," said Dr Jameson smoothly, as if he were used to difficult patients. "But you must trust us, Willie. We are here to help you. I sincerely mean that."

"Trust us, Willie," said Dr Grey kindly.

They must be stupid, I thought: trust them? In *here?*

"Tell us, Willie," said Dr Jameson, "whether you ever have a little private daydream about boys. A particular boy, maybe. Your cousin, perhaps?"

I could feel myself getting hot and angry. I flashed a glance at the warder, who was listening with interest, neither malevolently nor encouragingly, but listening nonetheless. I had to make my position clear.

"I don't mean to be difficult, sir," I said politely, "but I can't answer you properly. I don't know if you realise this, but in here I am considered to be pretty much of a beast, and I have been told plainly that I'm not wanted in Heaven. I'm in here to be corrected. Now you want me to confess to dreams about boys. If I say yes, and I'm not saying yes, and if you tell Mr Sheldon then I daresay I'll be in more trouble than I already am. *You* can get up and leave this place, but I can't. I s'pose you don't know how long I've got to stay here?" I added, not very hopefully.

"No, that's not within our sphere," said Dr Jameson, not in the tone of one who felt very concerned about it.

"His position is intolerable," murmured Dr Grey. Louder, he said to me, leaning forward: "Do you understand what the word 'confidential' means, Willie?"

"Yes: secret."

"Our conversations are confidential," said Dr Grey.

I coughed sarcastically and jerked my head at the warder. I do believe they'd forgotten his presence. They muttered something to each other and ended up with Dr Jameson beaming at me.

"I think there is the basis of many more discussions here," he announced. "We'll terminate this interview, but we may well be seeing you later on today."

II

THE WARDER took me back to the schoolroom. There I passed a dull time sitting on the end of a bench, ignored by the teacher, and listening to his monotonous voice taking a history lesson. It crossed my mind that he wasn't very intelligent or learned. I remembered my uncle saying that any fool could set himself up as a teacher, any oaf. Here was one, I thought. Though who in their senses would out of choice come and teach in this hole? They were lucky they'd got anybody at all.

After another scraggy dinner we proceeded on to oakum picking; but here a pleasant surprise awaited me. I was sent for by the doctors during oakum picking! I was so delighted that I entered the room in a very good mood, and they looked very contented too, for, as they explained, they had fixed it for our discussions to be private. No warder was in the room. When I was to be escorted back, they would ring a bell in the corridor.

Our mutual pleasure was short-lived, because I was obliged to point out in all politeness that although there was no warder I couldn't help wondering whether they would be tempted to reveal the substance of our talks to Mr Sheldon anyway. They assured me that they would not.

"Dr Grey and myself are not attached to this place as such. We are employed elsewhere. We are not answerable to Mr Sheldon. We are from outside, and therefore independent. Certainly we will make a report upon our findings, but that report can be as precise or as general as we choose to make it. Our interests are purely scientific."

"We haven't been sent to probe you for secrets that would get you into trouble," said Dr Grey. "We want to know how you think and feel. We are interested in you."

"Oh," I said flatly.

"Is there a problem?" Dr Jameson enquired.

"Only . . . I've never talked about my feelings, to anyone, ever – well, except to my brother, nobody since, not properly – well, perhaps my aunt. But in this place I don't know whether I could. I mean, whether I dare let go."

Dr Grey promised they would make it as easy as they could for me.

"Something I'd like to know," said Dr Jameson, "is why, or how, you have, as it were, two ways of talking. Had you realised? One minute you are a little terse, all aitches gone, and an accent I have heard in Smithfield; and suddenly you turn about and regale us with refined diction. It makes me suspect a basic disturbance and certainly a conflict."

"Well, it's easy enough to explain," I said. "I started my life talkin' ordinary. Then when we lived in Aldgate I spoke like the people there, and then my relations made me speak proper; worked on me day and night, like. I come in here and I started speakin' common. Everybody does."

"Which is more comfortable to you?"

"A mixture," I grinned.

"Good; I'm glad about that."

"I can't unlearn the cultural things I know," I said. "I mean, I can recite *Lycidas* all the way through! But I'm not naturally cultured, so I drop into the old."

"Do you feel resentment?" Dr Grey wondered.

"Who towards?"

"Towards whom," said Dr Jameson.

"Yes sir; towards whom?"

"So, resentment, is there some?"

"Nah!" I shrugged.

"Not to your uncle?" asked Dr Grey.

"Bleedin' hell!" I gasped. "Resentment isn't how I'd describe what I feel to *him!*"

"Ah," said Dr Grey, "I meant, in fact, resentment for taking you from your natural habitat. But, of course, I'd forgotten . . . I suppose it was at his instigation."

"Were you thinking of your uncle when you committed the offence upon your cousin?" asked Dr Jameson.

I burst out laughing. "No," I said, controlling myself.

He looked displeased. "I mean, of course, did you feel resentment which you suppressed, and which burst forth in crude aggression?"

"If I suppressed it, how would I know?"

"Did you want to hurt your cousin?"

"I don't want to talk about it," I muttered.

They shuffled papers around, looking thwarted, but trying to be patient and understanding.

"Tell us what he looked like," Dr Grey suggested.

I fidgetted.

"What is it?" Dr Grey asked rather kindly.

"I find it sort of painful," I answered, looking at him.

"Did you love him?" he asked, and in such a sweet understanding voice that a lump came into my throat and I couldn't speak at all.

"I see that he was fourteen," said Dr Jameson, looking at his papers, "and was called George. Try to describe him. What colour was his hair?"

"Yeller," I scowled.

"Eyes?" enquired Dr Jameson smoothly.

"Blue," I croaked.

"A pretty lad, I would imagine."

I covered my face with my hands, blocking out the image of Georgey. Above my head Dr Jameson observed: "Paradise Lost."

"Why not let your feelings out, Willie?" he said, too briskly; "Let them come; it's necessary."

I looked at him angrily. "Not in here," I seethed. "You wants a bleedin' suit of armour rahnd yer and I'm keepin' one."

"Let me ask you this then," said Dr Jameson. "If you could go anywhere, be with anyone, lay your head on a friendly shoulder, who would you choose?"

"My brother Charley."

"Now, he went to Australia."

"Last I heard." I was relieved to be off the subject of Georgey.

"You were very close to him."

"Close as can be."

"What was so good about him?"

"He was very strong. He looked after me."

"That's what you like, is it? To be looked after?"

"Charley said I had a leaning sort of character," I said, pleasantly relaxed at the memory.

"Of course, you loved Charley."

"Course I did. He was all I had."

"Was he a good-looking lad?"

"I thought so. It's hard to say, ennit? If you love a person they look handsome. He's my ideal; but I don't think he was exceptionally beautiful. He was just very comfortable."

"Nothing like George."

"Georgey. Nah, nothing at all. Georgey was weak, my Charley was strong."

"You like a man to be strong."

"Yes. Don't you?"

"And out of choice, you like a strong man's shoulder to lay your head upon," said Dr Jameson.

I felt threatened. I felt I was being pushed into a box and labelled. I went sulky.

"Willie, it doesn't *matter!*" said Dr Grey, half laughing.

"I s'pose you've proved I'm one of *them*, then, have yer?" I scowled aggressively. "Awnings or something."

"Urning," said Dr Grey. "What do *you* think, Willie? Let me read you a description from a book: ' . . . The type is instantly recognisable. Of pallid appearance, with a skin almost translucent, and generally marked in some way with spots, pustules, boils. Beneath the eyes, mauve shadows, the result of constant self-abuse. The hands, long and thin, never cease to twitch and scratch, nervous mannerisms due to poor sleep and dark ill-ventilated rooms, and lack of manly health-giving exercise. A shifty secretive look, a guilty gaze, a start at sudden movements . . . The type shows scant regard for standards of dress and cleanliness, and out of choice will be careless, shabby and down at heel. The type is always thin, with possibly a receding chin and bulbous eyes; constant blinking is also a feature. There is never personal beauty. The type is without fail repulsive in the extreme.' "

I grinned a bit. "I don't know," I said. "I think I'm pretty repulsive at the moment."

"What I've just read to you," said Dr Grey, "is a medical opinion on what these kind of men look like. For some reason, it is assumed that bodily manifestations follow diagnosis of the condition. Myself, I cannot help but feel that it isn't so simple. It would please me enormously to be able to prove that a man could have this propensity and look perfectly normal, attractive even. I have to admit that I would be delighted if you were one. It would instantly disprove the passage I've just read."

"You are probably aware," added Dr Jameson, "that you are, even to the most cynical and objective observer, a very beautiful young man. One is hesitant to use the word 'beautiful' of males, but I would use it in your case. This in itself would be a breakthrough, the proof that any normal-looking man could be the type in question, that he need not be instantly recognisable as the pallid twitching wretch described."

"You *want* me to be this type, don't you?" I said bluntly. "You'd be disappointed if I wasn't."

"I intend to try to keep my mind entirely open," said Dr Jameson pompously.

"Look, you may not know this," I said, "but in the rough parts of the town a lot of – that sort of thing goes on. It don't mean anything. People just do it. But they aren't what you call types. They go with boys because boys don't have babies, so they aren't trapped into having to look after a family. It's not that they like boys best. If I was that sort, you'd be wasting your time."

"Everything we know about you," said Dr Jameson, "persuades us that you have a complex personality, one facet of which is an inclination to other males rather than to females. Also," he added, with a little smirk, "you admitted as much to your cousin."

"What?" I gasped.

" 'With me it's boys'," he read from his notes. "You said that to your cousin."

"You ain't never been pestering Georgey?" I screeched.

"Of course not," they assured me placidly and firmly. "The boy repeated all that had passed between you to his mother, who confided the facts to her husband, and all of this was explained to Mr Sheldon, when you were admitted."

"Bloody hell," I said faintly. I felt surrounded by enemies, with all retreats cut off. My throat went bone dry. These gentlemen sitting there so neat and smart and collected knew the details of what I did with Georgey. It was viciously unfair.

"All I'm saying," continued Dr Jameson, "is that on your own admission you prefer boys to girls as wished-for sexual partners. Now answer me this. Suppose I were to paint you a picture of two alternate futures. Suppose we had a gipsy's crystal ball and could see the years ahead. Behold!" and he caught my attention by pretending to do hocus pocus things with his hands as if he was cleaning a glass of mystic mist. "I see a lovely wife. *Your* wife. She's small and graceful and exquisite. She has blond hair and blue eyes, and heavy womanly breasts. Three – four buxom little children accompany her. She needs you. She wants you to make a home for her. She will reward you at night with the welcoming softness of her pillowy breasts."

My eyes widened to saucers, possibly with alarm.

He continued: "The other vision. A tall strong man. He looks like your brother Charley. He's capable and manly, good-natured, and handsome. He'll look after you and hold you in his arms. Now tell me, which of those pictures holds most attraction for you?"

They watched me carefully. During his description of the tall strong man my guts stirred with longing. I daresay it might have shown on my face. I had the impression of having been beaten in a fair fight. "I suppose I could lie," I grinned.

"I want a clearer answer than that."

"Oh, all right, I'd prefer the man."

They tried not to look too pleased; but they were. It was obviously a breakthrough point for them; and with a lot of paper shuffling Dr Jameson said he thought we would leave it there for today. "Is there anything you need?" enquired Dr Grey.

"A free pardon," I suggested flippantly.

"Seriously, Willie."

"Yes please: I'd like a comb," I said frankly. "No one's thought to give me one; and I can't get me tangles out. My hair looks real nice combed."

This further indication of my Female Soul in a Male Body went down very well; and they promised me I should receive one.

III

AFTER BREAD and butter that evening, we all had to watch a flogging. It was the boy who tried to escape that morning. We were marched into a room, and in this room was the flogging box. The arms were fixed at the wrists into holes such as were found in old-fashioned pillories and the legs went into a couple of holes in the top of a box, which held the person still. The especially sickening thing about the event was that we were arranged as if for a Punch and Judy show, small boys cross-legged on the floor at the front, and us who were taller standing at the back.

The boy was led in without his shirt. He was thin and scared and half stupid. They fixed him in the flogging box and laid into him with a rod. They welted his back and he screamed. It wasn't just me who felt sick, I could see by the number of others who went green. Anyone who looked away got his face turned back round and a clip round the ear. We were all silent when we marched out again, past the privies in case anyone needed to throw up. Hammer said the boy would have to spend the night in the Black Hole. He was flogged as an Example to Us All.

"I'm glad you've come here," Bonnett confided to me. "Before you came it was me they all went for, and now I get left in peace."

Bonnett shuddered at his memories. He was a pretty boy, but that was his misfortune. He had taken no pleasure in anything that had happened to him in the dormitory. He had a sad little face, as if he was likely to start crying under the least pressure, and it was true what Hammer said: he often got picked on by the warders, and by the teacher too, and you could not help feeling that it was done for the enjoyment of seeing him cry. I felt modestly pleased that at least I had helped in easing his nights.

For myself I found only improvements in my lot when I became Hammer's moll. He looked after me in every way. Since the boys there were subservient to him they all worked together. They surrounded me if Firth was our escort, so I was less notice-able to be picked on. They slipped me extra slices of bread. Best of all, during oakum picking they passed me their own picked bits to save my hands. It thwarted Firth's nasty plans for me, because instead of being victimised for my long hair and rumours of effeminacy, I was protected. All I had to do in return was look after Hammer at night, and if he lent me out, it was all part of the deal.

Of the boys in the reformatory, Hammer was toughest and held sway over everybody. There were Larkins and his mate, but they weren't so tough, though they made life miserable for some weaker boys. Once they beat someone up, at night, and no one helped their victim. You didn't get helped unless you had a part in the system.

About half the boys there were in for a long stretch, and about half were short stayers, sometimes just overnight. A wide variety of crimes were theirs – one boy had killed someone, by accident; one had beaten up a crusher; but most had committed offences against property, for which the laws were very severe.

Meanwhile, the medical men pursued their research. Dr Jameson questioned me about my experience of casual couplings in Aldgate and how boys thought and felt, and whether both parties enjoyed the experience or whether one was taken advantage of.

"The world of science," he said, "knows so little about the human body in its acts of love. No one for instance is sure how much faculty the *woman* has for pleasure. A whole volume could be written on the subject – but how could one ever break through the bounds of propriety? How could one ever *ask* women what they feel? It isn't possible; society doesn't permit. Even with men . . . reticence, upbringing . . . one can only research with society's victims. And how exact a sample is that? If I sat discussing this with all the prostitutes in the cells overnight, how would that help me to understand the maiden at the piano, the matron in the parlour?"

While my heart did not exactly bleed for the frustrated man of science, I was nevertheless quite interested in his problem.

"I know what you mean," I agreed. "It really struck me going from Aldgate to Putney, how people just don't talk about that in refined circles. See, ordinarily, we were very free and easy, and no one got hot and bothered about screwing. But in Putney it was like you didn't *have* privates. You got no advice, nothing. Yet you still thought abaht it; nearly all the time!"

From the two of them, appreciation flowed, for my little honest outburst.

"You thought about it then, Willie," pursued Dr Jameson. "Can you tell us?"

"I just did what boys do," I shrugged. "And I know boys do it," I added aggressively, "so don't just say it's me being perverse."

"You made pictures in your head to help you?"

I suddenly looked Dr Jameson in the eyes; we held each other's gaze. Intuitively I knew that Dr Jameson had done it himself. It was a curiously levelling notion. In return for my realisation I offered him a confession. "Yeah. I thought about boys."

"Ah!" they said gratified, shuffling their papers about. "Ever girls?"

"I tried it with girls, but it didn't work. I don't seem to get excited by girls. If I think about girls, nothing happens."

"Instinctive, you see," Dr Grey said to him, pleased. "Just as the normal male instinctively finds girls attractive without needing to justify it or query it, the Urning's attraction to other males is also a natural urge."

IV

UNFORTUNATELY I wasn't sent for as often as I'd have liked by these professional gentlemen to further their researches. Most of the time I was obliged to carry on with what you might call Ordinary Life, enlivened only by small incidents like people being cuffed for answering back and being punished by missing meals or having to stand at the front holding a notice saying IDIOT or DUNCE. I never saw another public flogging but a lot went on all the same. Boys came back to the dormitory and sniffed in the darkness till they fell asleep. Sometimes a boy would be sent here specially to be flogged, and then released. This was the typical treatment of someone caught, for instance, breaking a window.

I still had to present myself to Firth, nights, to be handcuffed. If he was busy or not in the mood he just clipped them on, but sometimes if he felt evil or had time to spare I'd get a little performance.

One evening when I was safely restricted he got very funny about the medical men. "Our Willie's become very important," he sneered to the other warder who sat with him. "Ain't yer, Willie? He has these doctors come to see him, special doctors, interested in finding out what it's like to be a boy who likes boys."

I started to go out of the room; he grabbed me by the nightshirt and yanked me back. "*Come* here. I never told you to go."

He held my chin, a thumb by one ear, a finger by the other, and moved my face from side to side. "What's it like then, sodomite?" he leered, half knocking me out with his beery breath. "What's it like fancying other boys? D'you go around the dormitory at night pleading for it? Getting refusals? Is that how it is?"

"No sir."

"What? You don't get refusals?"

"No sir, I mean there's no one there I fancy."

You would have thought Hammer had never given me advice, wouldn't you?

"Ah, you admit it, do you? *Like* kissing men, do you? No one there you fancy, eh? How do you like 'em? Big and tough, eh? Like me, eh?"

"No sir."

"Come on, you needn't be shy with me. Them boys too young for you, eh? You like 'em big and dirty, eh? Gasping for a kiss from a real man — is that what you're missing?"

"Yes sir!" I answered recklessly.

Almost sensuously he ran his fingers round my neck and gathered up a bunch of my hair, holding it in a vicious grip.

"How'd you like *me* to kiss you then?" he leered, close to my face, breathing into my mouth, doing excruciating things to my hair which made my head twist about, my throat arch and my face contort with the pain of it. "Eh? Like to kiss a real man?" he breathed.

"Yes sir," I winced, "but you ain't it."

His eyes went all narrow as it dawned on him that he'd been insulted. His reaction was immediate. It seemed like he dragged me round the entire room by that fistful of hair; I know we knocked chairs over and I know there was a moment when I hung by my hair and screamed, and the other warder intervened to separate us. I was flung out into the corridor bruised and shaken and it was all my own fault. The characteristic of mine which Charley had called Askin' For It was out of place in here and I was stupid not to know it.

However, after a week or so, the pleasure of sending me handcuffed to the dormitory began to pall and he laid off. I suppose he'd made his point and the gesture began to seem empty. It was bleedin' marvellous to get a decent night's sleep.

CHAPTER TEN

I

I BEGAN to notice that when I was called a filthy sodomite it seemed to me like a statement, though it was supposed to be abuse. I was certainly, by my standards, filthy, and as to the other, it was like an identity of which I was becoming more conscious with each conversation with the doctors.

"Are there many of us?" I asked them.

"It's impossible to say," said Dr Grey. "Society being what it is, men tend to keep it secret."

"Society being what it is?"

"It doesn't take kindly to rebels and the unconventional. Oh, you can get away with being deviant on the sly, and if you're careful. But flaunt it, and you'll likely get a gaol sentence. Society calls it a vice. Society condemns it, and classes it with murder."

"But what *is* society?" I demanded. "A whole mass of people like my aunt and uncle, who live in a protected world of comfortable security, who know nothing of life on the street. Who are they to make statements on what is vice?"

"They are power," said Dr Grey, "the voice of government, church, institution. They make the statements within the framework where all of us live. And they are too big to go against."

"But they're wrong!" I said.

Dr Jameson intervened. "It is no good leading Willie along these lines. It is not within our sphere to question social morality. Our task is more specifically to help Willie *fit in*."

I sulked. All this bilge about society, as if society was someone else, somewhere else. Dr Jameson was society. He was a doctor in it. He took society's money. I was against him too.

As I went through the boring and degrading business of daily life at the reformatory, I thought a lot about the plight and situation of we sodomites.

Dr Grey told me that throughout history there had always been men who loved other men. He said they had existed in ancient civilisations – Egypt, China, India – and that he knew people who were doing research into the literature of the past and others who were involved in extensive surveys in the present. They wanted to know if it was an acquired or inherited condition, what caused it and was it contagious? He told me about Antinous, the beautiful favourite of Emperor Hadrian. So, it seemed, even emperors could be sodomites. He said that in ancient Greece, instead of it being a sin and a vice, love between males was accepted and idealised, and male love was considered to be an ennobling and uplifting virtue. Alexander the Great was a lover of males.

It was because of what was written in the Bible that people's attitude changed. Christian philosophers condemned men loving men as a sin against nature and sodomites were burned at the stake. In the law of our own country it was written that sodomy was an abominable sin of which Christians must not speak by name, and so if you were found guilty you would go to prison. In France, however, they were more enlightened, and such acts were permissible in private and only punished if others were offended or if anyone was hurt. Whenever a scandal occurred in London, gentlemen scuttled for the boat train to Calais.

Dr Grey thought it was important that I should know these things because I had been brought here for that offence, and it was right that I should understand how the law stood with regard to it, and society's muddled and hostile attitude.

Before I came to the reformatory I had not thought much at all about sodomy as a label or a fact. But here I was obliged to be obsessed with it. Every day I had to recite the passages about fire and brimstone to Mr Sheldon. By the two doctors I was obliged to analyse my feelings while they improved my knowledge of pederasty in all its aspects. I was called any number of coarse names by most of the warders who had occasion to speak to me. And I was a whore at night, at first reluctantly, and gradually with increasing enjoyment and skill.

The reformatory couldn't be blamed for making me what I became, because unless I was that way inclined before, it would not have had the effect it did and I would have shaken it off once I was free. But though I don't blame the place in itself, I see it clearly as a hothouse where blooms of my variety were given an opportunity to blossom and grow. Before I went in there I didn't know I was a sodomite; when I came out I not only knew it but was eager to practice what it meant.

My own opinion on the subject was that, far from being contrary to nature, it was natural, simply because so many boys did it and took to it so easily. They didn't need to read about it in a book, they just needed to lie in bed with another boy; that was all it took. Later on, those who wanted to marry and have children took it up with girls, and those who found they liked girls best, either for procreation or just for pleasure, abandoned boys because of how society was fixed. Expectation, social advancement, convention, all favoured union with girls. But the faculty for enjoying boys would always be there, dormant, even through a lifetime of loving girls.

I thought about the countless pederasts who'd been victimised and persecuted, burnt at the stake for the way they chose to love. I thought about the ones who even now were living secret lives, feeling guilt and dread, maybe believing what society said about them, that they were beasts and depraved. All the hostile feelings I had about society, which had previously been centred on the injustices of unfairly divided wealth, crystallised now upon how I felt about myself as a sodomite. It would have been a little dramatic to describe it as a sort of crusade, but it did feel like that. I wasn't going to be a social reformer, but I would fight society in my own way. Society meant people like my uncle and Mr Sheldon, even Dr Jameson, and their minions, the warders, the policemen, the church. Somewhere amongst them were other misfits like me, and we would have to seek each other out and help each other, and even find ways to be happy.

I felt a cautious optimism, totally out of keeping with my surroundings.

There was another thing too. It was the picture that Dr Jameson had jokingly painted: there is a strong man . . . like your brother Charley . . . he will take you in his arms . . . For the sake of that man I had to be true to myself, because I would never find him if I faltered. Gasping for the kiss of a strong man, jeered Firth – well, it was true; I was. I hadn't even realised just how much, until I came here, and they told me.

WELL, A very odd incident happened next. It was organised by
Dr Jameson on his own, and I honestly cannot believe that Mr
Sheldon knew about it. I feel sure he would have disapproved.

I entered the room almost jauntily. It seems strange to say
that, but since my sodomy had become political, I did sometimes
feel jaunty. But I was floored that day when I found Dr Jameson
had brought in a girl! He'd brought her in, not the way I'd come
in, but up from the courtyard. Sneaky, I thought.

"Willie, I want to try a little experiment," he said, bubbling
with excitement at his own daring. "Today I'm going to introduce you to Caroline, and I want you to establish a relationship.
First of all, I'm going to leave you alone, for exactly ten minutes,
and I want you to talk to each other, and see how you get on."

Without exactly rubbing his hands together and chuckling, he
left the room. Me and Caroline were left looking at each other.
She was sitting in the chair I normally sat in, and I was standing
halfway across the room. As soon as the doctor had gone out, I
flicked a glance at the courtyard door. "I shouldn't bother,
ducks," she told me. "He asked a warder to wait at the bottom
of the stairs; you'd never get past."

"What are you supposed to *do?*" I asked her.

"Hasn't he told you?" she shrugged, slipping her shawl off
and settling.

I stared at her, taking in her appearance.

She was about twenty-five. She had coal-black hair and wore
a dark red dress. Now that her shawl was off, it was apparent
that her dress was rather low cut and, as I suddenly recalled the
phrase "alabaster globes", I connected her with the gay ladies I
used to gawp at when I was a boy, roaming the streets of London.
Her lips were painted, and her eyelids were coloured blue. Her
appearance was much more muted than the ladies on the street,
who were out to dazzle, but the effect was the same. She was
taking in all my details too.

"You aren't very old," she observed.

"Sixteen."

"Don't know why, but I thought you'd be older. Come over
here; I won't bite."

I went over to her, astonished that something so bright and

alive and so patently from the outside world could be a part of this bleak room.

"What are you in here for exactly?" she asked.

"Rape," I said aggressively.

"Oh?" She frowned. "I thought he said you was – "

"I raped a boy," I said coolly.

"Yeah, that's it. You're one of them 'Mary Annes'."

"Sodomites," I said brazenly.

"Call it what you like," she shrugged easily. "D'you know Alfie Sadler?"

"No."

"I thought you would have. D'you know his place?"

"No, what place?"

She told me some address in Soho, and she explained: "He's got boys there, *you* know, same as you. Gents come for a good time. I'd have thought you'd have known it. I know a lot of his boys. D'you know what?" she chortled. "Some of 'em are my customers! Nothing like hedging your bets, eh?"

"*I'm* not like that," I said dignified. "I'm not half and half."

"I get a sovereign for coming here," she said, comfortably, "and another half if I can get you good and hard."

"What a bleedin' cheek!" I said indignantly.

"Ain't it!" she agreed cheerfully. "So have a heart, ducks, and don't fight it. I can do a lot with half a sov."

"Are you – ?" I began hesitantly, crouching down by her chair, " – a lady from the Haymarket?"

"Well, I ain't a bleedin' duchess," she remarked.

"Do you enjoy it?" I asked with great interest.

"What a funny question!"

"How much can you make, like, in a night?"

"Who's got a bleedin' cheek now then?" she returned.

"Me, I s'pose," I grinned, flashing her a glance.

"Blimey," she remarked, "You're too bleedin' pretty to be one of them nasty perverts. What a shame you're stuck in here; you could be giving girls a treat, you could. I think I'm going to enjoy having a go at you."

"Don't you care about my sensitive feelings?" I demanded, not very horror-struck. "How can you be a party to the further indignities endured by a poor boy who done no wrong?"

"For that amount of cash," said Caroline, "it comes very easy to me. Yeah," she added, "it's a hard life, mine."

"Garn – I've seen your sort, all dressed up and lovely, smellin' like summer gardens, standin' arahnd and doin' nothing, and then up comes a hansom and off yer goes. I don't call that a hard life."

"Well, it ain't easy! Keeping yourself pretty is no joke, and haggling with them horrible old women who let you have a room and charge the earth; and there's more I could tell yer. It isn't all what it seems."

"You didn't have to do it."

"Well, put it this way: it's better than being somebody's skivvy, or sewing shirts."

"*I* wouldn't mind your kind of life."

"You say that because you're in here. *Anything'd* seem better, wouldn't it?"

The door opened, and Dr Jameson returned. He bustled about a bit, rearranging us. He got me to sit in the chair while he sat on the edge of the table and Caroline prepared to set about earning her half sovereign.

Dr Jameson said to me: "Now! You insist that you're a self-confessed sodomite, and you vigorously maintain that you don't like girls – that when you try to find females exciting, in your words, nothing happens?"

"Yeah, true."

"In fact, it's only boys that excite you?"

"That's right," I said comfortably.

"Well, young lady," said Dr Jameson, "what can you do about that?"

Caroline sat on the arm of my chair and put her arm around my shoulders and into the neck of my shirt. Now that she was so close to me, I felt embarrassed about my condition. "I'm awful sorry about the lice," I muttered, "and the smells."

"What a mean trick!" she teased, "trying to put me off like that! Don't you worry, my lad, I'll have you roused."

"Undo your trousers, Willie," said Dr Jameson briskly.

"Oww," I wailed, "this ain't fair!"

"I need to observe . . . "

"Yeah, and I'd like to an' all!" Caroline grinned.

"I don't smell nice," I muttered.

"Don't be difficult," said Dr Jameson. "Why this sudden attack of modesty? Undo your trousers or I'll undo them for you." And so I did.

We all looked at my limp, unexcited cock lying curled up in its coppery backcloth, and Caroline whispered in my ear: "Ain't you pretty! You ain't a nasty old pervert – they only have little ones!"

"How do you know?" I scowled, but she ignored that and started kissing my neck. With a shock I realised she was an expert. I sat, intrigued, experiencing her warm confident hands, and the warmth moved over my body like sun on stone.

She knelt down in front of me between my opened legs. All my embarrassment returned. I was terrified there'd be lice in my crotch hair and she'd see. Intense misery was my uppermost feeling. She started a husky low-voiced patter and, as her hands did such nice things to me, there was suddenly a twitch. Attention rivetted on it as on to a figure riding out of a distant storm to bring news of relief to the fort!

At that point I knew I had a choice. If I kept on with my misery and dread, Dr Jameson's experiment would be a failure. But bleedin' hell, I wanted her to have the money. You could get an awful lot with ten shillings, and she'd come to this place and not flinched from my repulsiveness and she deserved it. So I shut my eyes and thought with all my heart about a vision of masculinity and me on my knees before it, and I was so successful I had them full of smirking delight and congratulation. Blinking, I shook myself free of the exquisite torment of my fantasy and gave Caroline a watery grin. I was generous enough to allow that she was at least half responsible, though the handsome vision had done the rest.

"H'm," said Dr Jameson. "That is actually all I want you for today, Willie. It was a point I needed to prove."

I laughed sarcastically. I looked down at myself. "And meanwhile – what am I s'posed to do with that?"

"I'll tell you what," said Caroline, pleased by her success enough to make a bold suggestion. "When you get out of here, you come and see me. You can find me any evening outside the Red Star. I'll give you a real nice time."

She thought she was doing me a favour. Cocky little tart!

Dr Jameson prepared to escort her out. "I'm very pleased

about this, Willie," he said. "You see, it proves that your responses are normal. You have the potential to be a proper straightforward ordinary male. The exciting thing about all this is that *now* we can treat your sodomy as a disease, a transient aberration. And we can set about *curing* you!"

He patently expected me to be overwhelmed and grateful and delighted.

"Cured?" I screeched. "I don't want to be cured!" To bring the point home I added firmly: "I *like* being a sodomite!"

But nobody took any notice.

III

IT WAS an incident in the schoolroom that set in motion the chain of events which culminated in my release. Unfortunately for me it was not without showing me the grim truth of the saying: "It is always darkest just before the day dawneth."

It was all for writing 1837 on a piece of paper.

I happened to be sitting next to Bonnett when once again the teacher continued his dreary victimisation. It all crystallised upon Bonnett's having forgotten the date of the Queen's accession, the upshot being that Bonnett would be caned if he couldn't come up with the date instantly, and I wrote 1837 on the corner of my page and slid it along to him, and the teacher saw.

Like a policeman's light in a dark alley, Mr Swale's full attention was directed on me. Bonnett shrivelled up in relief.

"What did you write on that paper?" I was asked.

"Nothing, sir."

"Give it to me."

I handed him Anstey's paper instead of mine. He went liverish and yellow and didn't take it, but seized the paper with the date on and read it.

"Vile, deceitful boy," he muttered, almost shaking. "You should never have been permitted into this class." His usual way of dealing with me was to ignore me completely, as if I was a mist wraith and subject to invisibility. "Since you like writing messages on pieces of paper," he told me, "you may write the word SODOMITE on a label and stand with it out of my sight."

Standing out at the front was common practice, though I'd avoided it up till now. I curled my lip with contempt as I looked up at him. Ugly, really ugly he was, and he couldn't see me for his prejudices.

"Yes sir," I said. "But if I write it as large as you like DUNCE and PIG, it won't fit on the paper. Shall I use two pieces?"

He didn't even want to contaminate himself talking to me. He could hardly bring himself to speak. He jabbed at the paper with his knobbly finger. I decided to help him out.

"Why don't I write PERVERT?" I suggested reasonably. "Or SLUT is nice and short."

"Write SODOMITE," he told me in chilling tones. "And you will be hearing more of this."

I wrote it in beautiful copperplate. Ah, I must be honest, it wasn't so beautiful. Nearly four weeks of oakum picking had roughened up my hands and it didn't come so naturally to hold a pen as a delicate instrument. I stood out over in the corner, being too vile to go near the blackboard, holding my piece of paper. There was no particular reaction from the class; it was so usual for someone to be out there with a derogatory label that no one paid any attention. I thought about persecution. I had this feeling of a great brotherhood, all through history, and holding up a notice was nothing compared to being burnt at the stake. I felt very proud to be identified with them. I stood there rather pleased and arrogant, with my head up and a rather mystic smile. Thoughts of glory kept me going; I even enjoyed being on show. Mr Swale looked at me covertly, a frown upon his face. I stared ahead in pleasant unconcern. Once again, I suppose, I was asking for it.

After dinner, Mr Sheldon sent for me and then I realised there was going to be trouble. "William Smith," he said, "I have been hearing some very disturbing reports about you. I can hardly bring myself to believe what I have been told. It concerns your *attitude*."

Naturally I didn't say anything but just stood staring straight ahead, keeping an expressionless face.

"I would have thought," he said, in an almost puzzled tone, "that being in here would have brought home to you in some small measure the enormity of your vice and the extent of your wickedness. In anyone but the most hardened reprobate, a sense of shame *must* have followed. But in you, it seems, it has not. Your teacher speaks to me of a certain *levity* in your manner. Let me ask you plainly – *do you feel shame?*"

"For what, sir?" I said boldly.

"For what?" he almost screeched. "Is that in doubt?"

"Yes sir," I said, gulping. "But I will try to answer honestly. I do feel shame for what I did to my cousin. I know that was wrong."

The tension eased just a fraction. "But," I said, inspired by the ones who'd died at the stake, "I don't feel shame for my condition."

"Your condition? What do you mean, boy?"

"Dr Jameson has shown me that my – my sodomy might be something I was given at birth, along with the colour of my hair. If that's true, then it's a part of me, like a leg or an arm, and if it's a part of me then I accept it and I don't feel ashamed."

"What nonsense is this?" he frowned. "I've never heard anything so ridiculous. Legs? Arms? Your abominable vice is in no way comparable. I will not have Dr Jameson blamed for your offensive behaviour."

"I'm not blaming him, sir. It's simply that he pointed out that it could be a sickness or it could be a state of being. I feel it's the latter. If it is, I ought to accept it. It would be wrong to deny its existence."

"Let me understand you correctly," he said in a low evil voice. "Far from experiencing shame, are you telling me that you are proud of yourself? That, armed with medical claptrap, you find yourself totally unchanged since you entered here, and feel free to continue in your deviant desires, even boastful of them?"

"No sir," I winced appalled. Whether I did or not, I would never dare admit it.

"This morning you flaunted your bravado in class, I am told," he said, "and I will not tolerate any kind of behaviour inconsistent with my policy of correction."

"No sir," I agreed anxiously.

"Since your annoying Mr Swale was a public offence, your apology will be a public one," he said, "and we will both be perfectly clear in our minds about the moral issues involved. I can see that like a vicious weed you have been flourishing unchecked, nurturing private opinions which seem to me to be contrary to both the laws of the Almighty and the laws of the land. It is fortunate this came to the surface in time for me to take steps."

I watched him write some words on a piece of paper, his pen scratching in the silence, the warder shifting his feet, boot soles scraping the floor. Mr Sheldon handed me the paper and asked me to read it out to him. I began.

In its entirety it read thus: "Sodomy is a vile abhorrent offence, against the word of God, the nature of man, and the health of society. The sodomite is lower than a beast, a gangrenous limb on the body of the whole, and therefore should be cut away. I am a sodomite, and in my shame I beg if not your tolerance at least your pity. Particularly of you, Mr Swale, I ask your forgiveness for my offensiveness and wish to inform you that I feel the deepest regret for my behaviour, and for what I am the very deepest shame."

As I read it my cheeks flushed, and I looked across at him horrified.

"You will read that in front of the class tomorrow," he told me, "and leave us all in no doubt."

"But it isn't true . . . "I gasped.

He stood up slowly. "You deny it?" he said.

"I have to," I said. "I *will* apologise . . . but . . . in a way consistent with . . . with dignity."

D'you know what he said then? Leaning ever so slightly forward, he said: "I *will* break you down."

I felt my face twitch, and I had fluttering feelings inside my guts.

"Dignity," he said contemptuously, looking at me. "You arrogant little fool. You'll read that paper out loud tomorrow, and you'll go where silence will help you consider your position. I will not be crossed by such as you."

He gave directions over my head to the warder, and without more ado I was taken from the room, unutterably relieved to be out of his presence.

IV

I WAS escorted down to the ground floor and then I was taken to the Black Hole. I knew about this place. It was where they put the boy who tried to escape, indeed, any recalcitrant boy. It was a small room with an earth floor, smelling of stale piss and damp stone. No windows or light, a small ventilation very high up, a wooden plank bed a foot off the ground and on it one blanket, stiff with ingrained dirt. I was put in this place and the door was locked, and I was in darkness. As it was about two o'clock I reckon I spent some twenty hours in there. All that time there was no variation in the darkness; I couldn't see my own hand – it was like being drowned in darkness.

Much of the time I slept. The walls and door were so thick that no sound came from outside, yet there was a consciousness of the weight of heavy buildings above me, so that although there was no danger of suffocating, I had the impression of being stifled. The darkness was like a cloth, blocking nose and mouth. And so for me the worst thing was panic, unnatural panic. I knew so many stories about people confined to dark rooms, only to emerge years later, crazed beyond belief, and that's what I was afraid of.

I had no idea of when I would be released and I assumed the worst. I'd been told I was to be broken down. How long did he think it would take? Would I be here more than one night? Two days. A week? In the silence mice rustled. Please make them mice and not rats, I prayed; and even as I lay there frightened I remembered that God wouldn't be answering because I was what I was and had no place in his scheme of things. The night was very long, and I lost all sense of time. When the door was opened, light hit me between the eyes, and I crawled off the bed, dazed and blinking.

It was Firth who stood there, no doubt having put in a special request to be the one to let me out. "Sharpish now!" he told me.

I stumbled through the door, and immediately my knees buckled and I dropped. I suppose it was hunger. I found myself kneeling in front of Firth, but instead of picking me up he got hold of my head and pressed it against himself. I put my arms round his waist and buried my face in his crotch, holding on to his leather belt. I stayed with my face buried; I didn't want to get up.

He unwound me from him and sat me in a chair. In the small bleak room where we were, an open door showed the downstairs corridor and let in the drifting sounds of a distant hymn.

"Is it day?" I said stupidly, looking around.

"Blimey," he muttered. Then he closed the door and gave me a drink of brandy from a flask. I gulped it down; it went through me like fire.

"Right," he said. "Are you ready to come with me to Mr Sheldon?"

"No," I gasped. "What, already? Don't I get no breakfast, nothing?"

"Breakfast's over," he said. "I was given no instructions about breakfast. Now, let's not keep him waiting."

With legs like lead I went with Firth up to Mr Sheldon's room and Firth, holding me by the elbow, ushered me inside. As soon as I got in the room my cheek started twitching. I put a hand over it. I felt very ill prepared for this encounter.

Mr Sheldon was sitting at his desk, and I could not fail to see the offensive paper there by his arm, just where it was left from yesterday. He raised his eyes, and said: "You have had the night to reconsider your disobedience and the folly of your attitude. The position remains the same. I asked you to read that paper before the class; you refused. What is your standpoint this morning?"

"I won't read it," I said, my cheek beginning to twitch again.

"You won't?" he said evenly. "You have a straight choice. You will go down to the schoolroom now and read that paper, or you will accompany this warder to the flogging box and he will be instructed to give you a heavy flogging. Which course will you take?"

I didn't need to deliberate. Gone were the images of my predecessors who had died at the stake. I just remembered watching that boy who'd tried to escape, hearing his screams, and the awful thwack of the rod on flesh. "I'll read it," I said.

He breathed out heavily, I can't tell whether from relief or disappointment. He handed me the paper and I took it. To my horror he stood up to accompany us downstairs. Hardly knowing how I arrived there, I found myself in the schoolroom and Mr Sheldon beside me, setting up the scene. The class looked blank and mildly surprised, and Mr Swale took up a prim self-righteous pose. As for myself, the personal humiliation I was enduring certainly outran the wildest imaginings of the people who had caused it. Reading the speech was an act of highly refined pain, but nothing compared to the knowledge that I was so weak. In the Pocket Gems, the hero cries I will die fighting; it is the villains who collapse. One night in a cell, no food and the threat of flogging, that was all it had taken. The self-loathing I experienced was almost too much to bear.

With a husky shaking voice I read the ghastly speech, nearly drying up as emotion choked me. It was not that any of the boys gave a tinker's cuss about what I was saying, and even Mr Sheldon could not have understood what I was going through. He had expected me to give in, boys always did. No, it was a personal thing, that I hadn't been worthy of my fellow persecuted. I'd stood there and degraded myself to people I despised, and I felt that if I'd been physically grovelling on the floor I couldn't have more satisfactorily showed my capitulation to the enemy.

I withdrew into myself from that moment. At dinner time Hammer and Anstey surreptitiously gave me their potatoes. Withdrawn I might be but fasting I wasn't, and I ate every lumpy mouthful. I was sent for by Dr Jameson in the afternoon. The warder laid his hand on the back of my neck, and I slouched along like a felon, not bothering to shake him off.

Dr Jameson was as beaming and brisk as ever. Either he was as sensitive as a post, or he didn't know about what had happened. "That's it, Willie," he said. "Sit down. Now! After our important breakthrough last time, I want us to proceed along the lines of treating your condition as an illness, and to think about appropriate ways in which to cure it. I'd like first of all to point out the advantage in it for you if you are cured. I'd like us to think about the situation of deviates in the world as we know it, and to ask ourselves whether it is the kind of life we want, when the alternative is so much richer, safer and more generally satisfying. I want you to think about the advantages in being normal."

"I have," I said quickly. "And I find I was quite wrong before. You were right; we all saw I get aroused by girls. I believe you. I was pretending before. I never was a pervert and I don't need to see you any more."

Somewhat naturally, he looked at me with disbelief bordering on amusement. "What *is* all this?" he asked quizzically.

"I'm just an ordinary boy. I ain't what you thought. So there's no point in going on with this."

"I fail to understand . . . "

"It's easy. I was playing around. It was just to get out of picking oakum. And now I've had enough of it."

"What game are you playing *now?*"

"No game. I just want to be left alone. I'm in here to pay, and I'll pay all right. I deserve all I get."

"You mean you feel *remorse* now?"

"Yeah, that's it," I agreed, "I was a beast."

"Is this some kind of trick?" he said, as if he'd suddenly seen the light. "Do you think you'll be allowed to leave if you pretend repentance, and if you repeat these glib and trite remarks? Because you *won't*, you know. Your detention is only just beginning. It will do you no good to act this way."

"It's the only way I know. I done wrong and I have to pay. I did a crime, just like the other boys. They don't see no doctors and I don't need to either. I did it to get at my uncle. And don't worry, I've seen the error of my ways and I'll be goin' after girls when I get aht've here. I'm going to be normal then."

"I thought you maintained that it was normal for you to be a sodomite?"

"It ain't. It's unnatural. I'm changing my ways. I'll be different when I get aht."

"This is rather a wasted journey for me," said Dr Jameson irritably, shifting his papers about.

I sat wooden and silent.

He tried again a few times, different tacks, but I sat like a stuffed sack and was of no help to him. Eventually he was obliged to give up, and we parted on poor terms.

V

AFTER MY public recantation – I felt it was nothing less – I was no longer sent for to recite the passages about the abominable. It was like I was considered to be one of the mass now, and not someone to be pressurised and singled out. That was how I felt. I behaved like an object in a group of objects, marching around when ordered, shuffling hunched and lifeless when not. And so it came as a surprise to me when I was removed from oakum picking to go and see the doctors. I thought they'd have the sense to give me up as a lost cause after my last interview with Dr Jameson.

As usual, I was escorted into the room; the warder withdrew, and I saw it was this time only Dr Grey. He had obviously only just recovered from at least influenza; his habitual snuffling was more pronounced than ever, and he mopped at his nose with a vast handkerchief. We were a fairly unsavoury couple, he dribbling and me scratching. He waved his hand loosely in the direction of the chair, and I slouched into it.

"What's all this nonsense I've been hearing from Dr Jameson?" he said. "Sulky denials? Sullen silences? H'm?"

'I ain't goin froo all that again," I scowled.

"You *are*, my lad," he told me. "When I last saw you, you were, if anything, peculiarly proud of what you had decided was a natural condition. Now he tells me you're insisting it was all a pretence."

"Yeah, that's right. I ain't no filthy sodomite. I'm in here to pay my debt to society, and that's what I want to do, so just leave me alone and let me get on with it."

"Willie, I don't believe you," he said.

"You'll 'ave ter," I shrugged. "I'm doin' like I'm told now. I seen I'm wrong. I just want to be normal now. I'm an ordinary boy and I want to be treated like everyone else."

I could feel my face starting to twitch again. I put my hand over it, annoyed.

"Look at me," said Dr Grey.

I wouldn't. I looked down at my knees instead.

"*Look* at me, damn you," he ordered. I jumped and looked at him, because orders I responded to, instantly.

'I want you to tell me plainly about your state of mind," he said.

We looked each other in the eyes. He seemed to be trying to draw out my thoughts from me, with his earnest penetrating gaze. I resisted; I put up a wall. Just ever so slightly I shook my head.

Suddenly his control broke. He slammed the table with his hand. I flinched. "You will answer me!" he seethed. "If I have to have the words beaten out of you I will have your explanation!"

That sort of talk got through to me. I stared at him quiveringly, and then my face crumpled and I sort of groaned.

"You turnin' on me too, are yer?" I said bitterly, and then I put both my hands over my face and burst into tears. I don't know what he did, I was too busy sobbing my guts out. I laid my head in my arms on the table. I had never cried like that ever. My head was threshing about, my shoulders heaving, it hurt my stomach, even; it was an all-over cry. At least he had the sense to let me get on with it. If he'd told me to pull myself together, I could well have strangled him. After a while he put one hand on my shoulder. "What's happened?" he asked.

I stuck my hand in my pocket and pulled out the crumpled up paper. I'd clenched my hand on it so hard it was screwed up in the shape of my fingers, ridged. It had been in my pocket those few days ever since I'd read it out. Without even looking at him I foisted the paper on him. Half incoherent I choked out: "I read it out. They said they'd flog me."

While I sprawled sobbing across the table, Dr Grey had come to a decision. But I didn't know that. I felt shaken by him turning rough on me. I'd thought he was on my side. Not Dr Jameson, I knew he wasn't. But Dr Grey, with his silences and his helpfulness had always seemed sympathetic to me. I wanted him to understand. I twisted my head up and looked at him, tears trickling down my filthy cheeks. "See, they got everything off me now," I said. "What I think about myself . . . it's all took . . . "

Dr Grey went over to the door and locked it. He handed me a large clean handkerchief, which I took and used.

"Listen to me, Willie," he said in a low voice, putting his face near mine. His eyes were very bloodshot. "If I took you out of this place now, this minute, would you be up to it?"

"Ay?" I said blankly.

"I want to get you out. Can you cope with that?"

"Yes," I said, thinking I was dreaming.

"We'll go out through that door," he said, indicating the one through which Dr Jameson had brought Caroline. "It leads to the courtyard. I expect you know that."

"There's always warders . . . "

"It doesn't matter. As we walk across the courtyard I will grip your arm and it will be assumed I have permission to take you out. If I am asked I will say as much. You are being escorted to a wing of the hospital for some kind of treatment. There is no precedent here. The warders will have no reason to doubt me."

"You ain't really takin' me to a hospital?" I said scared.

"No. But you must look as if I am. You must look cowed and withdrawn, and utterly harmless. You must show no emotion, no excitement, nothing. Don't even look about you. Keep your hands in front of you, so that from a distance you may seem handcuffed. Is there anything you need to ask me?"

"No," I whispered, shivering.

Dr Grey opened the door. A staircase led down spirally to the courtyard. With buckling knees I descended the steps. Dr Grey was nervous too. His hand gripped my arm too tightly; it hurt. I kept my head down. No warder stopped us as we walked across the great open courtyard. Near the entrance there was a hansom cab.

I have always loved hansoms. They are so beautiful, with their black lacquered doors, and graceful shape. Their lamps loom through the fog like suns in winter. Their bells jingle as they glide closer, their drivers discreet and all-knowing. I have no idea whether that particular hansom had black lacquered doors, or whether it was in fact pulled by cherubim on clouds. I suspect the latter.

As Dr Grey ushered me with a pretence of roughness into the cab, we were challenged by a warder, and Dr Grey told him we had permission. We were also questioned at the gate. Dr Grey remained calm, even brusque, as if they should know better than to query his authority. The frequency of his visits here, his professional status and the blatant unlikelihood of his wanting to abduct me, were enough to allow us through the gates.

VI

IT WAS late afternoon in the month of March. The pavements were of a blue transparency, from the rain. A gusty wind shook the trees and scattered petals of early pink blossom. Daffodils of startling yellow stood in buckets at street corners beside flower girls in long fringed shawls. We wound into the traffic. We became part of the bustling streets.

"Will they come after us?" I whispered, sitting small and hunched and low in my seat.

"No. They don't know where we are." Dr Grey suddenly laughed harshly. "I've no idea where to take you! I haven't thought of that!"

"Just let me out somewhere. I'll be all right."

"Don't be silly. Not only are you nauseatingly unhygienic, you would freeze in those clothes. Mm, yes, once again I think I must trade on my sister's good will!"

He told the cab driver an address and we set off at speed.

The place to which I was taken was a tall thin house in a terraced row, with pointed iron railings at the base, and three steps up to a front door. Within moments we were in a warm hall, and a gaunt spinsterly lady was hearing a muffled version of our story. It was odd to think of Dr Grey having a family life. I gathered she was his elder sister and I daresay she had sorted him out through childhood. I quailed under her searching glance. I felt the lice in my hair would be glistening and preening, and making cheeky signs at her with their skinny fists. I felt the stench of me would revolt her sensibilities.

"Upstairs with him," was all she said.

Oh! She had a bathroom! It had a blue and white tiled floor, and standing upon it I felt tears trickling out of my eyes. Crying, I ask you, at the sight of a bathroom!

"Am I to have a bath?" I pleaded, anguished and yearning.

Dr Grey's sister – Miss Agatha Grey – ran the bath for me, until the room was a fog of hot steam. I couldn't get out of my clothes fast enough. Miss Grey used a pair of wooden tongs to remove them from the room. Within the blink of an eye I was in that bath. It was deep and beautiful. I sank in it to my neck. With the heat of it and all, my reserve crumbled, and as I seized the scrubbing brush and soap I couldn't stop laughing under my breath and crying at the same time. I put my head into the water and soaped my hair till the lather poured off in great black dollops of foam, making islands on the surface. I sat there and scrubbed till my skin burned and the water clouded up with filth and sludge, and I snivelled quietly with indescribable relief, tears plopping into the water.

Suddenly I was aware of Dr Grey's presence. He had been there all the time but I'd hardly noticed. Now I saw him with clarity as he stood there watching me, a preoccupied and distant look on his face.

"Oh!" I wailed. "Why are you so good to me?"

He shook himself and looked at me and laughed. "Don't you *know?*" he asked.

"No," I said, wide-eyed. "Are you sorry for me? Is it your humanitarianism?" I grinned, showing off.

"Don't you really know?" he asked wonderingly.

I shook my head.

Dr Grey came and knelt by the bath.

"Why do you suppose I'm so interested in what makes a person sexually inverted?" he said, oddly bright-eyed. "Do you suppose it's a disinterested search for knowledge, as one might study butterflies and fossils? No! It's to help me understand *myself.*"

"You?" I gasped. "You're one too?"

"All my life," he said. "I couldn't believe my luck when I was told you were available for research. I thought that studying you would shed some light. Above all, I wanted to help you. I wanted to make you realise that you were not alone. Or that *I* was not."

"Is Dr Jameson one?" I frowned.

"Oh no. He's just interested in the research. He has a wife and two children. But he badly wants to be the one to make a breakthrough in the study of inverted sexuality. He is convinced it's a disease. He had elaborate plans to cure you. *I* was interested in how you *felt.*"

"Yes . . . I see."

"When you seemed to be so unrepentant . . . so delightfully normal yet persisting in your preference for males, I was elated. You seemed to have pride. I found it so cheering. All my life, you see, I've kept my secret . . . pretended . . . living falsely, fearful of discovery. Tonight I dared not take you back to my rooms. I have a bachelor suite . . . but I could not risk bringing a boy back there . . . my reputation . . . "

I watched the black foam circling around my knees. I was impressed at his confessions. He continued: "I am ashamed to say that it was not common humanity that induced me to take you from that place. One feels, I am reluctant to admit, that boys in reformatory are acceptable research fodder. I convinced myself that you must have been a tough little criminal to be in there at all. You seemed to be coping so well . . . It was only today that I realised what was happening to you. I thought: if *I* won't help him, I who share his plight, then who will? I brought you out because you were denying your true nature; not because you were suffering. I ought to have brought you out before. I took you out, in fact, because of what you *are*, because *we* must help each other, we who are bound by what we have in common."

"I don't care why you did it," I said frankly. "Will you get into trouble?"

"I could do; I don't know. But don't worry; I'm not sorry – there are many areas for a doctor to find work and I have no objection to going abroad. I have no fears about the future."

"Will they look for me? Will they fetch the police in?"

"No, I don't think they will," said Dr Grey. "I don't know if you realised this, but you were taken in there illegally. I didn't realise it myself at first. I thought that like all the other boys you had been up before the magistrate and given a sentence. In fact you were incarcerated at the wish of your uncle, who is a friend of Mr Sheldon's. If your escape is publicised, this fact must come out, and many other facts too which would result in just the kind of family scandal your relations would wish to avoid. I think they'll be happy to let the matter drop. Just keep well away from both the reformatory and your uncle's house. Vanish. They'll probably be relieved to have you off their hands."

Miss Agatha Grey was a distributor of second hand clothes for deprived children, and she had in her basement any number of garments to fit a slim boy, five foot eight inches high. Airing on a fireguard even as I bathed were a shirt, trousers, jacket and drawers. (I didn't take the drawers. I mean, bleedin' hell, they were somebody's cast-offs!) Dr Grey brought these clothes up to me where I waited, clad demurely in the towel.

"Oy, mister," I said, "can I have a mirror and a comb?"

He brought me both and left me to my own devices. I put the clothes on carefully. One day, *one* day, I promised, I'd buy something brand new in a style I liked.

Then I tried to do my hair. Oh! The pain! My scalp came half off and I broke six teeth off the comb and lost them in the tangles and knots.

I peered at my reflection in the dim light.

I was shocked at the black hollows under my eyes; I hadn't realised. I ran my tongue over my teeth. Now I was among people, I rather thought my breath didn't smell very good. I felt like an outcast, nervous, unused to civilisation.

I persevered with my hair and with considerable anguish I achieved success. Shoulder length, it hung in familiar smoothness around my face. I fiddled with curls at my temples, and I made a kiss at myself, impressed at how lovely my lips were.

I made my way downstairs and found my benefactors sitting in the kitchen, which was very cosy with a fire in the range. They made enthusiastic remarks about how well my clothes fitted, and Miss Agatha asked me if I was hungry.

"Yes, I think I am, please," I said, palpitating with excitement.

"I'm afraid it's only a heated up stew," she remarked.

"It smells beautiful," I groaned.

She smiled tolerantly and dished out a great plateful of this wondrous broth. I had three helpings; no one seemed to mind. Then I had four cups of tea and two slices of seed cake and a large apple. Dr Grey's sister suddenly took hold of my nearest hand, looked at it and tut-tutted, vexed. She told me I was to have some ointment on my blisters. I found myself blushing. I suddenly realised that anyone seeing my hands would know I'd had to pick oakum and what that implied. She doused my hands in transparent cream. I thanked her politely and with some embarrassment, hoping that Dr Grey hadn't told her what I'd been in for.

"I'm going to insist, Willie," said Dr Grey, "that you stay here for a few days while you recover. There is a little bedroom you can use, and I want you to get several good nights' sleep and to eat some nourishing food to build you up. You are in no condition to wander out into the streets as you are. I could not answer for the consequences."

He must have been right, because I hadn't the strength or will to argue, and I went meekly to bed as directed.

I stayed at Miss Agatha Grey's house for about a week. I didn't go out and I slept a lot. It was a dazed unreal time, but I needed it and I felt it doing me good. All the same, I was uneasy there. Although they assured me I was safe I felt too vulnerable – I was constantly expecting to be discovered and dragged back to the reformatory. I had to get away.

And then one evening an incident occurred which forced the issue. I was coming downstairs for dinner when I heard voices in the hall below. I looked over the bannisters, then froze back against the wall, my heart pounding violently. Dr Grey was below and Dr Jameson was with him. They were arguing.

"Really . . . "cried Dr Grey, much agitated. "It is intolerable that you should pursue me here and pester me with your accusations."

Dr Jameson's loud carrying voice rang out:

"I know the boy must be here! Or if not, you know where he is."

"I do not! He is not here. How many times must I – ?"

"It may suit Mr Sheldon to believe your story of the boy running off into the streets. But I feel so bitter. We were proceeding so well with the research – a few days more – we shall be most unlikely ever to get such a chance again. Of course I regret troubling Miss Grey. It is all most unfortunate. Are you sure he is not here?"

"I repeat," quivered Dr Grey, "he is not here."

There was an odd little silence. And then Dr Jameson lowered his voice and said in a vibrant and meaningful tone:

"Do I need to point out to you what it could do to your own reputation if it was discovered that you were hiding That Particular Boy?"

My knees buckled and I crouched down in a heap, hugging myself small. I heard the sounds of Dr Jameson leaving, of the door closing behind him. In a little while Miss Grey called me down to eat. I descended and we sat down to our meal. None of us ate much. Dr Grey was as white as a sheet; Miss Agatha was exceptionally brisk.

When dinner was over I stood up.

"I'm leaving," I said quickly. "I've been enough bother. It's time I was on my way."

"But you must stay," Miss Agatha protested. "Or at least wait until the morning."

"No thank you, ma'am. I'll be off. It's best really, ain't it, sir?"

"Have you got anywhere to go?" asked Dr Grey.

"Yes, sir; friends." I lied.

"Where do they live?"

"Best you don't know, sir, ain't it? Best I just clear out."

Dr Grey and his sister murmured to each other, about what was best and whether I'd be all right, and would I let them know how I got on. I assured them I'd be fine. I thanked Miss Grey for the food and clothes and for the kindness and shelter, and I had a warm by the fire to set me up. Dr Grey gave me five shillings. He saw me to the door.

"You're sure you have somewhere to go?"

"Yes, sir, honest."

"Goodbye then, Willie."

I suddenly reached up and kissed him on the cheek. The only time I ever said this and meant it, what I used to say in the old days, when I sold matches. I said: "God bless yer, mister."

Then I quickly turned away and ran off down the street.

PART FOUR

CHAPTER ELEVEN

I

A SENSE of freedom and elation I did not have; no, I was much too close to the pit to be able to smell clear air.

It was night time and the streets were quiet. These tall houses presented an impassive front, blinds drawn, doors bolted up. It was lightly raining, and chill. I headed what we used to call "up west".

For the first time in my life I was finding out that streets and houses, inert brickwork and cobblestones, could assume a character projected upon them by the state of mind you brought with you. This had never happened to me before, and it was startling. Oh, I'd been nervous of drunks, and concerned when Harry and I passed dark alleys, but not this shapeless fear I carried in my own head.

This was the first time I'd been on the streets on my own for four years, and I'd been weaned off them, softened up, made to fear them. I ran, scared by my own panic, fetching up against dead ends, retracing my steps, expecting pursuit at every corner. I passed the lamp of a public house, loud laughter wafting through its open doorway. Eventually I broke through into a little square of posh houses, and further down the street I saw a hansom parked. With a touching trust in the credibility of hansoms, I asked the driver: "Oy, mister, which way's Regent Street?"

Following his directions I found myself at the Marble Arch, and then I knew where I was. I went along Oxford Street, turned down Regent Street and started looking for the address Caroline had told me, Mr Alfred Sadler's house where gentlemen came for pleasure.

The glittering cafes and theatres had long since erupted their brilliant company, and it was quiet even in this most lively of places. Hansoms glided by from time to time, and here and there girls waited in doorways. It was raining hard now. In the light of the gaslamps the rain was like a swarm of golden dancing gnats.

I squinted through the rain, looking for the place I wanted. And now here it was. Squares of dim light chequered the blackness, a street of tall dark houses, rooms to let, and seedy hotels. Many doors were open, cascading beams of light through the rain. Luckily for me, two lads whom I was soon to know as Bobs and Sam were leaning in a doorway. Bobs was heavily made up and wearing a pink ruffled shirt. This had to be the place.

I walked up the steps, causing appraising stares from the boys.

"I have to see Mr Sadler. Is this where he lives?"

"Who wants to know?" demanded Sam aggressively.

"I do. Are you going to fetch him?"

"I might," he said, not moving.

"Soon?" I said, rain dripping off my eyelashes.

"He could see Miss Trixie," said Bobs. "I'll take him up."

Sam shrugged and stood back; Bobs gave a very graceful flounce and said "Follow me."

I went, dripping raindrops, into a hall that smelt of cigars and perfume. There was a little lobby with a curved desk, like in a hotel, and dark doors further down, but we went upstairs to the first floor, and Bobs tapped on a door and said as he opened it: "Miss Trixie? Is it all right if we come in?"

We entered. It was a large dark warm room, heavy curtains drawn, a fire burning in the grate, and lush ornate furnishings. At that first impression I took in screens of tapestry with curly leaves and lilies cavorting all over them, a bed with purple hangings trailing down like parted hair, a tigerskin rug complete with the tiger's head and its teeth, a vase of frothy plumes, a dressing table and mirror, stacked with scent bottles and jars and powder puffs; and strewn about the room some billowing petticoats and several pairs of high heeled shoes.

At a curiously masculine desk sat Miss Trixie.

Well, just for a moment I really thought she was a woman. She was wearing a rose-coloured dress with a little hedge of lace like blossom in May about the neck. She had rouged cheeks and a beauty spot and a painted butterfly of a mouth. Before her on the desk was a ledger in which she was making entries, and there was a slim glass of wine beside it. She usually wore a wig of incredible splendour but wigs pinched; when she was in private she took it off and her own short grey hair was revealed. She was in fact a man of about forty-five. She was the Power Behind the Throne.

"Yes?" she said testily, looking at us. "I hope it's important, Bobsy. I am trying to work."

"Someone to see Alfie."

"Willie Smith," I said eagerly. "And I'm fairly desperate."

"You're fairly *soaking*," she remarked. "Suppose you take off your jacket and dry yourself – and *don't* drip on that petticoat."

"I need a place to stay," I said over my shoulder, stepping over the petticoat. "I got five shillings on me for starters but if I can stay longer I'm a good worker and I do anything."

Bobsy giggled. Miss Trixie raised her pencilled eyebrows and stood up, and glided over to me. I warmed my hands, my trouser legs steaming from the heat. She took hold of my hands and sharply turned them over; the blisters showed. "Are you on the run?" she demanded.

"No."

"The police aren't after you?"

"I was only in a reformatory; nothing serious."

"What were you in for?"

"Breakin' winders."

"How old are you?"

"Sixteen. Seventeen if you like."

"And what about your family?"

"I got no family."

"H'm," she remarked. "A bit like an answer to prayer, aren't you, Willie Smith? Dropping in on us out of the blue, all eyes and promises! Is your hair colour natural?"

"Yes, ma'am! . . . sir?"

"Miss Trixie," she told me, without a flicker. "And who told you about Mr Sadler's establishment?"

"Caroline."

"Caroline? Do we know a Caroline?"

"I know her," Bobsy said. "She's just a tart."

"And you've nowhere to go, Willie Smith?"

"No, Miss Trixie, and it's very late and very wet."

"Don't flutter your lashes at me, you sauce pot. So, you're a little Orphan of the Storm, are you? Bobsy, go and fetch Mr Sadler. I believe he's being awfully masculine down at the card table."

Bobsy ponced off, smirking.

"You're a very pretty lad," Miss Trixie told me. "And there's nothing we older girls like better than a slim youth. Is your name *really* Willie? Amazing! So awfully appropriate for a male tart. As long as you have the goods to match!"

I fidgetted at this teasing. My future was too uncertain for me to be able to respond. "Will I be able to stay?"

"We'll ask Mr Sadler, shall we?"

"Will he say yes?"

"Of course he will, dear, unless you've got the clap."

She pinched my cheek fondly and flounced over to the dressing table, where she sat and fixed her make-up.

I grew to take Miss Trixie so much at her own face value that it's hard to think of her as in any way unusual. Yet there she was, her patently male head emerging from the lace of her collar, her short cropped grey hair and thick neck so obviously masculine, and a flowing dress billowing out from her hips. She applied her lipstick, powdered her face, and then, for my benefit, she put on her wig. Curly ash blonde ringlets brushed her cheeks. She looked gorgeous, like a big blowsy madame, younger and maternal. I've been out with her when she wore male clothes. As a man she was extremely stylish, the baby contours of her face the more apparent. No one ever called her "he" or "him". Indoors she always wore women's clothes, even first thing in the morning.

Mr Alfred Sadler came in, a much younger man than I was expecting. He was in fact rather handsome. He had a square alert face, fringed with little black curls. His features were attractive and his eyes were the hardest I've ever seen. Or maybe it seemed so because his cheeks were so bland and dimpled, his smile so disarming. He was a great gambler, and nights when the lads and I were entertaining gents, he'd usually be downstairs at the card tables. He looked me up and down. "I hope you aren't wasting my time," he said.

"No I ain't," I said sturdily. "I'm looking for work, your kind.

I need a place for tonight, and if you want me longer we can fix up something; I'm easy. And my name's Willie Smith."

He then shook my hand. "First and foremost, Willie Smith," he said, "I'm a businessman. That's what this is, here, a business. I make money, and I got standards. Sit down, will yer? Trixie, have you poured him a drink?"

"Oh dear! No! How awfully unfestive of me," murmured Trixie, bustling around and pouring out three sherries. "Be off with you, Bobsy, you nosey parker. You'll see Willie soon enough."

I sat sipping sweet sherry, close to the fire.

Alfie quizzed me closely about my immediate past.

"And what made you come here?" he said finally.

"Caroline told me about it."

"Yes, but, even so. What's in it for you?"

"I been a boy lover since I was little. I came lookin' for me own kind."

"You mean you *like* it? It comes naturally to you?"

"Yes, that's it."

"You do realise the kind of things that would be expected of you?"

"I ain't totally naive, no."

We had a little chat about Madame Rosa's.

"Willie sounds almost too good to be true," laughed Miss Trixie. "Almost *eager!* And with those looks! Wouldn't you say the old city oyster had thrown up a pearl?"

"Maybe. It doesn't do to get over excited," remarked Alfie drily. "Well. You can stay here tonight, and in the morning we'll get serious and talk business."

"Thanks, mister," I said.

Bobsy helped me to bed, a soft fat mattress on the floor in a room at the top of the house. I was asleep before he'd gone out of the room.

II

IT WAS the smell of coffee that woke me up, and I lay for a moment just taking that in. Having woken so recently to the sound of barking warders, I knew this present time was too important to let go by without paying it the compliment of awe and almost holy regard. I lay on my back, eyes shut, and just breathed.

"Come on," said Bobs, "I know you're awake."

I rolled on to my elbow and looked at him, savouring this miracle with very alive senses. "You've brought me coffee!" I said.

"Yeah, and more. Look."

"Breakfast – in bed!" I gawped.

He arranged himself easily beside me, sitting on the floor by my mattress. Now I was starting to observe things I saw that I'd spent the night in a communal bedroom, an eaved room with sloping ceilings, the pointed window barely above the floor. There were a couple of narrow beds and various mattresses, but all in such a jumble the effect was like strewn clothes, a mass of rumpled blankets and careless confusion. Daylight filled the room.

"What time is it?" I asked, in the time-honoured tradition of sleepers awakening.

"Afternoon."

"Bleedin' hell! Don't anybody mind?" I said, alarmed.

"Mornings don't *happen* here!" laughed Bobs. "Mornings is when we sleep. Having breakfast at half past two is normal. Mind, I shan't always bring it you! So you enjoy it while you can."

"Not arf I will," I muttered appreciatively, tucking into toasted bread and honey.

Bobs was awful sweet. He wasn't exactly skinny but he looked as if he was. He looked like a waif, or a pixie, with his pointed chin and sad and graceful face. He had thick pouting lips, a long turned up nose and sleepy heavy-lidded eyes. His hair was right short, and cut across the fringe like as if someone had cut it drunk. His face was spotted with moles which curiously made him more attractive. He was wearing tight white trousers and a Chinese smock in lovely shiny gold, with a dragon embroidered on the back. I praised it, and he said he liked Chinese things. He said he knew a Chinaman, *and* he'd been in an opium den and smoked opium. He said it was beautiful, like flying, but Mr Sadler wouldn't tolerate opium smoking and had strong views about it. Bobs had come from the country originally, real countryside with fields and cows; and he'd come in with his dad to bring veg to Covent Garden. He'd carried cauliflowers and humped sacks of potatoes which was heavy work, so he used to skive off. One day a man picked him up and took him down the docks, where he first took opium. He done some funny old things before he fetched up at Alfie's. I liked him best of all the lads there. I told Bobsy about my odd education.

"First common, and then elevated. And now I ain't one thing or the other; I don't belong nowhere. I'm in what they used to call Limbo, waiting to see if the next thing is Heaven, or somewhere else."

"That's awful, Willie."

"Nah . . . I'll find me feet; it'll just take a bit. Trouble is, see, I feel sort of peculiar at the moment. I just come aht the institution; it's left me a bit odd. I feel like I been done over, in my head. I don't feel sure of myself; I need time to pass."

Bobsy thought. "But when you start feeling all right again, won't you wish you hadn't spent time *here?* Wouldn't you be better working as, say, a porter or a roadsweeper? What if, when you feel better, it's too late and you're sort of – tarnished? Someone told me I was that."

"No, I won't be sorry," I said. "Here is just what I want."

Later that day I let Miss Trixie lead me away to her room where she opened a linen chest and said I could choose anything I wanted out of there to wear. Oh! It was like a pirate's hoard! And just the sort of gaudy flashy things I loved. I knelt down with cries of delight. I came up with a pair of cream coloured theatrical tights and a long purple shirt with a black silk scarf tied about my waist. Miss Trixie clapped her hands and said I looked like somebody's page.

"Those wicked old knights of old!" she cried. "They all took their pages along with them. And why? Not to hold their horses' bridles, that's for sure! All those fat little arses in those fleshy skin-hugging hose. They were no fools, those glamorous old crusaders. Do you fancy some make-up?"

"I wouldn't mind."

As I sat by the fire and Miss Trixie handed me crimson sherry in a pink-tinted glass, I felt I was a fantasy creation – a slim exotic painted youth, long-haired and half effeminate, something out of myth or mediaeval legend. I could be handing a cup of

poison to a lady or a love potion to a prince. Golden ornate
pillars might surround me and beyond, a low green grove. With
my huge slanted eyes and hollow cheeks I looked like a dark
duke's catamite at some lost Renaissance court.

I saw all this in a rosewood hand mirror; I liked what I
saw. I'll tell you something, they looked after me at that place.
Whatever happened, and whether or not it was all dreadfully
immoral and exploitative, they saw to it I was well fed and warm
and clean. When I left, in early summer, I didn't have a louse
on my body. Miss Trixie taught me what to use on my hair to
bring out its highlights; she educated me in perfumes and medi-
cines, and she softened and whitened my hands with ointments
and creams. They dosed me up with oranges and apples and
made sure we all got enough sleep; they looked after their own.

III

THE HOUSE was four storeys high. The top was little more than
an attic, and here we slept. The floor below had the rooms where
we took our clients. There was a sombre and elegant one, with
oil paintings by minor artists on the walls – vases of flowers,
winsome sheepdogs, the Thames by night – and a large dark
bed. You took the diffident type in there, the one who was
embarrassed at needing you. Then there was a room which we
were assured was modelled on the French. It had red wallpaper
and a red chaise longue, as well as a bed with satin drapes.
Every wall had a mirror embossed with gilt and above two fat
cherubs plunged downwards holding streaming golden torches.
One room was heavily pannelled in the fashion of the mediaeval
resurgence. The bed had four posts with dragons' heads on the
ends, tongues sticking out. Of course, it was extremely modern
really, but in candlelight it was helpful to spark off a sort of
otherworldiness and romance. There were also some smaller
bedrooms, more functional.

On the first floor of the house was the bathroom and the large
rooms of Trixie and Alfie. There were also two rooms leading
off which contained certain bizarre objects. One of them was
stacked full of cumbersome chains and manacles, leather straps

and collars, birch rods and canes. You could only open the door with a special key.

On the ground floor, by contrast, everything was incredibly discreet. There were two large tasteful rooms, with hunting prints on the walls and an old coach horn and reproduction pistols. There were gentlemen's armchairs and low tables. Drinking went on here, cigar smoking; and there were newspapers in wooden frames. Certain famous people came regularly to sit in those deep leather wing chairs and meet kindred spirits. Sometimes us boys would be sent for, and gents would buy us drinks and just talk to us, either not wanting or not daring to go any further, but seeming to derive pleasure from mixing with us lower classes and hearing how we spoke. I mean, they were real gemmun, quality, with gold cufflinks and collar studs, and speaking most elegant.

At the back of the house was the kitchen; some women came in to do laundry and cooking, great brawny types who looked as if they could pick you up under one arm and throw you. There was a breakfast room attached, a lovely friendly room with a huge rough wood table, and we mostly ate there. We could fix our own meals too, if we wanted, potter round the kitchen and do ourselves omelettes and make tea and coffee and chocolate. And if we fancied, we could have our meals out at the little eating place across the road. In our street during the day almost everybody walking about was a prostitute coming up for air, and I'll tell you, the girls looked worse in daylight than we did. At twelve noon these gorgeous creatures of the night didn't half look pale and pinched – bags under the eyes, no make-up and awful crabby natured. We got to know some of them quite well, eating at the same place.

In those early days at Alfie's I didn't think much. My mind floated easy, like a boat moored at the wharf, touched by swell and flow but tied and not drifting, nor under any kind of steam. It wasn't unpleasant.

That first night, Alfie asked to see me and received me in his room. He poured us both a glass of white wine and he teased me about the violets twined in my hair.

"I see Trixie's been at you. She is a one for floral display. She'll have you standing in a vase if you aren't careful, with one leg stuck out behind you and an orchid in your – ear," was what he said, but I think he nearly said something else. We drank our wine.

Suddenly he said: "Right, Willie, I'm a client of yours. It's my first visit and I'm a bit shy. Show me what you can do."

Quickly I controlled my initial self-consciousness. "Have you come for – everything?" I asked.

"No; I'd just like to be treated a bit special, and you might favour me with a suck." He added: "I shall only ask you this the once. It's business, that's all, dear. I need to see you on the job."

"Well, I'll see what I can do then."

Alfie was a good-looking man, though he didn't set me alight personally. It was no hardship to do as he asked. When I'd finished, Alfie took a few deep breaths of recovery, tidied himself up and poured us both another glass of wine.

I stayed kneeling and smeared. As I held the long stemmed glass with its dancing contents, the shapes at the base of the stem were reflected on my hand, a stained glass window shape, like four leaves coming out from one centre.

"Well, I'll tell you, Willie," said Alfie, "you got class, and a sensitive touch. I've got any number of gents on my books to whom you would be a dream come true. What it is exactly it's hard to say. You ain't as skilful as Perce or as confident as Noll. But you're very, very nice. You make it seem as though you cared . . ."

He studied me with a half baffled look. "And now I'll tell you something I shouldn't: I'm half tempted to tell you to go away. Yes, I'm a fool to myself saying it, and I'll only say it once: are you sure you're doing right? See, there's something about how you do it. Like as if you was *hungry*. As if you was searching, with your mouth, for – well, I don't know, do I?

"Look here, Willie," he snapped. "It's no use looking for love *here*. Are you stupid? No knight in shining armour is going to come through these doors and carry you away. Just a lot of mostly middle-aged gentlemen, and some not only ugly but very dull. Maybe I'm wrong about you – am I? It's your bleedin' *looks*. You're something special. You look like a painting, one o' them high-class mediaeval jobs. Even if you never did a bleedin' thing, a gent'd pay just to see you walking abaht naked."

"Do you want me to stay?" I asked.

"I do! But I don't want you to have no illusions, that's all. Yeah, I want you here all right. You'd be every kind of asset."

"Then I'd like to stay. It would suit me very well."

IV

I HAVE thought a lot about the element of detachment in connection with the life I led. I rarely achieved it. They made a great issue of it at Alfie's, that you kept yourself back, did the job in question, and went on to the next. Sam was the obvious example. He made no secret of the fact that he was working here to make money in order to get married, and that he felt nothing while he serviced his gentlemen. The others agreed with him to a greater or lesser degree.

It seemed I was the only one who genuinely loved men. And I wouldn't shy away from using that word either – love. Almost without exception I found that, every time, there was a moment – be it only the blink of an eye – where love was. And I'd maintain that it showed and was appreciated, and that was why they took to me. I had some basic affection for my gents, an awful sympathy for the life they led, the perpetual deceit.

I have heard it described as the sensation of being buried alive and suffocating, and yet expected to go about in pleasurable delight amongst the feast of life. If their true state had been known, society would have rejected them, and of course they risked prison if they were flagrant. But even *suspicion* could lead to loss of status, acquaintances and reputation. In extreme cases men committed suicide, either through threat of discovery or because the pain of secrecy and guilt was too much to bear. Very few of our gents were proud of their tendency, at best they were resigned. Most admitted that the strain affected their health and made them nervous and ill.

I should make it clear that in those days, the early 1880s before that Law was passed, it was a very much freer and easier world for male tarts. Certainly we had police raids and hassle from various quarters, but nothing like what happened after they passed the Blackmailers' Charter. It was tough on streetwalking lads after that and I believe they finally closed down Alfie's place. But back then things were more lax, as long as you weren't stupid. Live and let live it was.

The situation of our brothel was a good one for our gents, situated as it was amongst all the ladies' houses. It meant that our clients could pretend they were in this area for girls. Isn't it funny? If they were assumed to be going with ladies, their mates chuckled and wished them joy. If it was known they were after boys – recoil, disgust, ostracization. But screwing young girls was all right. A man's got needs, hasn't he, and that's what tarts are for! Besides, it saves him needing to bother his wife with nasty propositions, and ensures the sanctity of the marriage bed.

Miss Trixie was intrigued by what Alfie had told her, that he had the impression I was secretly searching for Love.

"H'm," she chuckled. "You're hardly likely to find the strong man of your dreams here!"

"I can't find him at all yet," I said, "because I haven't properly found *me*. And I wouldn't offer him anything so muddled as I am now."

"Silly boy," she said fondly. "That won't worry your real man. He'll look after you the more, in proportion to your needs."

"Oh," I sighed longingly. "That sounds nice."

"Indeed it does," said Miss Trixie almost wistfully. "It's a search I've been engaged upon all my life."

"Have you?" I asked interested.

"In vain! If they're big and beautiful they're about as sensitive as a navvy. If they're rich and delicate they're weak as water and likely to crumple up like a daisy. Ah, but it's cruel of me to shatter your dreams. You go on searching. You may be luckier than I."

"They do exist," I said earnestly. "I had a brother, Charley. He was like what I want. He looked after me. I want someone like that."

"It's strength you admire then, is it?"

"Yeah, that's it."

"Do you know, dearie," said Miss Trixie intimately, "between ourselves it would give me the greatest pleasure in the world to be the one who brought you your knight in armour, and see him carry you off to a life of bliss. I might even start believing in Love! Now look at me, getting sentimental in my old age. I'm afraid real life is very unwilling to live up to the world of Fantasy and, believe me, I should know!"

CHAPTER TWELVE

I

I NEVER had anything to do with the upper classes until I became a tart.

Suddenly I had glimpses into aery regions previously as inaccessible to me as Heaven. We never asked our clients' names, of course, but sometimes afterwards Sam, for instance, might say: "You know who that was? You know who you had tonight?" and he'd mention the name of a politician or a lord or a marquis or a famous explorer or a foreign diplomat. But none of us were ever sure — it was just rumour.

There were high-class gents who came in full of bravado and who particularly enjoyed bawdy talk and jokes and the conversation of the lower classes. These usually went with Leo and Sam who could pass for stable grooms and played up to the part. I was usually given the shy or cultured ones because, said Alfie, I had "nice ways".

One of the first things I learnt was that my gents needed, as much as anything, to talk. I don't mean they forsook bodily pleasure, oh no, but afterwards they talked. I had one gentleman, about fifty years old, who regularly reminisced in my arms about the war in the Crimea.

I had another gent who was tormented with guilt about deceiving his wife. He'd take his pleasure like it was brimstone and treacle. Sometimes afterwards he'd sit in the chair and weep, with his head in his hands. I'd sit on the chair arm and comfort him, and he'd hold my hand and snivel. A grown man, crying like that. And, dressed, he was someone important who gave orders and snapped his fingers for a carriage.

"I love her very dearly," he wept to me, picking at the hairs on my thigh. "She is everything to me. But I have this demon . . . time and again I fight him down . . . she wouldn't understand . . . my weakness, my cupidity. I am faithful to her, I am! This is an aberration, not my true self. I never betray her in my mind . . .

the torment is unbearable. Oh, what can you understand of all this? How can I make it clear?"

"I do understand," I said. To show him I did, I quoted soulfully:

> "Your honour rooted in dishonour stood
> And faith unfaithful kept you falsely true."

He looked at me wide eyed. If geraniums had dropped out of my mouth instead of words, he couldn't have looked more surprised. "How do you know that?" he demanded, incredulous.

"I know the *Idylls* almost off by heart," I boasted.

"But Tennyson . . . " he murmured. "*Here . . . *"

Several of my gents were travellers to exotic lands. Either in the army or on geographical expeditions they had been to India and Africa. One had skin that was all yellow and his fingers shook from recurrent malaria. Another had been in the Sudan for years. He said that there were deserts of red sand where wild tribes lived, and they were taken as slaves for the harems of sultans in Turkey. These sultans owned pleasure boys whom they dressed in silk.

The mysteries of the East were particularly revealed to me by a gentleman we knew as Mr Scott. I knew he wasn't a mister at all, because when he told me what to call him, the way he said "mister" in a gleeful savouring sort of way implied that he was toying with an unfamiliar title. Sam assured me he was a marquis and his brother sat in the House of Lords. Well, Mr Scott told me that in India and Persia there was a whole philosophy on the subject of how to please a lover and that a body was a world of erotic possibilities, not for using but for *pleasing*. There were things you could learn, about which parts are most susceptible to pleasure, and there were special things you could do to give the most sensation. It was an Erotic Science, devoted to the Art of Love.

Mr Scott had in his possession a book. It had been published privately and only circulated among a select few, of which he was one. It was translated from the Sanskrit in Seven Parts. He brought this book with him and read sections out loud, and I followed his directions.

Fortunately for me, Mr Scott was a very attractive fellow. Not of course my dream ideal, but delightful enough for me to take an earnest and conscientious attitude to exploring the intricacies of Kama. Yes! I must have been the first boy in England to know that word! Mr Scott was thirty-eight years old, lean and upright, slender and wiry, slim and muscular. He improved his biceps by lifting weights. Very many of my gents went to private gymnasiums to build their bodies thus. Mr Scott had a pleasant face with brown eyes and a sallow skin, and brown hair in no way thinning but turning slightly grey. If he noticed a grey hair he'd pull it out immediately. He was meticulously neat and had beautiful hands.

In order to keep our liaison exotic and sensuous he gave me a present of a Persian poem called *The Rubayyat*. This book had been published in the fifties, and at first had been a great flop, copies sold off at one penny. Indeed I half remembered having seen some on the bookstalls. But then it had been Discovered by poets and artists, and now everyone who fancied himself as a connoisseur of that sort of thing possessed a copy. Mr Scott made me learn verses to his direction, which I'd recite to him in artistic naked poses. Once he bought me an orchid and twined it in my crotch hair, and got me to lie stretched out on my back, one knee raised, while he leaned over me, absorbed, and listened to my recital.

When I grew to know the poem well, it concerned me some-what that old Khayyam did not believe in an After Life and saw no direction to this Sorry Scheme of Things. I tentatively asked Mr Scott if he agreed, and where did God stand in relation to this Living for the Moment.

"God?" he said scornfully. "Does any thinking man still believe in God, since Darwin?"

"I thought they did."

"They go through the motions, that's all. It takes a brave man to deny God publicly, this being a hypocritical age. It's easier to conform, be seen going to church and giving money to the charities. But who really believes, now, that a Being directs it all, and metes out rewards to the good in the After Life?"

"*Isn't* there God then?" I demanded aggressively.

"How do I know?" he shrugged petulantly.

"Well, people should know," I said angrily.

"What's it to you, lotus flower?" he teased. "What's so personal to you? Forget it – no one can know."

"Tell me what you think," I insisted.

"Me? Well, maybe there's something out there, who can say? But it isn't the God of the Bible, that vindictive old man who sent the flood. Now that we know that species evolved, we have to discard the fripperies of Noah's ark and the Garden of Eden. It all really started with fish!"

As I looked so blank, he kindly explained to me all about Mr Darwin's theories and I was grateful for his time. It left me very stirred up. No God? To be honest I didn't sleep all night, up there in my attic bed; the idea scared me silly. At first I thought even the Grim God, the one who hated sodomites, was preferable to No God. At least he was there, keeping an eye on us, even if it was a stern one. And there was always the chance he might relent, on the Day of Judgement, when he saw you were just ordinary though inverted. But – no God? Just a Nothing, a big black space, and no Heaven, no After Life – just the Now, with all its miseries and injustices and death?

Miss Trixie pointed out to me that a refined gents' whorehouse was not the appropriate place for a discussion on the existence of God, was it? Of course there's a God, she told me, and he loves all his little children, even his naughty ones!

Not very surprisingly, I could not sort out from the limited facts at my disposal whether God existed. I mulled over it constantly. I felt a monstrous sense of indignation and fury, about Mr Sheldon making me learn those verses, reducing me to tears – it was unforgiveable. It was bad enough what he did to me if there *was* a God – but if there *wasn't* – my blood boiled with rage when I considered it. So I had the same chance as anybody else, then, did I, of going to Heaven? And if none of us would go to Heaven – ho! what a shock for my uncle! Just to die! No eternal reward! I gloated fiendishly. He'd be just the same as us, an ordinary mortal. Wonderful! Oh – but not so wonderful. If we didn't have God we had such loss. We had to lose the good bits as well as the bad.

I didn't want there to be Nothing.

I thought about Mr Pearson, who'd given that impassioned talk in our church. I'd thought he was like Jesus and my uncle had caned me for saying so. Mr Pearson believed in God. He did good works in God's name. He made you want to help the poor. You *felt* God, listening to Mr Pearson.

If Mr Pearson thought there was a God, well, there probably was. I trusted him.

Easier to pontificate upon was Kama. You knew where you were with that. The enjoyment of objects through the senses, bound up together with the mind and the soul, and the awareness of the resulting pleasure.

And that was what I concentrated upon while I was at Alfie's.

II

SOON AFTER that, my mind was quite diverted from the subject when Alfie said he'd got an Intriguing Evening lined up for me. It certainly turned out so.

"It's right up your alley," said Alfie. "What you might call Romantic."

"Yes?" I said warily. "I suppose you've found me somebody who likes me to read Keats to him with the other hand."

"I don't know about that; this is more like Cinderella or something."

"What the hell do you mean, Alfie?"

Alfie poured me out a glass of wine and so I knew something complicated was on its way. I sat and sipped.

"I got a gentleman coming tonight who's so cautious about being here that he wants all kinds of precautions taken," said Alfie. "He's arriving about midnight. No one's to see him; I got to escort him in very private, and he's most particular about what he wants when he gets here. The type he described, well, it has to be you. He don't want just a lump of meat and muscle. He wants . . . well, it'd only go to your head if I told you how I described you. Only thing is, we got a little problem . . . "

"He wants to bring his horse as well?" I enquired flippantly.

"No; he wants you tied up."

"You know how I feel about that . . . " I began. "I'm not happy doing Perversions."

"I know you're not. I wouldn't ask you to. But this is something quite different. And Bobs'll be there to untie you, straight after. You wouldn't be left, word of honour."

"Why does he want me tied?"

"He's petrified of being seen. This ain't so strange; you know that. They're all very cagey, ain't they? Only this one's worse. He wants you laid out ready, and you're to have a blindfold."

"Anything else I should know?" I said sarcastically.

"And on your best behaviour."

"Why the secrecy and all?" I said. "Hey, Alfie, it ain't Mr Gladstone?"

"I wouldn't tell you if it was, now, would I?" said Alfie. "But just so you don't get ideas above your station, no it ain't. He just wants to preserve his identity against the likes of nosey little buggers like you. If you ask me, he's having a Crise de Conscience."

"He don't want ter wallop me, does he?" I said dubiously.

"Nah! He wants a Night of Love. You're going to be the Boy of his Dreams. So beautiful he'll come back again and again. He thinks he's only visiting us the once. He thinks it's to be a Once in a Lifetime experience, burned on to his memory for ever. One Perfect Night. But if we play our cards right, he'll be back. And this is why I particularly wanted *you* . . . "

Alfie leaned back and blew a cloud of cigar smoke upward. "I thought we'd spread a black velvet coverlet on the bed," he said savouringly, "and you would be tied by slim chains, face down, and blindfolded with black velvet. Your long burnished hair spread out, your slender graceful back with that little dip just above your bum, and the jewel of it all, your radiant arse itself, two perfect swelling globes . . . "

"Of alabaster?" I suggested, impressed and amused.

"That's right, of alabaster!" Alfie agreed. "An artist's dream – a lover's fantasy. He'll never forget you!"

"I *would* look nice against black velvet," I mused seriously.

"He looks to me like the sort of gent who appreciates quality," said Alfie.

"Is he a lord?"

"How do I know?" said Alfie, clamming up again.

"Alfie, he ain't a *monster?*" I said in alarm. "He's not a Beast In Human Form?"

"Would I offer one of my little lambs to a beast?"

"I dunno, Alfie, would yer?"

"Don't you *trust* me, Willie?"

"Couplar inches, no more."

"Well, he ain't a monster. So – will yer do it?"

"Yeah, I'll do it."

Alfie was right. The strangeness and the sensuous nature of the proposition appealed to my imagination.

The room in which the encounter took place was a small one on the first floor, at the back. The window curtains, of very dark blue, were drawn and there wasn't much other furniture than the bed and the washstand.

Around eleven o'clock I had a long hot bath and lay soaking, watching the interesting shadows from the lamp, billowing and receding on the ceiling. I was clean, I was comfortable, I was healthy, I was beautiful. I held up my hands – my nails had grown. Every nail was long and oval with half moons showing white. My oakum blisters were all healed and gone. I had been at Alfie's now longer than I had been in that place. Soon I would put months and more months between me and it. I sighed; I think I was content.

In her room Miss Trixie doused me in lavender water and combed my hair till it shone. When I shook my head I could feel the hair all light and silky like a breeze.

"Have you seen him, Trix, this gent of mine?"

"No, I haven't. But I've made up the room a treat. Let's look at you then, popsy – turn to me."

I gave her the benefit of my limpid gaze.

"Am I pretty then, Trix?"

"Yes, love, you're a picture."

She tucked her frilled dressing-gown tightly round her, and patted her hair, and I followed her out of the door and along the landing.

I gasped when I saw the room.

The bed was indeed draped in black velvet, but here and there on the drooping folds were pinned spangled brooches like stars. On each side of the bed, instead of the lamps, there were candelabra, with candles lit. The effect was stangely theatrical, like a set for a fairy tale.

"Do you like it?" asked Miss Trixie, who had been watching my reactions closely.

"Yes . . . it's . . . most effective," I said. "Trix, was you ever on the stage?"

"Funny you should ask," she smirked. "Yes, I was, for a time. My trouble was I liked the women's roles best and always clamoured to play Juliet. Then once I got into those lovely mediaevel dresses I couldn't help playing the fool. 'Else would a maiden blush bepaint my cheek' – can you imagine it? Nobody believed I was a maiden. In the end I was so outrageous I had to go. No company wants the audience in hysterics at the tragic bits, not even a ninth-rate little show like I was in!"

She'd made me laugh. She gestured to the bed. "On you get, fragrant one."

Cautiously I kneeled on the bed and dropped forward, spreading myself slowly. "Ooh!" I wriggled at the sweet touch of the velvet.

"Having a little thrill, ducky?" she beamed. "Let's have your wrists then, shall we, and get you arranged?"

A bit ruefully I extended my arms, and she put my wrists through circles of metal which clipped shut. A slim taut chain threaded each to a bedpost.

I turned my head in sudden panic. "There will be someone in call?" I gasped.

"Alfie – and Bobs'll release you when Alfie tells him."

"You won't leave me here all night?"

"Pull yourself together, ducky, you're being paid for this."

Her sudden harshness restored my equilibrium.

"And now the blindfold," she said briskly.

It was a wide ribbon of black velvet, gathered tight. Effective. I couldn't see a thing. I heard Miss Trixie move out of the room and shut the door behind her.

III

AFTER A while the door opened, and closed. There was a silence. My gent was staring at me. Time hung still, nobody speaking.

Then this low melodious voice said to me from beside the bed:

"Tell me . . . is this in any way against your will?"

"No, mister, it's all right by me," I assured him.

"I will proceed no further if you have any qualms at all."

"Honest, mister, it don't bother me a bit."

I knew I'd feel no end of a fool if he didn't go through with it.

I heard him draw in a long deep breath and give a sort of sigh. Then I could hear the rustle of his clothes as he started to undress.

He didn't speak. Hesitating?

"I been lookin forward to yer," I began conversationally. "It's nice, ain't it, with the candles?"

"Mm, yes, very nice," he said abstractedly.

"The velvet's lovely and soft . . . come and lie on it with me."

He moved over to the bed, and sat. He put one hand on my shoulder and stroked me, wonderingly, like he'd never felt young male flesh.

"Aah," I went softly, to show him it was nice. He stroked my hair, taking it between his fingers, lifting it, baring my neck. It was so gentle. Anyone'd think it was me that was to get the pleasure. But he continued like that, lightly touching me, my arms, my shoulders and down my back, first tentatively and then harder, in firm circles of spreading sensation. I began to moan and stretch. He stopped.

"Don't stop . . . " I murmured, forgetting. "Oh – bleedin' hell," I gasped then. "I'm awful sorry, mister. I didn't mean to tell you what to do."

"It's all right. Did you like it? I'll carry on."

He stroked all over my back – I daresay a full ten minutes passed, just in sheer bliss for me. I was writhing shamelessly now, under his touch. Then I felt his lips on my skin, on the back of my neck, and then down my spine. I was a mass of goose pimples, shuddering with pleasure. And then he lay against me. I felt his nakedness with a shock of excitement. He kissed my neck warmly, and wound his arms around me. He brought his hands down lower – oh I was real hard down there by then, velvet one side of me, him the other. He lay full on me, holding my cock for me, letting me push on his hands. It felt like an awful liberty; I was there for his enjoyment, not he for mine.

"Oh darlin'," I groaned, "please may I – ?"

"Of course – it's what I want."

I just went wild then. I plunged into the velvet, making ecstatic

194

noises. I could see spots and stars and zigzag lines in front of my eyes.

"Oh mister," I gasped. "You was lovely."

He gave me an understanding squeeze, and then he moved over to the table. The bed creaked and dipped as he climbed back on, and he began stroking my arse.

"Have me, mister," I invited. "I'm all yours."

I experienced great pride; I was really aware of the shape of him, this lovely quivering maleness moving inside me. I lifted myself to him, feeling the roughness of his crotch hair on my skin; his arms held me tight. I pressed against him, elated at his closeness. Into my neck I heard him murmur: "Oh . . . you're beautiful . . . beautiful" and I was enclosed in his powerful warmth. I gasped in sympathetic excitement and from my own delight. Our communal sweat ran between us.

"How are you, my dear?" he asked me, in a voice so caring that I could barely reply for the ancient stirrings it roused in me. Stupid, but I could feel a strong affection vibrating from him that reminded me of Charley. It was the way he held me close in his arms, as if he would keep me safe. The disturbing illusion made me half inarticulate. "Thank you . . . lovely . . . very nice, mister . . . yes."

We lay in warm silence and I listened to our hearts beating. I tried to breathe in time to his. I would have liked us to have gone to sleep together then. He moved suddenly, as if he too had been lulled into peacefulness. I felt him go tense, and he unwound his arms and disentangled himself from me.

"Don't go, mister," I cried, frightened suddenly at the prospect of loss.

He stood up.

"Take me blindfold off," I pleaded. "Let me see yer."

But he didn't speak and I heard the unwelcome sounds of his beginning to dress.

"Let me help," I offered desperately. "I always do that. I'll fix yer tie for yer."

But there was just the sound of the rustling of his shirt and him moving about, a little way off. I tried to get my wrists out, but I couldn't.

"Please, mister, will yer come back?"

"I can't come back," he said sombrely. "I shall never come here again."

"Wasn't I any good?" I demanded, pained.

He made a sort of gasp – irritation? reproach? "It isn't that, nothing like that. Don't you see? It's *me*. I should have never – it was very wrong of me. As if one *can* remain impersonal . . . "

"Ah, mister, stay!" I pleaded huskily. "Let me do things for you. Don't leave me; you were so nice."

"Don't!" he snapped.

"There's loads of things I'm good at. I'll do anything you want, for you to hold me again."

"Please stop it," he said, between his teeth. "I shall not return. It was a dreadful mistake. Please forget what happened; put it out of your mind."

"I never can – I'll never forget yer!" I wailed, shaking my chains despairingly.

"Then that must be my burden," he said in a low severe voice.

That was all he said. After that the door opened and closed, and into the silence I croaked: "Come back!"

I thought Bobsy would rush in immediately. I jiggled my chains about impatiently. Nothing happened. "Bobs, where are yer?" I said into the air. "Come *on*. Where are yer?"

I felt an urgent desperate desire to see him, the man who'd just left me. If I could just see his face . . . where he went . . . if Bobs was quick I might just do it . . . I heaved and sighed in exasperation and impatience.

I was deeply stirred and emotional. This stranger had touched some chord in me, picked up some thread. He'd come in out of the night, nameless, faceless, and touched me to the heart. He'd held me and cared for me, just that tiny while, and the damage he'd done to me was irrevocable. Not since Charley, no one had held me in his arms like that . . . All over again I knew what I'd lost. And now he'd gone off, back into the night, promising never to return.

"Bobs!" I screeched.

No one came. Then I got furious. I'd been told I wouldn't be left, word of honour, and here I was unreleased. I pulled and heaved – I would've looked a treat from behind, humping and bucking – and it did me no good at all. I hurt my wrists, and I wrecked the bed. The black velvet ruckled under me and worked loose. Suddenly it slid off one side of the bed and left me on a stiff mattress, and as helpless as ever. I hurt my neck trying to rub the blindfold off. Tears of rage and frustration soaked it. "Alfie! Come here yer bugger!" I yelled. "Get me out!"

I don't suppose it was more than fifteen minutes that I was there, heaving and yowling and crying, but when Bobs finally came to me I was half hysterical. The first I knew of his presence was when the blindfold came off. I twisted a wet flushed face round accusingly. "You little bastard, where've you been?"

"I've only just been told to come this minute," said Bobsy reasonably, patently woken from sleep, his hair tousled, a white dressing-gown around him. "I ain't undoing you till you're quiet; I don't want my head bashed in."

"I'm quiet," I wept. "I won't hit yer; they left me here ages."

All the candles had burnt to stumps, and the room looked bare and ugly, the mystery and magic quite gone. "Hurry, Bobs," I pleaded.

He unlocked me. As soon as I was freed I leapt up, pushed past Bobs, and naked as I was I belted along the landing and down the stairs. I ran like a mad person, right out to the front door. I stood on the steps, looking up and down the street. Cool darkness hit my skin. It came at me along with a sharp dose of realisation. I'd never find him. I was too late.

IV

"WHO WAS he, Alfie?" I begged.

"I don't bleedin' know who he was!" cried Alfie. "And if I did I wouldn't tell you. Let it go, boy, let the matter drop."

"Was he handsome?" I asked tremulously.

Alfie gave me a silly grin. "Have you got yourself involved?" he said. "Has he managed to touch your foolish heart?"

My sulky silence was answer enough.

"I warned you, didn't I?" said Alfie. "I told you to stay detached. I said not to use this place for your fantasies. So put this gent out of your mind. I ain't going to tell you nothing about him." He sniggered. "He could be a bleedin' werewolf as far as you're concerned."

My dreams that night were full of ships, tossing and turning on high seas, my childhood reaction to Charley's going. I always thought of him in a ship, permanently stormbound, far from land. I believe in my heart of hearts I still imagined him travelling, restless like he always was, never reaching harbour. I ached for him. I tossed around like the ship. His ship never stood still. It never waited for me. I never caught it up. I'd always be half a world away, reaching my arms out.

Bobs stretched out a hand from his mattress to mine. "Willie," he whispered. "Shall I come in with yer?"

"Yes please, Bobs."

He pulled his mattress closer, and we fixed the blankets so we lay in a double. Bobs held me and stroked my cheek. "You was askin' for Charley."

"Charley's my brother."

"Where is he?"

"In Australia."

"Where's that?"

"The other side of the world," I said very choked up.

Bobs was very understanding. He held me real nice and kissed me a bit, not for anything carnal, just for friends. We lay there close and warm.

"The gent I had tonight," I said, "reminded me of him. Stupid really. He wasn't nothing like him, just how he made me feel. You can believe anything in the dark I s'pose."

Bobs soothed me till I was peaceful.

"You ain't half nice, Bobs."

"That's all right. I like strokin' yer. You're nice too."

"Bobs, I think I love yer."

"Garn . . . nobody loves anybody *here*."

CHAPTER THIRTEEN

I

I T DIDN'T matter that Bobs was right to warn me off falling in love, or that we lived in a place where rewards, punishments and favours existed in terms of money, and that love was inappropriate. I badly needed to love somebody. After my Encounter with the Mysterious Stranger it was like a lid had been lifted off my emotions, and all the emergent feelings latched on to Bobs.

Oh, he was lovely, Bobs was! His scruffy mop of hair and his pointy pixie ears and his street urchin face which could look so sad, and his wide sensuous lips, and his heavy lidded grey eyes which had seen so much. I didn't mind that it was me that did the loving and Bobs who received. I couldn't do any longer without loving someone.

Days were warmer now; we were in the month of May. In our attic the sunshine came in real warm and spread on the sheets with their nice fusty smell of dried male juice. I'd wake up all tangled round Bobs and lick the sweat on his neck and suck the long strands of hair at the back. Being in love was very pleasant. It suited me; it made me attentive and thoughtful, almost happy. I'd take pleasure in helping him dress and making chocolate for us both at night. I brushed his hair for him and folded his clothes when he left them crumpled. We spent a lot of time holding hands, which we'd often done before, so no one thought anything of it. It was just the feelings in my head that were different.

I went soliciting with Sam.

Why did we do this, when we had everything laid on at Alfie's – comfortable rooms, a regular wage? Well, it was the independence. It was all very well asking Alfie for push, but what we picked up privately was all our own.

I was introduced immediately to Albany Street, along Regent's Park. Fitzroy Street, Cleveland Street, and Brunswick Square, these were all our stamping grounds. Up and down the

Burlington Arcade was a good place, and Fleet Street, Holborn and the Strand. These were the girls' territories too – they, of course, were everywhere.

Along with the ladies there were odd little knots of reformers trying to turn them back to the path of virtue. Funnily enough, these same do-gooders simply didn't seem to realise that some of the hansoms spilled out gents wanting boys, or that male flesh was on offer as well as girls'. In a way, it was one of the reasons why we were able to flourish so well – people didn't credit such fiends as us with existing at all. Yet sometimes you'd get this occasional little flurry, pamphlets circulating, warning people about Beasts who Prowled the Streets. Details were given as to how we were supposed to operate. Apparently, we stood with our fingers under our coat tails and wriggled them in a suggestive manner! We could be recognised by our pallid features, black-rimmed eyes and effeminate walk. Our heinous act was slangly termed "backgammon". Considering that we were always suffering nervous illnesses due to our misdirected urges, I'm surprised we were expected to be on the streets at all. Nevertheless, some of the public houses put up notices saying Beware of Sods. The pamphlets usually ended by declaring that the pillory was too good for us and hanging hardly severe enough as a punishment for our crime.

It wasn't true about the finger wriggling! We never needed to be so crude nor so explicit. All we did was walk. Having checked the parked cabs for lurking crushers, we just strolled up and down looking pretty. One of two things then happened. Either a hansom drew up and a gent enquired if he might offer us a lift, or one would walk slowly toward us and take out a cigar. Ever so polite and swift you'd offer a match and say: "Light, sir?" It was that easy.

In our street encounters there was no relationship and often nothing said. I remember my first because it was a thrill, not because he was unusual or unforgettable. We walked together into the park, silent and a little tense, past some children playing with hoops and past a hedge of rhododendrons. It was dusk. We found a sort of spinney where it was quiet, and I knelt down and unbuttoned him. There was just the sound of his harsh breathing and, as on the other side of a bubble, the distant shouts of children. Within a moment he was gone, and I stood up, thoughtful, a coin in my palm and a creamy stain on my lapel.

Although it was Sam who taught me the ropes, as it were, I never got on well with him as a person. Partly I suppose it was because I was a proper Urning and he was in it for the money. He seemed to look down on me, the way these so-called normal boys tend to do upon self-confessed inverts. He taught me the skills of soliciting as if it was something he slightly despised. He once said to me, real vicious: "I hate it that we have to go with men!"

It was the only time I thought about the street scene from that point of view. Logically, objectively, we boys ought to have been the pick-ups of older women, as the girls were for older men. Fleetingly I tried to imagine a world in which *women* cruised the pavements in their hansom cabs, choosing and buying pretty boys. How strange it would be if men and women had complete equality, and what was permissible for gents was perfectly acceptable for ladies too! What a different world it would be! I think we can be confident, though, that gents will never permit it. They enjoy their questionable advantages far too much to share.

One time we were out together Sam took me to meet his girlfriend. She was a milliner's assistant and as the shop was in a poky little street with a stinking gutter in it, I assumed it was Sam's earnings rather than hers that were to take them to Australia. His girl was very sweet, but terrified in case her employer thought we were taking her from her work. Sam made me pretend I was other than what I was. I thought it was immoral what he was doing. He'd told his Ellen that he was a gentleman's groom and I said I was clerk to a bookseller. But I ask you, what kind of a relationship will they have, starting off so dishonest? It wouldn't do for me, I know that.

II

ONE HOT night somewhere round the end of May, we got into a scrape – we were picked up by the police.

What happened was that Noll, Ally, Perce and I went for a midnight bathe in the Serpentine. Nights was awful hot in the attic bedroom and a bathe seemed like a good idea. Gents went bathing there in the daytime and swam in the nude, and any number of relationships were struck up over the pleasure of a swim. Well, we went at night, and we took several bottles of wine along with us to make it more fun. It was too cold at first, but so nice and the water that cascaded from your lifted arms caught the twinkle of moonlight in its spray. We passed the bottles round and got merrier, pushing each other about and splashing, giggling and, I cringe to remember, singing. I suppose I did gradually realise that the moon had grown very bright and was shining on us from three sides, but it wasn't till the voices started barking at us that it dawned on me we were being ordered out of the water and the lights were coming from policemen's lanterns.

Two large towels was all we'd brought and when we realised we had to get out, we raced for them and fought over them.

This whole event I remember for the one thing: the first time I had been vividly aware of being treated like a tart. It must have been something to do with being part of a group. We were treated with frivolous contempt. There were three crushers there, all uniformed and majestic, with the weight of the law behind them. They must have been watching us disporting ourselves, and recognised who we were. They'd got their van parked, a big dark box drawn by hulking great horses, the doors gaping open, and they'd slung all our clothes inside. They didn't tell us though; they watched us looking in the grass for them and amused themselves with cries of: "Lost something, boys? Picking flahs?"

I was wrapped in half a towel with Ally, half daft with drink, and honestly astonished not to find the clothes. We were dripping water and shivering noisily; they herded us into a huddle and told us we were being taken to the police station on account of indecent and disorderly conduct. Then they drove us towards the entrance of the van and hustled us inside. We had to get dressed in the dark with the van moving and that was no joke. When we were invited to descend we were still behaving a bit silly — Perce had hiccoughs, and we were giggling a bit and arguing. Then under the blue lamp we went, and thus I entered a police station for the first time.

We were put into a cell with a gas jet glowing above the door outside, and there we spent the rest of the night, singing and dozing. Nothing else happened to us. It was just an example of the crushers showing us that they could bundle us about. Bathing naked at night wasn't a crime; it was because we was tarts that we was taken in. It was a Little Warning. Shoving us about with rags of towels around us was what crushers could legitimately do to tarts; they could take liberties, and we had to put up with it.

Alfie had to pay a fine to get us out. That was the most painful part of the proceedings, because he took the money from our wages. I stood before his desk, sulky and glum, watching while he showed me how much the little venture had cost me.

The incident brought home to me that I didn't like being part of a herd. It was humiliating being hustled around in a bunch like that, and hearing yourself called "a cellful of Mary Annes" and "out you get, ladies". A person's individuality was stifled.

I found myself chatting about this to Mr Scott – the one who bought me an orchid and required me to learn the *Rubayyat*. It came up when he was mentioning the week after next. "I may not be here," I said vaguely. "I ain't going to always be here, you know."

We were lying on our sides, face to face, on the bed.

"Not be here?" said Mr Scott astonished. "Why not?"

"Well," I said reasonably. "A person feels restless."

"Do *you* feel restless?" he demanded accusingly.

"Sometimes I do, mister."

"But, Willie, I assumed you'd be here always!"

"Oh no." I shook my head.

He got up off the bed and started pacing about. He had nothing on. His rangy body looked so good in the nude I watched him appreciatively.

"I can't do without you, Willie," he declared.

"You don't have to," I assured him. "If I left here, I'd just be starting up on my own, that's all. You could still keep coming to me. I'd be pleased to keep doing for yer."

"It's most unsettling," he complained. "I like to think one can depend on things."

"You can depend on me!" I cried. "All I said was I wouldn't want to stay here for *ever*. Everybody moves on. Evolution," I swanked cheekily.

"What would you say if I offered to set you up in a place of your own?" he enquired thoughtfully. "Where I could visit you whenever I liked. A modest room, where you could live comfortably, and have your things about you?"

I stared, awed. Some whores had to work for years before anyone proposed that to them. For some it's a salvation, the summit of their ambition. Security, protection, a dream come true. I was impressed by the generosity of his offer; and my own value rose in my esteem, to think I'd been offered this proposition. "I'd say thank you kindly," I replied, "but I could not accept. That's what I'd say."

"Why could you not? Do you mean you want *more?*"

"No, mister! Less!"

"In what way, beautiful one?" he asked, running his eyes over me lustingly, and not really angry at my refusal.

"Have you ever been in somebody's power?" I asked seriously, though not expecting him ever to have been so. "I've known two kinds of subjection. One is where you're controlled by kindness and your own greed for self-improvement; and one's where they flog you if you step out of line. And now I'm beginning to see that paying wages is another kind of control. When I leave here I'm going to be my own man. I'm starting to understand that I need my independence. Not to be answerable to anybody, however nice he is. I'm awful fond of you, mister, and I like being your Lotus Flower and the Moon of your Delight. But if I was living in a room you provided, I'd be your kept boy and it would be a Tender Prison. And I must be free."

The sweet man did not laugh at my earnest declaration, but gave me a kiss, and said he respected my integrity. "Just as long as I don't have to give you up, my blossom," he murmured. "I could never replace your particular kind of sensitive beauty, and the delicate honeyed tone of your voice reciting quatrains in my ear as we make love."

Purringly I lapped up the compliments, immensely gratified at his need for me. "I won't be leaving yet awhile," I promised him as we settled into an embrace.

III

I SUPPOSE my feelings about Bobsy would have come to some kind of head even without the incident of the birch twigs.

He put this proposition to me. He said he was desperate to go and have a smoke that very night, and if I was a true friend I'd cover for him.

I knew he frequented the opium dens down by the docks without Alfie knowing.

He turned his lovely eyes on me.

"You don't know what it's like," he breathed, "when you've been smoking as long as I have. How you get to need it. I can't describe it, I've just got to have those dreams again."

He won me over. Our problem was that if Bobsy couldn't get back in time I'd have to cover for him by going with his gent. We were taking a risk here, but Bobs said all I had to do was give his gent a few sharp thwacks with a rod. It had to be me because anybody else couldn't be relied on not to sneak to Alfie, who'd forbidden Bobs to go down the opium den. It was easy, he said, and he knew I could do it. "You know I haven't had to before?" I said dubiously.

"What, never welted anyone?"

"Not properly. You'd better tell me how it's done."

I sat on the bed while Bobsy strode about with an imaginary rod, speaking the dialogue – acting both parts, squeaking and growling, and being so funny that I sat there laughing and enjoying it. I never really thought it would come to my actually having to do anything myself.

Imagine, then, my growing alarm when at about eleven o'clock that night I was watching out for Bobs and he had not come back. I couldn't even make my concern apparent, since no one but me knew that Bobs was even out. Well, I saw the gent escorted in. I was watching from the landing. The gent was in the bedroom. He was all ready, waiting for Bobsy, and Bobsy wasn't back. Groaning and wincing, there was nothing I could do but go downstairs and cover for Bobs, and hope the gent would take a substitute. It was with a horrible sinking feeling that I slunk down the stairs and put my hand upon the door.

Bobs's gent was a short dapper man of about fifty years old, and as far as I could guess, was one of those public school cast-offs who'd learned to love the birch and hankered after cherished memories. I half hoped he'd find me unacceptable. But after a short exchange of words, polite and detached as was proper, he said that if I could treat him exactly as he deserved, he would put himself in my hands. In the corner of the room there was a birch rod.

I had no trouble at all acting the part of the Young Master. Before I knew it, we were involved in a jolly little drama about my suddenly returning to the stately home and catching him stealing the silver, whetting his appetite with a description of what I would do to him. I was still the Young Master as I strode over to the birch and as I swished it down upon his bending shanks. It made a noise like a bucket of water thrown over a cat. Carried away with my role I swished him three times, hard, and then it was that I realised how effective I was being. He was cut all over; blood was trickling down his thighs. I stared appalled, frozen, the birch high like a sweep's brush.

"More, more!" he moaned. "My wickedness . . . "

My stomach rose up. I gaped stupidly at the lacerated flesh. The reality of birching stared me in the face. Of course I had no idea that this was normal punishment for schoolboys, nor did I understand the pleasure network involved in swishing. Half scared that I could be arrested for assault, half nauseated at the sight before me, I hesitated, dumbstruck and stupid.

"Why don't you strike?" he groaned.

I dropped the rod and ran, fumbling with the door and shoving myself through. I pelted upstairs, shook Sam awake and gasped out my awful plight, and to my heartfelt relief he ran straight down. There was a nasty hubbub of voices on the landing, at which my heart really plummetted, because one was Alfie's. As I crept to listen, I realised that Bobs had chosen that precise moment to stagger home. I didn't want him to have to take all the blame, so I went down too. Bobs had trailed off to the kitchen. I could hear him calling breezily: "I *will* have some coffee; leave off, Alfie."

Down in the kitchen we had a Horrible Scene. Bobs had slumped into a chair. I sat down beside him. Alfie was yelling something awful about opium dens and docked wages and *now look what he'd done:* Alfie had been Embarrassed in front of a Customer.

"It's not Bobs' fault," I began. "I should never have agreed."

"It *is* my fault," Bobs corrected languidly. "It ain't Willie's; he's just easily led."

Alfie lost his temper and banged our heads together.

I'm sure if he hadn't done that we'd have been able to sort it out civilised. But once he'd done that, both Bobs and I came over all emotional. I was in such pain. I assume Bobs was too; it's no joke having that done to you hard. We was clutching our heads and groaning and crying, and Alfie was hanging over us like an avenging angel. "Why'd yer do it?" he demanded of me, furious.

"I was helping Bobs," I snivelled.

"But bleedin' *why?* You hate flagellation; you're always telling us. What *made* yer?"

"Bobs wanted me to."

"What's his hold over you? Did he pay yer?"

"No!" I screeched.

"So what then? What was the arrangement?"

"None! I just said I would."

"But why? I will get to the bottom of this."

"Bobs asked me to and I wanted him to be happy."

"Why'd you want him to be happy?"

If I hadn't been so fraught I'd never have said it, but I was fraught and I did. "Because I love him," I wept.

"You *what?*"

I turned my face away from Alfie's incredulous scornful gaze.

"And what about *you?*" he demanded, with one almighty leer. "Is this romance a mutual thing? Hey, Bobs? Hearts and flowers, is it? How about you?"

"Well, I love him too, don't I?" shrugged Bobs with an aggrieved sniff. "We loves each other."

I looked at Bobs, astonished and grateful. I really have no idea whether he was speaking the truth. He could well have been just getting at Alfie after all – his vanity was smarting along with his head – for treating him like a naughty little boy.

"I don't believe this!" cried Alfie. "Have we been having a little romance going on under our very noses? Unobserved? Or is it that I'm the last to hear about it? I hope it isn't that. I don't like being made a fool of, you know. I'd be very, very cross if I thought some of my little boys had been falling in love under my roof, and turning a commercial level-headed venture into a sentimental novelette for ladies. That wouldn't please me at all, that wouldn't. Particularly when it's my two prettiest and most desirable bits of nancy. I think that might make me very annoyed."

"We can't help our feelings," said Bobsy pouting.

"Oh yes we can!" laughed Alfie nastily, "and we better *had*. You was all right, Bobsy, till this red-headed little bitch turned up with his Culture and his Religious Doubts and his Moral Scruples. You was a committed worker. It seems to me that things have got just a little aht of hand."

"I want Willie to make me some coffee," Bobsy sulked.

"Yeah, do that for him, Romeo, will yer?" said Alfie. "I s'pose young sweethearts like lookin' after the beloved's welfare when he comes staggerin' from the opium den. I'll leave yer to whisper sweet nothings. We'll have a little talk about it tomorrer."

IV

THE DAY that followed I kept out of Alfie's way, though he was of necessity in my thoughts because the side of my head remained tender all morning. I spent the afternoon lying on my mattress leaning on my elbows, reading all Keats' most melancholy poems while the sunlight moved slowly across the room picking out the stained and crumpled sheets, the strewn frilled shirt, the ribbon of dyed red fur, and a little spiral of flies that buzzed irritatingly over a couple of squashed strawberries trodden into the rug.

The poems had thoroughly depressed me. It may have been because I was reading beauty of language in the attic of a brothel and felt myself cheapened by comparison. Perhaps it was that I was sympathetic to the poet's words and longings and troubled by his early death. Certainly I was haunted by a sense of perfection that was out of reach and unattainable in life – never, anyway for me. All in all I was despondent and gloomy when Bobs came in and selfconsciously rolled up his mattress. "Sorry, Willie, I ain't allowed to sleep with you no more; he don't think it's good for me. I'm taking my bed down into Trixie's room."

I watched him, without saying anything. "I have to do it, love, he pays my wages," Bobs laughed brittlely. "I have to be a good boy now. What he's docked off me for yesterday's lark, he's left me beggared." He sniggered to make it sound suggestive. "We never meant it anyway, did we?" he said, fidgeting. "It was only play."

"It's all right, Bobs," I said irritably, to make it easier for him. "I never loved yer."

"That's it," he agreed relieved. "I never loved you neither."

Later that night I was down in the kitchen on my own, heating up a pie and letting my thoughts come. Cooking was very soothing to a person about to make a big decision. I pottered about, poking the fire, filling the kitchen with odours of pie and eventually tucking into a nice little meal. I had coffee as well, one cup, just for me.

It came over me very clearly that I wanted to be on my own, just look after myself. I probably hadn't really loved Bobsy anyway – just the idea of loving. We weren't suited. We had nothing in common except our beauty and our trade. We'd shared an affectionate warmth and I'd always be grateful, but I needed to leave. I'd had enough of being one of Alfie's boys; I was ready to set up on my own.

I felt content rather than excited. I sat sipping coffee and holding my toes to the embers – like Cinderella, though I daresay she had daintier feet. I sat, my mind swimming with half-formed plans, till my coffee dregs were cold and bitter and the embers burnt low. Miss Trixie came down to see to the fire, and said goodnight to me just as if everything was the same as usual; just as if my head wasn't full of the prospect of many wonderful changes.

CHAPTER FOURTEEN

I

THE NEXT few days I spent tramping the streets looking for a room. My problem was that I was very choosy and particular in my requirements; there was rooms and there was rooms.

What I had in mind was somewhere decent like, a haven, somewhere to retreat to, from my work. On the other hand, no respectable place would have me. Anyone with long hair and bright clothes who worked nights would soon be shown the door. Anyway, a respectable house I did not want – tea at four, and are you a churchgoer? I needed a place near the regular haunts, and not out in some well-mannered suburb like Camden Town or New Cross. Then again I wasn't having any truck with some thieves' kitchen or low nethersken where every other person was on the run and busy planning fresh crimes. So it was a hefty bit of tramping I had to do.

But I found what I wanted.

It was a little bit south of Covent Garden, a tall rambling old house in a narrow street of rooms to let, punctuated by little shops. On the corner of the street was a public house and its flaring light glowed through the dusky gloom. The pavement was narrow and uneven, awash with puddles after rain, and the road was cobbled. The carts to and from the market made a constant noisy clatter and the scruffy down-at-heels from the Drury Lane dosshouses were always passing. Whoring was not done so openly here but there were rooms available, with cards discreetly tucked behind ornaments which read "Beds" and offered simply that.

My place was run by one Mrs Dawson, who lived in the house next door and let this one. She was weird, she was. She made a great show of respectability and then for a couple of shillings she'd turn a blind eye. She'd say: "I hope you don't think this 'ere's one of yer common lodging hahses; this is a respectable place, this is!" And then out the corner of her mouth it'd be: "For two bob I didn't see that. For two bob I won't let on."

My room was at the side of the house. It overlooked an alley. I got sunshine from early morning till ten o'clock and then the sun could have been anywhere on earth; I saw nothing of it. To reach my room you went up a narrow stairway, along a landing, and up two little steps, and I had a sort of archway over my door, which was most pleasing. On the landing the wallpaper was thin green and cream stripes, moist with damp. My door was dark green, with a number seven in brass nailed upon it. When I was first shown inside, the room hadn't got a lot in its favour but I knew it would do; it just needed Touches. It was awful run down. Saggy net curtains hanging by a nail; horrible bedding spilling its innards from splits in the mattress. I threw all that out. Chances were someone had died on it.

The best thing about the room was it had red wallpaper. Dark musky red, almost burgundy, and I loved it. There was a bed and a wardrobe and washstand. I did a lot of cleaning and the woman who came in to do the rest of the place – she lived in Drury Lane, like the muffin man! – gave me a hand. I bought a secondhand carpet (red, with fringes), dark red curtains and creamy net ones from somebody's sale of house contents, and I bought new a real feather mattress and a dark green coverlet.

I bought a wicker chair to go by the fireplace, and a small swing mirror, and then an old lamp, with every bit as much delight as Aladdin. A bloke from downstairs put a shelf up for me and there I arranged my books.

Now what made me truly broke was that I started buying prints. Ah, there was any number of tacky little prints in the bookshops – praying hands and little girls with puppies. But in the posh shops, where you could also buy leather bound tomes edged with gilt, there were wonderful prints and that was how I first discovered works by Moreau. I bought two. There was Phaeton – golden plunging horses with flaming manes, a boiling sea dazzling with drowned sun and, framed in a scarlet cloak like a raging fire, the curved and gorgeous body of a naked youth, his long hair streaming, his shapely thighs arching forward, offering his loins.

That went over my mantelpiece.

The other, on the opposite wall, was called Hercules and the

Lernaean Hydra. A gruesome picture, I suppose, with its rocky
landscape and the mangled limbs half in, half out of the marshy
pools. But what drew the eye were the two naked men. Hercules
was muscular and pretty, decorated with accoutrements that had
the effect of ribbons and daisy chains. Not quite at his feet lay
a beautiful nude young man, victim of the Hydra – but oh so
graceful, so slender, lying like he was asleep and waiting for a
lover. He had sensuous lips and a sweet expression, and long
tresses of rich auburn hair. I have to admit it: I thought he
looked like me. The fantasies I wove around that picture! The
youth was not really dead . . . fainted . . . Hercules would kiss
him and take him in his arms. I was the nude young man;
Hercules was a mystery, a dark stranger, the lover who came to
me out of the night when I lay on black velvet, the strong hero
of my dreams.

Later I bought another print – Saint George by Mr Burne-
Jones, in black and white. A long lean lad in armour he was,
with close cropped hair, carrying shield and banner. He was the
soldier of my childhood hymns; he was Mr Pearson bringing
hope and help to the poor and destitute, scaling the strongholds
of the rich and careless, girt about with righteousness, strong in
the armour of truth. He filled me with yearning. I ached to be
a hero and to be better than I was. He tormented me with what
I ought to be and wasn't. It was painful and necessary. I wanted
to keep hold of it in the life of depravity upon which I was
embarked.

Here I was, settling into a room and making it habitable, and
for what? – a base from which to go a-whoring. And unlike when
I fled to Alfie's, I wasn't scared and abused and alone; I was
perfectly aware what I was doing. When I think how Aunt
Louisa had once had plans for me to set up in just such a little
room from which to emerge as a clerk in my grey suit and
cropped hair, I could not help but smile at the fulfilment of her
intentions.

To be fair to myself, it would have been difficult to break into
respectable work at that point. Decent jobs required a sponsor
and some influence, and you'd be expected to answer certain
questions about your background. I'd be obliged to lie through
my teeth. As for cheap labouring jobs, I never gave them a
thought. Look at the money I could pick up whoring – I could

earn in a night what honest toilers earned in a week. While I was young and pretty it seemed the best occupation for me – and bleedin' hell, I enjoyed it!

Yet there it was, that print. The pure and noble knight, the sword of righteousness. It disturbed me, it pained me, but I wanted it. It was like the thorns in a big luscious rose, its place in my life. Was it my conscience? A better self deeply suppressed? A sort of hair shirt to remind me I wasn't wholly convinced by my bravado and careless unconcern? Did I feel that as long as that picture still affected me I was not beyond redemption, I was accessible to moral feelings, and that there was a way back, a way up?

II

MY NEW-FOUND independence showed itself in my choice of clothes. In a stuffy little backroom in Whitechapel I acquired at last the image I had always longed for: a wonderful jacket in green corduroy, a buff-coloured brocaded waistcoat backed with brown silk, a cap of brown corduroy and a pair of cream trousers and a matching shirt, the whole being finished off with a dazzling silk neckerchief, one in purple, one in peach.

As I wandered out thus clad, I passed some flowersellers on a street corner. I bought a buttonhole of lavender from a lovely fresh-faced girl in a honey-coloured shawl. She fixed it in for me.

"It was *made* for yer, mister," she told me.

It seemed almost possible. A summer evening, the powdery dust churned up by the horses' hooves and the hansom wheels, the mingled scents of lavender, perfume, beer, rotting fruit and horse dung; the glitter and excitement of the start of an evening up west; everything blended for me. I was part of the street.

In my little room I spent my afternoons reading books. I read the works of Mr Dickens, but more particularly I liked *Wuthering Heights*, *Jane Eyre*, *Tom Brown's Schooldays*, and *Far From the Madding Crowd*. I also bought several pamphlets on social issues, remembering that Mr Irving had encouraged me to develop my political awareness – *Practical Socialism*, *The Co-operative Movement*, and *Towards A Brighter Future*.

I read relevant and irrelevant things; I even stacked up some of my old friends the Pocket Gems. And then I had a remarkable piece of luck. In a pile of cheap prints I came upon that old print of myself as a boy, in the goatskin, all bum and innocence. When I found it I blushed, as if all over the quiet refined shop-room everyone knew it was me. I bought it with a silly smirk on my face and feelings of elation in my heart. A treasure from the past indeed! I grinned at it affectionately, as if I was the older brother of that lad and would look after him to keep him out of scrapes.

Fond hope! I had a living to earn.

There was one particular time I remember. It was one night in August. I was up in Brunswick Square. It was about midnight, raining. It wasn't heavy rain, but a pittering drizzle that left your hair covered in fine pinpoints of gleaming moisture and dampened your shoulders. I loafed in a doorway for a while, but no one sees you in a doorway, and so after a time I emerged, pulling up the collar of my green corduroy jacket and adjusting my buttonhole of fresh lavender. I walked the pavement a bit, keeping an eye to the passing hansoms, my hands in my pockets, my walk just dainty enough to catch the eye. A bloke in a tall top hat passed me by bent under the rain and not paying me attention. I drew level with a lamp post, and I stopped, leaning slightly against it. In its light, the rain was an enchanted circle of glittering needles. The romance of it all was still with me then. I itched to be wanted.

A cab approached from behind, drew level and slowed, a face at the side window. The cab stopped. A man leaned forward, his hands in white gloves. In the gaslight now he could see me, my painted lips and shadowed eyelids, my frank assessive stare; he could be in no doubt. "A bad night to be abroad," he remarked.

"Pretty bad, sir," I agreed, lounging still.

"Can I offer you a lift?"

"Very nice of you, mister. I wouldn't say no."

So back comes the flap, and I gets in and settles myself, dripping a bit. "Sorry to be wet, mister," I grinned, looking at him.

He'd got a nice face, intelligent, alert-eyed. He was quite slight and dapper, little shoulders, hairy hands. His face was thin and pointed, and he had a small greyish beard, his hair greyish brown. He was very neat and clean. "Is there an address you know?" he enquired in a low and business-like tone.

"Yes, mister, but I charge a guinea indoors."

"Is it a safe address?"

"Perfectly safe."

"A guinea seems reasonable enough."

I told him the address and he announced it to the driver. Away we went, along the jewelled streets. I couldn't help a happy little sigh. "Ooh, mister, I love hansoms!"

I sensed his benign tolerance of my appreciation.

"Ooh, my hair's wet," I remarked. The gent passed me a white handkerchief and I was grateful, and set about patting the ends dry. I was conscious of my perfume in this enclosed space. Rain and lavender; that gent would associate those things with memories of me henceforth.

"Do you have a name?" he asked.

"Willie."

"You seem . . . young, Willie."

"Seventeen." (All but five months.)

"Do you . . . work . . . from need?"

(Yours, I thought lewdly.) "No, mister, I enjoys it."

A lot of them were like this. They wanted you to assuage their guilt, and not to be a poor desperate boy who sold his body to get hospital treatment for his widowed mother. My gent relaxed. "Have no fear, mister," I assured him. "I'm quality. You'll have a nice time with me."

The room I took him to was an address I'd got from Sam. I left my gent in the cab while I fixed things, and came back for him and helped him down. We slipped indoors, down the dim lit corridor and up the stairs, and there in a room at the back I gave him his treat.

"Tell me . . . would you really do anything?" he asked in simple amazement, as his eyes ran up and down my body.

"Yes, mister, only it's five pounds for perversions."

His lips twitched. "And what, pray, do you call perversions?"

"Anything which I consider unusual. Dressing up in corsets and stockings, or pretending I'm a colonel or a schoolmaster. Canings is perversions, and tying up, and having things thrown at you. They'd all be a fiver."

"What a varied life you lead! You'll think me very tame!"

"No, indeed, mister. I think you're real nice. What'd yer like? I'm good at everything."

Afterwards, I stood up and helped him become neat and proper.

"Alas," he said drily, "I cannot share your liberal views. Much as it was enjoyable to me, and not, I hope, too distasteful to you, what you have just done to me I count as a perversion." And into my hands he put five sovereigns.

I was torn. It didn't seem right for the little I'd done. "Mister," I winced, "it's too much, yer know."

"Accept it, you foolish child," he answered. "It is a way of thanking."

"Ta, mister," I said appreciatively.

"I'm ready to leave now," he said.

"There's a boy downstairs who'll go for a cab for you."

He went – I rushed to open the door for him – he gave me an odd sad look as he went through. But I had no thought to analyse it or dwell on such. I was elated. Five pound! Some folks had money to burn! I hurried into my clothes, licking my cheek and picking a hair out of my teeth before I laced up my shoes.

When I got back out into the street a sudden shock of how beautiful the night was hit me in all its wonder. A gas lamp opposite seemed to project a lilac-green glow, a heady triangle of mysterious light on wet pavements that rainbowed like spilt oil. In the irridescence the rain showered sparks like from a bonfire, myriads of them, dropping out of darkness. A cab passing splashed up an arc of silver spray.

I felt part of it all. There was gold in my pocket. I felt successful and free, a part of the glitter and the darkness.

I thought: I have arrived.

III

MY ROMANTIC nature and my awakened senses, still as yet unsullied by disillusion and disenchantment, found in the long warm nights of the fading summer images of beauty and a perpetual wonder. I grew familiar with the blurred green darkness beyond the lamps. So often did I ply my trade by gaslight I felt my silhouette must be a part of the whole picture. The smoky soot-stained bricks provided backdrop, and down the glimmering street the air was coloured with a wispy bottle green wash. Above the black jagged shapes of roofs and chimneys curled a murky haze, and a bright white moon shone. I became aware of the characters of lamp posts, as a painter would of easels, slender ones with elegant metalwork, others with broad bases and a ridge at the right height to lean an elbow, and those on street corners that curved ornately from the sides of buildings.

Sometimes I'd go with a gent under a bridge by the river, down the wet steps to the archway. If there weren't any dossers down there huddled in heaps of rags we could take up position in the gloom there, where the stinking water lapped, oily and black. Underfoot there'd be little heaps of rough stones, the rotted remains of a boat maybe, and broken posts sticking up out of the wet mud. A torn poster advertising entertainments far removed from here shifted in a windgust. Listening for the noise of any river barge – the crushers patrolled the water as well as the streets – I'd see to my gent. The wind came round whippy under the arches and you didn't stop for anything elaborate. Beyond him, the curve of the arch was dappled with the shifting shapes of water and a poster on the stonework behind his shoulder read "Excursions to Paris".

On a clear dark night the lights on the bridges glittered in the black water. There was a quiet time, a melancholy time, when the night's main business had been done, when men had gone with girls or gone home, when the workers were not yet stirring and the street cries still an hour or two away. I've trailed home in that half-silence, the passing hansom cabs no chance of trade but taking someone home, the blinds drawn in the sleeping houses and silver moonlight lightly touching the leaves.

To hear me talk you'd think I was the only male whore on the streets! No, there were dozens of us. We couldn't help but recognise each other, and we weren't half catty. "Fuck off, darling, this is my patch," was a common greeting.

One particular lean blond fellow crossed my working path regularly enough for us to have a superficial relationship. We might find ourselves leaning on the same railings, taking a breath between hunting, claws drawn in for the moment.

"How's business, darling?"

"Mustn't grumble."

And we'd be assessing each other carefully, sideways on. How much has he made tonight? Looking tired and drawn, hey? Must've been a good night.

"Crushers are all up and down Albany tonight . . . someone was caught with a soldier."

"Poor sod."

"How d'you get your hair that colour?"

"Mother Nature."

"Garn! It comes out of a bottle!"

"It does not! Mind, it ain't half a battle keeping it nice. All the dirt and smut. I s'pose you have the same trouble."

"Mine don't shine. Like a bleedin' thatch."

"S'pose it is!" I agreed cheekily.

"You know what they say about natural redheads?"

"No, what?"

He nudged me with a lewd mirthless chuckle. "They turn out to be perverts."

We shifted about, hands in pockets, backs against the railings, eyeing the street. A couple of cabs turned the corner, moving slow.

"See yer, Carrots."

"See yer, Straw Thatch."

We never fraternised. The joy of working on your own is its independence, and by its nature it has to be solitary. Unlike the situation with girls, no client of ours would accost us in a crowd and chat us up in public. So we had to put ourselves in the less populated streets, the ones where it was understood our sort of thing went on. The male tarts who worked the same pitches functioned like efficient shadows, prowling, emerging, disappearing, obvious enough, but not intrusive. There was no point in becoming matey and congregating; it was asking for trouble. You'd get noticed, hustled on, provoked. And if a hysterical do-gooder worked it out there'd be letters to the papers about the moral degeneracy of the nation, and the crushers would step up their harrassment. So we acknowledged each other, swapped insults, and warned where necessary.

Funnily enough, I had more to do with the girls.

For a start, you couldn't help it! Once you turned into the Strand or the Haymarket, or anywhere central west, there were the girls. They started walking even in the afternoon, and the action intensified as darkness came down and the mauve twilight poured itself slowly round the flaring lamps. It was awful noisy and amazingly shameless. Police were there, ineffective and grumbling, calling out "Move on now, move on," half hidden by the fancy ribboned hats and the tiered hairdos of the girls, and swamped by frills and feathers and streams of sewn-on lilies and roses.

It was only a matter of time before I bumped into Caroline again. I saw her first as part of a merry group outside a gin palace and she waved enthusiastically over somebody's head. Another time I saw her inside a coffee shop; she beckoned me in to sit by her and in I went. We had a nice chat about how life was treating us and the state of the game. She'd got a small apartment in Soho in a house full of other girls and no madame to boss them about, so she was doing very well. She was impressed at my setting up on my own and treated me all pleasant and respectful, without any jibing references to reformatories or lice or reluctant erections. She was ever so pleased to see me safely out.

I don't know why, but Caroline was a woman I got on tolerably well with. She wasn't silly with me like some were. Being older than me, she always seemed more understanding, and I particularly liked how she appeared to have accepted that I was a certain kind of bloke and not a challenge. She didn't pester me, though she did tease good humouredly. When we met we usually had a drink, and sometimes went back to her room.

Of course there I had to put up with her mates, and the whole business would begin again. "You really like *men*?" "What do you *do*?" "Is it true you – ?" I never answered properly, because they didn't want to *know* – they just wanted to smirk and laugh. They thought it funny and odd, and also, I guess, at heart they found it threatening and insulting to them. But in general they were friendly enough.

Caroline's room was lushly furnished. Her bed had peacock blue drapes and a coverlet embroidered all over with Chinese gentlemen and dragons and pagodas.

The amount of creams and potions she had on her dressing table! Ivorine cream and Essence of Tyre and oatmeal toilet soap, and French perfumes with glass stoppers as big as the bottles they stopped! One wet afternoon she made up my face for me; she said I had a fine bone structure which was wasted on a man. "Pity more blokes aren't your sort," she observed. "You're so easy to get on with, Willie, just like one of the girls."

The other girls seemed to treat me so too, because they strolled in when I was there without any of the change of atmosphere that occurs in a female group when a bloke enters. They came in half dressed and sleepy-eyed, without make-up, groaning and grumbling about gut-ache and pimples and putting on weight. In fact, I thought they looked better in some ways than in the evening when they sallied forth like ships in sail, impeccable, all blemishes disguised, half slaying you with perfume and half choking you with powder. Forgetting I was different, they sat about and drank coffee and dried their hair, loose dressing-gowns open over shifts and corsages, trying out false violet sprays in their hair, pulling black stockings on to long elegant legs.

I quite liked Caroline's friends. I liked them because they left me alone and just got on with their way of life. I helped them fix on fringes and chignons, and towelled wet hair, and pulled corset laces tight – girls who were wearing the stuff of Twilight Tale fantasies, silk drawers and stockings, and the famous alabaster globes half naked while they sat plucking eyebrows and picking their teeth.

IV

ANOTHER OLD acquaintance of mine I renewed contact with was Madame Rosa, who remembered me from when I was a boy. We assumed a reasonable working relationship. Her interest and mine was the earning of push and the servicing of gents, and we needed each other to provide the goods. She had any number of customers lurking in denizens of respectibility who were eager to frequent her dwelling in Holborn; me, I appreciated an indoor base. I saw her now not as an exotic gipsy lady in Spanish scarlet but as a hard and heavily-lined madame, having more in common with a shopkeeper than a dancer. I liked her better, uncluttered by my boyish ignorant fancies.

I also sometimes still used Alfie's place, mostly to continue seeing Mr Scott, he of *The Rubayyat* and Eastern culture. His guinea was a pleasure to earn.

He was most interested and amused to hear me describe my room. He said it sounded charming.

"I suppose you are furnished with the basics?" he enquired.

"Oh yes – I got a bed and a mirror."

He smiled, amused at my priorities. "You need never want, you know, Willie," he told me. "Autumn draws on. I have to assume you are comfortable – you'll be able to keep yourself in dull necessities – coal, lamp oil, blankets?"

"Honest, I'm fine. I live very cheap."

"Have you ever been obliged to look after yourself in winter?"

"Oh yeah, when I was a kid," I shrugged easily.

"What was it like?"

"Horrible!" I laughed.

"I'm going to give you the money for a winter coat, and you're to buy one – not dissipate it on silk scarves and flashy shirts. Is that understood?"

"It ain't winter yet."

"It will be, lad, soon enough. And you're to have some decent boots then, and put those dainty and inadequate shoes away till the spring."

"Hey, mister, who's going to pull up a cab to look at someone muffled up in a coat and big sensible boots?"

Mr Scott winced in distaste. "I wish you'd accept that offer of mine to set you up in a place of my choice. I hate the idea of you hawking on the streets."

I sidled up close and rubbed against him. "You're real good to me, mister; you're the best."

"But?"

"But it's nicest like this. How about you lying back and I'll kiss you real sweet, and we'll forget about nasty things. Unborn termorrer and dead yesterday, why fret abaht them if terday be sweet, hey?"

"Perverse and beautiful boy, then do your worst!"

"Ah, no – my *best*!"

When he'd gone and I was taking a bath – I always made use of Alfie's superb washing facilities when I worked there – I lay in the hot water and I had to give myself a good talking to. I sensed a vulnerable situation between myself and Mr Scott. I knew that I could fall in love with him. He was the nearest thing so far that I'd encountered to my ideal – the strong man who'd look after me. And obviously, this could never be. Mr Scott was a society gent, even a lord, and I could never mingle in his world. I could be his kept boy, a shut away thing; but from my Love I wanted more. I wanted to be his friend and helper, something valuable to him. Mr Scott certainly didn't want my love or to talk to me about his life and worries. I must guard against love sneaking in. My problem was I badly needed to love again. My love was like a coat looking for a peg to hang on. I had to be sensible and not use Mr Scott for my romantic dreams.

Mr Scott had obviously thought about it too and, sensible man that he was, he bought me presents. It was good; it put our relationship in its proper perspective. It reinforced the delights of what we had; I think it showed great maturity. It would only have led to unhappiness if he'd tried to uproot me and replant me in an alien setting. I was only a common ordinary lad and his world was not mine. So I accepted his presents, and that wasn't difficult as they were gorgeous.

He bought me a goatskin rug to go in front of my little fireplace, and a small cane sofa with two cushions. He bought me a strange and exotic indoor garden – ferns and leaves set in soil, and covered over with a glass dome. Ever so beautiful. It was the devil to carry from Regent Street down to Covent Garden, though. Noll helped. It's nice to have sturdy muscular friends.

And there was another present too, a necklace, which sounds effeminate but wasn't. It was made out of marcasite, a sort of crusty grey, a circle, thick and chunky like a coil of chain; you wore it against the skin, under a shirt. It was classy and subtle and unusual. He fastened it on for me himself. I kept it on all the time. I paraded for him dressed in nothing but it. He said I was frighteningly perfect.

CHAPTER FIFTEEN

I

IT WAS in the park that I first became conscious of the change of seasons. I'd been getting by with pulling my collar up, vaguely registering the sharp little wind and hurrying home the faster. But one evening I took a gent into the bushes where I earned a quick five bob, and he shivered as he tidied himself up. "What do you do in the winter?" he suddenly enquired.

"Mister?"

"Well, you won't be able to carry on like this, will you?" he remarked. "Within a month, where we're standing now will be open and bare. Winter – indeed, autumn – must take all the cover away. I was curious as to how you managed."

"I expect I shall work indoors."

"Oh yes, of course. Goodnight to you."

"Goodnight, mister."

I stood on my own in the park, listening to the leaves rustle, dry and brittle sounding, and a sudden gust swirled a little whirlpool of leaves ahead of me. I shivered. Suddenly I felt uneasy about the future. Soliciting in winter . . . what would it be like? I had no alternative but to shake the thought away. Thinking on those lines could scare a person.

However, I was off the streets that autumn, and it was influenza that did it. I was real awful for a week, and two weeks after that very shaky. When I was over the worst I caught up on my reading and began *The Poems of Byron*. After a while it wasn't so bad, and I sat by the fire with a blanket round me, reading *Mazeppa* and eating licorice, occasionally stumbling down to the kitchen to brew tea. Mr Scott paid my rent for nothing, and sent me hothouse grapes and a bottle of brandy.

It was well into November when I started going out again, and the world had slunk into that dull dark time of year, its gradual changes already gone. I emerged into the short daylight hours and the yellowy fog, having half forgotten how it made your eyes ache and stream, and stank its way into your lungs. I found it hard going walking around. I seemed awful tired just doing my shopping, carrying coal and kindling. My chest ached when I got home; my room was awful dark.

I stoked up my fire, and I thought about last year, when I'd lain in clean sheets and been looked after, and illness meant camphorated oil and hot milk with cinnamon, and people reading to us at our bedsides. Now I was paying out to a greedy landlady for having watery broth put on the floor by my bed. I was on the way to a fair degree of self pity. It was sordid being ill on your own. How had I sunk so low? I was fit for better things.

What could I do? How could I get out? But when I thought about trying to take on honest work I ended up groaning: I couldn't, I couldn't. That wasn't what I wanted to do with my life, and how could I ever find my Lover once I'd gone respectable? I'd *have* to stay with the street and the night and the secretive world of prowling inverts; once I'd left it I'd never find a man who'd love me. Ah, but would I anyway? Who'd love me, who'd risk taking a tart off the streets, who'd have the nerve to take me home? I was in a trap; I was caught. I was on a treadmill – I could never get off.

All right, so I was a tart, and the sooner I behaved like one the better. In the morning I pulled myself together and went up to Alfie's to wash my hair and make myself beautiful. To my dismay I found I'd gone very hollow cheeked and drawn looking, great black shadows under my eyes and my cheek bones too much emphasised. I went and found Bobs, and we sat at Miss Trixie's dressing table to see what we could do. "Makeup'll cover it, darlin'," he assured me. "Spots of rouge here, and here. You need a lot of sleep, I'd say."

As if it wasn't bad enough to feel ugly, I had still further cause for depression as the day progressed. When I was undressed for Mr Scott and told him how much better I was feeling, in answer to his solicitous enquiries, he said, "I say, boy, you've lost some weight."

I faced him accusingly, as if it was his fault. "How much?" I demanded. He strolled around me, touching me up and down my ribs. "You're a little on the wrong side of sylph-like," he said. "You really don't want to lose any more, you know."

"You'd chuck me then, wouldn't you?" I screeched.

"Oh, really . . . " he said in mild exasperation.

"You would! You'd leave me if I grew skinny. You only want me if I'm beautiful. It's true!"

"Why do you oblige me to admit the obvious? I do pay for you, and you aren't cheap, you know! Yes, I do prefer you plumper. You were quite perfect before, and at the moment you are somewhat more bony than I like. But I'm sure we can get you swiftly back to health."

"I am healthy," I snapped.

"I've a proposition to put to you," he said, sitting down and watching me.

"What, a trip to the knacker's?" I sneered.

"No, no, quite the opposite," he smiled. "Why don't I take you away to the country? I have a house in Hertfordshire, surrounded by fields. You need fresh air and good food, and I'd see you received it. It would be a great pleasure to me to take you away and fatten you up. What do you say? The city in November is no place for anyone convalescing. And really, Willie, you're looking pretty rough."

"Oh, I couldn't," I said, not really taking him seriously. "It's good of you, but I'd lose my room – and – " my independence, I was going to say. I never wanted to be his kept boy. I was still smarting from him admitting in so many words that he only liked me for my body and would leave me if I grew ugly. I resented his money, the power he'd got to buy pretty boys, and more than one house. I felt sullen and hostile. "Take a couple of East End kids," I said rather sarcastically. "Give 'em a treat. Then you'd feel real pious and good."

He shifted irritably. "I myself intend to leave town. I advise you to reconsider my offer, which is not ungenerous. If I am out of town, which I may well be till after Christmas, I shall not of course be frequenting this place and you will lose my custom. Think about it."

I turned away, a lump rising in my throat. Everything, but everything, was reduced to barter, to commerce. Human emotions had their market value. Life was the passing of a guinea from one hand to another. I could keep my principles, risk my health, lose his very welcome payment and his interesting company; or I could give up my independence and recover my fitness in comfort, a rich gent's boy. What did it matter anyway? "Please may I consider it, mister?" I said in a subdued voice.

"By the end of the week. We'll say no more about it tonight. It's very much in your interest to accept, as you must surely see."

I could not imagine living in the country; and I decided to put the notion from my mind.

And then I had a very strange night, which even now brings a shiver to my spine.

II

IT HAD upset me quite a bit, the feeling that I was ugly. I hoped that at Rosa's the gents would be less discriminating. But I was in a disturbed state of mind, I knew. I'd been sleeping badly, my nightmares a regular event now. Warders and policemen pursued me across my dreams, with ridiculous chases that I could marvel at in the mornings but which at night were grotesque and terrifying.

I knew I was disturbed, because a small incident occurred that should never have troubled me. An open carriage drove past me one day, and in that carriage there were a gentleman, a lady and two children, all laughing lightheartedly, with parcels on their laps. I had such a feeling of pain and loss as they passed. That could never be mine. Family, wife, a position somewhere, coming home at night to a cosy home, kids with red hair pestering for stories – I was denied all that. Up till then, of course, I hadn't even wanted it. Suddenly it seemed to me the essence of happiness and I felt like the little match girl. I walked along the street with tears running down my face. I never asked to be different. Why had I got to be an Urning? Who in their right mind would ever choose to be one?

That evening I went to Madame Rosa's, where I had a gent booked. "Oh, Willie!" cried Rosa pulling a face. "You been ill or something? You look awful tired."

"Ta very much. You make a person feel wonderful."

"Come and have a sip of something. You got a rather demanding gent lined up."

Fortified with her best Bewjolly I went in to face this monster.

Ah, he was no worse than others I had had; but ain't it so, how if you're down everything conspires to make it worse for you? He was fat and puddingy with no finesse; I found nothing there to love. I shut my eyes in his embrace. His plump sausage fingers pinched my flesh and his saliva trickled down my neck. I hurried my way down his bulbous belly, kissing through gritted lips. His stomach gurgled throughout, little watery noises like plumbing makes. He heaved and churned like a whale. I suddenly remembered that time when I'd been placed on the black velvet and surrounded by stars, and that gent had come to me out of the night. My eyes filled up with bitter tears. I should never have got into this business. I was a stupid sentimental believer in love. What was I doing *here?*

"I so enjoyed that," said my client. "You were most acceptable. May I expect to use you again at a future date?"

"I don't know, mister; I work irregular hours."

"I'd be glad to visit you again."

"Ta, mister, I appreciate that."

When he left I spent a lot of time cleaning myself up, laying the soap on thick, erasing the memory of his touch on my skin. I felt mucky. I didn't stop for a drink with Rosa; I just wanted to get away from there. I went out and started walking.

It was a stinking night, thick mushy fog that tasted damp and rank and went into your nose with the consistency of curds. Under a street lamp I paused and took out my mirror and touched up my lips and eyelids. I made a fine purple shadow above my still haggard eyes and brightened my pale lips with scarlet. I looked like some decadent boy from ancient times, overpainted, available. I dabbed my ears and throat with lavender water, and looked about me. Where was I? I'd struck out north-east; there could be trade round here if I was lucky. I paced about, keeping under lamps. At the sound of wheels I'd stay in the light, posing. I wanted to find a gent, quick, to wipe out the other. I'd have liked a little triumph, one that made me feel good, somebody classy . . .

I could hardly believe my luck when the double lights of a hansom came swaying through the fog, slowly, along the kerb's edge, as if the gent was looking. I stared, eager. I could smell the horses as they passed. The cab drew up, and I walked towards it. A head leaned round, in a high hat. "Can I offer you a lift?" said the gent.

"Thanks, mister."

"Dreadful night to be out, eh?"

"Bitchy."

He opened up the front and I climbed in beside him. The fog had made my nose ache all the way down to my lungs. I sighed and leaned back. He got the cab started, the way it was going. "You were going in this direction?" he enquired.

I blinked, surprised. "My ultimate direction," he continued, "is an address in Whitechapel – not a salubrious area, I know, but that is where my business takes me. Perhaps you'd be so good as to let me know where I can put you down?"

I didn't know whether to laugh or cry at the ridiculousness of my position; the foolish gent was genuinely giving me a lift. I sat tense and hesitant, waiting for the moment when the truth would dawn on him. As always in a hansom, my heady perfume began to make itself felt. The confined space reeked of lavender. "I think you better put me down here," I said in a gentle resigned tone. At that moment I could feel him working it out, as if a series of clockwork stirrings were set in motion. He was staring at me, appalled. "My God!" he said, in a choke, twitching back in revulsion, as if I was breathing clap all over him.

Then I did start laughing, a cynical brittle laugh it was, but I could see the humourous side. He could not. He banged on the roof almost hysterically, till the cab slowed down and brought us to a standstill. "*Get out!*" he spat. "*Vile thing!*"

"You want to be more careful who you pick up," I remarked. "You might be luckier next time and just find a nice wholesome murderer."

"How *dare* you?" he murmured, shaking. "How dare you walk our streets?"

I undid the flaps and climbed down. I said, over my shoulder: "They're *my* streets, mister."

"Drive on!" he ordered.

As the righteous vehicle swam off into the fog leaving me in the quiet street, I found I was shaking too. I had never been so close before to someone who'd radiated such hatred. He knew nothing about me and he'd called me a Thing! He'd seen the paint on my face and that was it, I was damned. He probably went to the same church as Mr Sheldon. He'd hardly wanted to sully his mouth by talking to me. He'd have felt contaminated even ordering me to get out. I sniggered to think of him alone with the scent of my perfume, edging himself into the corner away from where I had vilified the seat with my filthy obnoxious presence. Instinctively, to cut out the pain I knew I was feeling, I drew my prickles about me and kept on walking.

I knew where I was now. These streets were familiar to me from when, as a scruffy kid, I'd trailed up west from Aldgate. Ah, I'd come too far over; there'd be no trade for me here. I slouched my way to the next lamp post, and leaned, floating and disembodied, as if the fog was water and I was adrift.

Gradually I became aware of footsteps coming nearer, a slow measured tread which instantly suggested the law. Who else would walk the foggy streets so self-assured and unafraid? As the figure drew into the gaslight's glow I saw that it was not a crusher, since he wore a tall hat and an overcoat; moreover, he was carrying something bulky in his arms. I stood still and stared.

With a hard sharp physical shock I realised who it was. I recognised him. It was Mr Pearson, my hero, my ideal who had stirred all my boyhood longings so long ago, and now he was here, real, just a few yards from me, coming out of the fog. In his arms he was carrying a boy. And there was another boy trailing slowly along beside him. And I knew that I could not let him go by. I knew that I would have to speak.

I'd had a bad night, remember. I don't know what devil got into me. He looked so upright, so law-abiding and so obviously Doing Good. And yet seeing him carrying a boy, I suddenly had a warped and twisted vision of his being a bad baron carting off boys to a secret stronghold to satisfy his perverse desires. I wanted to tarnish his image. I wanted to shock him and disturb his complacency.

I strolled coolly towards Mr Pearson. When I drew level I stepped out insolently in front of him and let him see exactly what I was. "Oy, mister," I said cheekily. "Can I give yer a light?"

He looked at me blankly. We stood there, staring, illumined by lamplight. I could see I had surprised him by my sudden appearance out of the fog and I smirked, gratified. He looked so taken aback, so startled and astonished.

I repeated my offer, smug in my success at disconcerting such a hero. "Light, mister?"

Quickly he recovered. "No thank you," he said, frowning a little, his eyes never leaving my face, as if he must convince himself that this odd little encounter was really happening. Now it was my turn to feel disconcerted – the intensity of his gaze was curiously disturbing. So I leered provocatively, hand on hip.

"Go on, mister. Ain't it wotcher want?"

He looked me swiftly up and down. "I'll tell you what you *can* give me," he said, "and that's the help of your strong right arm. Carry this boy."

And he handed me an armful of boy, so authoritatively that I instinctively clutched hold of the little blighter before I knew what I was doing. "Oy, mister," I protested.

"Too heavy for you?"

"No, but – "

"Then be so kind as to step along with us. This little lad here," he indicated the one on foot, "is falling asleep on his feet. We can be quicker with two." He picked up that boy, who in fairness was a whole lot bigger than the one he'd given me, and lodged him so he could sleep against his shoulder.

"Do you know Goff Street?" Mr Pearson enquired.

"No. Where is it?"

"Shoreditch. Not too far. If you will be so kind as to accompany us I will give you the fare for a cab up west."

I blushed in the darkness. His covert reference to my trade embarrassed me, his assumption that that was where I functioned. I bit my lip.

I settled the boy in my arms and we started walking. Both boys were ragged, filthy and barefoot. Mine weighed no more than a mongrel, all skin and bone, his little knees jutting up through rent cloth. He smelt foul. I was concerned about my corduroy jacket. His nose streamed; he was not endearing. Five years old, I thought. "Where'd you find 'em?"

"Under half a sack," he said expressively. "They are brothers."

That was all we said the whole journey to Goff Street. *Under half a sack* – the way he said it carried the whole weight of what he thought about society, as if I didn't know already. The boy he was carrying was wheezing something awful. He looked about eight, and every bit as blatantly destitute as the one I held. Mine clutched at my lapel. I sneakily unpicked his fingers, but he put them back. I never got that lapel straight. He gripped it like it was a lifeline.

After my initial ghastly behaviour in the gaslight I sank into tongue-tied shyness. I never thought I'd be forced into his company after my awful cheek, and now I felt depressed beyond words. Against all odds, I was in the company of my hero, my Jesus figure, the one I'd got caned over, he who was valiant against all disaster. And here I was in my true colours, excessively painted, stinking of perfume, a street whore by action and appearance; I wasn't fit to be near him. I was an outcast and he was half captain, half missionary; a passionate apostle, glorious and good; and I was a worm.

Silently, we plodded through the fog. I kept an eye on our route, working out where we were. Shabby streets, narrow, ill lit, the usual intermittent night-time stragglers. The boy in my arms fell asleep and grew heavy. My arms hurt, but I'd never have admitted it. The fog was making my chest ache. I'd pay for this stupid act of humanity; I'd be lucky if I didn't get another bout to lay me low. I resented Mr Pearson and all other do gooders. They waltzed into your life and traded on your good nature, catching you by surprise. I bet he was never ill. I bet he had a Dear Wife to mop his brow.

We arrived at Goff Street. I was curious to see this famous Boys' Home, the one he spoke about so caringly in my uncle's church. *If we gave all we had, it would not be enough.* The fellow was exaggerating, said my uncle, he was after money.

There was a high brick wall and a gateway – no gates. We went through into a yard and there was a tall gaunt house stretching up, dark, fog wisping about it. Some little stunted trees rattled bare branches. We went up the steps to the front door and he pulled a bell. Very shortly a light appeared, the door opened and a woman stood there, a broad squat lady in an apron and striped dress. She had a square sensible face, and I irrationally hoped she was his housekeeper. Their conversation gave nothing away except that the lady's name was Elizabeth, and there I was handing over my dozy boy to her, and she took him indoors.

My arms hurt and hung down heavily. I took a breath. "Well, I must be going," I said hesitating.

"Listen," said Mr Pearson, "wait."

We stood on the step, he still holding his boy. We faced each other; he was taller than me, six foot I shouldn't wonder. I actually dared then to look into his face. He looked kind. And troubled. "About your question," he said.

"What question?"

"Whether you could give me a light."

I felt sick with shame at having it brought back at me. In the light of his glowing gaze I felt myself paling. "Yes, what?" I said roughly.

"I wish," he said, in a gentle voice, "and I hope . . . that you are able to find a light for *yourself*."

I wasn't stupid; I was educated – I knew about symbolic language. His meaning got to me straightaway. Ah, how easy it was for him to talk about light. Safe in his big house, doing good, with Elizabeth to help him and make him cocoa, one of God's pets, the sort that got a pat on the back on the Day of Judgement. Well done, thou good and faithful servant, you gave a home to destitute boys. Whereas you, Willie Smith, you hawked your body about and cheapened yourself in vile brothels.

All I'd got, in the face of his obvious care and concern, was my bravado. "Offer still stands, mister," I said, real coarse and crude. "Garn, give yerself a treat, you deserve it. I'm real good. Only five bob out of doors, and I can't say fairer than that."

Suddenly his face filled with a sort of loathing. Hatred even. He looked shockingly different. Across the sleeping boy he said in quiet venomous tones: "How dare you? I think you'd better go."

I turned. I looked over my shoulder and sneered nastily. "Everyone knows why older men take an interest in boys. Pervert!"

Then I just ran.

III

I POUNDED down the foggy streets of Shoreditch, running till my chest hurt and my breath was coming out in sobs. What had I done? What had I said? I didn't *know* myself. I was like a Roundhead pissing on an altar. What was I becoming, what would happen to me? In my head I was hysterical, thoughts bashing against my skull like trapped sparrows. I had to stop running; I ached all over. I felt awful. I thought I was going to drop; I don't know how I got back up west. I collapsed in a doorway. I fell over my feet, anyone would have thought I was drunk. My breath was coming out like the sound of an old saw. I had pains inside my ribs.

I made it to Caroline's.

It must've been about three in the morning. The house door was open, and the hall was lit, but it was quiet. A plump old lady was sitting knitting. Her lips were painted scarlet on a face dead white with powder. "I got ter see Caroline," I choked.

"She's with a gemmun."

"I'll wait."

Caroline saw her gent off with polite kisses, and screeched when she found me practically under her feet. "Willie! What you doin' here?"

"I need yer, Caroline," I pleaded hauntedly.

"Ow, Willie," she groaned. "I'm tired, I need a wash, I can't see yer now."

I staggered to my feet, clutching her. "I don't want to go home."

"Are you ill?" she frowned. "All right, come inside."

She closed the door and folded her arms severely. "Now, what is all this?"

"Can I stay? I can't bear goin' home, I don't want to be alone. Please let me stay," I said, starting to cry. She still showed no reaction, and in my desperation I said something awful. I said: "I'll give you a guinea for your time." And then I broke right down, my arm leaning on the wall, my face hidden in it, choking on my sobs. She came and put her arms round me. "I hate myself," I wept into her shoulder. "I can't stand who I am."

There was a whole lot more of this. She had to put up with me writhing about and moaning and telling her how vile I was

233

and how I couldn't take any more and no one should have to live like this and I couldn't go amongst decent people; I just went on and on. She sat beside me on the bed and held me; she was used to being silent and consoling difficult gents. Somewhat later she washed my face for me and creamed off all my makeup, and said I could stay the night.

"You won't seduce me, will you?" I quivered. She seemed so powerful I believed her capable of any miracle.

"I do have my standards," she replied huffily. "I draw the line at little boys."

Rather chastened, I went off to have a piss. When I came back she had found a nightshirt for me, and she helped me get undressed and into it. She tucked me into bed and pattered about washing; she brought us cocoa and put on a nightdress and climbed in beside me.

That was my first night with a woman, and I know it was nice because I slept all through it. It was my first proper night's sleep for many nights. Desire never entered my head and probably, in the state I was in, hers neither.

In the morning, when I was coherent, I told her some of my troubles, and I asked her what she thought about Mr Scott's offer. "I think you'd be a fool not to accept," she said.

PART FIVE

CHAPTER SIXTEEN

I

HALF COURTESAN, half patient, I was Mr Scott's kept boy for two whole months, a length of time that at first alarmed me and which I later grew to accept. I could not settle for resentment of the fact that I was still paying Mrs Dawson so much for an empty room. Eventually probably to silence my repetitive complaints, he paid off the lot in a lump sum, a gesture which bound me to him for as long as he wanted me, for indeed I was bought, as surely as any shop object. For the push he spent on me I accepted his ownership. Objectively I hated it; but my resources were low, and at the time I could see no other course open to me. I can't pretend there was not a deal to enjoy. I had never lived in such luxury in all my life.

"Bring nothing," he told me – as if I had anything to bring or a bag to carry it in. However, everyone told me it was cold in the country and so I went down Whitechapel and fixed myself up with some black corduroys. I asked my tailor to make them to the same measurements as the cream, confidently expecting to return rapidly to my original voluptuousness; consequently they hung on me a bit, making me look thinner than I was. I also bought a strong pair of sturdy boots, and as to a warm winter coat I found one I liked down the old clothes market, black cloth, lined, padded round the shoulders, and coming to just below my knees. I can't say it was the last word in elegance but it was warm, and with my cap pulled down low I was all set for wintry weather. I tucked my purple scarf in to the neck to break the blackness, and I thought I looked rather artistic – I even had the proper pallor and the mauve circles below the eyes.

Well! I was to go on a train!

I was given the fare by my lover, along with copious directions, for of course he could not travel with me or be seen in my company in a public railway station. I did not mind. I was as excited as a child, and would only have embarrassed him by my elation and nerves. As it was, I found myself entering under the archway of Saint Pancras station and mingling with the crowds, trying to look as if I made this trip every day, working out where to buy my ticket and where to wait for the train. Wait I did not need to, because it was in the station, belching out steam like a story book dragon. I went up to look at the engine, and gawped at the huge wheels and the great funnel and the fire, and the stoker who looked little older than myself, though all muscle and brawn. A sudden burst of steam entirely covered me up, alarming me that the train was about to leave without me and I hurried to take my seat.

I must admit to a sudden jolt of panic in the stomach as the train set off. It was so fast! I swallowed and coughed to control my nervousness, but as we pulled out of the station I relaxed and lost myself in the wonder of the experience. How amazing it was to see houses pass by at such speed, and then to see fields, real fields. The compartment was full; unfortunately everyone wanted to talk and so I was obliged to invent a kindly uncle and all kinds of other fanciful extravagances to explain my journey. And all the time I was staring about me like a newborn babe seeing the world for the first time. It was a dull day, twilight at midday, with heavy banks of cloud. How enormous the clouds looked, seen over fields, no houses in between! How huge the sky was . . .

I had not a long way to go – so said Mr Scott who had travelled to Arabia – but it seemed quite far to me who had been no further than across London. I was leaving behind me all that was familiar. Gone were the high houses and the crowds. To either side of us were only fields and woods, a small village, a river – things I had read about in books. I felt curiously inexperienced out in the world. Darkness began to descend, though it was only afternoon. As we drew into the station I felt oddly shy, and had to ask which one it was, learning as I expected that it was the one I wanted. Others were descending too as I climbed down onto the platform, the lamps already lit, the air striking cold and fresh. When I made my way out the train started up, real loud, like nothing I'd ever heard, and hissing steam.

I was met outside the station by a servant from the hall. He came unerringly towards me. One thing about having auburn hair, it tends to make you an accessible landmark. He'd got a small carriage waiting, a little way down the road in the gloom, I was uneasy. I had no idea how to behave with servants. I knew he could have no jot of respect for me, and yet he behaved as if he had – that is, falsely. I sat on the worn leather seat, and the carriage creaked into life and swayed and set off. On either side there were trees. The carriage lamps lit up snatches of hedge, a clutter of undergrowth, and bare angular twigs against a dark sky. The branches rattled, one bare stem against another, like bones. The moon rose.

I had to laugh at myself, because I was aware of my imagination coming to the fore, as if I was the heroine of some melodramatic novel – plucked from her hearth and home to go as governess to mad Lord Somebody's crippled son. He would of course have a Gothic mansion; there would be a secret room and a secret passage; on the first night there the candles would all blow out; I would hear the clanking of chains; and one or two drops of blood would drip from the ceiling on to my pillow. The wicked lord would be Sinister, Brooding and Severe, and he would either turn out to be a vampire, or, won over by my sweet ways, would fall in love with me, and make me his bride. I couldn't think of any tales like that where the protagonist was a bloke; they were all earnest and vulnerable young girls.

The ambiguity of my position confused me. I should certainly never have come. I blame it on my illness that I felt so negative about what was after all rather an adventure and laden with benefit for me. But I wasn't at all happy. I knew I was deeply entrenched in a situation I had never wanted to be in and had sworn to avoid, and yet a situation I landed in time and time again, obligated, dependent. What was it about me, some weakness somewhere, that pulled me back into dependence that was no good for me? Some need I had, so that given a chance I always abandoned the integrity of independence and plumped for a protector, a sort of womanly wish to be cherished? It depressed me immensely.

Eventually we arrived at some tall gates. The moon hung like a lit pumpkin on a navy blue backcloth as we turned into a drive which continued for some while through parkland smudged with the shapes of trees.

As I soon came to know, the house was Georgian. It was, at least downstairs, elegant and uncluttered and tasteful. It was not large, I was told, and I accepted that as true, even when I was strolling through vast rooms and corridors as long as a street and looking through full-length windows at long clear vistas of lawns. That first night, however, it was simply a black shape with a wide open door through which light flooded. In front of the servants Mr Scott shook my hand, but in his grip I could sense his suppressed exhilaration. I hardly felt I merited it, a hunched and chilly bundle in a long overcoat – but maybe he saw me different.

II

THAT EVENING we ate in the dining room at a polished table beside a bright fire of logs – apple, he told me – and I was impressed to hear that different boughs give off different scents when burning. An odd meal it was, exquisite food, which a silent servant brought, and between ourselves clipped polite conversation, on his part with an underlying amusement, and on mine with general uneasiness which made me sound sullen.

In all fairness, my benefactor took very seriously his role of returning me to health. The fact that he was doing it for his own benefit I pass over, since after all it was for my benefit too. For probably the first three weeks I could almost have been at a luxurious sanatorium. I was sent to bed early every night, and to sleep an' all! Oh – and the bed – never seen one like it! Huge! Old! Brocaded drapes, and so high off the ground it was almost a climb, and a feather mattress so deep you sank to your own weight in softness. I had my own room, with a fire lit, and a servant to see to it. I slept late and the servant brought breakfast in bed on a tray. He said nothing, except to tell me what the weather was like as he drew aside the curtains, and I never replied. I felt foolish being called sir, particularly first thing in the morning. In this household the coffee and the hot chocolate were out of this world, and served in wide cups with saucers, painted with gold and dainty figures dancing. The boiled eggs came in silver egg cups, while the salt and pepper were to be found in an elaborate contrivance with lions' paws at each corner.

In the mornings I spent my time in a leisurely fashion till lunch. I could read anything I wanted from his library, though he saved his pornography until I was fitter! At first I read books on Indian philosophy, but he also possessed all the works of Jane Austen, which were of the same age as the house, and I read all of them, curled up by the fire.

In the fly leaves of these books I saw many times over his real name written. Yes! He really was a lord. That did my self-esteem no end of good. In the afternoons I had to go for a walk in the grounds; I had to stay out for at least an hour, and later when I'd lost my pallor and such, he was insistent I ran as well. Sometimes I felt like I was his labrador! I mean, he came walking with me sometimes, and he'd order me when to run and take out his watch to make sure I kept on for half an hour. He never ran, he just loafed, leaning on a stile, warm in a fur-edged coat, watching me run.

I was fed on wholesome food at regular intervals, including milk and cordials and concoctions from the mysterious East, which were mixed and brought to me by his manservant whom he called Jamshyd – the name of a mythical Persian king. Jamshyd spoke no English, and I found him very unsettling and disconcerting. His skin was very dark, and he wore a long robe, sandals, and a turban. His eyes, alert and watchful, flickered over me with, I could have sworn, contempt.

Evenings were spent in Mr Scott's upstairs study by the fire, sitting in leather chairs, while he attempted to teach me chess and backgammon, at which, although he teased me lightly, I was not good. Dominoes was what I was best at but, after all, I wasn't well! When he judged I was getting drowsy I was packed off to bed like a seven year old, sometimes as early as half past eight.

Bodily contact between us was almost non-existent during the early part of my stay there. But I felt like the cherry who was left on the plate for last. I knew he was looking at me proprietorially, comfortably, knowing I was ripening, assessing my bloom. It amused me. I would have gone with him on that first night if he'd asked; he had that right. I broached it to him one day, in the evening, when he told me it was my bedtime. "Look, mister, I ain't pulling me weight. I don't want somethin' for nothin'. Why dontcher come in with me and I'll see to yer?"

"It's a matter of principle. A bargain with myself, almost. I have resolved to restore you to health. It will be my reward when I am satisfied with your progress. It is for me even a discipline, a virtue, to look at and not to touch. Do you understand?"

"Oh yes. I used to be the same at my uncle's if we had cream on the stewed apples."

I didn't see much of the servants, but the house had such an empty feel that I believe we only had as few as were needed to run the place at basic level. The rooms weren't well dusted, I noticed, but we always ate well and had good fires in the hearths. Mr Scott was not always at home, and while he was away I read and took tea, and lazed, and ate oranges and nuts and apples, and washed my hair.

In my long rambles round the estate I felt my vitality returning as clearly as if it had been visible. I walked miles over the parkland, discovering a small lake and copses, and following little winding lanes that caked my boots with mud I didn't even have to clean off! To my delight in the month of December we had a sparkling frost. The sky was pale blue, and every hillside looked as if it had been dabbed with a huge white powder puff. To see white fields was magic to me. I found a puddle frozen over with ice so thick that even standing upon it did no more than slit the surface into cracks. Beneath the ice, brown mud-flurried water stirred. I kicked a hole in the ice with my boot heel for birds to come and drink – whole ranks of crows there were, and also seagulls. That day for the first time I ran for the pleasure of it, breathing in clean cold air with none of the pain the fog had caused, and blowing out white steam of my own. I came home so sparkly and rosy that Mr Scott gave me a peculiar look and said he thought it was time our celibacy came to an end.

I wasn't at all sorry. I felt strange being a guest there without doing what I'd come for, and also as a proof that I was indeed recovering, I was hungry to get back into that action; I was eager for it. He came to my bedroom and we made love by the fire. It was so very pleasant that I had the illusion we were really lovers, and that money and possessions were not involved; he was a considerate and refined paramour, and gave as well as received. "Oh," I said, "won't you stay?"

"You need your sleep," he said firmly. I felt regret. It was not to be the sort of relationship where we slept in each other's arms. I sighed, but I accepted it. We were never close; and it was foolish of me to want it. Lovemaking for him was almost an artistic pursuit. Under his roof it took place in the daytime and out of bed; it wasn't a friendly thing you did before falling asleep. We never slept together, but retired to our own bedrooms. I must say I slept very well while I was there. I had no nightmares and rarely any dreams at all.

III

WHEN CHRISTMAS came, Mr Scott was obliged to go away and spend time with other members of his family. I could not help but reflect on the strangeness of life, to think that last Christmas there had been all the festivities at the Armitage household – holly boughs, decorations, plum pudding and parlour games. And now here I was, one year later, the catamite of a cultured gentleman, in solitary luxury and somewhat lacking in integrity.

I didn't mind being on my own for Christmas; it was strange but pleasant. I was well looked after; the servant brought meals unobtrusively and retired. I went for long walks on the estate and fed the ducks on the lake, returning to sit in the study by the fire. There I drank port and ate turkish delight and oranges, and leafed through Mr Scott's pornography – Indian drawings and photographs of copulating statues on temple facades, and extensive literature on the cult of the phallus. Outside, great white snowflakes tumbled past the window, whitening the lawns and the tall old evergreens; inside, the firelight glowed and I lazed in a low leather chair like a pampered cat. From far away came the sound of church bells carried on the wind.

Since it was indeed Christmas I wanted to give Mr Scott a present. Hampered by being in the situation of owning nothing, I had the idea of copying out one of our favourite verses from *The Rubayyat* (in my best copperplate) and folded it over a lock of my hair.

When on his return I handed this gem over to him – sitting

on his knee in the study by the fire – he was very pleased and touched; he said so. I was daunted by the generosity of the gifts I received in return, a startling mixture of the practical and the extravagant. A gold ring with a curvaceous W engraved upon it; two nightshirts in warm flannel, a dark blue muffler and lined gloves, a carved Indian box for my jewellery and an ivory bracelet inside it; several pairs of socks, and an illustrated book of Persian fairy tales. As if this wasn't enough, he told me he had put one hundred pounds in a bank for me, which I could claim when I was twenty-one. We had a serious talk about banks and money orders, while he explained to me how I was to collect my money when it was due.

Behind his gifts, I know, was the implication that I might fall upon hard times. The gold ring I could sell, and of course the other things too – indeed he told me which shops would take them. It seemed curious, and sad, to be giving presents on that basis. As to the hundred pounds, I don't think anyone who's been poor would refuse that. I certainly didn't. I just set about convincing him I was worth it.

Now that he was back to stay and I was so patently recovered, our life then centred around the main reason for my being there. He was able to indulge his favourite fantasy; we retired to the mysterious East. In the room further along from our bedrooms he had had an oriental tent set up, an amazing embroidered creation with a pointed roof and yards of billowing cloth sloping down. Inside were carpets and cushions, and here we spent our afternoons. He dressed in voluminous trousers and gold slippers and wore a brocaded fringed waistcoat over his bare chest. Me, oh I didn't wear anything, except jewellery. I was a slave, see, and he was a sultan. He taught me how to show my obedience by a deep salaam, and after that I spent a lot of time worshipping him. My lips used to taste of the odd pungent oils with which he perfumed all the crevices of his body. Afterwards he liked to smoke an opium pipe, and I had to help set it up and pass it to him. I learnt how to roll the brown pellets and to keep an eye on the flame so it didn't go out. All the time Jamshyd sat outside and played Indian music on a sitar, and handed me the plates of sweets I sometimes had to pass to my sultan.

Yet these forays into the perfumed garden were also alternated with the kind of innocent exertions that a chaperoned girl could have shared unblushing. Mr Scott was a sultan within the tent, but out of it our relationship was as of guardian and ward. He was caring but severe. We went for snowy walks muffled up against the cold. He still made me run but I didn't mind by then; I was very much fitter and it was no hardship to run around the lake, which lay cold and glassy, smudged with gold from the blurred wintry sun.

"Ah, mister, it ain't half clean here," I couldn't help remarking. "All this space, all this white . . . I never tasted such clean snowflakes!"

"I knew it would do you good . . . " he purred.

"I s'pose," I said eagerly. "I s'pose we couldn't have a sledge? I could make one if yer like, I wouldn't half fancy it."

"I assume you imagine it's just a question of slinging a few bits of wood together!" he said reprovingly.

"Ain't it?" I enquired cheekily.

"No indeed. It's very skilled work. The runners have to match exactly; otherwise you go round in a circle. Why, my brother and I – " and he stopped, laughing at the idea of chatting to me about his childhood.

"You had a brother, did yer?" I asked interested.

"Two, and two sisters. I daresay the sledge is still somewhere about . . . I think it's time you had another run."

"Run with me, mister," I challenged.

"Me? – I'm far too old and dignified . . . "

"Race yer!"

He must have been inspired by his reminiscences. He pelted off after me and caught me up, but I ran faster and left him behind. I stopped, laughing and gasping, to wait for him. "Yah, mister! I'm fitter'n you! Early to bed for you tonight!"

I'd have gone on jeering happily no doubt, except that he reached down without saying anything and scooped up some snow. I saw it coming and ducked, but he kept some in his hand and flattened it on my face. I let him. I was still sparkling and grinning, and I lifted my face up to his snow and let him smear it. It made me gasp, it was that cold – but so clean, so pure. I felt it on my eyelashes and licked it off my lips. That part was nice, but the trickle down my neck wasn't, and I pulled away and rolled a snowball of my own. I had it in my hand, aiming, but I hesitated. I knew he wouldn't like it. I had to respect his dignity. It was part of the hundred pounds in the bank deal. I slung the snowball at a tree. In our relationship it was my place to receive – snowballs, money, presents, lust, and his to give. Even out here in all this powdery purity, my function was the same as when I was on the streets. Nothing changed.

Mind you, he found the sledge for me. That servant must have been a bit astonished, being asked to root out and dust down an ancient toy from the woodshed. So off I'd go, nice and warm in my long black coat and cap, the blue muffler streaming and gloves on my hands, pulling the sledge over the snow to the slopes. It was a funny thing to be doing on your own, like a private ceremony. I saw nobody; I was alone with the trees, the heavy white sky, the lump of misty sun and my own footprints. I learnt for myself that the climb up the slope is long and hard and the short rush down is always over too soon. And I learnt that for the sake of the swift exhilarating rush of pleasure, so wild and so soon over, you make the slow laborious climb again and again.

Mr Scott was waiting for me at the big front door, looking out for me. I kicked the snow off my boots against the wall, and as the servant hurried forward to relieve me of the sledge I suddenly felt sheepish with the string in my hand. My ears were burning with cold and my nose dribbled and my coat was powdered with snow. "My goodness," said Mr Scott, smiling and shaking his head. "I sometimes forget, Willie, how *young* you are."

Young I may have been, but he seemed to have no difficulty exchanging the scruffy kid with the sledge for a partner in pleasure, and inside the brocaded tent he kept me in erotic subjugation. Not a day went by but I saw to his delight on the Persian carpet and the Indian cushions. By now he had abandoned any pretence of our being lovers, never returning the favour to me but enjoying his satisfactions much as any sultan would. I began to feel like I had been purchased in the Darfur desert for the markets of Turkey.

Nor was Mr Scott impervious to the implications of our roles for, once over dinner, he talked about the concept of slavery, reflecting on how it had always existed, wondering what exactly was the obscene thrill one being took from dominating another, and how the notion was objectively revolting and yet personally compelling, particularly in terms of the erotic. I said rather stuffily that I did not approve of slavery, and he just smiled and said he was probably speaking on a hypothetical level and I need not concern myself with actualities. I tried to point out to him that slavery was all around us, that the poor lived in bondage, and that the upper class and the factory owners were almost as bad as the tyrants of Arabia, but he frowned, and said this kind of conversation was inappropriate between us.

IV

ALTHOUGH HE was a sultan to his heart's content with me, Mr Scott still had his commitments in the outside world. Sometimes he would be obliged to spend time away, and then I would return to my solitary existence with the polite servant, and the long walks in the January fields. It was on one of these occasions that I walked further than usual and out of the estate, making my way to a village. I was now returned to full fitness and it came easy to me to cover distances, and I was getting very bored with the parkland. I had a good look round the village, staring and being stared at, for to me country people were like visitors from another planet, as I must have been to them. I noticed an inn and longed to go inside. I could see a fire within, and a warm beery smell wafted out as the door opened. I minded not having any money. I had to trail back to the house, irritable and fidgety.

When I got back I surprised the servant by lurking around in the kitchen and asking him if he could lend me a shilling. He said he didn't think the master would like it, and it crossed my mind to search the house and see if there were any loose coins lying about. As it happened I didn't, but merely having considered it made me realise that if I was left here much longer I'd be obliged to give in to the temptation. I thought then about Bluebeard's wife who, left alone, goes rooting about and finds a secret chamber. It occurred to me that a room full of dismembered bodies would be a welcome diversion.

"And what use have you for a shilling, Willie Smith?" enquired Mr Scott on his return. We were sitting in the study in the evening.

"I was going to buy a drink," I said frankly.

"Buy? A drink?" he frowned.

"Yeah, at the village. They got this little place . . . "

"You've been to the village?" he said angrily.

"Yes," I said defensively. "Why shouldn't I?"

"Aren't these grounds big enough for you?"

"No. Why should they be? I'm used to the whole of London."

"You must not go to the village, Willie. I'm very displeased about that. I forbid you to go again."

"Oh? Why?"

"It's obvious, surely. I can't have you sitting in the village inn with your long hair and your London accent, chatting to the villagers and explaining who you're staying with! Use your common sense."

"Ho! Surely you ain't ashamed of me, mister?" I sneered.

"Are you spoiling for a fight?" he half laughed. "I shouldn't advise it. I hold all the advantages."

"Yeah, like money," I scowled. "What d'you imagine I'd tell your precious villagers, hey? I'm his lordship's kept boy?"

"I insist you give me your word to stay within the grounds," he said, his lips tight with annoyance.

"And you'd take it?" I said cynically. "And what if I said no?"

"I suppose I could chain you up," he drawled.

"You'd only do that once!" I gasped.

"Listen here, my lad," said Mr Scott comfortably. "I've no wish to fight any more than you have. I believe we've come to the natural break, and I think we should recognise it and act accordingly. You are well now, Willie. I pulled you from the slime of your natural habitat and it's time I dropped you back in. Attractive as the idea is to me of keeping you chained up for my own personal pleasure, I am still just about able to separate fact from fancy. If I can no longer be sure of your remaining quietly here of your own free will, then I must allow you to leave, which in fact suits my own plans. I shall be returning to the city next month. Then I shall make preparations for a long journey abroad. Our time together has been of mutual benefit, and the wise know when to separate."

I sat and thought. He was right, of course.

"Do I still keep me money and me presents?" I asked.

"Certainly," he said, looking surprised.

"When shall I leave?"

"Within the next day or so; however long it takes to arrange."

I felt suddenly despondent at the ease with which he seemed able to dispense with me. "Will you be sorry to lose me? A little bit?" I hoped.

"A great deal, you engaging imp," he said warmly.

I was pleased about that. "Since we are talking to each other tonight," I said, "I'd be curious to know what you think about me going back on the streets."

"I'm sorry you have to," he shrugged. "What more can I say?"

"But you wouldn't persuade me against it? Or advise me to do something else?"

"My dear boy," he laughed. "I can't imagine you *doing* anything else! What else are you so good at?"

"I write a fine copperplate."

"Ah!" – but he wasn't taking me seriously – "so you fancy being someone's secretary, or clerk?"

"No, not really. I just wondered whether it bothered you that I was going back into whoring, after you'd cleaned me up."

"But it's your life, Willie. If that's what you want . . . "

"Just tell me something. If I wanted a reference from you to get me into a clerk's place, a nice place, not something common, would you give me one?"

"Oh, come, Willie," he declared. "You don't even want to *be* a clerk!"

"No, but would you?" I persisted.

"I would not. Now are you satisfied? Are you nicely upset? What did you expect me to say? It's more than my reputation's worth to place you among genteel people who might make enquiries – moreover, I genuinely believe you wouldn't take to it."

"So far as you're concerned then, all I can ever be is a whore. You get uneasy when I'm anything else – if I'm a kid pulling a sledge, or if I talk to you about social conditions. You're uneasy *now*. You don't even like me talking about it. You're only comfortable with me when I'm your own pet prostitute."

"My dear boy – if you had not been a whore you would never have met me! It is the only level on which we could meet. Socially we would never have spoken. Or maybe one day you might have cleaned my shoes on the pavement. I suggest we both be grateful that the money which passed between us was for something very much more enjoyable. And now, a glass of something before bedtime, I think."

It was a goodbye drink, our position clear, our business stated. Myself, I think he was more immoral than me, but I have an odd view of morality. I cherish a fondness for him though, and I know that on the whole he was good to me. It makes me laugh to think what his hundred pound was eventually spent on, when I had access to it at twenty-one. Maybe it put the balance right. To me it was very pleasing.

February saw me travelling back to the smoke. I felt jaunty — now I was all confidence and ease about the train ride, carrying a lady's bag for her and playing five stones with her little girl to keep her amused. I felt I'd had a strange little holiday; strange indeed.

CHAPTER SEVENTEEN

I

WHEN I arrived back in London, they'd had snow too but it was grey snow. The roads were awash with filthy slush, and the pavements were packed with lumpy ice and spaded heaps of old hard snow, speckled with gutter mess, that flaunted its obscene remains and would rot and mulch when the snow heaps melted. And yet I was happy to be back, gladly exchanging the sparkling fields and wide pale skies for the chimneys and dirt, eager to root around for the next scraps of my life.

I went first to Caroline's for my key and all the news. She was toasting her feet at a fire, eating marshmallows and nursing a streaming cold. I felt disgustingly well by comparison, and she instantly sent me out to do some shopping for her and not to forget throat lozenges and whiskey. Then she told me to push off, as my rosy cheeks and cheerful attitude were getting on her nerves, and so I obligingly set off for my place.

Apart from the bleak, cold atmosphere of unlived-in rooms, and the appearance of several large patches of damp on the walls, nothing had changed. I flung my coat off and set about getting a fire going. I unpacked my clothes and presents, and I sat up half the night airing my bedding, drinking brandy and reading Persian fairy tales. All my old depression and doubt had dispersed, and I felt comfortable and optimistic.

When I got back to work, blokes thanked me for being out on the streets.

"I say," one breathed, "I'm awful grateful to you. It can't be easy on a night like this . . . I do appreciate you being out . . . I needed it so badly tonight."

"My pleasure, mister," I said modestly.

In many ways the winter nights were more beautiful than the summer. On cold clear nights the sky was so starry and I never tired of gazing up at infinity. Was God really up there, I wondered, looking down on us, all seeing, all knowing? Why didn't he reach down and give me a punch? I felt more comfortable just taking the stars at their face value. They were impressive enough even without God behind them. I tried to remember their names, but the only one I was sure of was the Plough, and the way it pointed to the North Star.

And the stars were not the only lights, oh no. As the gas lamps were lit, the whole city bloomed like an exotic garden – lights, lights, as far as the eye could see, dancing in the black silk of the river, strung out in streaming rows like a necklace. Lights on the bridges and under the trees, lights to illumine a young male tart, and lights to hide from when he's picked his plum.

One night a gent in a hansom picked me up and began chatting to me. He was tense and anxious. He asked me if I knew a place to go, and when I suggested addresses, he kept telling the cabby to drive on. He kept asking me if they were safe, if they were ever raided by the police. However much I assured him, he wouldn't let the cab be stopped. He began querying whether I believed in eternity. I said I did. We continued to drive around. "But damnation?" he persisted desperately. "Hell fire?"

"Yeah, I know, the lake of brimstone, I've heard all about that," I growled. "Forget it, mister. Take your pleasure if you wants it. God'll understand in the end."

"How do you know? How can you be sure?"

"Well, he's Love, ain't he? Love understands all things."

"You say that because you want my money!" he accused.

"No; I say it 'cause it's what I think."

"But how can you be sure?"

"I *ain't* sure."

"The Bible tells us it's a sin. If it's a sin and we commit it knowingly, then we are damned," he shuddered.

"Why did you pick me up, mister?" I asked reasonably.

"The urge was too strong . . . I gave in . . . I knew what you were. I wanted it."

"D'you still want it, mister?"

"Yes! But it's a sin – it's wrong."

"Look here, mister," I said kindly. "How about if the people who wrote that part of the Bible got it wrong? How about if they didn't understand what it feels like to want to love a man, and how about if they made a muddle working out what God planned? It's a very complicated world, and God made all of it – maggots and flies and scorpions and all kinds of *things* which are hard to explain. So why not other things? Just cause people think things are bad, it don't necessarily mean they *are* bad; it just means other people don't understand them. Honest, if God's got a soft spot for maggots and vultures he ain't going to turn against nice blokes just cause they like to cuddle men. He probably knew what he was doing when he made us what we are, hey?"

"Don't you worry about hell fire? Doesn't prostituting your body make you tremble for the consequences?"

It was hardly politic to point out that the consequences were more likely to be the clap than hell fire and that I worried about that all right.

"No, I don't bother about hell fire," I replied. "I don't know why, but I just don't believe in it. And if it did exist, believe me, it wouldn't be a lonely place! We'd be burning in very illustrious company."

II

IN WINTER the darkness is a cloak. It performs the same function as greenery does in summer. In the darkness, protected only by the dark, I could take gents to places not possible in summer – behind a wall, a few steps down an alley, in a dark doorway down deserted basements. I've been on my knees before a gent under the main steps when boot heels clomped up the steps over our heads. I've been up against the sides of houses thinking we was unobserved, and only noticing afterwards that our two shadows had been relayed in quivering magnitude by a wicked lamp and strung out across the street.

I wasn't always lucky. Many nights I paced the pavements for hours till my heels ached, my ears burned with cold, my nose dribbled and my numb fingers ached for the feel of a friendly fire. If I was fortunate I'd find a coffee stall or a baked potato man. I'd warm my hands there and buy a hot mug to hold, and we'd exchange grunts about the cold. You never could tell with traders. Some were glad of your custom and company, and would give you their entire philosophy of life; others treated you like filth. I've had times when a street hawker would squint at my painted face and shake his fist at me: "Be off with yer, yer little beast! Scum! Get off the streets!"

"Scum yerself! Shove a tater up your arsehole for me!"

In the spring for a time I attached myself to an introducing house in a little street off Millbank. It was an upstairs room with drawn curtains where they burned incense, which fugged the atmosphere with a heady stink. The boys who offered themselves here were free-wheeling and irresponsible, and I could not help feeling that in this company I had come down in the world. These boys blackmailed their gents to strike it rich. I heard them boasting about it while they sat playing cards and waiting for customers. They had no scruples or morals; they were like Fadge, working in flesh rather than pickings, in principle the same.

I began to worry that I too had maybe got that hard look about the eyes, the blank unthinking cynicism so apparent in the lads who worked for money, trading first on their clients' needs and then on their guilt and fear. I used this base only a few times, taking each gent back to an address, and it felt sordid. I began to realise that the problem was myself.

You might say that the last entire year of my life had been sordid, but I didn't think so. At night out in the streets I'd felt like a prince. I'd been desired and beautiful, and I'd grown richer both in pocket and in what I'd learned. But if you lose that feeling – that buoyancy, the tingle of power, the awareness of beauty, the bravado – if that goes, then it can be sordid. It can be the full repulsive horror which do-gooders tell you it is. I got so I was thinking things which before had never troubled me. I was slouching round the streets thinking how ugly was man. I no longer felt excitement at the thought of uncovering a new pulsating prick, and when I looked at gents in the street, dapper in their dark suits and tall top hats and white shirt fronts, I saw so many penguins.

Whatever I'd proved by whoring I didn't need to any longer. Whatever identity I had been seeking, as a person or a type, I'd found. The enjoyment had gone, and the obvious fact was thrusting itself to my notice – I was young and pretty and I wanted what anyone would want, someone else young and pretty to love. Why should I have to be a boy to troubled middle-aged perverts? I wanted something different.

"Don't you ever get tired of it, Caroline, whorin' and such?"

I wondered, lying on her bed and watching her make up her face. "I know *I* do! I'd love to get off the streets, I really would!"

"Oy, Willie, move yer boots; that's a genuine Chinese coverlet! Yeah, of course I do. In fact I'm branching out. I've got myself a nice little side line now." She looked smugly mysterious. "An Afternoon Employment!"

"What?" I said curious.

"Guess!"

"How can I? It could be anything."

"It's Modelling!"

"How d'yer mean, Modelling?"

"For artists, in an art school."

"Huh," I said disparagingly. "A lot of dirty old men who come to gawp at nude girls and pretend they just want to draw them. We all know about artists and models."

"Your mind is like a sewer, Willie," said Caroline with dignity, fixing her chignon. "In fact it's all very proper. One works in a room full of students, with a professor. *And* one can earn three guineas a week!"

I whistled impressed. Then my cynicism returned.

"Ah, but it is nude, isn't it? I was right, wasn't I?"

"Yes," she conceded. "But it's not like you think. They sit yards away, chewing their paintbrushes; they never touch. They're all too shy and nice."

"They watch you undress. It's like a strip show."

"It isn't!" she burst out laughing. "Haven't you got some funny ideas! I undress behind a screen and come out with a cloak around me. I only take it off when I'm actually posing. They don't speak to me and I don't speak to them. And then I collect my money. And Mr Franklin is ever so nice, a real gent. You'd like him. No, come to think, you'd probably like Mr Charles better."

"I thought you didn't speak to anybody!"

"Ah, but these are *real* artists. I went round to their house once. It's like a palace. I had my portrait done in a garden, holding some primroses." She added archly: "I was personifying Spring."

Now I really did roll about laughing, and she tipped me off the bed for ruckling the coverlet.

"If you really want to see what it's like," she said loftily, "you can come and meet me out of work. You'll find it's all Extremely Civilised and Cultured. And they need boy models too."

I crossed the huge tiled hall and entered the cool salon where the students took their lessons. The class was packing up for the evening. I weaved my way between the students. I saw Caroline retiring behind a screen to dress. Sketches of her body lay strewn casually upon table tops and drawing boards.

"Oh yes," said one of the students as he passed, "it is imperative to spend at least six months in Paris. One has not lived until one has visited Montmartre."

I lodged on a desk top and folded my arms. A certain theatrical exhibitionism prompted me to arrange myself in a great dusty shaft of sunlight.

Caroline emerged from behind her screen, patting her hair, saw me, smiled and waved. I stood up and she came over to me. I gave her my arm, and we made to leave. A voice called "Charles! Stop that boy!" The voice was so authoritative and urgent, you'd have thought I'd stolen something. The words were to change my life.

The person coming towards me was a black haired gent of about thirty. He had a hefty black moustache, and I summed him up swiftly with a tart's appraisal – good body; dark, attractive eyes; intelligent, worldly.

"Caroline dear, is this boy anything to do with you?" he enquired.

"This is my friend Willie Smith, Mr Charles. Ain't he pretty!"

"Willie Smith," said Charles, smouldering shockingly. "What shall I appeal to, your vanity or your greed? Which is your weakness, which the fatal lure? I have a house in Kensington. Will you come home and pose for us?"

Caroline nudged me meaningfully, her face wreathed in knowing smiles and I-told-you-so glances.

"He will!" she nodded.

"I will," I agreed, embarrassed because it sounded like a ceremony.

"You see, Willie," began Mr Charles, "you are exactly what we are looking for. It would be easier to explain if you were to come and see our establishment. It's not far away. I suppose you couldn't accompany me there now?"

"I can find my own way home, Willie," Caroline assured me cheerfully. "You go with Mr Charles. You won't be sorry, Mr Charles. Willie's a lovely poser!"

III

IT WAS a walk of only a few streets. I noticed with pleasure the warmth of the light evening, and the little flurries of pink blossom that fluttered down in the sudden breezes. The month beloved of my Arthurian heroes had crept up on me unobserved – it was May. I began to experience a pleasant sense of importance at being chosen by this elegant gent. I say elegant, but he was not finely dressed; it was more an elegance of nature. He walked well and had a confident and self-aware manner, like an actor might. He asked me a few questions as we walked – was I in employ, how old was I, where was I living, had I posed before, and did I like art?

I told him I hadn't posed before – a little bit of fibbing seemed appropriate here – and I said I wasn't very well educated as regards art, but I liked the works of Monsieur Moreau and Mr Burne-Jones. "Indeed!" he observed. "Amazing!"

He peered at me earnestly and finally said: "I do hope you don't use henna."

"No, mister, I've always been a natural redhead," I replied.

"You know what they say about redheads," he smiled.

"Oh – it's like left-handed people, I think," I laughed. "Everything short of Satanism, and all the perversions in between."

I bit my tongue. Blimey, that was stupid, chatting about perversions with a stranger. But far from shocking him it seemed to draw us closer together. "And is it true what they say?" he enquired suavely.

"Er – no," I mumbled swiftly, wondering whether he was an Urning sounding me out. He just laughed and didn't probe further. We continued to walk, past some very posh houses, until we turned down a quiet road and then took a side alley past the back walls of gardens. We entered through a green garden door, and so it was that I saw the garden first of all, and the house from the back.

As we walked down a path of amber gravel, my senses were

assailed with delightful perfection. Massive white and purple lilacs were in bloom, and all over the wall were creamy white heavily scented flowers as big as fists. Thigh-high bronze wall-flowers overhung the path, and there were bushes and trees and clouds of pink blossom, and everywhere such perfume. A mauve twilight now gathered. I felt a thrill of expectancy.

As we entered the house Charles called out: "Maurice! Where are you? I've brought you something astonishing. I've brought you a Parsifal."

Thus was I announced to the artistic world. A Parsifal – as one might say: I have brought a loaf, or a roll of material, or some nice buns for tea. They always pronounced it like that an' all, very purist, never Perceval, and even Mr Tennyson never wrote it like they pronounced it.

Maurice was an ordinary affable fellow, brown-haired and bearded; he was never anything more to me than a dedicated artist. You would never have thought he created mediaeval idylls to look at him. He lived in two downstairs rooms of the house, with Clara, his woman. No one in their establishment bothered with marriage; it was very important to be Free. Clara was a beautiful and wholesome-looking girl, much younger than he; she had long loose corn-coloured hair. She was sweet and earnest, and she wore mediaeval clothes all the time. That first evening they both came through at Charles' declaration. We stood there in a sort of hallway, the floor of worn stone, a green light filtering through some stained glass, the door to the garden open, and the perfume of the flowers floating on little waves of breeze. They gasped over me and handled me with their eyes, every bit as if I was an Elgin marble fresh unpacked from Athens. "Just what you wanted!" Clara said, awed.

"But he's perfect – and is he willing? He's exactly right."

"Ah, you'll have to share him," Charles laughed. "Everyone'll want him when they see him. I do myself," he added enigmatically.

"Could he possibly move in?"

They looked at me as if the fate of nations hung on my reply.

I could hardly believe my luck. I was hesitant to assume what it was exactly they meant. "Yes, move in, sleep here, occupy a little trundle bed," explained Charles, a little sarcastically, as if it should have been obvious to all but the idiotic. "Unbeknown to yourself, Willie Smith, you are the fulfilment of our artistic dreams, largely through no fault of your own but simply through being endowed with auburn hair. These days we are all painting auburn hair; it is our fantasy of perfection. Whether Parsifal had auburn hair it is impossible to say, but that we like to assume he did causes us to pursue the image with a tremulous intensity. Speak to us, o mystic child. Nothing enigmatic or oracular: will you become our model?"

"Will I be paid?" I said cautiously.

Charles shuddered. "That something so beautiful should be so mercenary!"

"I have to earn my living."

"I hate this," Charles apologised to us all, "but we must talk terms."

There followed a swift clarification. Three guineas a month it was to be, with my room and food free. I thought that was pretty good. It was exactly what I needed at this phase of my life. I hardly needed to mull it over at all. It was a beautiful place they owned. I fancied living there. I agreed.

Well, Charles said we must celebrate our new arrangement with a drink, and he took me inside the house. He did not turn up any lights, and so that first evening I simply had an impression of mysterious splendour. We went into a room which opened into the garden with casement doors. A flowering bush grew outside, with tendrils hanging down over the open doors like yellowy green ringlets. I heard the sound of water; there was a fountain *inside the room*, tinkling and splashing. Birds were singing in the garden. The walls were hung with huge pictures, and there were cushions and rugs strewn, and a long low sofa covered with a shimmering spread.

Charles lit three candles on a cumbersome three-pronged candlestick and gave me wine in a pewter goblet. I sat upon a heap of velvet cushions, and he talked to me about Life and Art while I drank and listened.

"It's an ugly world, Willie, ours," he said. "We have come so far from the old innocences when the land was pastoral and the soil was blessed. Now the earth is branded and plundered, and fettered with iron, and the wrong things are valued. We the artists have to make our own world."

He showed me paintings of exotic landscapes with yellow skies and gilded pillars, burning rocks, and monsters rising out of the sea. He read me a description of Love, who was embodied by a beautiful youth from whose steps flowers sprang, who wore violets in his hair and trailed a wonderful veil the colour of saffron. The ideal young man, he said, had an almost girlish beauty, of stature slim and willowy, with large melting eyes and sensuous lips, and silky flowing auburn hair.

"It could be you," he said. I wondered for a moment what his intentions really were but instantly he returned to the philosophical.

"The only true reality," he said, "is what we see with our souls. In the dark places within there exists beauty and splendour, melancholy and languor, and decadent inexplicable emotions which are sometimes falsely called Sin. We mustn't be afraid of what we find. It is all Art's realm. It is the Mystic Truth."

I sat and listened, very aware of my own being. I felt very much in this century, someone who knew the price of groceries and who had read *Practical Socialism*. I sensed a falseness in Charles, a pose. I thought I would easily retain my rational capacities. I should have realised I was susceptible. My old passion for the world of the *Idylls* should have warned me. In Charles there was a certain jarring quality, but later I was to discover the potency of his creed when love dazzled me.

"I'd like you to move in immediately," he said. "It should be a very fruitful partnership."

I walked home through the gaslit darkness, the lamps glowing like magic apples.

Next day I moved into the house in Kensington.

CHAPTER EIGHTEEN

I

I WAS given a little attic room, a boxroom almost, next to the studio which ran across the top floor of the house. High wide windows had been set into the roof for better light, and the studio was a workshop all day. Canvasses hung on easels, the room smelt of oil and paints, and exotic objects lay in casual abandon – a lyre, a metal gauntlet, a carved chest, old bound books, goblets, long rotted fruit in a silver bowl.

All the rooms in the house were luxurious and artistic. The walls were covered with paintings and with Japanese plates. There were screens and fans and vases, and the wallpapers vied with each other for unusual and beautiful designs. In the downstairs room there were low couches covered with black fur and Indian rugs. Peacock feathers were somehow suspended from the ceilings and shivered in the breeze from the garden. The main front hall was tiled in black and gold, with a squarely Greek intricate pattern. At the foot of the wide staircase was an alabaster statue of Antinous naked. (The only genuine alabaster globes I've ever seen!) To me that was the best thing in the whole house. I wandered past it time and again, and touched his finger tips caressingly. He was a reproduction, but I didn't mind. He was beautiful.

The bathroom was like a pagan temple. The floor was tiled to make a picture of ladies and lilies. The bath stood on curved metallic feet in the shape of lions' paws. All around the walls there was a frieze of white roses and green leaves. And I could have a bath whenever I wanted!

The house I believe was Mr Franklin's, the one who had called out: "Charles, stop that boy!" He looked like pictures of the young Beethoven, and always wore those wide open collars. He was painting an enormous mediaeval scene, tapestry like, in which a train of nobles was riding through a forest. For him I modelled page boys, a minstrel and two young lords. For him I stood for hours with a lute, and sat astride a bench which he later transposed into a horse. He rarely spoke to me but I loved what he made of me. Once he enquired whether I was happy, and I said yes. He did not want to bother with details.

Also living in the house was a tormented guilty poet named Strode. I can't speak of him without a certain cynicism. He was an Urning all right, and he made a profession of suffering. "Unnatural vice", as it was called, was freely discussed in this liberated atmosphere. Indeed it seemed almost an obligatory characteristic of being free that you had to discuss the plight of the Urning in Society, and Mr Strode bowed his head and suffered for us as a victim should rightly do.

It seemed that along with the fascination for a jewel-encrusted Sodom and for slim effeminate youths with bluish tinges around their eyes, there went an interest in the depraved world of the lone Urning – someone who frequented this mystic landscape, a quivering moaning outcast, sitting beside tombs and autumnal watersides, crushing fistfuls of translucent black lilies and orchids, his distracted eyes ever graveward. Mr Strode sat around like melancholy Jacques, peculiarly respected, half pitied, half admired. Physically he was about forty, with black hair streaked with grey, and a small moustache, drooping shoulders and heavy eyes, somewhat baggy and wrinkled and seeming to give truth to the picture of the sad unfortunate perverted enough to love his own kind. In his company I struggled to seem ordinary. I was alarmed to think what might begin to happen if I admitted that I was one too.

The house was full of hangers-on to this artistic circle. I was by no means the only model, and others also stayed the night. The profession of modelling was perfectly respectable – I knew that, of course, in spite of my bitchy remarks to Caroline. Italians were much in demand because of their dark beauty. An ice cream seller and his entire family came in and out all day and lovely black-haired kids ran around in the garden. Pretty girls were also always about, coming in discreetly, with neat shawls and gentle nervous eyes. Later they would be transformed into paintings of slave girls and medieval maidens, and Sappho with her friends.

There were other kinds of girls too, free-thinking upper-class ladies, who liked the company of artists and had artistic pretensions themselves; they sat and sketched, mostly in the garden, since the weather was now very pleasant. As a gesture against the part society expected them to play, these ladies did not dress as the fashion of the day directed. They wore blouses and skirts (and No Stays! You could tell!) and sometimes loose Greek tunics with a cord at the waist. They looked very charming and comfortable in these white flowing dresses, and the men brought out fruit drinks on trays into the garden to share the idyllic and pastoral atmosphere.

Mr Strode and I, in our own different ways, were also on the look out for beauty. I fancied an Italian lad, but he always came with his mother and I daren't make any moves. Glumly I saw that he was covertly eyeing the loose-robed ladies under the lilacs.

In the evenings, the artists sat around by the fountain in the room downstairs with the garden doors open to the sweet perfumed twilight, and smoked hashish and read Baudelaire out loud. Naturally the meanings went over my head, my French being limited to *la vache* and *la fenêtre*, things which did not overmuch interest Baudelaire. Taking amused pity on my bafflement, Charles translated a verse for me, which began *Je suis un cimetière abhorré de la lune*. Ain't French musical? Well, I'd sit there, thoughtful-like and dreamy, listening and watching the evening darken and the moon rise, and the scents of the stuff they smoked making me drowsy. I'll tell you, it wasn't hard to forget you were in London. It was like a waking dream, and it was starting to work on me.

"Try this," Charles said. The voice he used, I half expected him to be passing me a drug. In fact it was the poems of Swinburne, and for me the effects were the same, a drug. I read the poems last thing at night, by lamplight, and I made love to myself in a heady sensuous passion. I was like a garden ripe for the seeds of love. My little room was warm and dusty and my senses were very much overheated. If anything I was in love with Antinous by the stairs – not a day went by without my touching his alabaster arse. (I was more daring now: I had progressed beyond the finger tips!)

No reality at all was allowed to permeate our lives. At first I thought Maurice and Clara were in the real world. Maurice made furniture, and one of his rooms was stacked with wood and tools. Clara used the cellar as a pottery. She had a wheel down there, and covered the wine racks with the pots she'd thrown. We ate off them – they were real and useful. Clara and Maurice ate rice and beans and no meat, and cultivated herbs in the garden. They believed the Middle Ages was a kind of Garden of Eden, when England was a green and flowery landscape, unpolluted by factories and machines. But the mediaeval was also the mystic. And so although they worked with their hands with wood and clay, they also spoke intimately about the Soul. The Holy Grail to them was as real as the hunk of cheese on the board. They chatted pleasantly about visions and legend.

It was startlingly obvious that the portrait of Parsifal that was slowly taking shape was the best thing currently emerging. Really – it was uncanny, it almost glowed. The others used to pause and look at it, not even jealous. Because of the portrait I sensed a curious possessiveness in their attitude to me. I wasn't just another model but their pet model. Handle carefully, nurture along, feed his mind. In a way, just as they created images from me, they created me too, or tried. It went to my head. My appalling vanity made it easy for them.

I was released from all necessity to concern myself with ordinary things. I never needed to spend money. Food was always there. From taking personal responsibility for myself, I was swung to the other extreme. I floated about in mediaeval garb as a minstrel or pageboy. If I went for a walk in the evening, although I was in the London streets, I carried the world of the house round in my head.

For Charles I posed as the living reality of his bizarre dreams, and always naked. He talked to me throughout, conveying to me what it was exactly I was representing. He talked a lot about Byzantium and "the mysterious road that leads to the interior". His voice purred as his brush painted. He spoke about the Soul and white azaleas. He said: "Natural things exist only a little. Reality lies only in dreams", and he said: "The road of excess leads to the palace of wisdom" – but Blake said it first, and at that time I hadn't heard of Baudelaire.

It was eerie being deluged in the fantastic and told that you embodied it. Sometimes I would come away from him feeling like someone who'd overindulged in treacle.

Maurice was the antidote. Posing as Parsifal for him was what suited me best.

Charles said Maurice was old-fashioned, and that his naturalistic mediaeval works were too pre-Raphaelite. He said the world was moving to a strange new disillusion, and real flowers and honest knights were already passé. With Maurice I discussed the *Idylls*. We talked about the Holy Grail, and life being a journey. He had a knack of making me pensive, and when I was lost to myself in thought he caught the expression, so in a way I wasn't posing at all. It was a portrait of me, or how he saw Parsifal – human, hopeful, conceited, sad, and needing counsel. Parsifal goes upon his quest in confidence, but he remembers all his sins, and becomes despondent. Things he meets – apple trees, a kind old woman, a house – all turn to dust. Worse, a golden knight who opens his arms to embrace Parsifal turns to dust also, and Parsifal in despair feels that the Holy Grail itself will crumble to his touch. A hermit tells him he has not true humility, like Galahad.

Then one morning as he was painting me, Maurice said casually over his shoulder to Clara: "Speaking of Galahad . . . when does Algy get back from Greece?"

II

SUDDENLY EVERYONE seemed to be talking about Algernon, or "the dear boy" as he was termed. He had spent spring touring Greece (in the company of a friend from Oxford) and because of this it was decided to hold a Greek banquet in the evening in his honour. They discussed it around the fountain that night, in sleepy tones, the ideas permeating through the hashish dreams, so colourful and quirky that I half wondered if they would be forgotten in the morning.

It seemed we were all to dress up in classical Greek garments. "The advantage of this," Charles slurred, "is that anyone who feels his limbs unsightly may legitimately appear delicately draped! How are *your* knees, Franklin?"

"Very fine, Charles. Alexander's generals would have been proud to own such knees. And you?"

"I think I would grace a small tunic – how vain we all are! Maurice?"

"Believe me, I shall be enveloped in a decorous sheet. I shall spend the morning decorating it with fine designs from the hall tiles."

"Parsifal of course can go naked. He has nothing to be ashamed of, as we all know. Charles has painted that boy nude from every angle."

"I hope I have the choice," I said haughtily.

"Oh – come, this is no time for modesty. Old men like us are obliged for the sake of good taste to cover up our slightly bulging midriffs – "

"Franklin! Speak for yourself," protested Charles.

" – but you must grace us with your young perfection. At banquets young boys strolled around quite naked for the delight of the older admirers. Have you not seen the pots? Charles, has he seen the pots?"

"Strode, I believe *you* have them."

Poor Mr Strode was obliged to go in search. Vaguely I wondered what he would be bringing. I half expected to hear the sounds of crockery. But in fact it was a pile of pictures, and Mr Strode sat down by me, extremely close, and let me look.

I was spellbound. It was like Mr Scott's pornography. Naked youths there certainly were in abundance. I knew of course the *Ode to a Grecian Urn*, but surely Keats had not been thinking of something like this! Boys were bending, all curves and genitals, boys were being pursued, tempted and seduced. Older men were bringing them gifts – cockerels particularly – and touching their sweet little cocks. Boys and men were kissing and drinking wine, and doing all the other things; indeed, one scene showed men queuing up to take a turn!

They laughed at my absorption. "See how fascinated he is! Are we corrupting him?"

"Do you find it shocking?" Strode asked me anxiously.

"No," I murmured, hot. I sensed his quickening interest and his body now brushing against mine. I shifted slightly. The pictures aroused me. I wanted to go to bed and stroke myself.

"So you see, Parsifal, a pretty boy was perfectly at home in his birthday suit," laughed Franklin.

"With what result!" I observed, but Charles remarked: "Please don't pretend to be shocked. I have never had the pleasure of painting anyone so completely at ease in the nude as yourself. You would make a delightful boy at a banquet."

"There will be girls there," Maurice said. "Maybe we should not encourage too much Innocent Depravity."

"The girls have all seen him naked," Charles shrugged easily. "I don't recall a single case of fainting. Does anyone know," he went on, "whether dear Algy found the modern Greece in any way the same as the ancient?"

"Ah!" they smirked meaningfully. "Did he find a present-day Ganymede? No, I haven't heard."

I went to bed tormented with excitement, awfully aroused with images of sweet Greek boys and bold seducers and the prospect of Algy.

In the morning, Charles got me posing indoors, up in the studio. I posed as Saint Sebastian, whom everyone knew as an excuse to paint a naked boy writhing against a tree. Charles slung a strand of twine across to hold my wrists in place. I didn't think he was in a funny mood, since his conversation was always a little risqué and provocative. He was chatting about the Greek vases I'd been gawping at last night; I had the feeling he wanted me to say straight out what I felt at the effect of so much explicit detail. I wondered why we weren't out in the garden, where everybody else was, and the sun was going to waste. I leaned in my nakedness, my arms above my head, my throat arched, looking at the heavens. Charles pattered on about Eastern Climes, and how the hot sultry countries seemed more prone to natural urges than we in our fog-bound isle. I fidgeted. The sun was shining outside.

With no more ado than the sound of swift footsteps along the landing, Algy came into the studio. I would have known who he was even without Charles' cries of delight and the offering of his hand. Me, I was so stunned it was like the roof had suddenly blown away. Algernon was the most beautiful being I had ever seen. The sun was shining through his fine blond hair. He wore a white suit, exquisitely tailored, white gloves, white shoes and at his throat a pale green silk tie. His face was flawless, his eyebrows fair and beautifully formed (he plucked them) and his lips full, sensitive and perfect. He was the same height as me, and his build was slim.

I was struggling from my stupid bonds as Algy approached holding out his gloved hand to invite a formal handshake, and

I was consumed with embarrassment. There was more to follow. "Bleedin' hell!" I yelled at Charles. "You fixed this! Didn't yer?"

Charles raised his eyebrows and smirked. "Algernon, my dear, this is the young Parsifal you've heard about. Currently Sebastian, as you see."

"My name is Willie Smiff," I squawked, yanking my wrists painfully past the cord, furious with myself for being caught like this, with Charles for laying it on, and with Algy for being impeccable and a lord.

Scarlet faced and mortified, I shook hands with Algernon and then pulled away. I hadn't even any clothes in the room.

"Excuse me," Charles murmured, retiring for no obvious reason at all, and leaving us alone.

"I have heard so much about you," Algernon murmured in a most cultured upper-class accent that made me dismally aware of the unbridgeable gap between us, the more obvious for my street howl just now. He laughed delicately. "Really – you are not as I imagined, somehow."

"Don't even start to tell me – I can't feel any worse'n I do," I groaned.

"Oh, please," he said politely. "There's no need. Tell me, are all these paintings you?" He started walking purposefully around the canvasses, staring at them pointedly. "Ah, yes," he laughed nervously. "They are, aren't they? It's quite obvious . . . Charles has been looking for an auburn-haired boy like you ever since he discovered Moreau. You must have been the answer to his prayer."

"I believe I am," I said unhappily, feeling anything but, my hands clasped over my crotch, my shoulders hunched and, I daresay, my feet turned in.

"Who are you here, on this one?"

"Ganymede," I mumbled.

"How appropriate for me!" he said smoothly. "I am recently returned from Parnassus."

Peasant that I was, I did not connect that it was the mountain where one might find gods walking, and anyway I couldn't flirt, feeling how I was. "Owww," I wailed, "he did it on purpose to me. It's wrong playin' with people's feelin's."

I turned right round and wiped my fist across my nose – I

was full of such tasteful gestures – my back to Algy, my head full of misery and gloom.

"You're right," he said, coming and standing behind me. "It was mean. I suppose I am partly to blame. They all wanted our meeting to be natural and in private. Of course I was consumed with curiosity. I had no thought for your feelings and now I feel ashamed."

"I can't help you much there," I shrugged.

"Listen. I will go down into the garden and find a charming rustic bench and wait for you. Get dressed and come down to me. Come soon."

And off he tripped. I'd have kicked the easel if I'd had boots on. I went to my room and, abandoning any pretence of medi-aevalism and Parsifal, I put my tight green corduroys on and my white shirt, open at the neck. I hesitated, squinting at myself in my mirror. Algy was a lord. He was not for me. He was exquisite and reeked of breeding; I'd sworn and I'd talked common. And people had teased me, setting me up like this. It crossed my mind to walk out of the whole business; they weren't my sort of people. What was I even doing here?

I thought a whole lot more on similar lines as I walked down to the garden.

Algy was surrounded by girls.

He was sitting on the bench as promised, girls in white on the grass clamouring for news of Greece, and roses all around him. I scowled across at him uninvitingly. He stood up, placed a white broad brimmed hat on his blond locks and wove a twisty path through the girls to me. As we started walking along the amber gravel, he handed me a white rose. "Will you be at my party?" he enquired sweetly.

"Yes."

"What are you going as?"

"As someone in a sheet," I muttered sulkily.

"Oh come on now," he reproved. "You must enter into the spirit! I'll help you."

"I'm goin' as someone pure, chaste, moral, and *clothed*."

"Hm," he smiled. "I see – a gesture of defiance and daring!"

I didn't respond but walked, twiddling my rose.

"I think I shall go as the Baudelaire King," he said, resolute to remain pleasant. "Do you know the poem which begins *Je suis comme le roi d'un pays pluvieux?*"

"No."

"Shall I speak it?"

"What, all of it?"

"I recite exquisitely. It's beautiful to hear me."

The honourable Algernon launched into poetry. I didn't understand a word. Later, when I looked it up, I found it was about a king of a rainy land, wealthy but helpless, young but moribund; nothing can cheer him, no one can make him smile, his bed now decked with lilies is a tomb, in his veins not blood but Lethe water flows. All this I learned painstakingly with a dictionary.

"What do you think?" he declared, his performance done.

"Very nice."

"You are not free with your compliments, Parsifal."

"Oh, please don't call me that," I wriggled. "It feels false."

"But I can't call you Willie – not here! It doesn't sound right. Let me call you Parsifal – or even Ganymede," he added, looking winsome.

"No!" I snapped. "You call me that and I'll be fighting off Mr Strode and he don't need any encouragement."

Algy looked thoughtful, and we crunched up the path.

"How old are you?" he asked.

"Seventeen."

"I am twenty-one. School and university are done, and the world is my oyster."

"What do you mean to do?"

"Travel, and laze. Eventually farm."

"Farm?" I sniggered.

"When I say farm, I do not of course mean lift a spade," he said loftily. "Our estate is in Bedfordshire. Land economy is a complicated business."

The gap between us yawned again. For about twenty minutes he talked to me about the problems of managing land. I listened, as one might to the rustle of trees, the words a soft blur. We paused. A riotous clump of scarlet poppies blazed beside us. I picked a poppy and threaded it in his buttonhole. The smudge of colour was exactly right. He looked at it, then at me, and I saw his eyes were an enchanting and delicious green. "Be there tonight," he murmured, "clothed or not."

Then he let himself out of the garden door and was gone.

III

I LEFT the heady garden and went indoors. I ate my way through a hunk of bread and cheese and poured out a bottled stout. Clara was painting Greek designs on a sheet. She said I could have a couple of yards if I wanted. We sat at the kitchen table and looked at pictures of Greek costume. "But what do they wear underneath?" I grimaced.

"A sort of cloth, I think," she said doubtfully, and we started to giggle.

But she was very helpful; she said she'd make me a garland if I picked the flowers, but wait till dusk, she said, so they last. She said if I didn't mind wearing make-up it would add a pleasant decadent touch; I assured her it would be no bother. We made a sort of tunic for me and painted a Greek border along it.

In the twilight I stripped the garden of daisies. A sweet little moon rose, and I felt like a secret votary casting spells. From the house came the pleasant sounds of people getting ready: laughter, the rattle of plates, the uncorking of bottles. I made a garland of daisy strands, which amused me for its curiously virginal quality, and as for make-up I lightly laced my lids with violet, and glossed my lips to dark pink. "How fresh and pure you look," Charles said.

The room filled up with blokes and girls in tunics and togas and flowing robes, speaking exactly as they did on ordinary nights, confident and cultured, drinking wine and champagne, eating all kinds of posh food that had no relation to the shores of Hellas. But the fountain was lovely and rose petals had been scattered around its marble edges, and the moon shone over the garden.

Algernon came late. He was wearing a long peacock-blue cloak, and he glided amongst the guests accepting compliments most graciously, everyone wanting to say how glad they were he was back and eager to hear all about Greece. The party being in his honour, he was constantly surrounded by well-wishers and his health drunk many times, and ours by him. When I was beginning to wonder whether I had dreamt his urgent voice asking me to be here he floated over to me, and lifted his glass. "Are you tipsy yet?" he enquired.

"I don't think so."

"I am – a little," he said, with sparkling eyes.

"Algernon!" I gasped. "What have you got on beneath your cloak?"

"Not very much," he grinned. It was the first time I had seen his wide smile – he cultivated a pose of languid sensitivity as a rule. He inched his cloak aside and showed me. I stared. It was a long wide belt, slung low on his hips and up over his crotch. The belt was sewn with blue gems that matched the cloak, and I was petrified they were real. That was all he had on! His slim bare chest showed, and his luscious belly and his thighs. I could see the fuzz of little blond hairs on his legs. I began feeling breathless just looking. I looked back to Algy's face and our eyes met, lust-laden. "I'm pretty, aren't I?" he said.

"Yes," I gulped.

"You too . . . The daisies, so innocent, the make-up so alluring, giving the lie to the daisies. If I were to say to you 'Come into the garden', would you solemnly swear to make no jokes about the black bat, night?"

"Yes, solemnly," I said in lugubrious tones.

Algy giggled and gave me his arm.

"Algy, is it wise?" I hesitated. "With people seein' us go?"

"Do you know," he said seriously, "I half believe it was the reason for this party."

Palpitating somewhat, I took Algy's arm and we walked out into the garden. He led me to a dark secluded place behind the tool shed! A trellis dripping with honeysuckle was over our heads.

"I am afeard being night all this is but a dream," Algy murmured comfortably. "Too flattering sweet to be substantial," he added.

"You ain't half a show-off, Algy," I remarked.

Algy just looked at me and suddenly we found ourselves kissing. Weak with delight I pressed against him, slipping my arms under his cloak to close upon the warm flesh of his back.

I tasted the soft fine strands of his gold hair and breathed in the sweet scent of him. We sighed.

Eventually he said: "You aren't as I imagined. But this is very special. Will you love me, do you think?"

"I will, yes; I do. I love you."

"I love you too," he said.

"Algy, I ain't never said that to anyone straight out like that . . . not since . . . since I was little."

"No – one doesn't ever say it to many people."

Then he hugged me. "Let's not become morbid and melancholy. I have an idea! We'll make an offering. Come on, help me to pick some flowers."

"Flowers, Algy? What for?"

"Do as you're told. Don't my years of autocratic aristocracy count for anything?"

"What kind of flowers?"

"Any kind whatsoever – roses would be nice but they do prickle. The one I gave you earlier made me bleed."

"Oh!" I gasped. "I'm sorry."

"Not badly," he purred. "Just make a small bouquet."

By the moon's light we picked flowers, laughing as we encountered hazards that never seemed there in the day – brambles, canes, a little trowel. "Franklin'll kill us," I muttered, tugging at poppies.

"Nonsense; flowers exist only for the pleasure of man."

"And for bees," I corrected earnestly.

"Oh yes, and bees. And butterflies."

"And insects and slugs." One had to be fair.

"Slugs! *Must* we?"

We made ourselves as decent as we had been, and went indoors by the kitchen door and padded through to the hall.

I thought Algy's idea was beautiful. We laid our flowers down at the feet of the statue of Antinous – rose petals in abundance, honeysuckle, daisies, poppies and lilies – and then we knelt down ourslevs, excited at doing something so perfect. Our eyes sparkled with newly discovered love and childish delight in the ceremony. We held hands, and looked up at the superb nude figure, and smiled in happy anticipation. "O Antinous," said Algy, "beautiful boy beloved of an emperor, to thee we dedicate our newfound love."

"Amen," I agreed, and Algy laughed and cuddled me.

"I thought we might sleep together," he suggested.

That Antinous may not have been the best of persons to pray to – did he manage to share a happy old age with Hadrian? – and that Algy had needed drink to spark his courage, never occurred to me that night; why should it?

As we knelt there amongst the rose petals before Antinous, hand in hand, I was completely happy.

CHAPTER NINETEEN

I

A PAIR of young lovers in their first flush of love was all the artistic community needed to put the finishing touch to its way of life. They gave us every encouragement, leaving us alone and vacating the most idyllic spots in the garden so that we could pursue our relationship in the situation of most perfection. Plans were instantly afoot to paint studies of David and Jonathan, Apollo and Hyacinthus, Herakles and Hylas.

But Maurice had the best idea. I wondered whether he had seen us kneeling before Antinous, because he conceived the notion of painting Parsifal and Galahad praying before the hermit. This caught the imagination of them all. Algy was just right for Galahad, they said, so pure and golden. This pose had everything – two beautiful young men in holy rapture looking soulful, a chapel (ruined), an altar, plenty of ivy and decay, and how about a raven or a crow? One was found (a crow), a hideous thing that lived in a cage and cawed like Macbeth's doomy messenger, hoarsely. Charles was chosen to pose as the hermit, having the best bone structure, and he lurked at the altar when required, a chalice in his hand, reminding me more of a magician than a hermit and hardly a person of whom one would even ask the way, let alone absolution. However, this picture was the background to our new love and important to it. With aching knees we gazed into each other's eyes for hours on end. Only lovers could have posed so long.

Franklin gave what was to Maurice the highest praise. "Very Burne-Jones," he said.

While I continued to live in the house and sleep in the little room by the studio, Algy lived the peculiar double life of the artistic bohemian rich – one moment he was with us, and then he disappeared on some mysterious engagement necessary to the upper classes. Algy had a dominant mother who seemed to be showing him off to half London. He attended dinner parties and Occasions, theatres and balls. He was being "matched". His mother had in mind an honourable named Claudia. I was sorry for him. To be the heir to estates seemed to carry with it such peculiar responsibilities, not the least being to deny one's true self and to function for the gaze of the masses.

It meant for Algy that the times with me were doubly precious.

"It is curiously relaxing," he said, "to be not just timeless but classless. How wonderful it is that my lands and titles don't impress you, and we can simply meet as persons in a garden. I have never had this experience in my whole life before."

Algy could wheedle any secret out of me. Lying with him on rugs upstairs in hidden corners we shared all intimacy. "Why were you in the reformatory then, Parsifal . . . come now, tell."

"I can't. It's too . . . I don't know what you'll think."

"You surely never murdered anyone."

"Of course not."

"What then, you stole a crust?"

"Don't laugh if you don't know what it is to be that hungry."

"Tell, sweetheart . . . it's horrid when you're so mysterious. I tell all."

"I was in love with my cousin. You're awful like him, Algy. You could be him grown up, except he was so plump. He was like a fresh little rose with the dew still on it."

"I was never plump! At school they used to call me Peaseblossom."

"Peaseblossom!" I hooted happily.

"I was light as thistledown."

"You still are."

"Nonsense, I am nine stone six."

"We are about the same weight," I marvelled.

"But to your cousin – your plump cousin."

I told all. ". . . I kept my love for him secret. And at night I made up stories about him, mucky stories, Algy, to bring me off. I had him every way imaginable."

"You're exciting me, look. If I'd been in your fantasies we could have shared him, *and then had each other!*"

We trembled. "Well, one night I went mad and lost control. I wanted him *real*. I was sick of dreams."

"Like the Lady of Shallott."

"I was a bit rougher'n her," I said modestly. "See, you know, it wasn't an act of love. I did love Georgey, but I hated him too.

I hated him because I was poor and he was rich. I could have gone to university if I'd been born rich. I was going to be a social reformer."

"Oh ho! And put me in a tumbril, hey?"

"I never thought about it like that. Anyway, I said reformer, not revolutionary."

"Fibber. You've got *Practical Socialism* amongst your books."

"Ah," I said, touched that he'd noticed. "Would you like to borrow it and see what it's about?"

"No, of course not. It's something one jokes about, not reads."

"Well," I said uncomfortably, briefly aware of the gap again. "To be a reformer in this country you need money or education or both. I could have given the world so much. But I was denied. And Georgey who was as intellectual as a plum pudding was to go to university. So I just went crazy. Years of frustration erupted in one night."

I told Algy the whole sorry story.

Algy suddenly kissed me. "He deserved it," he said. "He had no business frequenting your fantasies in slave gear. He was asking for it."

I grinned. "Algy, I never seen it as in any way funny. I always thought of it as tragic. I never thought I'd smile about it. You ain't half good for me.

"Algy," I went on, "why don't you go into politics instead of farming, and change a few laws so they put an end to grim places like reformatories?"

"I'd do it to win your regard. If it was humanly possible and easy to do I'd do it gladly, and I'd hand it to you on a gold plate. If I could wave a wand I'd do it for you."

"I wasn't serious. And somehow, my sweet Galahad, I don't think you're the bloke to do it. I don't think you'd know a social condition if you saw one."

"I can't help my upbringing. I refuse to feel inadequate because I've never been down a coal mine."

"It don't matter; I'm in no position to talk. What social reforming am I doing, hey, lying in the lap of luxury and taking my baths in a work of art?"

"Have you ever made love in the bath?" Algy asked.

"Only to myself," I grinned.

"Would you like to try it with another person?" he smouldered.

"Have you anyone in mind?" I quivered.

"Now?"

Thus it was we were able to stave off any intrusion, any unwelcome subject, anything that hinted of differences in our viewpoints. There was no doubt that we were both bursting to get each other to bed – or bath – and needed no persuasion to leave off talking to lose ourselves in the joy of each other's desire.

"I feel I can hardly believe my luck," Algy marvelled, as we dried each other. "All those years of suppression and fear and secrecy, and then to meet someone so abandoned, free and natural – someone so eager for pleasure and so good at it, so physically beautiful."

We stood together before the full length mirror, narcissistic and adoring. "We are awful perfect," I remarked, awed.

II

ONE DAY we were sitting on the grass in the sun, bees buzzing in the lavender. We were making a long, long daisy chain. Algy wore his broad-brimmed sunhat, with two pink carnations in the band. We talked about our early feelings of love, and I told him about Charley. "He sparked off love in me," I said, "and then left me. I feel I've carried round this void for ever. Like as if my life is a search, and one day a person will come and fill it, and then I shall know I am at home."

"What was he like?"

"Oh – very strong, and laughing, very caring. He could punch any boy who bothered me, and he'd always look after me and sort my problems out. He knew the world was a bad place with so much wrong in it, and he knew that two people close together in bed could deal with the world from a base of love. Ah, I did love him so!"

"It must be obvious to you, Parsifal, that I am not this ideal. How do you explain the deviation?"

"Oh darlin', I ain't criticisin' *you!* Don't ever think it. It's possible to love different sorts of people."

"Do you think in me you love a reflection of yourself? I sometimes think that."

"I don't know. There's all kinds of love; all real."

"I know. I suddenly wondered, you see, whether it could be that you've outgrown Charley? You say you liked his strength and being looked after. Maybe now you have your own strength; maybe the void has closed up, unnoticed by you. Maybe you can look after somebody else, instead of seeking protection."

"I don't know."

"You seem strong to me."

"Oh, I ain't!"

"Well! In comparison with me . . . " he said, with an expansive shrug. "You have to know something about me, Parsifal. I have always been afraid of things. As an infant it was ghosts – and believe me, we had the pick of them at home – wounds that bled, chains that rattled. Ghosts, storms, the dark, my father – I was afraid of them all. And then at school . . . "

"What happened?"

"At my public school I was awfully bullied, and dreadfully miserable because of it."

"Couldn't you have told?" I demanded.

"Surely you don't mean sneak?"

"I s'pose I do."

"No – no – I became the bitch of a strong protector: that was the answer. They were called bitches, you know, pretty boys who were used for favours. It was quite respectable then, you see, like being the king's mistress. You were given a girl's name and you had specific duties and an easy life. And then you grew older and no one pestered."

"Did you then pursue young boys yourself?"

"No. It's odd, isn't it? You see, by then I knew it was serious. I read Plato and worked it all out. It was profoundly depressing."

"Why?"

"Because, as I have told you, I am so timid. A life of conformity lay ahead of me, the estate, marriage . . . This discovery seemed a burden I could do without. I found that instead of running wild with all the enthusiasm of a Roman tyrant on Capri, I retreated within myself. I looked at the other boys, and if I wanted a particular one I avoided him as if he were a case of rampant cholera. I would have been terrified of being rejected, and even more terrified of being accepted."

"I don't really understand, you know."

"No more did I. I could not have forced myself on a lower

277

boy as was done to me. I was far too proud. I found that with my self-awareness came respect for others. I would have liked to give and receive love on equal terms, but I was too unsure – it was too important. And so I looked and dreamed and yearned, and wrote a lot of ghastly poems in what I thought was a fair imitation of Shelley . . . There was one boy . . . "

We threaded our daisies thoughtfully.

". . . Altrincham . . . we had a very beautiful friendship. Yes, like you and Georgey on your omnibus, we sat thigh to thigh. How erotic that is in summer trousers! The mutual heat! To see the perspiration gleam on his open palms that rest upon his well rounded knees . . . the golden hairs on the pale brown arms . . . his shy half-smile, the little curl of hair on his smooth neck. I did no more with that boy than yearn and lightly touch, yet his image is engraven upon all my senses, and the little we ever did assumes to me a height of erotic fulfilment I doubt I shall ever achieve again."

"It sounds beautiful, Algy."

"It was. The unattained may remain ever so. One takes no risks.

"Ah," smiled Algy, "you and I did not make that mistake. Look at us – we made love the first day we met. How easy it was . . . "

Like a bell clanging off key, a sour note struck my thoughts. Did we find it easy because neither of us is truly what the other wants? If one of us had rejected the other, we could have coped with it. What do I want with a lord, I could have said, he is no good to me – or he could have said I am well rid of him, he is a streetboy. I shivered at this frightening sacrilege.

"I was no more successful at the university," Algy said cheerfully. "I sat and gazed at choirboys, never daring to pursue. There had recently been a scandal of that nature. The man in question was obliged to leave. His reputation is for ever tarnished. He will always be avoided in the very best society. One has to tread as if through broken glass."

"It ain't easy," I agreed. "I don't know what the answer is."

"Well, one solution is to go abroad."

"Oh yes, so I've heard. You can buy boy slaves in the Sudan, and by all accounts the Eastern countries make a speciality of male brothels."

"Oh, Parsifal!" Algy chuckled. "What extremes! I simply meant a trip to Italy."

"Oh, well, I don't know nothing about Italy," I muttered, embarrassed at the extent of my sordid knowledge.

"On the continent the atmosphere is much more lax," said Algy. "Paris is ideal. There is so much bohemian society and café life. Male lovers can pass almost unnoticed. In Italy and in Greece almost every man is as handsome as a god. Adonis and Apollo walk the streets. Also, there is such poverty, a peasant lad will sell himself." Algy sighed. "It's horrid, isn't it, the way love is debased."

"What?" I muttered. "Is it?"

"I mean, to sell your body for money," said Algy, with distaste. "To be beautiful, and cheapen yourself that way."

I felt anger welling up. "You saw it happen, did you?"

"Yes, and in Greece too."

"You didn't make use of it yourself?"

"Oh!" said Algy blushing. "Would it make you despise me?"

"Tell me what you did," I insisted.

"I can't. You're looking so fierce."

"I ain't fierce; how can you say that? How can I be fierce makin' a daisy chain?"

"You're dropping your g's. I can always tell with you. When you feel angry or socially aware, g's fall from your words like spilt buttons," Algy fluttered sweetly, trying to make us laugh. "Come on, now, the daisy chain is long enough to join; give me your ends."

Algy took the thread of daisies from my hands and joined them to his. We sat there silent and, removing his sunhat, he lifted it over our heads so that we were delicately chained together round the shoulders. Daisy-white, shirt-white. Algy looked so wholesome and clean; the sun picked out the lights of his golden strands of hair. We couldn't help kissing each other inside the daisy chain.

"Ah," said Algy fondly, "see how closely we are tied. Neither of us can break away. It's like enchantment, look. We are inside a mystic circle, safe and protected."

"We are similar, aren't we?" I sort of pleaded. "It's only superficial things that seem to separate us. I want us to be close. Not just because daisies bind us."

"Our lives do have things in common, yes. Considering that our backgrounds are so different, there is a pattern. We were both pretty and exploited for it. We both loved a boy as beautiful as ourselves, innocently almost. We both could hardly believe our good fortune in finding each other. And now we are posing as Galahad and Parsifal, two knights seeking perfection."

"I would hate anything to be false between us. I was angry with you just now."

"But we are different too," Algy declared. "Can't you see it? How we reacted to those things which were the same was different, very different. We were both picked on for being vulnerable — but you seem so capable now. Then take the boys we loved. I said nothing to mine. I let him go, all words unsaid. You wanted Georgey, so you took him. You're strong, that's the difference. I'm still afraid of things. I daren't admit outside the daisy chain what sort of person I am. I didn't even find you for myself. My friends found you, and handed you to me. Life happens to me, I never make it happen."

"Oh, Algy," I groaned. "I ain't better than you. I'm very much worse. I got to tell you. I was angry with you just now because you said it was cheap to sell your body. I was angry because if you went with Greek boys for money you were equally to blame. Prostitutes get the abuse, not the gents who use them. No one should despise the boy who sells his body unless they despise the buyers too. And I know about it because I did what those boys did. And that's it, I've said it now." I ended defiantly, but my heart was sinking at the look on his face.

"What do you mean?" he said, pale as a sheet. "You did what?"

"Sold my body," I said bluntly. "Went with gents. Picked up trade on the streets. I was a whore."

"Oh — no!" he groaned.

Close to him, every bit of revulsion was obvious to me. Simultaneously we pulled away, and all the daisies broke. "It isn't true!" he choked.

"Don't worry: I never caught anything," I snapped.

"I don't mean that," he gasped. "I mean — I mean the love — that I thought I'd found somebody who felt the same as I. But a whore could do it with anybody — you wouldn't have to love me — you'd only have to make me *believe* you did!"

"But I do love you. I told you."

"How can you *mean* it? Isn't it a stock in trade?"

"No it ain't," I cried affronted. "I've never said it not meanin' it. I never said it to a gent, never in my life."

"But – looking as you do – posing as Parsifal – you are utterly false."

"I know. That's why I had to tell you. I don't want you to love me for a saintly image. If I didn't love you I wouldn't have told you. You don't know what it's costin' me. Seein' your eyes change."

"How long were you – that?" he demanded.

"About a year," I muttered.

"Oh, God!" he moaned. "All that time!"

"I'm sorry," I said, starting to cry.

"Oh, stop that," he seethed. "Everything about you is false. I daresay you have taught yourself to weep; it's very affecting. You solicited, did you? This business of offering a light?"

"Yes, I did that."

"Where did you take them? I imagine you were quite a success, you looking as you do."

"Yes, thank you, I did quite well," I sniffed, half wretched and half aggressive. "We went behind walls and down alleys. I also worked in a high class brothel. I got a guinea a time."

"You – rat!" he gasped. "I believe you're boasting."

"I won't be judged," I wept angrily. "Tell me what's the difference between what I done, and bein' a bitch for older boys to save your skin from the mob? I'll tell you for nothing, Algy – if you'd have been me, and even if you'd been you, without money to protect you, you'd have done the same."

"How dare you!" Algy stormed. "It is not the same at all. Everyone at school is a gentleman's son. On the streets you pick up anybody, the dregs of society – I thought you were special. No wonder you are so good! The practice you must have had!"

He stood up quickly and turned away, his hand over his eyes, daisies trailing from his shoulders. The other ends of the daisies trailed from mine, the torn stems dangling where there used to be a join. Then Algy, as if he'd been realising it too, lifted the daisies off himself and dropped them. Without even looking back he strode away and out of the garden.

I didn't blame him. I blamed myself. Reality was catching me up. All very well, this king-of-the-street philosophy, rhapsodising about the lights on the water and the gentle glow of the gaslamps. I'd been in a stinking trade and my lover was revolted. Any decent person would be. At least, I thought, sniffing, if he thinks I'm strong I can try to be. Enchanted circles are no good; you cannot live inside one.

So I took my daisies and I laid them with his, and I wiped my eyes on my shirt sleeve and went into the house. I had a good wash and went down to the kitchen. I sat at the table in the green gloom, drinking stout. Fresh tears dropped into the froth and made little hollows. I could not hide my distress from sympathetic Clara. "All lovers quarrel sometimes," she said.

"I have lost him for ever," I replied.

"Believe me, I know Algy. He doesn't give his heart lightly."

"Well, he is sorry now that he gave it at all."

"One has only to see you together . . . "

"Nothing is as simple as it seems."

I must admit I was in no frame of mind to pose when I took up my kneeling position by the mediaeval altar in the corner of the studio. "Mm!" cried Maurice rapturously. "That expression – perfect! Try and hold it – if only I can catch that nuance of pain . . . "

I daresay I could have held it with no trouble. My heart weighed a ton and my eyes were swimming. The tinted sunlight fell upon me, dazzling me the more. Tears trickled down the well worn paths across my cheeks. I thought I had my emotions in check, but my eyes were like brimming wells. "Do you want me to stop?" Maurice asked nicely.

"No."

"I know you and Algy have had words . . . "

"It's all right. I might as well cry here as anywhere else."

"I am concerned – but your expression is superb – I'd hate to stop. Your pose is perfect."

"I'm glad somebody benefits. No, I don't mean to be bitchy. It really does please me we can turn it into art."

Because of my watery vision and the sunlight that cast what Charles would call a Florentine gilt, I was not aware of Algy entering, until he came and knelt beside me in his pose as Galahad. I gasped. Maurice swore lightly at my change of expression. Algy took my praying hands in his, and we knelt there like two halves of the same whole, joined at the palms. He even had identical tears. "I'm sorry," he whispered, as if he was interrupting a performance. "I'm so sorry . . . forgive me."

It was strange and really mystical, like the picture "Galahad shone before us". We just continued to kneel, all sensation in our palms and fingers. We looked into each other's eyes, watery gold framing our vision, causing translucent brilliant mobile effects, his beautiful pale tragic face seeming like Narcissus in the pool. All the while, Maurice kept on painting, the sound of his brush busily scratching, his palette knife tapping and his voice sounding in ecstasy and annoyance – seemingly we had achieved the perfect pose and he doubted his capacity to translate it to canvas. Everyone who saw it afterwards said it was a masterpiece.

III

ALGY FELT that I had been badly disadvantaged culturally and he set himself seriously to put me right. He took me to see the Elgin marbles and the Lindisfarne gospels and the Egyptian antiquities. We went earnestly round Westminster Abbey and the Tower of London. We visited the South Kensington museum on a day when sunlight filled its huge arched hallway with shafted light. One very hot day we went to Kew Gardens and peered at the foreign trees and entered the hothouses, smiling and perspiring, fanning ourselves with handkerchiefs. We saw exquisite lilies and strolled around the leafy grounds. I ached for us to hold hands, but of course we could not.

Algy found me a suit of his and took me to concerts and once to the opera. I am someone whom opera seems not to touch. I sat there thoroughly ill at ease amongst the cultured ladies and gentlemen and the glitter of jewels, and the unintelligible Italian from the stage. A young girl near me was so affected that she cried. Myself, I sat obsessed with Algy's thigh. My fingers itched to stroke it. His knee was just the right shape for my hand. I clasped my fingers together, my palms sweated. The music was so loud, the heroine muscular and immense. My collar scraped my neck – it was like wearing unplaned wood! I threw Algy an appealing glance. He smiled ruefully. He understood – but we still had to sit it out. Concerts I found easier, but it made me fidgety having to sit quiet for so long.

Artistic activity went on as usual at the house, and in connection with this something occurred which roused me to anger.

Franklin suddenly decided to break from his immense mediaeval canvas to paint some Sentimental Scenes of London Life. Now what he did was to stroll about the streets until he found people who were destitute, ragged and poor, and bring them home and paint their picture. They were given an insulting pittance and then cast back into the maelstrom. Old men, out of work husbands and, worst of all, scruffy little kids. Now why did I get so livid, hey, when as a scruffy little lad I posed for an artist for half a crown? As an urchin, morals never troubled me and I loved posing. So why now? These brats weren't complaining – they came in, posed and went, glad enough for the pennies. But it disturbed me, seeing it.

"It's wrong!" I told him stoutly. "They aren't fish, what you catch and then fling back in the river, they're humans. You bring them into the house and let them see all your wealth and then toss them away – you *use* their poverty to make yourself richer. What are you going to do with the proceeds from selling those portraits? If you ain't givin' it to charity you got no business doin' it at all."

"Have you quite finished?" he drawled.

"It's immoral. It's usin' people who are down."

"There is no morality in art."

"In art maybe not. But in life there is."

"I had not realised you were such a prude."

"You should be more so. You should *care*."

"Care? How can one be so altruistic? The problem is too large. But from the artistic point of view, all life is the artist's medium. In the streets of London I sketch water, windows, flowers, carriages, dungheaps, beggars – all with the same equanimity, as legitimate objects for my artistic skill. It's not my business to enquire how life came to be so; life *is*, and as such I may paint it. I need feel no guilt, I need not trouble about social conditions. They exist, and I translate them into art."

"It isn't *right*."

"Parsifal, you're irritating me. I pay them, don't I?"

I blushed, angry and aware that I had overstepped the bounds of politeness. Real sharply it struck me that the artists, while seeming to be free thinking and above the law, aerial spirits of no time or place, were living in a dream world of their own creation, as if in a golden bubble, and I had been as guilty as they. They were selfish and careless, rich and unthinking. They had a lot to say about trends in French literature and liberation of the mind, but all around them, not so far away, the slums existed still, kids starved and played in rags, barefoot, and died of diseases induced by filth and poverty. What had happened to my own principles? Where had my idealism gone, my hopes to change the world, things my dad believed in? *What was I doing here?*

It troubled me no end. I did feel bad about my luxurious existence. In a way I was a sort of kept boy still. My body was still in demand for money, though now for the artistic world not the sexual one. Rich blokes could always buy me. I felt depressed and morose.

I thought that maybe I could put the balance right by helping the models Franklin brought to the house. What I did was give them a meal. Anyone who looked scruffy I took to the kitchen after and gave 'em an omelette or something on toast and a nice mug of tea. Well, what happened was that word got around.

I wasn't surprised. I knew the poor had a system of communication as gipsies do, and I wouldn't blame any of the models for passing on the word. Within the week I had folks knocking on the kitchen door and soon we had a string of them. I decided it would be simpler if I kept some soup on the go, preparing it in the afternoon and feeding it to whoever came in the evening. I felt benign, munificent and warm-hearted as I ladled out soup to the poor. I took a lot of trouble with that soup and all, flavouring it real nice and shopping for cheap meat. I hadn't realised how much I'd missed being out in the real world and it felt real good to be back. I spent happy afternoons chopping veg, and at night a trail of destitute folks came gratefully to my door and sat around the table eating soup, while the artists were getting heady on hashish and Baudelaire by the fountain.

Oh! The eruption when I was found out!

Franklin was furious, Clara upset and Charles rampant with sarcasm. I was accused of ingratitude, of bad manners, of giving open house to all the riffraff of London. There would be fleas, lice, cholera, dysentery, we would be robbed and murdered in our beds. "Oh," I yelled back, "it's all right to paint them, is it? But not to feed them?"

"It isn't even your own house, your own food – "

"I bought it out of what you pay me!"

"You use my kitchen utensils!"

"Are they sacred, your pots? Are they all holy grails?"

"How dare you? You should be grateful, living here. Instead you abuse your privileges."

"So frow me aht."

"We haven't finished our paintings. We shall have to settle it amicably," he said vexed.

Well, I stuck up for my point of view. Since the artists still needed me I could make conditions. There would be a soup kitchen once a week. The artists turned it to their advantage by sitting in on it, and sketching heads for crowd scenes.

Algy thought it was endearing of me, and a little incomprehensible. "They're so – dirty," he said. "How can you bear to be near them? And how do you know they aren't cheating you and pretending to be poorer than they are? Good nature is always exploited by its recipient."

But for pure love of me he rolled up his shirt sleeves and ladled soup, and I laughed out loud when I heard his high-class cultured voice call out: "Seconds, anybody?"

The artists became goodhumoured about it in time. They made a collection box for me with a label: Saint Sebastian's Soup Kitchen, and they put coins in it for me to buy the food and boots and extras. They weren't bad-hearted really; they just hadn't thought about poverty much. I know I felt a bit easier in my own mind helping whoever came to the kitchen. I felt less of a parasite, and full of love for Algy who passed around the soup with a fastidious fixed smile on his face, and who always had a bath afterwards.

CHAPTER TWENTY

I

GREATLY DARING, I took Algy to Spitalfields.
My love for Algy was like drinking at a magic fountain.
You needed more and more, you could not wait to return
to it, and you could not trust the evidence of your senses. Could
it really be as beautiful as you remembered? Neither of us had
ever known before the astonishing rapture of loving and desiring
somebody who returned love with equal need and fervour. Sometimes we were scared it was just a mirror image and we were
simply loving the beauty in ourselves. I started to distrust the
atmosphere of that place. I was afraid we had become unreal. I
found it scary always to make love in perfect places. It reminded
me of those fairy stories when the palace vanishes and the
dreamer is left alone on a bleak hillside. I found the enchanted
circle of the daisy chain a dangerous place. How could we ever
abandon æry regions and come down to earth?

So I took Algy walking round the streets of my childhood. We
went by hansom across the city and alighted in Aldgate. Riding
in a hansom with Algy was one of the most beautiful experiences
of my life. The cab was glossily black, like the satin flanks of a
quality horse. In the shadows we held hands, our legs touching
from ankle to thigh, my black velvet jacket against his exquisite
suit. "I love you," I said.

"I love you," he replied.

No wonder I have always adored hansom cabs. Could such
perfection ever be repeated? Was I at the summit of my life?
Would it all be downhill from now on?

I showed the house I grew up in to Algy. It looked extremely
horrid; the street was even narrower than I remembered. It was
just the antidote I needed to the house in Kensington. Walking
here with Algy, it had to be real. No one dreamed up these
places.

He remained detached and polite. He certainly hated the whole
business. At times he put his handkerchief to his nose. He stepped

carefully around the filth in the street. Kids followed us and I gave them pennies. We came to the house where Harry used to live – I knew that Algy had never been anywhere like it in his life. I would have thought twice about bringing him there at night. He was so golden; he looked so rich. I pictured myself defending him from robbers. I'd murder to save him, I thought.

I realised that for him the experience had been a shock. He must have been feeling contaminated. He had never seen streets like the Lane. I sympathised with him, the effort he was making not to appear nauseated and repelled, not to hurt my feelings by his revulsion.

And now I came up against a difference between Algy and me. Because I wanted our love to be based in reality, I'd obliged Algy to walk through Spitalfields and I'd made him face up to where I'd come from. But he never dared return the compliment. Algy never took me anywhere near his family. Probably it was to spare me discomfort rather than because he was ashamed of me, but the fact remained Algy knew I would not fit.

"Right!" said Algy triumphantly. "You've shown me the East End; now you can take me to a music hall. That is something I've never done."

And so we did. It was about as successful as the concerts. It took me by surprise that Algy didn't know the words of even the most well known songs, so out of politeness I didn't sing either. That way, though, you miss out; it's peculiar not singing and yelling and stamping your feet. I can't say I enjoyed the music hall in Algy's company. It seemed more than usually coarse. I saw the familiar look of mild distaste on his lips, contained by the same fixed smile he showed when he ladled out soup to my weekly poor. I smiled wrily, as he had to me at the opera. But then I embarrassed myself by a snort of a laugh at a crude joke from the stage and I winced to note that Algy wasn't laughing. With some relief I saw that the next item was a sentimental song. When I'd been there before with Sam and Leo we'd sung along in beery unison, but Algy behaved like he was the Angel Gabriel come down to earth in the wrong place. I was nothing but relieved when we came away.

We took a hansom back to Kensington through the warm summer darkness. As we came in through the garden door, Algy held me where the peacock feathers were floating and used one to tickle my face. He snapped the feather from its string. I gasped: "Vandal!"

He giggled. "We're going up to your little room," he said, "and I'm going to take off all your clothes and I'm going to tickle you all over with this peacock plume. I shall reduce you to a hysterical jelly. Giggling at the smut we heard tonight will be as nothing to how you'll be when I've finished with you. You're *common*, you are. You're a ragamuffin, Willie Smith, and all my attempts to civilise you have failed."

He hugged me against him tight and close. "And I do love you," he said.

The next day Mr Strode came into the kitchen where I was making potato soup for the needy, and he lurked.

It's funny, people who lurk. They fiddle with things, pick things up, drop them, fidget. He even began a conversation about greenhouses. "I think it's wonderful what you are doing for the poor!" he suddenly blurted out.

"Oh no," I insisted, "it's a drop in the ocean."

I launched into an account almost verbatim of what Mr Pearson had said to us at church, about the ragged boys in the streets and alleys of our city, and how if we gave all it would not be enough. Mr Strode ogled me and my words passed over him. "You and Algernon . . . " he began.

"Yes?" I said prickling.

"I too, as you know . . . " he continued, twiddling with a fork, "and I have never found it easy . . . a terrible burden . . . I wondered if, Parsifal, you could help me to ease it . . . "

"Um, how d'you mean?" I asked naively.

"Oh, now, don't torment. You must know I'd very much like to know you better. You are a very beautiful boy."

"Thank you," I said politely.

"Is there any chance? Could you – be fond of me?"

"I'm sorry, Mr Strode. I appreciate the compliment."

"Oh – please don't refuse me out of hand. Take some time, consider it."

"No, you see, I love Algy. When you're in love you just want the beloved," I said proudly.

"Quaint," he said, with a crooked smile. "All right. I accept that you could not love me. But surely you could bring yourself to – just sometimes – "

"No; I want to be faithful."

"How about if I were to offer you money? Would it change your mind?"

"It would be the worst thing you could do," I said stiffly. "What do you think I am, a street boy?"

"No – I don't mean to insult you. I simply desire you so badly."

"It's real nice of you, mister, but no."

"A guinea?" he tempted me, and my heart hardened.

"No, and that's final."

As I stirred the soup I reflected that the joy of not being a tart was that you could enjoy the luxury of saying No. I savoured that moment.

II

IT WAS when my cat ate the raven that I knew I had stopped being welcome at the house in Kensington.

I should explain how I came to possess a cat at all, let alone one who so made his mark on the artistic community. It was as a result of one disastrous night when Algy and I went to see Mr Henry Irving at the Lyceum Theatre and whilst coming home encountered trouble.

The evening had started so beautifully.

Wearing my borrowed suit of Algy's, I had met him in Trafalgar Square. Much as I found the suit constrictive it was a most elegant thing and I very much fancied myself. It was pale brown, with a matching buff-coloured waistcoat and a brown silk necktie; the only odd thing being that on me the suit looked quite different from on Algy. Don't they say fine feathers don't make a bird? I don't know if it was how I walked, my long flame-coloured hair, my cheeky stance or my sweaty uncomfortable neck that wriggled around like a villain in the stocks: I looked more like a "swell masher" than a nob. Nonetheless, I was a fine sight all right, very flash, and as I leaned against a lion waiting for Algy I was pretty content.

As usual when I saw him coming towards me it pained me

that I couldn't run to him and kiss him. Our eyes met, and I knew he felt the same.

Algy said smoulderingly: "O boy with the virginal eyes, I seek you but you do not listen, not knowing that you are the charioteer of my soul." Then he added: "Now would you like to hear me say it in Greek?"

"Yes please," I said adoringly.

He frowned endearingly, concentrated and spoke some words. I grinned. "Don't you realise you needn't strain so hard? I won't understand a word."

However, that evening I was conscious of mental closeness. In Shakespeare we had found a common ground, and we sat enrapt. We were spellbound by Mr Irving, who was all presence, with a thrilling melodious voice. It made your spine shiver. Transported into such a different world, I believe we had momentarily forgotten our surroundings, and outside the theatre as we were walking I suddenly blinked and laughed uneasily. "Hey, not up here – this is Bow Street."

"Oh, is it?" said Algy blankly.

In the jostling throng we had been carried as on a tide. All was bustle as gents shouted for cabs, and the pavements were packed. Rapidly returning to my senses I stared at my surroundings, the streets round Covent Garden, easy walking distance from my little room at Mrs Dawson's.

At that instant I was assailed by a familiar voice. "Willie Smith! Where yer bin?"

Caroline! She was there with a bunch of her cronies, soliciting for theatre traffic under a lamp. I was torn. My feelings on seeing her were first of all horror, because I was with Algy, but this unworthy response was rapidly overtaken by frank pleasure at seeing her again. Genuine delight of recognition passed between us. She was a good mate.

"Will you wait for me?" I whispered to Algy. He nodded and I ran over to Caroline. Within minutes we had slipped into companionable chat, gossiping merrily; she was laughing out loud, her hands on her hips and her long fanlike ear rings jiggling under her tinted curls. Then one of the girls groaned: "Oh-oh: company!"

Behind me, unnoticed, two crushers had come strolling up. "Move along ladies," I heard, "nah then, move along."

Suddenly I felt my ear gripped – my *ear*! This dirty great finger and thumb turned me right round using my ear as a handle, till I was facing this leering mug. "Willie Smith, I do declare!" he beamed. "Up to our old tricks again, are we? We hoped we'd seen the last of you!"

"Get your bleedin' hands orf me!" I gasped, white with rage. Naturally enough, he took offence at this, and did not relinquish me but pulled my head about a bit by the ear. He was one of the policemen who'd brought me in for bathing in the Serpentine with the lads from Alfie's. Just my bad luck he remembered me so well!

"Ah, leave him!" Caroline cried. "He ain't even working. He was just chattin' to us. He's given it all up now. Stop pickin' on him, yer big ugly!"

"Given it up?" said he scornfully. "*He's got a gent waiting!*"

To my appalled horror they all turned to look at Algy. I kicked the constable hard on the ankle and pulled free from his grasp. "Run!" I choked to Algy, shoving him, and we both took off down the street. They didn't follow, but the pig who'd held me called out in ringing sarcastic tones: "Good night, *gentlemen*!"

Once we were well clear and safely down a grimy little side street, I flung my arm against the wall, buried my face in it and burst into tears. I was so ashamed and embarrassed and angry at having involved Algy in such a tawdry little encounter. Breathless from running, Algy stood behind me, patting my shoulders inadequately. "Don't," he said, "oh, please don't."

"Now you've seen the lot," I shuddered. "Now you've seen it all. I never told you, did I, that I was known to the police?"

"Oh come on," he pleaded. "Let's find a cab. I'll take you home."

"I ain't fit to come home with you; leave me where I belong," I wept. This was when I was first aware of the cat rubbing against my legs. I kicked it away. It miaowed and came back.

"You can't stay here all night," said Algy reasonably.

"I can – these are my streets. I'm a guttersnipe like this bleedin' cat. Seems like I can't never shake the past away – seems like they won't let me."

"Oh, cease these histrionics," Algy snapped.

I knelt down and stroked the cat. Blimey, he was thin. When had he last eaten, poor little blighter? He began to purr, an awful hoarse rattle. I felt desolate and lonely. I knew Algy had detached himself from me and was unable to comfort me because of his own state of shock. I knew he wanted to get home and have a bath and wash his hair — all the things he did when reality intruded — and that he needed the reassurance of his home, the safety of his property about him. He had all that to fall back on, I'd got nothing. That's why I took the cat home. I'd got more in common with that cat, I thought, than with Algy. At least I could give him a decent meal.

I stood up slowly, cradling the cat, one of my tears plopping on to his mangy fur.

"Ugh, put it down," Algy grimaced.

"I'm takin' it home," I muttered.

"It'll be diseased," he assured me.

"I don't care. It's lonely."

"How do you know? Cats don't have feelings."

"*I* feel. I feel it's lonely."

"Well, it's your problem," he shrugged.

My ear lobe ached. I felt thoroughly miserable. "Yeah, all right, let's go home," I said.

I was surprised the cat settled on my arm. He latched on to my shoulder, his defiant purring close to my ear, his claws gripping the cloth of the suit. He impressed me with the way he adapted to circumstances. What a sneaky little opportunist!

Algy procured us a cab, and laughed at me for chatting to the cat. "Who's ridin' in an 'ansom then? Who's goin' up in the world? Who's goin' ter Kensington?" I cooed, cuddling it.

"I'm callin' him Thrummer," I added.

"Oh?" said Algy, arching his exquisite brows.

"It's a word as means threepence. It's a street word."

"Willie, listen . . . it doesn't make any difference what happened. You don't have to take on this aggressive stance, you know."

"What?"

"This 'I am of the common people'. You can talk and act perfectly civilised when you choose. I know it was unpleasant, that stupid policeman, but it was just a silly incident and it's over now. We won't go there again."

"Algy!" I wailed. "It was the one place we both were comfortable. We loved it. We mustn't be frightened off."

"We can't take that kind of risk just to see a play."

"What risk? I wasn't arrested. We just got to run if we see a policeman, that's all. It's pathetic if we let crushers stop us enjoyin' an evening at the theatre, and we did enjoy it, both of us."

"I know. But I found it upsetting seeing you in a policeman's grip; it was so degrading. And also," he added in a subdued tone, "somebody I know might be coming out of the theatre and see it happen. I can't take that risk."

Thrummer had all the grace and charm of an alleycat and an alleycat's winning ways. He pissed on the tiles in the hall, and spent hours of ingenuity lying in wait for the oriental goldfish in the marble fountain. Everyone hated him. He wasn't even mediaeval. He fitted no image. He caught birds in the garden and he rolled on the seedlings, he scratched up the herbs and dug hollows under the mint. He brought his half moribund prey into the house and left them on the Indian rugs. Charles included several in his pictures of decay and gloom, as symbols. I was secretly delighted at every fresh crime of his. I was beginning to find the artists pretentious and amoral. Thrummer was doing the kind of things I'd like to have done myself. Well, maybe not bringing in mangled corpses, but I wouldn't have minded casually knocking over a vase or two and bagging a goldfish. Even pissing on the tiles, now I come to think of it . . .

In a couple of days Algy appeared, contrite and loving. He handed me a tiny box, a present. Inside there was an amethyst ring set in gold. I was awed. Of course it fitted; Algy had used his own fingers for measurement. "Will you stay tonight?" I said.

"Yes. And I have an idea to put to you. You must tell me what you think."

When I reflect upon it now, Algy's idea that we should go to Paris together seems to me the craziest idea I've ever heard. A lad from Aldgate whose experience of travel was darkest Hertfordshire and whose knowledge of French could have been written on a postage stamp, planning to live in Paris – the idea is quite bizarre. And yet, so help me, I let him convince me; I believed it possible. It even seemed logical.

England, that is, London, he said, was no place for two men in love, two men of different classes. We could not fit into each other's world and so we had to go where we could make our own. It was common practice amongst English Urnings to take to the Continent. It was different there. In Paris we would walk along the streets and allow our love to blossom gently.

The artists declared it was a charming idea and how like Algy to come up with such a beautiful solution. If I had misgivings they were drowned in the river of delights that seemed within my grasp. Suddenly everyone was talking about Paris in October, the tall beautiful houses, the green shutters, the tubs of flowers in the street, the window boxes with the pink geraniums, the pavement cafés where one sat and sipped the stuff of dreams. One didn't even need to know French, they told me. English was spoken by all the cultured intelligent people; besides, Algy spoke the language fluently.

"But what will we *do?*" I asked.

"We will *be*," he replied.

All around me it was evident that my usefulness to the artists had all but run its course. The studio dripped with auburn-haired lads in every conceivable pose and legend. They writhed against pillars, they lay in ecstatic nudity, they offered chalices to Zeus; they lay wounded beside fountains, roses and briars brushing their pallid hands, they held swords whose blades they kissed in earnest of holy intentions. The picture of Parsifal and Galahad wanted only the last touches to the ivy.

It was at this stage that Thrummer finally achieved his ambition and knocked over the cage where they kept the crow. The door flew open, but the wretched creature was trapped and doubtless stunned. The result was so horrible I will pass over describing it, but Thrummer's presence was treated henceforth with chilling resentment and by implication I too was under a cloud. To all things a season, they say, and summer was drawing to a close.

III

AND SO we made our plans for Paris.

Clara, the most practical, sat with me in the kitchen, and helped me to learn French phrases from a book. "Monsieur, I do not wish this wine. Kindly remove it. Where is the station? I am lost. Here is my baggage. That is my hotel. I am English."

Algy was pleased but sceptical, teasing me shamelessly. He slung his arm round me and giggled to Clara: "Where is my hotel? I am lost, but," and he indicated me, "here is my baggage!"

We decided that I would wear his pale brown suit to travel in; beyond my personal effects I would take nothing. In Paris he would buy me all the clothes I needed, in the styles current there. At first we would stay at a hotel, in separate rooms, and later we would look for an apartment. He would show me the delights of Paris and for hours at a time we would devote ourselves to making love. That part of our life never palled. If ever I had any doubts about the wisdom of our venture I lost them when we lay in each other's arms. "Parsifal," said Algy, "you taught me how to love – I never had that gift before you."

Algy would hear nothing of my contributing to the venture from my savings and so, flushed with the triumph of giving, I took what was left of my sovereigns and pressed them all into the hands of a Quaker from the north who was raising funds to save poor boys from going down the pits.

It gave me a real thrill to be so munificent.

By then Paris was taken for granted by all of us. But Algy was having bad dreams. I would hear him whimpering in his sleep like a little boy. I remembered what he'd told me about his childhood – "I was afraid of everything" – and I'd take him in my arms and hold him tight.

"Was I dreaming?"

"Yes, darlin', but it's over now. I'm here."

"I'm shivering."

"Lie close to me; I'll warm yer."

"I was frightened."

"I'll look after yer; yer got me now. There ain't nothin' out there we can't beat."

". . . so threatened . . . things closing in . . . " he shuddered.

"I used to get bad dreams too."

"You, Parsifal? You seem so strong."

"I ain't. I'd wake up shiverin'. Half the constabulary and the prison service would be chasin' me, with hands big as cauliflowers. I'd be backed against a wall screamin'. I know about bad dreams."

"I'm so sorry to be so weak."

"I'll be strong for yer. I'll fight 'em off," I promised.

"How did your bad dreams stop?"

"Mine stop when I sleep in the arms of the one I love."

"Why don't mine?" he quivered, tears wet on his cheeks. "Why don't mine?"

I just held him tight and kissed him better. I see now what I couldn't see then. His bad dreams were caused by me. They couldn't be stopped by the act of being close to me and lying in my arms. He went ahead with planning Paris; he booked our train, our boat, our rooms at the hotel, and all the time he was in a panic of terror and dread. My bad dreams had been caused by fears that were *over* and so love could soothe them away. But Algy's dreams were in the future – our future, the commitment he was scared of making.

I didn't see much of Algy for the week before we were due to go. He had his own arrangements to make, people to see. Myself, I packed up all my dear possessions and took them to Caroline's, pictures, ornaments, clothes and books, and various portraits of myself from the artists; my little swing mirror, my winter boots and of course Thrummer in a closed basket. Franklin gave me a porcelain cup, which was very decent of him considering what a Philistine I was; Clara gave me some pottery plates, and Charles the copy of Swinburne. I also took the peacock feather with which Algy had carried out his wonderful erotic promise to tickle me all over, and many pressed daisies from the garden, for sentimental reasons.

"Don't you worry about a thing," said Caroline cheerfully. "I'll keep your things safe and you can send for 'em when you're ready. Let me know how you get on. Oh! I do envy you, Willie. It's a chance in a lifetime!" And she went into great detail of what I could bring her back from Paris. I'd have needed a couple of trunks!

The artists gave me a good send off with a superb meal the night before, and lots of wine. It was late September, the time we'd chosen for our flight to a new life, and I was to meet Algy on Victoria Station where we'd catch the boat train.

I hate that station worse'n any place in London except the

reformatory. It's a very public place to be abandoned. I was there hours. Several trains went. I got so its details were engraved on my vision – the cabs in rows at the great arched frontage, the dining room and refreshment room, the notice saying Main Line Trains, the ironwork of the roof, the stink of soot. Steam billowed out in clouds entirely obscuring the trains themselves. It made you cough. Every time it cleared, my romantic mind expected Algy to be standing there like an angel bringing me my release and my passport to heaven.

I must've had a dozen cups of tea from the Temperance Society's mobile stand, and the lady gave me a leaflet to read for the good of my soul. At first I truly believed that night I would sleep in Paris in the arms of my golden-haired beloved, that we would walk by the Seine and see October in from the slopes of Montmartre. I would not allow the truth to dawn upon me until many bleak hours had made it seem inevitable. As long as there was another train I hoped. I wouldn't wish on anybody the kind of day I spent on Victoria Station.

It was dark when a telegraph boy found me and handed me a note. It just said: "I can't go through with it. For both our sakes. Forgive me."

And the crazy thing was, my first reaction was immense pity for him, that once again his nerve had failed, and that he was still the frightened boy who lay and shivered in the dark. I knew he would have suffered, writing that note, that he would have spent as tormented an afternoon as I had. I remembered to give the boy a tip; he was good lookin 'n' all, and telegraph boys had a bit of a reputation.

I was immensely relieved to have a reason to leave that station. I took a cab to Blackfriars Bridge, and as the journey progressed I was aware of an ache in my body from chest to guts, real sharp around the heart. When the cab put me down at the bridge, I crossed halfway over and into the black waters of the river I dropped *Useful Words and Phrases for the Traveller in France*. The ache grew stronger, and I wondered whether I was hungry. The idea of stuffing food down myself nauseated me. More pressing, I had nowhere to sleep and it was night. I also had no money.

I would have died rather than go back to Kensington. I wondered briefly about Caroline, but my mind just numbed over.

The rejection I had suffered so crippled me that I felt the other side of a chasm from all human contacts.

I walked up Ludgate and on to Holborn.

After a while I saw a likely looking gemmun, and I offered him a light.

PART SIX

CHAPTER TWENTY-ONE

I

TOOK ME three goes before I latched on to one. Ho, losin'
your touch, Smiff, are yer? I thought grimly; maybe you
don't look so promisin' in your suit. However, I did my
best and I strolled off to Rosa's with my catch.

"Hello, my dear," she declared, like I'd never been away.
"Yes, I can find you a room, Take him along; I've got just the
place."

I can't say I remember his face at all. He was a cipher, that's
all, the means for the price of a room. I didn't even bother with
my fancy skills; it was a real sloppy performance he got from
me. As he began to pant in my ear I buried my face in the
pillow. The ache in my guts spread all over my body and my
eyes filled up with tears; I couldn't help it, they came spilling
out. I bit my lip till it hurt but the tears still came. "Oh Lord,"
said my gent, concerned. "I'm not hurting you, am I?"

"No, it ain't you at all – you don't hurt a bit."

"What is it then?"

"Nothing," I wept. "It's just . . . I thought I'd be somewhere
else tonight."

"What shall I do? Would you like me to stop?"

Was he a saint or something? "Of course not," I said fiercely.
Poor sod, hey? A weeping tart, where's the joy in that? Not
much of a night's pleasure, was it? "I hope it gets better for
you," he murmured solicitously.

"Thank you, mister."

I was pretty glad when he left. With push in my pocket I
bought myself the use of a seedy little room in a rundown place
in a back street, and took a bottle of gin up to my room and
proceeded to drink myself to sleep.

I stayed there for a week or so, hardly ever coming out or even bothering to get dressed. I lay in bed mostly, drunk and very smelly. I went to seed almost enthusiastically. By the end of the week I was picking lice out of my crotch hair. Truly the memory of that week is unclear. Once or twice I bought a sandwich from a street stall and crawled back inside. Honestly, I did not know where I was half the time. It was only running out of money for the gin that brought an end to this dismal phase of my life.

Penniless, I sat on the end of the bed, staring vacantly ahead of me. Rain on the window made a sound that was like the slapping of wet fish. I did not want to think; I could not even frame the words that caused me pain. I needed another gin-induced stupor. I'd have to go out. That night I dragged my clothes on and went into the dark. I hardly noticed the rain. I traipsed the wet streets with my collar up, ugly in my uneven beard; I got five bob from a gent I did with my hands behind a wall. Now I could retreat again into oblivion.

The next two bottles of gin left me feeling so ill that I had to stop this horrible binge and attempt to pull myself together. My hands were shaking, my head ached, I was dizzy when I stood up and I could hardly see. I tried to look in a mirror, but I couldn't focus; I got a pain between the eyes. I had to hold on to the wall when I staggered to the privy and I couldn't aim straight when I got there! Bleedin' hell, I was a mess! I had to lie in bed and wait till I felt better. Partly I didn't want to feel better; I knew there was something nasty I'd have to face when I became human again.

One morning I woke up weak but clear-headed. The gin effects had eased off and now I'd just got heartache. I lay there; I ached. My body was one complete ache.

Algy had left me.

Algy had left me, but I'd got to eat.

I got dressed and combed my horrible hair. It hung lank and flat and itchy. My mirror showed me a ghastly pale face, hollow-eyed and bloodshot, with ginger stubble reminiscent of Macbeth's blasted heath, uneven and clumpy. I was awed by its ugliness.

I slunk out, mingling quickly with the street crowds, and walked the long dreary distance to the public baths. I was unsteady on my legs, I felt weak and queasy, but better when I was clean. I had a bath and shave and washed my hair, cocooned against the world by the hot steam. I went out and had a cheap meal but it was all I could do to eat. Each mouthful felt like a great hard lump, and tasteless as dough.

I eventually ended up back at Madame Rosa's. I hoped she could fix me up with something regular. One night a week would see me all right till I'd got myself sorted out. She said she'd see what she could do.

By some quirk of chance as I was coming away from Rosa's, I happened to bump into Sam and Noll out walking in Holborn. I hadn't seen them since I stopped going to Alfie's and they wanted to stop and chat and ask how things were going. Half incoherently I muttered some reply, but I was totally disconcerted by the contact and couldn't wait to get away. I badly needed the privacy to go to pieces on my own; I wasn't up to that kind of chance encounter. I turned my back on the familiar haunts and hurried down a horrible side street into the filthy maze around St Giles, a place to go to ground.

Those streets and alleys still had a bad reputation, left over from before they slashed 'em open with New Oxford Street. They were no longer the vile rookery they used to be, but they were about as nasty as you could get except for some places in the East End and down the docks. I hunched my shoulders and slouched into obscurity. I found a public house and started once more on the gin.

I slept that night in a low dosshouse – the bed cost me fourpence; it was no more than a stiff straw mattress with a blanket, and I kept my shoes on in case they were pinched. The bag I'd been carrying around with me I used as a pillow but stupid with the effects of gin, I went out like a light, and in the morning it had gone. I was astonished, and almost full of admiration for the skill of the thief, prising it out from under me. I rolled onto my back and lay there, looking thoughtfully at the low beam that was seeming to hold the roof up, and the cobwebs hanging like mosquito nets around each individual palliasse. I reflected that I was curiously close now to Willie Smith aged ten. Here I lay, with just the clothes on my back, stiff from a hard bed, itching from lice, alone.

Was it worse, I wondered, when Charley left me? I tried to compare the pains. My body had ached then – oh, but this one was much worse. Algy was my lover. He'd shown me what life could be like, and then snatched it away. What tormented me was that I knew perfectly well that we *could* have had a life together if he had dared. Being an Urning is only dangerous when you have to solicit. Two gents can be secret if they trust each other. Two gents can even live together. The public doesn't assume sin; it only gets angry when the sinners flaunt it. Algy and I could have been discreet, if he'd wanted me enough. But he didn't.

He had wanted me, but he'd wanted safety too, and the good regard of his family whom he'd spent a lifetime pleasing. We could only have had a future together if he had been different. But he was weak. He was like Georgey. Funny, so often I'd thought he was like my little cousin – blond, adorable, spoilt, indulged, protected, delightful, beautiful – and like Georgey he was weak, and in each case I'd been left beaten down from having loved them. How mischievous love was! All along I'd known that what I wanted was a strong man who'd look after me, like Charley, and there I went pursuing indolent nymphs. A weakness in me, maybe, a quirk that caused my own undoing.

The ache of my body became unbearable; I drew my knees up to my chest with the pain of it, hid my face and cried. No one took any notice; this was the kind of place you could lie and rot as long as you paid your fourpence, and there in that horrible dosshouse surrounded by coughs I abandoned myself to my misery.

No commonsense answer suggested itself. No voice said go round to Caroline's and have a wash. Those voices are very silent at times like these. I cried for hours on end. Once, a mug of coffee was put down by my elbow but who did that kind thing I have no idea. I drank it – it was hot and bitter. As well as lice I caught a head cold; everyone round me was coughing. Again I ran out of push. I had to leave the dosshouse. On the streets it was shockingly cold. It struck my bleary senses and added shivering to my general malaise, as I shuffled along hands in pockets looking for a gent.

That night I did something I'd never ever done before: I pleaded. I encountered this gent who hesitated. I thought he wanted me but he dithered. There in the street he stood and frowned, balancing the issues. "Please, mister," I snivelled, "I'm down on me luck at present."

It was the wrong tack. "Ah, I think not," he said, and hurried on.

I slouched away, up and down, up and down, between lamp posts, now and then essaying a not too hopeful: "Light, mister?", expecting refusal. It was like when I was a scrap of a kid, selling Lucifers, screeching my wares to trouser legs and coat hems, hopeful of a gloved hand descending with pennies. Oh, Charley, I thought, if you could see me now, the wheel come full circle, your ragamuffin brother still hawking on the streets.

Mechanically I offered my light; I received polite refusals and pointed ignorings, and so when one accepted me my hands trembled with astonishment. I took him down a vile alley. He asked how much I charged. "Five bob," I said, ashamed at my nerve.

We went behind a wall in an unpaved little court pitted with puddles, a broken drainpipe gushing nearby, and light rain pattering beyond the overhang of the low roof where we sheltered. I attended to him swiftly, and we separated. The gent sloped off; as for me, I needed the sweet dulling haze of gin and a bed to drink it in. Five bob – I was rich now for a while – and I turned back into the sprawl of St Giles.

Before I reached a public house three blokes got hold of me and hustled me into a doorway, and the next thing I knew I was being robbed. I was slung face against the wall, my pockets were pulled inside out, my five shillings was swiftly appropriated, and then my left hand was lifted up and slammed against the crumbling brickwork. I struggled. "Keep still; it's the ring we want."

No use telling me anyone who slouches round St Giles with an amethyst on his finger is asking to get done; it was too late for that. My wrist was twisted round, my finger half dislocated, and they scratched and tugged at Algy's ring. I kicked and screeched, my hand clenched in a fist, my mouth bleeding from being slammed against the brick. They held my hand against the wall by the wrist and just welted it till I unclenched, and twisted the ring off my limp finger. "Don't – leave us me ring," I howled huskily, but they had it. Then one of them looked right in my face and pointed a horny finger close to my nose. "I know you!" he said, a statement of surprise and threat.

They ran off along the street, jumping over the slouched hunched forms of the ragged bodies sitting on the pavestones. I was left shaken and wretched; I sat down where I was and put my head on my knees.

Some time later, a hand shook my shoulder. "Oy," a voice said, "d'you want a place to kip?"

II

I LOOKED up uncomprehendingly. I saw a ragged pale-faced youth of about my age. As far as I could tell he was the bloke who'd helped scrape my ring off and reckoned he knew me. "Come on," he invited cheerfully, nodding, and I got up and followed him. We went down the street and turned into a dark alley whose walls streamed water which slopped around our feet. We crossed a court where beggars lay sprawled on the cobbles and dogs sniffed at the rags. We went down an alley no bigger than a corridor, and down some dark steps into a cellar.

It was one of them old kitchens, and the first thing I noticed was that it had a range and a fire and they were cooking sausages. It was a biggish place, straw on the floor, dark crannies and corners, shapes and shadows, and various humans sitting about and standing. In a moment or so I saw that the bloke by the fire was Hammer, my protector at the reformatory. The one who'd brought me here then slotted into place, a boy who'd slept in the dormitory, whose name I didn't know. I had the reformatory then to thank that I had a place to sleep that night. But it was a very mixed blessing. "It *is* you then!" Hammer said. "Ain't you learned nuffin'? Sleepin' in a dosshouse wiv a bleedin' ring on – bleedin' barmy!"

"Is it you who's got it?" I demanded aggrieved.

"What if I have?"

"Have yer?"

"I have. Larkins!" he called. "Remember Larkins, Willie? The one who wanted ter beat you up? He's my partner nah. Show 'im the ring, Larkins."

Larkins strolled over, twiddling the ring provocatively. "What, this?"

I looked at it unhappily. "Give it back, will yer? It's precious to me."

A cheerful chorus of guffaws greeted this naive remark. "Precious? Yeah, I'll say. It'll buy us a coach 'n' horses!"

"You won't be able to sell it," I declared, in sudden inspiration. "It's famous. It's part of a collection. No fence'll take it; it'll be traced straight back to you."

"That's what I said," claimed one of Hammer's lads. "I said it was too valuable. It's in the wrong class for us."

"What's it worth to yer, Willie?" Hammer asked.

"I want it back," I admitted.

"All right, I tell yer what: you can buy it back."

"How can I? You took all me money."

"Yeah, five bob. Very decent of yer. Ow'd yer get it?"

"I got it off a gent," I muttered.

"Ah!" he crowed. "Tartin', was it?"

I scowled in an expressive silence.

"Ho! So you took it up serious, did yer, after you got aht?" Hammer declared interestedly.

"Nasty little runt," said Larkins, predictably, and pocketed the ring.

Hammer chuckled comfortably. He asked: "'Ow much can yer pick up? 'Ow much a time?"

"Depends."

"I bet you're real good," he said contemplatively.

"I used ter be. I've gone off a bit. I've had me troubles."

"Ain't we all," Hammer agreed. "Well, look 'ere, sweetheart, let's turn our meetin' to advantage, eh? You want this ring? I'll sell it to yer. Flack's right, we can't sell it easy. But hard push nah, that's different. You can 'ave yer ring back – you can earn it. What'll we say, Larkins? Five pahnd?"

"Six," said Larkins sadistically.

"Where am I going ter get six pound?" I blanched.

"Earn it," he shrugged. "Bendin' yer arse."

"It'll take me ages," I groaned.

"We can wait. You can stay 'ere, you'll get food, we do all right."

"Oh yeah," I sneered. "You always talked so big. I thought you'd have had a bleedin' mansion by now, all your bleedin' plans. All this time you're livin' in a cellar in St Giles."

"I ain't been lucky, that's what. I got nabbed, twice. But I'm doin' all right. I get by."

I looked around resignedly. I was starving. It was either Hammer or the streets. The smell of the sausages was tormenting me. My eyes kept straying to the range. It was for that smell that I made the deal. Hammer observed it all, and slapped me on the back. "Oy, Joey," he called. "Give our new boy a sausage."

I took it greedily. At that moment I was very close in kind to the urchin who went with Fadge for peaches.

I slept in Hammer's bed. "Go on," he advised me. "It's the best. It's the only one wot's off the grahnd."

This was true. The others slept on straw mattresses or wooden boards or on the straw itself, which was damp and dirty, like in a drawing of the interior of Newgate. Hammer's bed was a couple of boards slung between stone shelves which had been ancient wine racks. The names of the wines were still scrawled in chalk. It was a basement alcove and pitch dark. Half a window showed higher up, but it was boarded over and let in no light. On the floor mice busied themselves all night, and I am sure rats too, but I preferred to ignore that.

In the morning I insisted on having a wash. I put it to Hammer that he could give me money to go and have a bath or I wanted some water boiled at the range. "You was always fussy," he remembered. He gave orders to his minions for pails of water from the pump. I shuddered to imagine what kind of pump it would be in these streets, but as Aunt Louisa often told me, water boiled for two minutes is clean water, and I was grateful when it appeared.

Hammer's urchins had obviously never seen somebody taking trouble over cleanliness, and my morning washes were a matter of public interest. I had a chipped bowl on the floor in front of the fire. Time and again I was reminded of our way of life in Aldgate when I was ten years old. I kept remembering how our mum made us keep our standards up even though we'd fallen on hard times.

Not at all embarrassed in my brisk and lathery nakedness, I said severely to the nearest urchin: "And when did you last wash?"

"Me? I never wash! Lawks!"

"Was it you as brought the water?"

"Yeah."

"When you bring me some tomorrow you bring some for yourself as well – and for him."

"Blimey! You ain't goin' ter wash two days runnin'!"

"Listen to me," I said sternly. "If you don't wash, d'you know what happens to yer?"

"Nah. What?"

"See this," I said, picking out a louse. "You get these all over yer. You've got 'em all over you and so've I. I can feel 'em in me hair. I'm goin ter wash my hair in a minute and they won't like that one little bit. If you don't wash, you stinks. And you get scabs on your body. And when diseases come looking for a place to live they think Ho! that's a nice dirty body, I think I'll go and live there. But if you're clean they pass you by."

"Cor!" he remarked intrigued. But his friend was more sceptical. "How come you got such a bad cold then?" he asked. "If you're so clean!"

"'Cause I only started washin' today. If I'd been clean before I daresay I wouldn't've got it," I said virtuously.

"I wouldn't mind washin'," said the one I'd convinced. His name was Peter. "'Ammer's trainin' me," he boasted. "'E's goin' ter teach me all 'e knows!"

"All he knows?" I said scathingly. "How to get nabbed by the crushers and stuck in stir!"

They grumbled at such a misrepresentation of their hero and told me proudly of all the amazing things he'd done – daring little robberies, lock-picking, breakings-in and street hauls. Everyone ate well if they knew Hammer. "He don't buy you boots though," I remarked.

They shrugged. They'd been barefoot all their lives.

I got dressed in my horrible clothes, noticing how rapidly a decent suit can go to pieces when one is living rough; it was dirty, torn and stained. I did some washing and dried it and my hair by the fire. People came and went on mysterious errands, and now and then handed me food to cook. I fried a lot of sausages and fatted a lot of bread. When Hammer came in he brought me a bottled stout and a bun, and I sat barefoot by the fire with my feast. Later on I went and had a shave at a barber's.

That night I went out to try my luck.

III

IT WAS perishing cold, October, and damply misty, and I wasn't
warm enough in the suit. I have to admit something: when I
was in the barber's I nicked a cap. It was hanging up with the
coats and I just took it as I went past. I'd never stole before,
and I was interested to find how easy it was, that sort of casual
one-off stuff. I was glad of it now, as I pulled it down low and
turned my collar up, and slouched around a bit, propositioning
when a gent loomed out of the fog. The second gent I asked
agreed, and pleased, I minced off down a backstreet with him.
I saw a good place, a thin lane between the backs of two privy
walls. It stank, of course, but it was private. At the end of it was
another wall, and a sort of hutch. I didn't pay much attention;
it was like a dog kennel. My gent and I embraced, and I dropped
to my knees and began to undo his trousers. Then I heard this
sort of scuffle, like rats, and a sort of sigh. I paused.

He heard it too, and tensed up and snatched my hand away.
We waited nervously. I stood up. "It's in there," I said and the
little sounds came once again from the heap of wood. Annoyed,
I went and had a look. "Blimey!" I said, floored. "It's boys."

My gent stood behind me and we squinted down into the dark.
I lit a match. Two – no, three little boys were squeezed in this
tiny space, terrified eyes peering up at us, and this faint squeak
said: "Don't 'it us mister, we're only sleepin'."

"What you doin' in there?" I said. "Ain't you got no home?"

"This is it," he said.

I gasped, and turned to my gent. "They *live* there!"

"Well, either turn them out or let us go somewhere else," he
said testily.

"But mister, we can't leave 'em there!"

"Can't we? I can!"

"It's just two pieces of wood sloping together," I cried. "That's
no place for boys to sleep!"

"Oh really!" he snapped. "This is too bad."

"Maybe there's a place nearby," I said, "where we could take
them, a soup kitchen."

"I've no idea. I didn't accompany you to clean up the problem of the city's poor."

"Look, mister, I know a place where these'd be welcome. Will you help me take 'em there?"

"No, I will not! Are you so rich that you can afford to throw away the chance of earning five shillings?"

"Oh! I couldn't do it while I was worrying about these."

"Very well," he said icily. "Goodnight then."

For a moment I felt rather foolish, standing there, having chucked that chance. But I knew I was right. I knelt down by the boys and started chatting. I knew this nice big house, I said, and a real kindly man who cared for little boys and gave them shelter, and I'd take them there; we'd go now.

I must've been convincing, because the oldest very wearily wriggled out, and brought his two mates. They were aged nine, seven and three. The three year old was asleep. I picked him up and carried him, like Mr Pearson had done that night when he'd asked me if I'd got a light for myself.

So, off we all went.

Bleedin' hell, I'd forgotten how far it could seem walking to Shoreditch and carrying a kid. And yet I didn't seem to feel all that tired. I felt possessed by a strong sense of righteousness. I felt like my print of Saint George. It was so lovely to be doing something good, instead of drinking myself senseless and sitting on kerbs in despair. Cautiously I thought I wasn't aching quite so much, the Algy ache, the one in my guts. But I put Algy from my thoughts; I wasn't ready to face up to all that again; better numb the mind.

I chatted to the boys. They were all orphans, and awful tired. We walked slowly, and to cheer them up I told them the story of Puss in Boots. It passed the time and then we started looking for Goff Street. Fortunately I remembered where it was.

We stood at the gateway. "Now you go up to that door," I said, "and knock very loud, and say you've come to see Mr Pearson. Can you do that?"

"No," they quivered reasonably.

I gulped. I didn't fancy any more encounters with Mr Pearson, holy chat and questioning. But what could I do? The boys were too scared to go in, and I supposed some explanation was due.

Carrying the one, I hustled the other two up to the door and

I pulled on the bell. It made a pleasant jangle, and a light showed upstairs and then in the hall. I meant to run away then, but the boy I was holding was still asleep.

The door was opened by that lady – Elizabeth – who had opened it before. She had probably got up from bed. She was wearing a dressing-gown. "I've brought you some boys," I said.

She put her lamp down.

"You have, haven't you!" she laughed. "And who are these? Come on, give that little one to me."

I handed him over thankfully.

I was a while at the door, explaining where I'd found them, and like I said, I was a kindly passerby who happened to notice them.

She said: "I'm sure Mr Pearson would like a few words with you too. I wonder if you'd like to call round again tomorrow and – ah no, here he is," she declared.

She turned, having heard Mr Pearson coming down the stairs into the hall. I heard too and what's more I saw. For a moment our eyes met. I couldn't face him, and I just took off. I'd done my bit and I didn't want to stand there chatting. I pelted off, my feet pounding in gravel. But I didn't run far. I hid round the gatepost. I stood there in the dark and the fog, my heart thumping, edged up close to the wall. I pressed my face to the gatepost and peeped back into the yard.

Light from the hall was wisping through the filmy darkness. Against the light I could see Mr Pearson standing there in the doorway, looking out. I could see his broad shoulders silhouetted. He looked to one side, then another. "Willie!" he called, rather authoritatively, like he was my teacher. I gulped. *How did he know my name?* My mouth dropped right open in disbelief. I nearly came creeping out, like a bad boy discovered; it was that sort of tone. But I stayed where I was, not breathing, just watching.

Then he said again: "Willie!" only this time it was more of a quivering cry, real intense, or, as they sometimes say, thrilling. I know it thrilled me! I'd never heard my name called like that – like he was Mr Rochester calling Jane, and she hears it in her mind, and comes.

But then Elizabeth started bustling – I could hear her in the hall being brisk and cheerful, yes, I even heard what she said. Nice mug of cocoa . . . soon have you tucked up safe and warm.

And Mr Pearson turned back inside after her, and the heavy door shut, and the light went with it.

IV

IF EVER I felt like the little match girl it was then. I just stared at that closed door, green with envy at those ragged boys who were going to have cocoa. I do believe I stood gawping at that house for almost half an hour, just standing looking, watching lights on in different rooms, thinking about the warmth in there, and the beds and the cocoa. I gave a great sigh.

Coldness got to me and I turned away and started walking back to St Giles. I felt peculiar, sort of melancholy. I hadn't got the heart to try soliciting. I never saw no one anyhow. It was pretty late by then, two-ish, the lean time, when they'd mostly gone home. I trailed back leadenly to Hammer's kitchen, losing my way a couple of times, remembering it when I found the public house and the doorway where they got the ring off me. I was perished as I slouched down the cellar steps. There was a group closely packed around the fire.

"What did you get?" Hammer demanded eagerly, coming forward and practically holding out his palms. I imagine he thought I was going to drop silver into his hands like he was a bleedin' gipsy.

"Get? Nothing," I said shrugging.

"What d'yer mean, nothin'? Didn't you go with no gents?" he bellowed accusingly.

"No," I snapped.

"What've you bin doin' then? You bin gone hours."

"Walkin'."

"Look 'ere, Willie," he scowled hardening. "You ain't here to waste my time. Everyone 'ere pulls their weight. No push, no perks."

"I'm sorry. I'll have another try tomorrow."

"You better. You want yer bleedin' ring back, dontcher?"

"You know I do, else I wouldn't be here."

"Well, get off to bed. At least you pull your weight there."

"Oh, Hammer, I'm cold and hungry," I wailed.

"There ain't no room at the fire for layabahts and loafers. I said get off to bed."

He raised his fist nastily and I backed. I slunk off to bed and crawled into the rugs and I realised the ache in my guts this time was hunger, not emotion. I cried sniffily onto my arm at the mess my life was in. When Hammer came along he said it was my own fault if I was hungry; didn't I know nothing? No one strolled home empty-handed, they stole from each other rather than admit to no pickings. That was how it was. Then he reached for my hand and opened my fingers and put half a baked potato in my fist. "And it's more'n you deserve," he added gruffly.

"Oh, ta, Hammer," I slobbered gratefully, sinking my teeth into it. He climbed into bed beside me, and I fell asleep with my mouth tasting of spunk and potato.

In the morning I stayed in bed. I was so miserable I was prepared to lie and rot. But I had a bit of a surprise. Peter came in and shook my shoulder. "Come on, mister; I got yer washin' water, and mine too. We'll both 'ave one today – and you can show me ah ter wash me hair."

I blinked through the gloom.

"Ain't this wot they says?" he said cheerfully. "Good morning my lord. Huntin' today or shootin', what'll it be?"

"Oh, let's go and bag a pheasant or two," I grumbled, accepting the new day. "Ta for running me bath."

We had a lot of fun, him and me, washing. He even made me laugh; he was so funny. I scrubbed him down and washed his hair for him, and he liked it, and spiky-haired and chirpy he went off to pursue petty thefts all over the city. I couldn't help thinking that I had once been like that, a personable perky lad who got into bad ways, and now look at me – what an example! What would it be for Peter – a dose of reformatory and ending up like Hammer, a dealer in small-time crime? Was it all inevitable?

Well, me, I was clanking with hunger and I'd had enough of it. I went out, up into the world, and sold my waistcoat to an old clothes dealer. After haggling a bit I got a decent price and treated myself to a hot meal and a glass of stout at a chop house. I went and had a shave, and then called in at Madame Rosa's and made my position clear. "Look, Rosa, I need a gent. I want one tonight; *get* me one. I'll do the works, he can wipe the floor with me, but I want one now. I need the money. *Look* at me, look how I'm dressed!" We contemplated my appearance.

"You come back tonight, dear, I'll have one for you," she said patiently. "Don't you worry about a thing."

She managed it too. That night I gave a good oldfashioned servicing to a straightforward client, all very civilised and polite. Afterwards Rosa let me sleep in a boxroom – no rats and no Hammer – and in the morning I had toast and coffee and the pleasure of her nice bathroom and the luxury of a clean lavatory.

The sanitary arrangements for Hammer's crowd were the worst I'd ever seen in my life. Down the end of the street there were three privies in a state of nightmare filth and slime. They were so bad that rather than make the effort to use them, folks pissed in the alley and shit in a trench the other side of a hole in the basement, in the cellar of the house next door. Doing that, I thought, well, I can't get no lower than this in the great social scale of which her majesty is the pinnacle. I always maintained that where you shit is a good indication of how well you're doing in the world.

Five more gents at Rosa's and I'd be quit of Hammer. She laughed at my earnestness. "Come back here tonight," she said. "If you're really so short of push and down on your luck, I might have a way of bringing you a little windfall."

I was able to take a clear pound back to Hammer then, when I went back there midmorning. It got me a place at the fire and two sausages and half a cup of gin. Hammer was pleased with me. He said I was learning fast.

To my surprise, Peter was all over me, like a puppy when his master comes back. "I fort you was gawn," he said. "I was goin' ter get yer washin' water, and mine 'n' all. I'm real keen on bein' clean."

"Come on then," I said. "Let's boil the water up, and I'll wash yer, same as I did yesterday."

You can get real friendly, washing hair. We chatted about our backgrounds, about griddlin' and stealin', about Hammer, and life generally. He reckoned he was seven years old. All he'd known was St Giles. Thieving for Hammer was his big break, his gateway to a golden future.

I dried his hair on a dingy scrap of towel. He was a sweet little scruff. If he was me, I thought, and I was Harry . . . I thought of the peculiar power I had, to be good for him or bad. He trusted me now. If I said to him come here and I'll show you something nice, he would have. I could ease him into the ways of whoring, take him to Rosa's with me. He could make a whole lot more than Hammer. He'd got a good little body, thin but nicely shaped. I could teach him all I knew. I could be for him what Harry had been for me. A glorious future would be this little lad's.

I ceased my cynical reflections. "How'd you like to learn a trade?" I said. "Something decent, like a cobbler or a carpenter?"

"'Ow could I? Oo'd 'ave me?"

"Come out with me; I'll take you for a walk."

V

WE LEFT Hammer's domain and started walking. I felt like the Good Angel, warring with the Evil over the soul of mankind. I talked to Peter about his future. I let him know what it was like inside a school of correction and I painted it very black. I chatted to him about society and what was wrong with it, and how filching gold watches wasn't the answer. I knew this house, I said, where there was a lovely gent who helped poor lads like Peter and gave 'em a start. What exactly did he do? I frowned to try and remember what Mr Pearson had said in church — what, only three years ago.

"You cán go farming in Canada," I said, "or join the navy and be a sailor, sail in a big ship, or join the army and see India. Or just stay at home and learn to read and write, and then you can read story books, and that's real nice!"

"Would *you* be there?" asked Peter.

"I'd visit. But you'd like Mr Pearson. He's tall and strong and ever so good-lookin'. And he really cares, he does."

With a whole lot more of that sort of talk I seemed to have convinced Peter that a better life could be his. The final clinch was this: "And every night, you get cocoa."

"Oy, mister," said Peter, "can we go there nah?"

In the daylight! In the October afternoon! What would it be like? — no darkness to hide in this time. But maybe he wouldn't be there — maybe he'd be out talking to congregations, telling them what it was like on the dark forgotten streets. I'd be all right; I needn't see him.

"Oy, mister, Hammer won't like it, will he?"

"No," I grinned happily. "But he won't know."

By the time we had walked to Shoreditch I was getting on real well with Peter. I found kids easy to talk to, and I had awful strong urges to take him to the zoo and show him the parrots. And wouldn't he love going on a train?

"This is the house," I said. "It's got a real nice bell, and I'll lift you up and you can pull it. It makes a real pretty noise, you listen."

We listened, our eyes bright with expectation. The bell jangled, and we waited on the step.

The door opened.

I blushed. I was so sure that it would be Elizabeth that the sight of Mr Pearson completely floored me. There was all kinds of sounds from inside – the buzz of talking, some hammering, the rattle of plates – also there was a luscious smell of cooking. Stew, I reckoned, with puddles of gravy, and hot soft potatoes . . .

"I brought you a boy . . . "I croaked.

Mr Pearson carefully took Peter from me, and placed him on the step. "I lifted him so he could ring the bell," I explained.

"If you run away this time," said Mr Pearson sternly, "I shall come after you. I want a word with you, William."

"Um no, I won't run off," I said meekly.

Mr Pearson called for Elizabeth, and she came with soapsuds on her arms and her sleeves rolled up. They had a swift domestic chat, during which arrangements were made about Peter, and Peter explained who he was in a competent manner.

"He ain't like the last three I brought," I grinned, "he'll steal all yer silver, he will."

"I won't," Peter protested.

"No, don't do that, Willie," said Mr Pearson frowning. "Don't bring a boy's character with him – let me find out. There's nothing of value here, nothing to steal. But there's plenty to do, and Peter isn't going to be bored or idle if he wants to stop."

"I do want," Peter assured him.

He went off cheerfully with Elizabeth, and Mr Pearson eyed

me quizzically. His eyes were brown. "Willie, what are you playing at?"

"Hey?"

"Why are you bringing me half London?"

"You want boys, dontcher?" I demanded aggrieved.

"Oh yes," he smiled. "But why are you making it your personal responsibility to keep me well stocked?"

"I dunno," I fidgetted.

"Come on, you can do better than that."

"I s'pose I want them to have chances I never."

"What – was your background the East End streets?"

"Yeah, Aldgate and Spitalfields. I reckon if someone'd brought me here I'd've gone right. Only I wasn't as muck snipe as you like 'em."

"As what?"

"Muck snipe – as low down as you can get. That's how a kid's got to be, ain't he, to come to you?"

"Well, yes. There are the board schools for the deserving poor, whose families care for them. My lads are the desolate."

"Yeah, that's it, that's what I thought. You has to be desolate to come here . . . Well, I was never that bad. I had a ma and we had a place to live. So I was never sent here. But I could've bin!" I boasted.

"You mean I very nearly had the privilege of providing a home for you!" he twinkled.

"Yeah," I smirked. "I used to see you walkin', dark nights, all tall and upright, castin' a strong bold shadow. I was hid in a doorway. I'd have been nine or ten. My mate said you was a bleedin' do-gooder."

"Well – I hope I am," he said quite seriously.

"*And* I heard you in church," I continued, mildly surprised at how much I wanted to talk to him. "I gave pennies for your good cause . . . I thought you was like Jesus!"

He raised his eyebrows.

"Yeah," I laughed, "my uncle caned me for saying that. But you didn't half make a big impression on us all . . . I never forgot yer," I added earnestly.

"I'm gratified," he remarked.

There was a pause. "It's true, you do send 'em to Canada?" I prattled. "I told Peter you did and he's counting on it."

"Yes, it is true – but today we are being more modest – our visiting shoemaker is in residence teaching a trade . . . Willie," he hesitated, "you're not wearing make-up as you were last time. May I hope you've given it up? I only ask out of a very deep concern."

"Given up wearing make-up?" I said lightly.

"No, given up asking for lights and offering," he said darkly. Bleedin' hell, he was handsome close to, and real masterful when he frowned. I remembered quite clearly how I'd had an erection from staring at him and I'd had to hide it under my hymn book. I coughed.

"Look," I said, "I was rude to you when we met before. I don't know why I did it. I feel real bad about what I said to you. I ain't really so bitchy, well, only sometimes. That's why I ran off the other night. I was embarrassed about seeing you again."

"It's all right," he said. "I apologise too. I overreacted. I felt angry with myself afterwards. And very worried about you."

"No need," I laughed unconvincingly. "I can look after myself."

"Where are you living now?"

I gulped. "Oh – I've got a place . . . real nice . . . "

"Willie, listen," he said. "I have to get back inside." There were indeed some crashing noises and the hum of voices was very much louder.

"Yeah," I laughed brittlely. "A lad's got to be on his bleedin' knees before he gets your full attention, ain't he? You ain't got no time for the ones who can still stand. The ones who ain't quite – what was it? – the desolate."

He tightened his lips, vexed. The noise behind him increased. "I must go," he said. "But do come again."

"Nice meeting yer, Mr Pearson," I said brightly, and I touched my cap politely and turned on my heel. I heard him make a noise of irritation. But neither of us spoke, and when I turned again to look he'd closed the door.

THAT NIGHT I went round to Madame Rosa's as planned. A windfall, she'd said.

She gave me a glass of wine and we sat down before her fire, as I had when I was a lad with Harry, and she put this proposition to me. "Willie," she said, "I know you've always said you wouldn't do perversions. But I've got you this lovely gent. All he wants to do is give you a swishing, like they give boys at the public schools. Do it, dearie. He'll give you the full five pound."

I sat and sipped my wine.

Five pound. My debt to Hammer paid off in one fell swoop. My freedom; my ring back. "What would he use?"

"A birch. Real upper class."

"Tell me honest, Rosa, does it leave scars?"

"No!" she beamed, looking as plump and benign as a lady in a cake shop.

"You bleed though, don't you?"

"Yes, but it heals up."

"Afterwards could I stay here and would you patch me up?"

"Of course I will, dear. I've often done it to the girls."

"And will you be outside the door, and come in if I yell for yer?"

"I'll be right here."

"How much d'you get, Rosa, for providing me?" I said bitterly. "More'n five pounds, I'll bet."

"I'm in business, dear, I have to live."

"I'll do it," I said grimly. "I s'pose you knew I would."

He was a perfectly ordinary-looking bloke, no fangs, no forked tail, no cloven hoof. Quiet, soft spoken, gentle hands. I let him tie me over a chair and, no doubt about it, I was scared.

The gent laid his hands on me.

"I want to see you bleed," he murmured.

Next thing I knew I heard the swish of the birch. I gasped. He brought it down again and again, panting and sort of snarling. I was in pain; I writhed all over the chair. I yelled. I was terrified. Pleasure? They must be crazy. He was welting me all over my back and my behind, and I could feel blood running down my leg.

"That's enough," I said, but he went on.

"Rosa!" I screeched. "He's killin' me."

I struggled, beside myself with terror, twisting my head about. That was a mistake because out of the corner of my eye I saw blood trickling down my shoulder, and I was so scared I fainted.

Well, he was certainly shocked at that, and serve the bastard right. When I came to I was already untied, and Rosa was lifting me off the chair and over to the bed. I lay on my front, icy cold and shaking. They fed me brandy and hot milk which must have been dosed with something, because I fell instantly asleep. In the morning I was stiff and it hurt. I throbbed from neck to arse, I couldn't sit down, and I felt sick. It was a hard won five pounds for me. I had black coffee and toast, and I felt weak and light headed and scared.

Walking gingerly I left Rosa's and made my way cautiously to St Giles, and there in the cellar I handed over five pounds to Hammer. A lad was sent to find Larkins; he arrived and he gave me back the ring. They were astonished at my achieving so much push, and seemed curiously awed and admiring. "But look 'ere," Hammer said, "don't wear the buggerin' thing on your finger. Give us your pocket." And he ripped a hole in the lining, so that the ring dropped through to the inside.

"'Ave yer got any gin?" I said.

They laughed, and poured me a mugfull. I drank the lot. I couldn't bear myself, my body and my thoughts; I wanted nothing to do with either.

I left St Giles, not even remembering parting nor what was said. I wandered about, stupid from the gin, weak legged and throbbing. Waves of nausea now started up and I had to clutch at walls for support. I was frightened, and even through my gin stupor I knew I needed to be inside and seen to. I forced myself to remember the way to Shoreditch. It seemed to take me all day. Somewhere along the way I had to drop to my hands and knees and throw up. People walked round me in a wide circle. Someone over my head said: "Drunk!"

I thought grimly — on my knees, puking in the gutter, will I be desolate enough for him now?

Somebody lifted me to my feet. I was shocked to find it was

the lady from the Temperance Stall, the one who handed out leaflets about the dangers of drink and sold us cups of tea instead.

"Ta," I said with gin-soaked breath.

"You'll give it up now, won't you?" she said. "You'll give up the demon drink."

"Yes, ma'am," I promised.

I staggered along to Goff Street, and made my way to the open gateway of his house.

My legs gave out halfway across the gravel and I sank to my knees and then flat, with a sigh. I'd arrived. I was here. I was destitute. He would have to take me in. I remembered his words in the church: "No boy is ever turned away". I'd be all right now. I shut my eyes, almost contentedly.

Strong arms were picking me up, and eagerly I fitted myself into them. My head nestled on to a strong shoulder, a hardness and a strength I'd never experienced since . . . "Charley?" I said dozily, opening my eyes.

It was not of course Charley. It was Mr Pearson, and he'd lifted me up off the gravel and folded me in his arms, and he was carrying me inside. "Oh, Willie," he said. "What have you done? Did it have to take so much to bring us together?"

CHAPTER TWENTY-TWO

I

IALMOST wonder whether I drove myself to degradation from a deep and unformed need to be taken in and nurtured by Mr Pearson. I see now that I had loved him all my life. He was never far from my thoughts ever since that day when I had heard him speak in the church, an unconscious influence on me, a true knight when I had been merely posing as one, an ideal causing me alternate guilt at my way of life and joy at the memory of him.

When he carried me in his arms and spoke to me so sweet, reproachful, angry and sad, I had been limp and groaning. I daresay he assumed I could not hear the remark of his which intimated that he too had sensed we were destined to be close. He was quite justified in supposing I was deaf to coherence, since I asked him in all seriousness whether he was Charley. How odd that was! They were not alike, except for both having brown hair and strong shoulders, and yet the one reminded me of the other; it was an assumption of trust.

Wincing with pain as his strong arm shifted against my back, I was carried into the kitchen.

It must have been about five o'clock. Elizabeth was preparing the meal, two small boys were helping her, and the room was warm and full of the wonderful scents of dinner.

Mr Pearson deposited me in a huge old armchair very gently; but I tensed rigid and gasped, and had to stand up. Around me they were making arrangements to give me a bath, but he had become frowning and alert now. Vigorously he sent the two boys running off somewhere else. "What have you done?" he said, taking me by the shoulder. "Blood – ?"

I let him take my jacket off and I realised some of last night's stripes had broken open. He undid my shirt and took it off carefully. Here and there it stuck to me. His unshockability, his total acceptance of what must have happened, lashed me all over again. I blanched to think he might believe I'd done it for pleasure.

"I owed someone money," I blurted out. "I did it for the money. You don't know what desperate straits I was in."

"Yes," he said in clipped tones. "Well, we'll start with a bath. Every boy I take in begins that way and you'll be no different. However, in your case we'll have the doctor in as well. Now let's get you into that tub."

It was a tin bath from off the wall. I kneeled in the water. My wounds were stinging, alarming me. Elizabeth tut-tutted over them, and while I was crouched there, Mr Pearson dosed them up with medicaments. I howled.

"You know why it hurts," he commented. "You've birch fragments left in the cuts, and they have got to come out."

I wept with pain while he did it.

"Am I very bad? Will I be marked?" I moaned.

"No, no," he assured me, dabbing. "A rich crop of cuts but they're only shallow. It seems worse because there are so many; he really had a field day, didn't he? Barely left an inch . . . No, you'll be fine, as perfect as before."

I gasped – he thought I was perfect!

"I don't understand the mentality," he murmured, "faced with young clear skin, to want to . . . well! I am not the one to judge . . . "

He concentrated upon washing me. I kneeled upright, helping.

"Well," he said, "is there anything else I should know?"

"How?"

"No suspect consumption? No underworld associates coming to look for you? You know I do question my new inmates pretty thoroughly on arrival, as a rule. Parents? Employers? The law?"

"No one's coming after me. I'll be honest, I'll tell you anything you want to know. I'd be glad to. I owe it you – and anyway I want you to know about me. You can't imagine the relief this is for me. It's like laying a burden down and handing it all over to you. I've made such a mess of my life!"

I groaned. How could I do this to him – how could I admit to such a tale of depravity and sin? Surely there was a limit to even his caring tolerance? I wasn't just a victim of poverty, like the lads he found under sacks. I was *bad* – I must be! He'd throw me out. He'd *judge* me.

"I'd like to hear," he encouraged.

"Although I started life Poor But Honest," I began, in the manner of a Pocket Gem, "I got into bad ways as a boy. It was through being pretty, see. Someone I knew got me involved in servicing gents. There was this place in Holborn; just a couple of times. I needed the money, see, for my books – I was always reading. But I got scared and told my brother. He put me right. He looked after me, sorted me out, got me work. Ah! I wish you could have known Charley!"

The sudden tears that dropped from my cheeks and into the bath water must have prompted Mr Pearson's reaction. He stopped dabbing, all startled and concerned.

"Willie – you don't mean he died?"

"No! He went to Australia. Comes to the same thing, I suppose," I sniffed ruefully. "I did love him so much. Actually," I admitted, turning a little, "you remind me of him."

Mr Pearson avoided my gaze and began dabbing again.

"But he left you alone?"

"Not alone exactly. After we lost our mother I was handed over to an uncle to be Bettered. I learned civilised ways and was educated. My Aunt Louisa mostly civilised me. And then there was my cousin Georgey."

"Are you warm enough?" he asked suddenly.

"Yes. It was a different kind of shiver, that – an emotional one. Georgey was very sweet and nice and I fell in love with him. I don't know if you can understand what I mean, one male falling in love with another. You'll be shocked, I suppose. But honestly it's perfectly natural. History tells us – "

"Never mind about history, Willie," he said quietly. "I do know what you mean."

"Doesn't anything shock you?" I marvelled. I added bitterly: "Try this one then. I screwed my cousin Georgey and they put me in a reformatory."

"*Who* did? What for?" he frowned.

"For what I did to Georgey. My uncle."

"Your own flesh and blood? Put you in one of those – *institutions?* Ah, no, that I can't believe – "

"He didn't like me and I didn't like him. He knew the governor, see, so he could do it easy. It's all right now, it's a long time ago." I peered at him, surprised. I said, with a peculiar

325

twinge of gratification: "I have managed to shock you. I have, haven't I?"

"If it was up to me," said Mr Pearson, "I'd have every one of those places blown up. I'd light the fuses myself."

"I'd help yer!" I agreed feelingly.

"And how long did they leave you there?"

"A few weeks. I don't much want to talk about it. But at least I learned about Urnings. There were these two doctors who came to ask me questions. That's when I learnt about myself, see, that it's *natural* to be like I am. They call it being an Urning. There are books about it. Alexander the Great was one," I added with justifiable pride.

"Really?" said he smoothly.

"It was one of the doctors who sneaked me out," I continued. "He was an Urning too, but secret. He reckoned we Urnings must stick together. He Risked All To Save Me."

"Possibly even you, Willie, will never understand what that exactly means," said Mr Pearson gravely.

"I do!" I protested. "And he knew I was grateful. I owed him everything. I left his house so as not to get him into any more trouble. I went – I went where I knew I'd be welcome. I needed my own kind. I started up whoring, in a place in Soho."

My narrative, punctuated by gasps, paused there for a yelp of pain. I suppose his fingers must have slipped. He apologised.

"I was there a couple of months, and they were pretty good to me. It wasn't a bad life at all, considering. I was very popular with high class blokes – I had Nice Ways. One of them was quite fond of me and looked after me real well. But I liked being independent so I took up on my own. I was on the streets for about a year. I did all right. Then I got sick of it. Last of all I was a model. I posed for artists. I had a lover, Algy. We were going to live together. We were going to go to Paris. But he left me. That's when I took to the streets again. I got real down and low. I lost heart. That's when I came to you. Ah, Mr Pearson," I cried, "I'm desperate to go straight. I don't want to keep whoring. I hate it now. I want to start afresh. It's tearing me apart having to meet you this way. I wanted you to like me. How can you ever?"

"I do like you. Be assured of that. Listen," he said, making me look at him. "At this stage, shame is irrelevant; forget it. You are here with us now. Let us simply concentrate on making you well."

He dried me gently and put me into a clean starched nightshirt – grey flannel! I grinned. "I do like being made a fuss of," I admitted, "I feel like a little kid, being bathed and all."

He grinned as well. "I'm treating you as one," he said. "How old are you, by the way?"

"Seventeen and a half."

"A babe in arms," he teased. "Now, let's have your head in the bowl."

Mr Pearson washed my hair himself. He had a lovely touch. Afterwards I was given a blanket and I knelt by the fire, my hair in a towel, while Elizabeth carried on with the dinner and boys came in to help. Mr Pearson disappeared to supervise dinner, but I had mine by the fire – broth and bread, and a mug of tea and a biscuit. Ginger!

Life went on around me placidly while I dried my hair. Mr Pearson studied my clothes. "Is there life in this jacket? Yes, we'll keep that, and the boots are all right."

"Ohh! There's a ring in the pocket!" I squeaked. I had forgotten about it!

"A ring?"

He found it for me, and now his eyebrows did rise as he saw the amethyst and gold. He handed it to me and I put it on.

Mr Pearson explained to me that he wanted a doctor to see me and he asked if I'd object to an all-over examination. He said I'd be foolish to reject the opportunity. I said I'd be relieved.

I was taken upstairs and shown to my room.

The house had three floors. On the ground floor was the kitchen, the dining room and the schoolroom and workrooms. On the first floor were the dormitories and small schoolrooms. On the top floor was Mr Pearson's room and study and spare rooms. Mine was one of these.

This room, which came to be my home, was of a medium size, with a good window looking down on the neighbouring roofs and chimneys, and the wall that hugged the street. This didn't show on the first night. I just saw the little brass bedstead, with the sheet pulled back invitingly.

Before I could go to sleep, the doctor came.

I cringed to think he might suspect the kinds of things I had been up to lately. But he made no comment after his examination of me and merely asked: "How have you been eating recently? What has your diet been?"

"Sausages and gin," I admitted.

"Foolish child," he reproved.

He reckoned that sensible living and early nights would pull me round. I heard him mutter to Mr Pearson on the landing to make sure I had no access to gin. I blushed, and vowed never to let a drop pass my lips again. Fortunately he did not forbid bottled stout.

When the doctor had gone, Mr Pearson brought me hot cocoa and tucked me in.

"You know," he said, "I shall not do this for you every night! But are you comfortable? Will you sleep?"

"My skin feels tight," I said. "Like someone's taken a handful of it and gathered it up."

"You seem to have had a good report," he said. "Nothing nasty. All we have to do is nurture you – and keep you off the bottle."

I lay on my elbow and sipped my cocoa. "I'm so happy," I confessed. "I'm on the inside tonight, not the outside. You ain't half good to me, Mister."

"I was worried about you on the streets. You seemed so vulnerable. I'm relieved to have got hold of you at last, where I can be sure you take care of yourself."

"I'll make it up to yer," I assured him.

"I have taken the liberty of throwing away your lipstick," he said loftily.

"Oh! Have yer!" I said. I don't deny it – I felt a little pang of regret. "I look nice in make-up."

"You don't *need* to wear make-up," he told me.

"But I like wearing it!"

"What, arguing already?" he teased. "That's no way to behave. Drink up your cocoa – and there's also a course of medicine I'm instructed to see you take."

"Medicine!" I screeched.

"Pills *and* liquid. You *are* going to be fit, aren't you!"

I muttered into the cocoa. He helped me settle down and when I was comfortable, he leaned down and kissed my forehead in a chaste and – I'd say brotherly fashion if my brother hadn't been Charley!

"Goodnight, my dear," he said.

He left me to my solitude and thoughts. My head was very full, and it was a long time before I fell asleep that night.

II

ONE OF the first things that became apparent to me when I was on my feet again and back to my former strength was that Mr Pearson needed some help. "Oh I've tried working with assistants," he grumbled, "but I never get on with them. Young men with uppity ideas and unwilling to get their hands dirty. I usually let the brighter boys help. But it's true I need a secretary. I have to waste so much time writing humble begging letters. I hate that – I resent it, for a start, and that makes me untidy."

"Oh!" I beamed delighted. "I'm very good at writing humble begging letters! I'll do 'em for you."

"You write, do you?" he enquired.

"I have an exquisite copperplate," I boasted.

"Show me."

We went into his downstairs office, a sort of cubbyhole with a writing desk, which I was soon to know very well. I sat in his chair and on a piece of paper I wrote: "All are at one now, roses and lovers." I handed it to him. A lovely expression came over his face – pleasure, surprise.

"Where is this from?" he asked. "You know poetry?"

"Mr Swinburne."

"Ah – yes. Of course."

"I've liked poems all my life," I said modestly. "I know *The Idylls of the King* very well, and I progressed to Keats and Byron and Shelley, and the *Rubayyat* of Omar Khayyam. I also know several novels."

"Indeed! Well, your handwriting is exquisite – you are quite right. And presumably you can add up?"

"Oh yes. I know about accounts. They once intended to see me settled as a clerk."

"I had no idea you were so talented."

Really he was genuinely impressed. We bent our heads over

his writing desk and involved ourselves in earnest discussion. An awful lot of paperwork went into running the home, and I was keen to prove my worth. I wrote letters of various kinds, some to his dictation, and later by myself, and I kept the accounts and balanced income and expenditure.

Joseph Pearson had been part of the army in India when he was young. He was something to do with administration. His work took him all round the Indian villages making notes, rather like an Indian Domesday Book! It was in India that his conscience was awakened to poverty. Recurrent fevers obliged him to leave the army, and he devoted himself to the alleviation of poverty on his return. Although he had been to Eton and Oxford and came of rich parents he now considered himself classless, and so I think did his relations, who did not visit.

We relied for money on grants from a board of gentlemen, and all the extras we could get from charity and Mr Pearson's impassioned eloquence in churches, mission halls and Ladies' Circles. Our board of gentlemen were a very mixed blessing. They popped in unexpectedly and criticised. They made suggestions and pontificated. They stipulated that there must be prayers twice daily, and on Sundays we had to go to church and be *seen* to go to church. Not that anyone could miss us! Mr Pearson always found other useful things to do now I was there to supervise the procession; I grumbled, but I was rather proud shepherding my flock, and cuffing the stragglers.

Mr Pearson behaved to me somewhat like an older cousin. He never treated me like one of his foundlings, but more like his lieutenant. And I was happy. Content, like. I was safe and warm and I had a room of my own and a bed to sleep in. The rain could patter on my window at night, the wind could rattle the bare branches of the November trees: I was inside. Because of that I increased in my concern for the poor homeless boys out there, and when Joseph brought lads home or if they just arrived, I helped him bath them and wash their hair and found them a nightshirt and a place to sleep.

In fact I felt so comfortable and settled at Goff Street that I began to want my possessions about me, and yet I hesitated to ask for any clarification of my position in case Joseph became severe and practical and told me that if I was recovered then I'd better leave and find work.

But trusting my instinct that he didn't want to lose me, I started talking to him about it. We were in the kitchen, the boys tucked up for the night and us about to go upstairs ourselves.

"A friend of mine has got a stack of my things, keepin' 'em for me . . . books and ornaments . . . and I was wondering if I can fetch them and bring them here, put 'em in my room . . . "

"I don't see why not."

"Yeah, but is there any point? Am I stayin'?"

I swallowed nervously. My future hung on his reply.

"Ah, I knew we'd have to talk about it sooner or later. You want to leave, do you?"

"No! I want to stay!"

"You do seem to have found a niche for yourself. Frankly, Willie, I can't imagine how I managed without you. I rather think you've made yourself indispensable – very unobtrusively, so that I hardly noticed it happening."

"Really?" I beamed. "What, particularly?"

"Oh," he said airily. "The letters you write . . . the fine copperplate."

"I knew it would come in useful one day. Are there any other parts?" I enquired archly.

"Your obliging readiness to take the boys to church. I always hated that weekly duty."

"Ain't you a religious man, Mr Pearson?" I teased.

"I heartily resent having to parade my holiness for the gratification of our benefactors. I'm sorry – I don't want to put you off doing it."

"It's all right. I'm pleased to be helpful. Any other reasons why you like having me here?" I asked hopefully.

"You won't rest until I've said your sweet personality, will you?" he said fondly. "If you want to stay I'd be only too grateful. The room you have now is yours for as long as you want it."

"Wonderful!"

"Do go and fetch your things," he said. "I'm really happy that you feel at home. I really am," he added, almost emotionally, "most happy about it."

He always drew back from intimacy, and I never pursued. I felt that my position there depended on us being business partners and that I would do better to build up a relationship based upon our care for the boys and our working side by side. So though my love for him grew stronger every day I said nothing about it, and each night we went to our separate rooms on the attic floor, saying "Goodnight Willie", "Goodnight Mr Pearson", very civilised and proper. Not that I didn't ease my need in bed; I did. But I noticed that Algy had faded in importance in my thoughts. I could see now that Algy and I didn't have much in common, particularly that harmony of attitude which I shared with Joseph; you couldn't imagine Algy wanting to look after a houseful of street urchins. I could think about Algy clearly now. I had stopped wearing his ring, but that was because I usually peeled potatoes and took a turn washing up, and you couldn't keep leaving an amethyst beside the sink.

The clothes I was wearing now were from the home wardrobe, a collection of fiercely washed cast-offs from charitable families. I was looking forward to wearing my own things again. Joseph had been amused at my mild disdain for the garb he provided. "Don't you like it? It fits well – what's wrong?"

"I pride myself on being rather a flashy dresser."

"Honest workmanlike cloth should never be despised!"

"I believe you're getting *pleasure* out of seeing me in plain and sober gear!" I accused.

"Indeed," he said, "I am."

It was in this outfit – grey trousers, white shirt, a neat and slightly old-fashioned dull blue jacket and the cap I'd filched from the barber's – that I set off walking to Caroline's place in Soho. It was a bleak cold day, the wind wisping up scurries of dead leaves and making you shiver.

I was so glad to see Caroline again. I told her the gist of my recent doings, and where I was now, and she marvelled and laughed and gasped, and asked probing questions about Joseph which I avoided answering and probably fooled her not at all.

"Ah but you're happy, Willie, and that's all that matters," she told me, hugging me. "To think how I first met you – *and now you're a schoolteacher!*"

It was lovely to have my clothes back – my black velvet jacket, my green corduroy and all my coloured silk neckerchiefs, my corduroy caps, brocaded waistcoat and all. And the delight of pinning up my prints in my little room! My Saint George had pride of place, but my two Moreau pictures caused me some twinges, and I was half laughing and half crying all evening as so many memories assailed me.

The present intruded noisily as the boys stomped up to bed, and I pulled myself together quickly in case I was needed. I finished arranging my room, hammering some nails in for my pictures. I arranged my books with loving care. How beautiful my room looked! How very much at home I felt here!

I felt real tired from all the arranging and the emotion, and I was sitting on the floor, contemplating my blue porcelain and the pottery from Clara, when Mr Pearson knocked at my door and brought me in some cocoa.

He came in and sat on the bed to drink his. "It's a treasure house in here!" he marvelled. "As wonderful as an Egyptian tomb!"

I showed him all my exotic ornaments, and my less so. "The box is from a gent of mine," I confessed. "I hope you don't mind. Only he was real good to me when I was needy. He saved me from bronchitis, influenza, consumption and death," I added earnestly.

"Then he is to be highly commended," Joseph agreed. "And all out of the kindness of his heart, no doubt."

I blushed. "You mind me having been a tart."

"Yes, of course I do. I mind that anyone *need* be a tart, and I mind that gentlemen resort to deception."

"I hope it doesn't offend you to talk about it," I began. "Although I am ashamed of some of the things I've done, I also believe I did a service. It wasn't all sordid, you know. Sometimes it was very beautiful."

Carefully I continued: "I hope no gent who came with me need ever feel guilt or shame. I respected my gents. I always tried to give them my best."

"Do you recall any particular encounter, more than any other?" he enquired.

The air quivered with the unspoken but my nerve failed me. The pleasant intimacy of his company in my room was enough and more. I daren't risk the deep waters we'd be in if I said what I was thinking. "Yes, I do," I said. "But all were special to me."

The moment passed.

III

AS CHRISTMAS approached I was teaching.

How strange life turns out to be! Long ago my tutor Mr Irving, one of the men in my life whom I truly respected, told me that he would like to see me teaching poor boys and I was fitted for it by my background and social principles. I would be ideal, he said. But I had been unwilling to go straight back to the East End, and my uncle had been scathing about the low status of a poor teacher. And now here I was, fulfilling Mr Irving's hopes and enjoying it. I really cared about them scruffy lads.

Because money was always a problem I went out and sold my two rings – Algy's amethyst and Mr Scott's gold with the curly W on it – and slapped the money down on Joseph's desk. For a moment he looked at me with a flash of horror. "That's right," I remarked. "I just been hawking my bum round the House of Lords."

It was such a large amount of money, however, that I was obliged to explain how I had acquired it.

Mr Pearson was moved. He said he realised what a sacrifice that must have been. He gripped my hand and held it in a warm emotional clasp. "But don't do it again – please!" he begged. "I know how much you value your treasures – please don't pawn your beautiful box or sell your porcelain. I know we're poor, but you can't take on that burden. I won't say I wish you hadn't sold your rings; I know you meant well, and believe me, I'm grateful. But I won't stand by and see you impoverish yourself of your memories."

He said he understood my sacrifice; but the astonishing fact was that it had not been so. Algy's ring, that I'd sweated to regain with Hammer as my ponce, had been easy to sell, emotionally. Mr Scott's gold ring an' all, I'd lost no sleep over that. We needed push and so it just didn't matter.

I wrote begging letters to worthy individuals, and both of us gave speeches at church halls and societies. I was nervous about public speaking at first, but I found that if you care enough you lose your butterflies and simply talk. The hard part was the social chat before and after, when you had to be pleasant to Ladies and Gentlemen in fur-collared coats who are doing you a favour by speaking to you, but you need their money and so

334

you have to be dutiful. Hard times brought Mr Pearson and me very close together.

Things were worse, being winter, as it was very cold and there was the cost of coal to reckon with and boots for the boys, and illness and ailments, and we had bedsides to sit by along with all the normal work. It pained me to see Joseph working so hard, and tired, and I longed to comfort him physically. I realised as we worked together how much I loved him. It was everything – the big things, like he was dedicated and selfless, tender and caring, calm and strong; the little things, like he would turn his hand to anything, even washing up. I was happy just being with him, and even if he never loved me in return, I'd still have stayed by him. I looked after him as best I could, and of course I mustn't underrate Elizabeth, who was wonderful; and we all struggled on bravely, and did our best.

Well, one day in January, I was writing yet another begging letter when the doorbell rang and Elizabeth came to find me to say I had a visitor. The boys were in the workshop, with Joseph organising, and a couple of craftsmen hammering and explaining. I got up from my chair at the writing desk in a state of shock and trembling, because my visitor was Algernon.

He had been shown into the dining room, where we received our visitors.

I closed the door behind me, and we faced each other. He was as nervous as I was.

"Willie . . . I wasn't sure whether you'd see me," he began.

He was as beautiful as ever. He was dressed warmly against the cold, in a dark grey overcoat and silk top hat which he had placed on the table, with an elegant walking cane. I could see a pearl grey cravat at his throat and the stiff white collar of his shirt. He wore gloves, and his black shoes were highly polished. He had certainly come here by cab.

His soft fair hair lay lightly waved on his collar. The elegant outfit flattered his trim body. I felt a curious little flicker around my heart. I walked towards him. We were very close now. Close! Ironic – we who had kissed every inch of each other's skin.

"I'm happy to see you," I said awkwardly.

"I've been abroad," he said.

Uneasy at our communal discomfort, I held out both my hands and he took them gratefully, and for a while we stood like that.

"How did you know where to find me?" I asked.

"That black-haired girl who models at the art school . . . I remembered she knew you. I asked her."

I smiled weakly at the idea of Algy talking to Caroline. I was in a terrible flutter at seeing him again.

He pulled away from my grasp and turned his head.

"Oh, Willie . . . you cannot believe what I suffered that day as I paced up and down, realising I had not the courage to go through with our venture. As always in a crisis, my nerve failed. I penned that letter in a state of acute despair and self loathing. I simply did not dare take the risk . . . I wanted to talk to you about it. I wanted to explain. I went to Franklin's next day. You were not there. I longed to make sure you were all right. But I was so ashamed – I hesitated. I thought you must hate me. But I badly needed to see you. These past few months have been dreadful for me. I missed you so much. I had to see you again. I had to know you were all right."

"I'm glad. It was kind of you."

"Kind!" he shuddered. "I have not been kind, have I? Do you hate me?"

"No. I never have."

"Where *did* you go?" he asked hesitantly.

"Some old friends gave me a bed," I shrugged.

"And you despised me for my cowardice."

"No, not really. I simply missed you."

My voice quivered. He could still affect me.

"Oh, Willie! I missed you too! Dreadfully! You've no idea how much."

"I have," I laughed weakly. "I had a physical pain from missing you."

"Did you? So did I. Oh Willie, we did have a very beautiful love."

"I know."

We moved close to each other and then both leaned till we were pressed against each other, cheek against cheek. We stayed like that. I felt him stroke my hair, and I smelt the cold damp outer world of his overcoat, rain-touched cloth. Tentatively I held him around the waist. His clothes were stiff and I did not fit. We moved gently apart, but our hands held, our fingers twined, as if unwilling to admit separateness.

"And are you happy here?" he asked. "Is this what you want?"

"Yes," I said nodding. "Mr Pearson is a very good man and I'm his assistant. I do all the correspondence, and I even teach!"

We laughed politely at this phenomenon.

"I imagine you're doing good work here," Algy said looking round. "It's an awfully worthy cause."

"Well, it's hard work! But yes, it is worthy. I feel good, involved in it."

Algy said carefully: "And do you need anything?"

"Yes," I said bluntly. "We need money."

"Oh, Willie . . . let me help."

Well! I ain't proud! I told him frankly how much we lacked, and Algy said he would see his bankers that very next day and he would settle a grant upon our boys' home. In Perpetuity – did I know what that meant? It meant For Ever.

Unable to help myself, I hugged him. "Oh, Algy! You don't know what this means to us!"

"I'm envious," Algy said, "of your commitment."

IV

SHORTLY AFTER that, he left, and I leaned against the mantelpiece and had a little weep. Not my last. I would always cry a little over Algy, over poems that reminded me of him, over chalices and peacock feathers, fountains and daisies.

When I was composed I went to look for Joseph. Elizabeth said he was up in his room. I mounted the stairs and knocked on his door.

Joseph was sitting at his table, but not I think reading. He did not turn, but said in clipped tones: "So – your exquisite boyfriend has come back for you, and you want to leave. You've come to tell me the world is a wonderful place, and how perfect it is to be in love."

I laughed out loud.

"I watched him go," said Joseph. "He *is* beautiful; there's no doubt about it. You'll make a very handsome pair."

I made sure the door was shut.

I put my arm round his shoulders and nuzzled his ear. "Did

you think I'd leave you, darlin'?" I said bold as you like. "Nah! I'm stayin' wiv you."

He held on to my hand, but he was very stiff and tense. "Are you sure? Didn't he come to take you away from all this?"

"Well – I think he would have if I'd wanted to go," I replied. "But mainly he wanted to be sure I was all right. I told him I was very happy, and it's true – I am."

"Willie," said Mr Pearson looking into my face. "It isn't a straight exchange, you realise that, don't you? I can't give you what you had with Algernon. However much I may love you, there can never never be that relationship between us."

"You love me then? Do you? You do love me?" I gasped, pouncing on his words and grinning into his face like a happy idiot.

"Yes, I love you," he told me almost unhappily. "But we can never ever do more than speak the words. Anything more than that is out of the question."

"Why?" I demanded.

"Be sensible! I'm the head of a boys' home and you're my assistant! It would be the scandal of the decade."

"Listen, darling," I purred. "Before these things become a scandal they have to be found out. And how can we be found out? We have rooms on the top floor. No one else sleeps up here. I can come into your room and go out again just as if I was a little draught under your door!"

"It's unthinkable!"

"I'm thinking it."

"No!"

Shamelessly I sat on his lap. He liked it, but he was controlled and uneasy. "Any boy might come up . . . "

"We'd hear him. He'd knock."

I put my arms round his neck and kissed him. I stroked his neck. His hair was silky. I kissed him very lovingly. He let me. I kept on until he responded. When we had had a long sweet kiss and I was sure he was mine, I whispered: "I love you. I've loved you ever since you came to me in the candlelight and made love to me on black velvet. You were the best lover I ever had."

At the shock of my revelation his body tensed so rigid I nearly fell off his lap. I jumped up and began to walk about. What if I was mistaken, I thought in a panic, what if he denies it?

"How did you know?" he gasped. "How long have you known?"

I breathed in relief. I went and stood by him, my hand on his shoulder. It must have been the first time I'd ever seen him lose his composure. I was not exactly calm myself either.

"The first night I slept here," I replied.

"My God! So long!"

"At first I wasn't sure. It was very gradual. That evening when you brought me in, the touch of your hands when you bathed my back, and talked to me so gently . . . It must have stirred a memory. And then you kissed me goodnight. You called me your dear. You did the same that other night. I think I started to realise it then. But of course I couldn't be sure . . . I thought it was just my *wanting* it to be so, making me just a little crazy. But then, living with you, day by day, hearing your voice . . . A couple of times I came close to asking you outright. But I daren't. I knew you wanted it kept secret. I supposed you were ashamed . . . But you needn't be. Everything will be all right, I promise."

"I need to think – " he said.

I squeezed his shoulder and kissed his hair.

"By the way," I added, at the door. "Algy is going to give us a grant in perpetuity. I hope you're not a proud man. Algy is very rich and will hardly miss it. Our money worries are over."

I closed the door and slipped away.

V

HOW WE got through supper and bathtime and evening prayers I do not know. We did talk about Algy's money over washing up. Joseph said he would need to talk to Algy about it; a sum of that amount was no light matter. But I knew he would agree.

I lay in bed and watched the moon through my window. It was chilly in the sheets but I was warm with excitement.

Well into the night I padded along to Joseph's room and let myself in. I knelt by his bed and whispered: "Mr Pearson, I'm a lonely boy afraid of the dark. Can I come into your bed?"

"For Christ's sake go back to your room!" he whispered appalled. "What do you think you're doing?"

"I'm visiting my lover."

"Wretched boy, go away."

"And you *are* my lover," I smirked. "You made love to me on black velvet. I remember every detail. You were beautiful. You – screwed – me!"

"It was despicable of me."

"No!"

"It was," he groaned. "I've fought against my natural urges all my life. I've suppressed them. I've always won. Except for that one time. It was just too much to bear. I thought: just once. Just once I'll give way. I'll do it, and I'll have the best. A perfect boy, he must be perfect . . . and he was. Too perfect. I wanted the memory to last all my life. Indeed, it has. But not in the way I imagined. I wanted no involvement, simply a moment of sweet passion, a boy I would never see again, a dream to conjure with. Instead, we made some kind of contact, reached each other. Tenderness. You begged me not to leave. I knew then how wrong it was of me, toying with emotion. I knew I'd left you sad and bereft. That place then seemed a monstrous place, and it tormented me that you were there, receiving other desperate men. The guilt I felt for that lapse . . . "

"I never forgot you."

"You must forget it! All we can hope for is a distant relationship, nothing more."

"Let me come into bed; I'm cold."

"Please go. I have long since decided that I can bear it, that it would be enough just to have you near me under the same roof, working together, sharing everything except . . . that."

"I thought it was enough for me too, Joseph, but it ain't. I want more."

"Go back to your room, Willie. I order it."

"Tell me when it was you first knew you loved me," I said comfortably, my chin burrowing into his sheet.

"I suppose it was when we met that night and carried the boys home. It was your hair I recognised first, for as you'll no doubt remember, I hadn't properly seen your face! What do you think it was like for me, wicked urchin? Plodding homeward mechanically, tired and oppressed – suddenly to see this apparition in the gaslight? To realise that, just as I'd imagined, you were altogether beautiful, in features as well as in body . . . to find that I was face to face with you – in the night, in the fog – the boy of my dreams, no less, painted and provocative, offering me with casual unconcern what I had already bought so dearly and could never put out of my mind . . . "

How altogether different that encounter seemed, now that I knew what had been in his mind! I wriggled.

"I'm awful sorry. I acted real cheap."

"I am ashamed to say I was glad of the excuse the boys provided for keeping you with me. All the time we were walking I was trying to think what I could legitimately do for you. I wanted to ask you in, but it was too difficult. You seemed so cynical – and desperately unhappy. I hated the way you were cheapening yourself. You looked ill. I felt so guilty, as if I were partly responsible. And all the time, I was tormented with . . . a most shameful and unworthy desire for your body."

"Oh!" I gasped, delighted. "If only I'd known! You should have *said!*"

"For Heaven's sake, Willie!" he said sarcastically. "Have some sense! What should I have done – sat the boys on a couple of dustbins while I took you behind a lamp post?"

I sniggered.

"Yes," he agreed. "And your accusation in the doorway didn't help. You were a very uncomfortable companion. And when you ran off I was left so anxious and disturbed that later on I went back to Mr Sadler's to enquire about you. *That* wasn't easy."

"No, I can imagine!" I said, impressed.

"Mr Sadler told me you were fine. He said you had been taken into the country by a gentleman."

"It's true; I was. Fancy you asking after me!"

"I too never forgot you. I learnt that your name was Willie Smith, and I thought about you so regularly that it seemed perfectly natural to call your name as if I knew you. When you began bringing me boys I wished you were younger, so that I could bring you in myself, and bathe you, and put you to bed . . . I longed to make a fuss of you and comfort you. You had a hard edge to you that prevented closeness. You seemed encased in prickles."

"Yeah, I know. And *you* seemed awful holy."

"Holy! My God! I am a mass of guilt and weakness."

"You seem so calm and strong."

"It's a perpetual battle."

"Yeah, it shows, now I know you better. It isn't right to fight yourself and dam up your natural urges. It makes you unhappy. It ruins you in the end. You need to weaken, mister. You know what you need? You need *me*."

"Willie – you're so young – I'm twice your age."

"I'll grow!" I assured him. "How old are you anyway?"

"Thirty-four."

"That's young! You're in your prime! And I know you're good at loving!"

"Please, don't refer to that!"

"I will! I will! I remember everything about you, and you remember me an' all. You're picturing it even now."

"I admit it. Willie, do you know what a succubus is?"

"No."

"They come at night to poor tormented novices as they lie on their beds wracked with desire. They take the form of beautiful naked women – or I assume beautiful naked boys, depending upon the kind of imagination that summons them!"

"Do they ever come in nightshirts?"

"They do! They have tonight!"

"Please let me in bed, Joseph. My toes are like blocks of ice. My beautiful bum is freezing up."

"And you want to get into my bed like that!"

"I want you to warm me, and love me."

"Suppose one of the boys was ill and came up here to ask for me."

"Then you would go to him."

"But if he should see . . . "

"I've locked the door. He needn't enter your room."

"Oh – I don't think – "

"Joseph, it's just boys you're worried about, is it? Not divine wrath or hellfire or anything like that?"

"Curiously enough, Willie, I assume God understands. Human weakness and human love I believe to be his deepest concern."

"Nothing then really stands between our two selves and very great happiness, darlin'."

"Willie, it isn't that easy, and you know it. We shall have to be so careful, under constant strain, always on our guard. No mistakes – the revealing glance, the careless touch, anything that might give us away . . . "

"Ah, I'm not stupid. I know it'll be hard. But all we have to do is be sensible over appearances. It's worth the risk, darlin'. You *know* it is."

"I almost dare believe you."

"Joseph, I can't wait for you to do battle with your scruples. I'm young and eager and I'm freezing to death. I love you and I want to live with you and be your helper. Sometimes at night I want to come into your bed and lie in your strong warm arms. Tell me to come into your bed, because I'm coming in anyway. But I'd prefer to be invited."

"Come into bed then, Willie," said Joseph, turning back the sheets.

With an ecstatic sigh and an icy body I climbed into Mr Pearson's bed and he took me into his arms. Shuddering, he rubbed my hands and feet. As our shared warmth percolated I nestled against him and found I was a perfect fit. I began to make love to him. We lay close and warm, whispering tender words. The future, with all its joys and sorrows, was not much in our thoughts that night; only the present, where all we had ever dared hope for had become a sweet reality at last.

AUTHOR'S NOTE

The following books were useful to me as background to the story:

Victorian People by Gillian Avery
The Devil Drives by Fawn M. Brodie
Homosexuality – A History by Vern L. Bullough
The Victorian Underworld by Kellow Chesney
The Victorian City, Images and Realities edited by H.J. Dyos and M. Wolff
Victorian Olympus and *The Aesthetic Adventure* by William Gaunt
The Dark Angel – Aspects of Victorian Sexuality by Fraser Harrison
Victorian Patchwork by Cyril Pearl
The Worm In The Bud by Ronald Pearsall
The Romantic Agony by Mario Praz
Victorian England by W.J. Reader
Victorian Life In Photographs introduced by William Sansom
Eminent Victorians by Lytton Strachey
Gustave Moreau by Jean Selz
Seen And Not Heard – A Garland Of Fancies For Victorian Children selected by Nigel Temple

Also by Chris Hunt
N FOR NARCISSUS

If you enjoyed *Street Lavender*, you will want to read this sequel, following the subsequent adventures of Algy and featuring several of its characters (including of course the irrepressible Willie Smith).

It is 1895 and Lord Algernon Winterton has long settled down to respectable married life, taking on the role of the perfect Victorian gentleman. Anything in his youth which might have suggested otherwise has been forgotten. Until an old associate makes an unexpected appearance, stirring up disquieting memories that cause Algy to try and recapture former passions -- which proves a highly dangerous step to take at the time of the trial of Oscar Wilde.

A fin de siècle love story taking the reader from elegant English homes and Paris salons to the slums of East London and Montmartre. Once again Chris Hunt has painted a revealing portrait of late 19th-century life, charting the persecution of gay men in Britain in the wake of the Criminal Law Amendment Act.

"Chris Hunt has carved a comfortable niche as the author of highly readable historical epics set against a well-researched historical background... Writes in a fluid vein that admirably encapsulates the time, well positioned with myriad details which bring the period vividly to life for today's reader" -- *Gay Times*

ISBN 0 85449 139 2   UK £7.95 / US $12.95 / AUS $22.95

MIGNON

The glittering Paris court of Henri III provides Marc with ample chance to advance his fortunes, as a *mignon*, one of the king's pet boys. But when a threat is made on his life, he flees his native France to seek refuge in the England of Elizabeth I. Here life proves just as dangerous, when he encounters a celebrated new playwright by the name of Christopher Marlowe and is quickly drawn into an underworld of spies, crime and political intrigue.

"Finely researched, deeply detailed. You will find no better novel (certainly in the gay genre) which deals with this particular piece of English literary history" -- *Frontiers*

"A rattling good read which adroitly mixes an entertaining plot with plenty of authentic historical background" -- *Gay Times*

"A well-researched book with a genuine feel for the period in which it is set, manifested particularly in its accounts of historical perform- ances, its use of puns and its ear for the speech of its French hero; amusing, and at times moving, (it) contains serious explorations of questions affecting the lives of homosexuals" --*The Historical Association*

"A rich and detailed picture of Elizabethan London is revealed. Chris Hunt includes the minutest details of life at that time, contrasting the overcrowded squalor with the vast stretches of open space that still remain in what we now know of as central London, highlighting the stark contrast between rich and poor" -- *Him*

ISBN 0 85449 066 3   UK £6.95 / US $10.95 / AUS $19.95

THORNAPPLE

A renegade monk; a scheming lady of the manor; a mysterious old woman and a beautiful boy guarding magical secrets -- these are just some of the intriguing characters encountered by a young pedlar as he journeys through the east of England in 1204. Their stories intertwine to form a fast-moving tale of romance, murder and witchcraft, taking the reader from Norman castle to Saxon hovel, from the studios of Paris scholars to the dens of London thieves. Once again Chris Hunt has created a unique work of historical fiction, weaving a rich and imaginative tapestry of people and places to bring the early 13th century vividly to life.

"A romantic epic as any historical romance is... Hunt has once again created a historical novel from a homosexual standpoint... Replete with convoluted plot, plenty of action and loads of love and lust...Hunt writes a mean page-turning tale" - *Gay Times*

"In a language rich and lavish (it) carries you along, moving quickly from start to finish. Compelling and highly enjoyable"
-- *Northwest Gay and Lesbian Reader, USA*

ISBN   0 85449 104 X   UK £6.95 / US $10.95 / AUS $19.95

GMP books can be ordered from any bookshop in the UK, and from specialised bookshops overseas. If you prefer to order by mail, please send full retail price plus £1.50 for postage and packing to:

GMP Publishers Ltd (GB),
P O Box 247, London N17 9QR.
For payment by Access/Eurocard/Mastercard/American Express/Visa, please give number and signature.
A comprehensive mail-order catalogue is also available.

In North America order from Alyson Publications Inc.,
40 Plympton St, Boston, MA 02118, USA.

In Australia order from Stilone Pty Ltd,
P O Box 155, Broadway, NSW 2007, Australia.

Name and Address in block letters please:

Name _____

Address _____

_____

_____